# NOBODY'S CHILD

*The Pandora Files*

# NOBODY'S CHILD

## AUSTIN BOYD

ZONDERVAN.com/
AUTHORTRACKER
*follow your favorite authors*

ZONDERVAN

*Nobody's Child*
Copyright © 2011 by Austin W. Boyd

This title is also available as a Zondervan ebook. Visit www.zondervan.com/ebooks

This title is also available in a Zondervan audio edition. Visit www.zondervan.fm

Requests for information should be addressed to:

Zondervan, *Grand Rapids, Michigan 49530*

Library of Congress Cataloging-in-Publication Data

Boyd, Austin, 1954–
    Nobody's child / Austin W. Boyd.
        p. cm. — (The Pandora Files)
    ISBN 978-0-310-32819-3 (softcover)
    1. Birthmother—Fiction. 2. Mother and child—Fiction. 3. Human
reproductive technology—Moral and ethical aspets—Fiction. 4.
Ovum—Transplantation—Moral and ethical aspects—Fiction. 5.
Bioethics—Fiction. 6. Domestic fiction. I. Title.
PS3602.O928N63 2011
813'.6—dc22                                                    2011012194

Representation by the Leslie H. Stobbe Literary Agency.

*Cover design: Curt Diepenhorst*
*Cover photography: Caleb Rexius*
*Interior design: Michelle Espinoza*
*Editorial: Lori Vanden Bosch and Melissa Lowe*

*Printed in the United States of America*

11 12 13 14 15 16 17 18 /DCI/ 19 18 17 16 15 14 13 12 11 10 9 8 7 6 5 4 3 2 1

*With love to my mother, Joanna Calvin Boyd,*
*an enduring and creative woman*
*who loved the people and mountains*
*of Tyler County, West Virginia.*
*You left us too soon, and you are sorely missed.*

# NOBODY'S CHILD

# CHAPTER 1

DECEMBER 21

Laura Ann reached for a tissue, wiping away wetness in deep ravines at the corner of Daddy's mouth. Labored breaths measured his final hours, lying on a handmade rope bed in the farmhouse where his mother bore him. Walnut posts, worn soft by five generations of lingering hands, defined the corners of his world.

"Let's give him a little morphine. Perhaps he'll rest," Pamela whispered as she drew the solution into a new hypodermic, her gentle voice a sigh against the background of the night's frigid silence.

Laura Ann nodded where she knelt at his side, Daddy's limp hand sandwiched between her palms. Fingers of December cold plucked at her, working their way under leaky windows, death struggling to snatch him away. Her eyes never left Daddy's face, willing him through each ragged gasp that pulled them both closer to Christmas, four days hence. An eternity.

"You need rest too," Pamela added, adjusting his pillow. She faced Laura Ann for a long moment, waiting for some response, then shook her head as she worked down the bedside, tucking Daddy's quilt in a futile battle against chill drafts. A tireless hospice nurse, she slew demons of fatigue with her helping way, encouraging father and daughter through the tortuous last hours of his life.

Each minute defined by the spasmodic cadence of her father's struggle to breathe, Laura Ann McGehee knelt at his bedside, coaxing out the next seconds of life with the squeeze of a hand and a muttered prayer. Breath by breath, she anchored Angus McGehee to the world of the living. Death hovered, a wispy shroud poised to spirit away the last male in the generations of family who'd farmed this land.

"I need to stay," Laura Ann said when Pamela finished adjusting the covers. She squeezed Daddy's hand one more time, pumping the next breath into failing lungs. "The evening news will be on soon," she added, dipping her head in the direction of a muted television. "Daddy never missed it."

The thin nurse nodded and set the volume on low. Like a prod, television roused him. Morphine-dulled eyes stared ahead as he spoke, breathless. "News?"

Laura Ann marveled at her father, one moment clinging to life while lost in a drugged haze, then conscious the next, unaware he'd reemerged from a morphine netherworld. "Stefany's show will start soon, Daddy. Want to watch?" Stefany Lukeman was hometown material, another of Laura Ann's many third cousins, born and raised only a few miles away in Sistersville.

His head bobbed on the pillow, attentive to Laura Ann's presence for a few precious moments. Brief seconds of clarity with Daddy that she treasured in these, his last days. She wiped his mouth again, dabbing at the red-flecked stream that oozed from him, unabated.

Images of pilots and aircraft filled the television screen as Stefany recounted the story of a local Navy pilot, now an astronaut. Flashy red hair cascaded over Stefany's shoulders, framing a perfect freckled face and green eyes.

Daddy's eyes closed again. Eyelids shuttered on consciousness, the morphine drew him into a land of fitful dreams.

*Please, Jesus. No pain.* She prayed in silence.

The chill and stiffness of death crept into his frame, her skin to his. She determined to delay his passing as long as possible using her own warmth, pressing his hands between hers, or laying an arm across his chest. As immodest as it might be, she'd even drape herself across Daddy's body to pour her life into his, suffering any embarrassment to regain one more moment as a little girl on his lap. To relive one minute beside him on the tractor. To experience one more caress of his rough hands on her face.

Daddy roused and coughed yet again, this one a hacking rattle from deep within. Both women sprang to his side, turning him slightly, draining the bottomless well that threatened to drown him. Neither woman grimaced, their nurturing impervious to the squalor of her father's self-inflicted disease.

Minutes later he settled back into labored breathing and Pamela carried away the soiled remains of their latest care. Walking back from the kitchen, she pulled a chair up behind Laura Ann, coaxing her to sit while the young woman prayed breath into failing lungs.

"Treasure every moment, dear. It won't be long."

Laura Ann nodded. The nurse's empathy for the needs of the dying blessed many in this little valley of the Middle Island Creek, a forgotten backwater in this rural corner of West Virginia. The wife of a local pastor, Pamela Culpeper ministered to those on the threshold of the next life, while her husband shepherded the rest.

"Christmas?" Laura Ann asked, her wet eyes pleading. She wiped at salty cheeks with a forearm, unable to let go of her father lest he slip away for good. Pamela walked around the bed and stood by the window, shivering as she stared out at the night.

Winter's breath found its way around loose panes, feeding a river of frigid air that flowed across the old bedroom.

"Are you sure you want this to drag out that long?" the nurse asked with a shake of her head, her face washed in the pale white of bright moonlight on a winter solstice evening. "Let God take him. In His time."

Laura Ann shuddered, looking away from the window back to the purple chapped lips of her father. "I'll care for him tonight. You take over in the morning."

Pamela's shoes clacked on well-worn oak as she crossed the room in silence. Passing Laura Ann, her hand lingered on the girl's shoulder, strong warmth that radiated "I understand." They connected for a brief moment, and then she departed.

Looking across the bed, her head cradled into Daddy's side, Laura Ann stared at the full moon where it rose above a ridge to the north. Stark poplars silhouetted against the white orb stood like soldiers arrayed about their small farm, a tiny island of life in the middle of the frozen Appalachians. Tall woody guardians basked in the brilliant cold, holding death — and the mortgage bankers — at bay.

But for how long?

"I'm sorry, Daddy," Laura Ann cried, her tears wetting her father's bony hand where it lay under her face on the bedside. "For so many things. I've done something you wouldn't approve of, but I did it for a good reason. I need you." She wiped his skin dry with shoulder-length brown hair, never moving her head from its place atop his wrist.

"I know you want to go. Please forgive me for holding you back." Pain clawed its way out of her, sobs dislodging themselves from a place deep inside, a crypt so hidden she'd never known it existed. A place he'd told her of once, when talking about her departed mother. A place she'd never understood—until now.

"Your momma ...," he'd said so many times, then turned away, chin quivering. Laura Ann and Daddy were kindred now. She would soon lose what Daddy forfeited so many years ago when Momma died—a best friend. But unlike Daddy with a daughter to raise, she would stand alone.

Through tears and a runny nose, she smelled him. The familiar fragrance of wood dust on his overalls—and the acrid tang of death, a scent that permeated his right hand, no matter how much she'd cleaned it. Even in the light of a rising moon, she made out the distinct yellowed callous between his index and third fingers, the death mark he'd so diligently burned into his skin—the tattoo of his destruction. She covered it with her hair, hiding the callous from view lest she slice off his hand to cancel the smoky poison his fingers fed him for a lifetime. A poison she would hate forever.

His breathing stopped. Laura Ann's heart leapt and she jerked upright, his hand in hers. Perhaps he'd heard her, but decided it was time. She squeezed harder, hanging on for his wisdom and understanding, yet regretting her last words.

"Please, Daddy. Don't leave. Not yet," she pleaded, wiping his hand against her face one more time before his pulse faded forever. "There's something I must tell you."

"Laura Ann?" His lungs sputtered to life once more.

She stood up, her face over him. "I'm here, Daddy." She battled to face her sin, to tell him how she'd violated her sacred place. To repent, that he might forgive—before it was too late.

"The farm?" he wheezed. His eyes danced around in the moonlight, unable to connect with her. "Chain ..."

Lost words drowned in the gurgle of his throat.

Laura Ann shivered, the last word on his lips expressing his greatest fear. Their farm, generations old, poised to flee from McGehee hands in order to pay medical debts — and his daughter left alone, with no means of support. No means, at least, that she dared confess.

"You and me, Daddy. Links in our family chain." She choked back sobs, the unspoken sin burning deep within her. "I won't break it," she promised, burying wet cheeks in his shoulder. She dared not face him, not now.

His breathing calmed and he whispered words she might not have ever heard, even inches away. As though God knew that Daddy needed her to draw close.

"It's okay ... You've done ... enough."

Her eyes dried and her hands grew small. Laura Ann stared at tiny fingers as she walked along the ridge, in wonder at the strange pain that she'd bottled up only moments ago. Now she felt free, a lifetime away from the ache and foreboding that niggled at the back of her mind.

A voice whispered to her spirit. *This is not real.*

Honeysuckle sweetness filled the air, her feet squishing along a damp forest path. Mayapples carpeted the floor of the wood with their twin green umbrellas and first buds of coming fruit — West Virginia manna. A winged streak of red and gray flew through the trees ahead of her, alighting on dead limbs to peck for worms. The rapid knocking advanced with her, an airborne escort to the woodland edge.

Standing under tall poplars, their perfect straight trunks shooting up a hundred feet above her, Laura Ann lingered at the edge of her heaven. Rolling down from the ridge top and its bounty of timber, pastures filled with fat cows and late spring grass waited for her to cut a path to home. Daddy would be there, his rusting red pickup parked in front of the farmhouse in the distance, beyond fields swollen with the lime-green leaves of young tobacco. He'd be waiting for her in the wood shop, a little white box beside the big red barn. Daddy, her protector. He'd know what to do.

Magically, the next moment she transported to his lap, seated on his stool by a workbench laden with wood shavings. The pungent odor of poplar filled the air, sanding dust from his lathe settling on her like wooden rain, covering them both in a beige film. Freshly turned stair balusters stood arrayed along the wall, each draped in the same gentle coating. When he smiled, dusty cracks formed in deep folds of his face, ravines weathered by nearly fifty suns in the rocky fields that he and his fathers carved from mountain forests.

"Okay, Peppermint. What's the problem?"

Daddy could read minds. Other dads were good with cars or computers. Hers knew everything about life.

"The McAfee brothers. What am I going to do?" As she spoke, she felt something strangely wrong. The voice, disembodied, whispered to her again. Like a reminder that she'd uttered this question many thousands of days ago. Foreboding tugged at her and she pushed it away. She felt so safe in his lap, rough hands cradling hers. Hard biceps, tough as hoe handles, pressed into her sides where he supported her.

"Are those boys bothering you again?" he asked, his voice strong and gravelly like a tractor, with the power to plow through problems and make her safe.

"They both say they love me. I have to choose one tomorrow when I get to school. I don't know what to do."

He smiled, dust cakes shedding from his face like so much

man-glitter. The essence of wood permeated him, trees-become-stair-parts now wrapping their soft warmth around her. She hugged him close.

"Do you love them?" Bony cheeks round as plums rose up under twinkling eyes, shedding more poplar dust.

"No!" She pinched his arm and he pretended to flinch. Invincible, Daddy shrugged off pain. He carried an entire farm on his shoulders, with never a complaint.

"Then tell them you love *everyone*. The same way God does."

His words hung in the powdered air, interrupted only by the occasional burp of the air compressor coming up to pressure. The heartbeat of Daddy's shop.

"You're so smart," she said, leaning into his chest.

He patted her on the knee of her jeans, smiling. Blue eyes the color of faded denim flashed love, pale blue suns embedded in a leather-brown face that thawed the deepest recesses of her fear. Daddy kissed her on the forehead. "We'll get through this together, Peppermint. We're a pair, you and me."

"Like bread and jelly?" she asked, feeling the warm joy of a smile.

"For aye. We're a team."

She pulled him tight in a hug, wood dust clinging to her arms, then slipped from his lap, headed for the farmhouse and a snack.

Daddy evaporated, yet somehow she felt him, could still smell him. Her neck creaked with stiffness, her back in pain where she leaned over his bed. He gasped for breath, grabbed for her hand, and then cried out. "Laura Ann?"

She awoke. Her protector and the wood shop disappeared in a mental mist. A dream.

Daddy's gentle eyes stared at her, no longer dulled by drugs. He recognized her at last. Her hand in his, he squeezed hard, strength he'd not shown for days. Not since his ugly slide from life commenced its terminal phase.

He smiled, staring for a long silent moment into her eyes. The old daddy had returned, grinning through yet another of those long pensive looks he'd once said were his only chances to reconnect with Hope, her mother—a woman who'd replicated herself in Laura Ann's face.

"Yes?" Laura Ann's voice cracked, her skin tingling in the moment. They were not alone. There were three in the room now. She could sense it.

He turned his head, staring at the full moon where it soared over poplars lining the distant ridge. Perfect cylindrical trunks that awaited transformation into furniture and millwork under the curling bite of his lathe tool. He turned his gaze back to her, his face wrinkled with the biggest smile she could remember.

"Goodbye, Peppermint." He paused, then squeezed her hand one last time. "I just flew out the window."

The moonlit spark in his eyes faded, and with it, her last chance to share a secret pain.

With a long gentle sigh, Daddy let go.

# CHAPTER 2

DECEMBER 24

"You can't stay here," Uncle Jack said, waving a pudgy hand toward the pasture, then pointing at Laura Ann. "A mortgaged farm with no means of support." He huffed, shoved his hands in his pockets, and stomped out of the front yard of the farmhouse. "Just like your old man. Stubborn and stupid."

Auntie Rose straightened up as to object, and then shrunk back, head lowered. In words too soft for Uncle Jack to hear, but perhaps for Laura Ann's benefit, Auntie Rose spoke up in her meek way. "We just buried my brother, Jack. Let him rest."

The seven visitors at Laura Ann's side drifted apart. Preacher Armstrong and his wife followed Uncle Jack to his car, parked nearby. As if to summon a dog, the elderly preacher hesitated at the yard gate and shot a glance back at Auntie Rose, motioning with his head toward the automobile. A clear message, but Auntie Rose stood her ground.

Preacher Armstrong's iron gaze melted for a moment, confronted by her disobedience, but then he set his hands on his hips and spoke a second time.

"It's time to go, Rose," he commanded. His own wife nudged him with a loud huff, and then headed for the sedan where Jack stood, door open to the rear seat. Preacher stood alone a moment longer, eyes on Auntie Rose and shaking his head, then retreated to the car.

Pamela Culpeper approached Laura Ann, extending a hand in fellowship. "Ed and I can be reached any time. You too, Rose. You call if you need anything. Hear?"

Laura Ann threw her arms around Pamela's neck in a tight hug. "You've done so much already," she said, and then took Pastor Culpeper's extended hand in a long embrace.

"She's serious," Pastor Culpeper added. "We know you'll find a way through this, Laura Ann. Let us help where we can."

"False hopes." Preacher Armstrong's voice broke the cold night air like smashing icicles. "Don't be messin' with God's design, Laura Ann McGehee. No matter what Culpeper says, you listen to your uncle."

"God's design?" Pastor Culpeper shot back, turning away from Laura Ann. Pamela put a hand on his shoulder, but he moved forward to the yard gate, his eyes riveted on Laura Ann's family preacher. "His design is that she trust Him for all her needs. That's a message you might have shared at Angus's grave today, Phillip."

"False hopes," Preacher reiterated, pushing his wife into the backseat. "Face the facts, Culpeper. Angus is dead. That girl's life on this farm is over. It's time to move on."

Pastor Culpeper shook his head. "The word that comes to mind is *grace*, Phillip. Wouldn't hurt you to show a little. Like now."

Preacher tarried at the rear door, shrugged, and then ducked into the car.

In the silence of the tense moments that followed, Laura Ann watched her surly uncle kick frozen clods with his dress shoes where he stood in the drive beyond the fence. The frozen red-brown mud, a palette of country color, reminded her of earlier times this very day. Red clay, the soil of a fresh-dug grave, steaming in the bitter afternoon air at Preacher's church in Alma. The brown of Daddy's simple casket, lowered into the ground he'd loved so much.

"Don't mind them," Auntie Rose pleaded, her eyes glistening. She reached out and laid a hand on Laura Ann's forearm. "But I'm worried about you, sweetheart. Not for now—I mean, I know you have food and transportation for a while, but what about—"

"The bank?" Laura Ann interrupted.

Auntie Rose nodded. A solid band of grey streaked the middle of the part through Auntie's brown hair, one of those odd hygiene items that sent Uncle Jack into a rage. If he saw it, he'd drag her from the porch, berating her for "skunk stripes." Laura Ann reached up and adjusted Auntie's hat, pulling it down a bit in the front to save her a repeat embarrassment. Auntie Rose's lips pursed in her look of submissive resignation, a silent "thank you."

"I have a backup." Laura Ann pulled her aunt close, shielding her only blood relative against the bitter chill of Christmas Eve. "You'll see," she added in a whisper, lest Uncle Jack hear. "Pastor Culpeper's right. God will provide."

Auntie Rose released Laura Ann's hands and took her in a tight hug. She held on as if she'd never let go, perhaps struggling to hang on to the only home she'd ever loved. Laura Ann gripped her tight, watching Uncle Jack from over Rose's shoulder as her aunt clung to her, a prolonged hug that cried out, "Please, let me stay."

The moment wouldn't last. Preacher said something to Uncle Jack that she couldn't hear. His countenance soured and he dropped a rock, then stormed through the fence gate, headed straight for Auntie Rose. As he approached, a quiet young man to Laura Ann's left stepped forward, planting himself in Uncle Jack's way.

"You're not on duty, Ian," Uncle Jack said.

Ian locked eyes with Uncle Jack. "Far as you're concerned, I am. Don't try something you'd regret, Mr. Harris."

Laura Ann could see the pulse pounding in Ian's neck, only a few feet away. Yet he seemed so calm, an impenetrable barrier between Auntie Rose and her thundering husband. How many years had she watched him stand up for underdogs in class or in town? Now her friend stood up for Auntie Rose. And for *her*.

Lowering his gaze, face red, Uncle Jack spun about, kicking at the air, then walked straight to his car. He lingered at the driver's door, half-open, nearly yelling his next words. "It's a sad day, Preacher, when a husband's authority is undermined this way. Don't you think?"

Laura Ann watched Preacher's head bob up and down. Muffled by the closed door of the car, only one word stood out. "Sad."

Jack took his seat in the car. Moments later, the horn blared — Jack's first line of defense when he didn't get his way.

"Let him go," Laura Ann begged. "I'll drive you home later."

"You know Jack," Auntie Rose replied with a sniffle, dabbing her nose with a crumpled napkin. She smiled a pasted-on "See? I'm happy!" resignation that Laura Ann often saw below a bloodied cheek or swollen eye.

"You don't have to leave, Auntie Rose. This is your home too. Please. Stay a while."

Rose shook her head. Her chin quivering, she pushed away. She squeezed the hands of the Culpepers, and Ian, the young lawman who'd taken a stand. The shake of her head as she left screamed stories of suffering, of betrayal and abuse.

The car door slammed behind her, and chunks of slag flew out from behind Uncle Jack's wheels when he spun away. Pamela put an arm around Laura Ann as they watched the sedan make its way across the pasture and up a frozen hill in the darkness.

Ian turned to face them as a sense of calm returned. "I'm sorry it came to this, Laura Ann. You didn't deserve that. Especially not today."

"I'm not sorry," she replied. "You saw my life for what it is. All of you did. But thanks for stepping in."

She caught Ian's eye, and he nodded, with the hint of a smile. "Call me if you need anything. Promise?" His eyes spoke words of comfort he'd left unsaid.

"I will," she replied.

Ian's smile faded with his next words. "Now that your dad's not here to stand up for her, I'm afraid Rose won't have a day of peace."

Laura Ann folded her arms against the chill and turned to watch the last glimmer of red lights heading over the ridge. "No." She shook her head. "She won't. And neither will I."

## DECEMBER 25

Cows' breath fogged the air inside the barn where the big creatures pushed their heads into feed stalls, maneuvering for first position to reach Laura Ann and a fresh flake of hay. Oblivious to her pain, two-dozen Black Angus woke to a new day like they did every winter morn, pushing and shoving for their five a.m. feed. Warm breath spewed damp clouds in the bitter cold predawn air of Christmas Day.

Laura Ann took her time as she tore at the hay from her perch above the cattle in the loft, holding each section of the bale to her face before she dropped it to hungry beasts. She breathed in memories of summer. Clover, dried in crisp pale-green shamrocks, flecked the bale with its sweet flesh, a cow dessert. Straws of timothy—cow salad—held the bales together with their pithy shoots, miniature stalks the grass equivalent of sugar cane. Every bale carried Daddy's touch. From the first fertilizer and lime application early in the season, to the roaring slice and crush of the mower-conditioner in June, Daddy crisscrossed that pasture time and again, year after year, to prepare the meal she would serve each morning all winter long. Love, laid up in long grassy bales, fed Angus beef stock, their second-best source of income after the tobacco.

Every bale carried her touch too. She and Daddy put up hay the "old way," square bales plopped one by one from the back of an old red McCormick baler, forty-pound bundles of hay thrown by Daddy up to her on the wagon, then stacked in the barn by Laura Ann. Each summer she pitched as many as ten thousand bales with Daddy, laboring in barns hot as ovens, sweat drenching her shirt and layered in the prickly grime of hay dust. Hay elevators creaked over rusty rails, bearing bales from wagon to Laura Ann, where she stacked for hours, a girl piling up forty-pound blocks. Those were summers filled with flies, barn snakes, mice, aching shoulders, blistered hands — and Daddy, encouraging her with the daily reminder that "hard work is the essence of the good life."

Laura Ann held another flake of summer above jostling black heads, its color stopping her: the dry crumbling remains of a pasture flower. Red pain. In it she saw Daddy, pitching a bale to her in August, his last day throwing hay. The bale missed the wagon and he fell, knees buried in fresh-cut grass, bent over in a horrible cough.

Laura Ann dropped the hay, tumbling into the face of a heifer that pressed against bovine sisters for a meal. She stared at her hands, the red of Daddy's blood on her fingers a vivid memory. Like the crimson that splattered his hands and mouth that day in the hay pasture when they first met his disease. It started that afternoon, in the dog days of summer. Daddy's end.

Minutes later, she shoveled more feed to swollen mothers who would drop calves within weeks. Corn, more of Daddy's labor, nurtured new life in a circle she'd been part of for twenty years. She shoveled from bins that stood brimful with brilliant yellow cobs, laden by a father who wheezed through every load they'd gathered this past September. Nights were shorter then, with no strength for talk, unlike the years of her past with a vigorous daddy who loved their evenings together after a full day in the field and wood shop. Nights spent reading stories to each other from dozens of books, their favorite escape.

A cat nudged her leg, drawing her back from the memory. Black purring nuzzled against her ankle. Laura Ann shoveled cobs to another waiting mouth, then took the barn cat in her arms, one of a dozen pets she'd never named. Arched in a bony inverted "U," the cat purred as she stroked black fur, her hand raising crackles of static as she rubbed from head to tail. The barn cat pushed its head between her arm and side, seeking some warmth in the folds of a dusty brown barn coat, layered in hay dust from a thousand cold mornings in the loft.

September had transitioned from the gathering colors of fall and bounty of yellow corn, to the beige of hospital corridors, pale blue of doctors' scrubs, and the white of paper. Sheaves of paper. Documents to sign, authorizations to treat sickness that might recur, waivers, addresses, and always—promises to pay. "No insurance?" a voice asked nearly every day, incredulous. Day by day, she bore the epitome of hospital shame: a patient without health insurance. Too poor to buy a policy, unqualified for Medicaid because they owned a farm. Day by day, Daddy fought the disease while she battled the healthcare bureaucracy.

Laura Ann set the cat down and walked along the feed trough, scratching heads. Dusty and spattered in dried mud, the Angus acknowledged her with a brief look up or the wink of a wet eye, and then crunched away on the next cob or flake of dry grass. She dove her fingers into warm thick hair between black ears, scratching hard, working her fingertips down long faces toward wet dripping noses.

"Merry Christmas," she wished each cow as she made her way along the two dozen pregnant mothers, the last of Daddy's once proud herd. The fog of bovine breath enveloped her in a cow cloud as she ran her hands over massive black foreheads with hair dense as carpet, this her ritual morning goodbye.

Laura Ann knelt in the living room at the base of their meager Yule tree. Despite the water in the feed bucket that held the tree, fragrant needles cascaded to the floor at her touch. Death found its way into every facet of Christmas.

Three packages waited under the tinsel and lights, wrapped in paper she'd horded each year and stored for future gift opportunities. Three packages — but only one she'd wrapped herself. Laura Ann's hand lingered at the first parcel. Pamela's handwriting adorned two of the gifts, part of her helping way. Weeks before his slide into the end, with Pamela's help, Daddy took the time to make sure his daughter had something waiting under the tree.

Laura Ann took the first gift, a thick heavy one. A perfect bow, creased paper folds, and neat tape cuts were Pamela's signature wrapping. No doubt she'd prepared the gift while sitting with Daddy through long painful days while Laura Ann worked the farm.

She released the bow and folded it with the ribbon in a pile, her annual rite of thrift. Dissecting the tape joint like a surgeon, she disassembled the paper, determined to save it for yet another year. This wrapping was holy, the dressing on her last gift from him.

The heft of the gift, and the embossing she felt below the paper, left no doubt as to the contents. She slipped the wrapping free to expose this year's dream, a leather-bound copy of the Lord of the Rings trilogy. Her lifelong favorite, three precious books bound in one.

Tears welled as she opened the book to the flyleaf, fingers running down the sharp edge of leather that defined the binding. She'd longed for this book, a sacrifice too dear in their rough months making medical payments and sustaining life. Daddy's scrawl adorned the first page and Laura Ann choked, closing the cover for a moment to seal him in her treasured gift.

He called to her, reminiscences of strong hands holding her through long cries about clueless boys or the pain inflicted by petty girls. His memory beckoned her to open and read. She lifted the cover of the trilogy a second time, anxious for Daddy's resurrection on the page. Shaky letters penned by an unsteady hand adorned the leaf.

*Dear Laura Ann,*
    *Every word of this book took us on adventures to strange new places when we read together. I will always treasure the gift that God gave me in you, my best friend.*
    *Keep reading, Peppermint.*

Laura Ann drew the book to her, closing it slowly as she inhaled the perfume of ink and leather binding. She held Daddy's favorite escape from farming—and her imagination quest—bound up in one volume. Within these pages lived their nightly travels together, experiences in distant lands, in wonder at the fantastic exploits of hobbits, warlords, dwarves, and elves.

The second package beckoned her. Wrapped in the colored newsprint of a *Wheeling News Register* Sunday comics, and bound with baling twine, this would have been one that Daddy wrapped—his annual joke about her "ridiculous thrift with wrapping paper." She straightened up and pulled the second parcel into her lap, tugging at coarse hemp wrapped about it, then curling the baling twine into a ball.

A second leather-bound book fell open, this one a journal filled with blank lined pages. An envelope dropped on the floor with her name penned on the front in Daddy's hand. It was a steady cursive, handwriting like the kind he'd used before the bedridden phase of his sickness. Laura Ann picked up the envelope and pulled out a simple card. The words stole her heart.

> *Write me letters, Laura Ann, and save them for my grandchildren.*
> *I love you.*
> *Dad*

# CHAPTER 3

Cold gripped the motor of the old pickup, icy tendrils wrapped around cylinders that screamed their complaint when she engaged the ignition. After feeding the cows, she'd planned to take a ride around her land. Not now. Laura Ann kept her eyes focused on a truck parked on the ridge above the farm and the trespasser who stood beside it. Poachers. Her ears pricked for the telltale moment when she needed to pump the accelerator and urge the old truck to life.

"Please start!"

As the first cough of an engaging motor gave her hope, she saw a man move back toward the vehicle. In the rising sun she could see better now. A *blue* pickup.

Uncle Jack?

Before her engine warmed to a semblance of reliability, the trespasser was on the move. He'd heard her truck start, no doubt, and had the advantage. She determined to catch him.

Laura Ann jammed the truck into first gear and broke the tires free of their frozen grip in red clay. As she sped up the hill, the mysterious pickup pulled out of sight. A blue truck, for certain. If it *was* Uncle Jack, he'd never wait on her, and if confronted, he'd never admit to visiting the farm on Christmas morning. That was his way. Once she heard him refer to his little lapses in honesty as "white lies." "Don't hurt nobody," he'd said.

She bounced up the farm road toward the top of the pasture, frozen ruts jarring the ride as tires dropped into steel-like gullies, then jerked back out again. Minutes after the trespasser pulled away, she passed the spot where melted snow showed in a perfect rectangle beneath the missing warmth. Five minutes further down the road, she'd driven the length of The Jug, their unique farm locale in the midst of a creek-bound island. But no sign of the intruder, and no proof it was her uncle.

Laura Ann gave up the chase at the low water crossing, the creek's unique geography where it doubled back on itself. Crushed white ice in frozen potholes proved the passage of the visitor. Undisturbed snow meant that no one pulled off the farm road into the wood to avoid her. The more she thought on it, she was sure. It was Uncle Jack's gaudy Ford, the only showroom-new electric-blue vehicle in a county full of dented red or white pickups.

Laura Ann stopped when she reached the creek and turned off the ignition. Frigid greenish-grey water tumbled along the Middle Island Creek, flowing around her farm, the creek's largest island. She walked out on the low water bridge where the creek turned hard to her right. Three miles downstream, it would pass the farmhouse. Four miles farther, after its loop about their unique hilly island known as "The Jug," the stream would return to a place only twenty yards to her left, but thirteen feet lower in elevation. Laura Ann moved to the downstream edge of the bridge and sat on mud-stained ancient concrete, watching icy water wind its way to the tiny hamlet of Middlebourne, two miles away.

How many times had she floated this loop of the creek? A hundred? She'd toss hay for a day in the summer, or work with Daddy in the shop, then pull the canoe into the stream. Pick any spot on the farm to start, go downstream, and eventually she had only to portage the low water crossing and jump to the upstream portion and float back to her point of origin. An endless circle of solo canoeing, the ultimate solitude.

Here sat once-proud milldams over two hundred years ago. Generations of water wheels churned in this perfect place for waterpower, each destroyed by flood and rebuilt by sturdy folk. Daddy's people. The McGehees, and the Greggs who came before them to build those mills, were the stuff of lore, hidden in time. All of them — along with their industrious handiwork — had long since departed. Now, muddy brown logs jammed themselves into disheveled piles above the deep hole to her left, a churning hairpin turn in the creek that gathered flood trash when waters raged over the concrete crossing. Like matchsticks piled up by a wet hand, they endured wintry cold, waiting on spring and the next flood. Every curve in the Middle Island had its share of logjams, a sight so commonplace that it never turned a head.

Seated on the concrete dam, Laura Ann pulled her legs up close, wrapping her arms about her shins. The trespasser forgotten, she buried her face into her knees, desperate to shut out the world, determined to bottle up her pain. Daddy's passing only added to her guilt, a discomfort so deep and so sharp that it would not pass.

Words bubbled up in the cauldron she'd sealed inside. Daddy's words about "letters to my grandchildren." Preacher Armstrong's words, Sunday after Sunday — and again last night — stern warnings that screamed "don't mess with God's design!" And Pastor Culpeper, in his caring way, reminding her at the funeral that "the Lord will provide." But here she sat, huddled against the cold, pinned in a desperate corner of her own making, her secret far too terrible to share.

Deserted in the back of beyond, Laura Ann closed her eyes in prayer.

"Are you a troll?" a voice asked sometime later.

The question jarred her out of another world, the mysterious twilight of deep prayer. Laura Ann looked up from her cold seat on the causeway, blinking against the sun. A man in green and khaki stood over her, lit up with smiles.

She wiped her eyes, self-conscious about any wet in them. "Ian?"

"I asked you a question," he said, his smile brimming ear to ear. "Are you a troll?"

She dusted her pants as she stood, tilting her head.

"You know," he said. "Guarding the bridge. From the Brothers Grimm? We read those stories when we were kids."

Laura Ann smiled. "What's the password, Officer?" she asked, crossing her arms and staking a claim to the middle of the concrete.

"That's easy. Hot biscuits."

Laura Ann shrugged with a shake of her head.

Ian put a finger to his temple, then replied. "Biscuits and gravy!"

"Got it. But you're early," she responded, extending a hand. His grip was strong and warm. Inviting.

"Been out since five. Most poachers can't wait to hit the woods with their new rifles on Christmas morning. Probably figure I'll be home snoozing on a holiday."

"Any luck?" she asked, remembering her reason for leaving the house. The intruder.

"I wrote three tickets before seven. So, what's got you down here? It's too cold to be out watching the creek."

"Thinking," she replied, hands shoved into the pockets of her coat. She looked away for a moment, sure her expression would give her away.

A hand touched her shoulder. "I'm sorry, Laura Ann. For

your loss. Your dad was the best." Ian faced the ground, perhaps to save her the embarrassment, perhaps because he felt her pain. "I wish there was something I could do."

Laura Ann watched him, a tall drink of water with tousled brown hair under a West Virginia Department of Natural Resources ball cap. His badge rose and fell with the deep breaths of a man who didn't know exactly what to say, a man who exhaled deep with each frustration.

"Thank you, Ian," she said, moving toward him. She put a hand on the forearm of his brown official coat, squeezing through the insulated sleeves. His eyes met hers, and understanding flowed in the silence between them.

A long moment later, Ian motioned to his truck. "I'm starving. Biscuits and gravy?"

Laura Ann smiled. "I saved some. Hoped you'd drive by."

"Every Christmas. Are they still warm?"

"They were when I left," she replied, climbing into his vehicle.

As they drew abreast her pickup near the bottom of the hill, Laura Ann touched Ian's forearm a second time. "Let's ride to the farm in your truck."

"Suits me," Ian said. He shifted down a gear to climb out of the low water crossing and head up the first hill of The Jug.

Laura Ann turned and looked out the back window at her truck, aside the road near the bottom of the grade. "I want to leave it there for a while. As a warning."

"Warning?"

"Someone was in here this morning, Ian. Taking pictures, I think."

His countenance changed like summer weather. In an instant he was serious, his law enforcement face. He stopped the truck and turned in the bench seat to face her. "Pictures?"

"I saw someone up on the ridge above the farmhouse forty-five minutes ago. I took off after him, but he got away."

"Any idea who it was?"

"Uncle Jack, I think."

"You're sure?"

"No," she confessed. "But I saw his blue truck. It had to be him, right?"

"Not because of the truck. But I'll bet it *was* Jack."

"Why?"

"Saw him up the road. On my way back from Big Moses."

"You saw Uncle Jack?" she repeated, incredulous.

"Yep. And he had company. Two of 'em, plain as day." Ian laid his arm on the seat back, turning her direction. "Had a gun in the rack, and Jack was wearing a tie."

Laura Ann took a deep breath, trying to remember. There could have been two of them. But Uncle Jack in a tie? Never.

Ian smiled, lowered his arm, and put the truck back into gear. "Let's go grab those biscuits," he said with a chuckle, "and we'll figure this out together."


Eight hours later, the farm kitchen brimmed to overflowing with food. Auntie Rose's turkey simmered in a pan of blistering hot drippings, fresh from the oven. Salad, cornbread dressing, pole beans, fresh-baked bread, and mashed potatoes all waited to be heaped into serving dishes. Laura Ann surveyed the feast and cooking utensils, then joined her aunt at the window.

Laura Ann broke the silence with the question that no doubt hung on Auntie Rose's mind. "Do you think Uncle Jack got your note?" Laura Ann asked, certain she didn't want him here for dinner, and hopeful her aunt would say "Let's eat without him."

"I called twice, Laura Ann. He won't answer his cell phone."

"Should we start without him?"

Auntie Rose lowered her head and shook it slowly. No words needed.

"Fine," Laura Ann replied, pulling her in the direction of the living room. "Then come see what Daddy gave me for Christmas. It's amazing."

Auntie Rose brightened and dusted her hands on an apron, then followed.

Together, they squatted at the foot of the Christmas tree and shared stories about the leather-bound book, Laura Ann's favorite. Auntie Rose told stories about her brother Angus and his love of reading to his daughter. Stories about his experiences traveling the world through books.

Daddy lived again in her words. She could see him in Auntie Rose's face, shared genes expressed in her aunt's cheeks and eyes. Daddy's laugh mirrored hers, and it felt good to giggle again. To share the living room floor as family. To hold someone close, warm skin embracing hers. She relished every one of Auntie Rose's stories, tales of Angus McGehee, and his conquering ways as a young man in a post-Vietnam America. The farm boy whom every girl pined for, but only one woman captured. Stories of Hope and Rose, sisters in spirit and marriage. Idyllic times.

Uncle Jack might not have entered the story had he not arrived at the door. The bang of a fist meant he came to be served, not to dine.

Auntie Rose stopped in midsentence, sharing another memory of Hope and their youth together as schoolgirls, the tender middle-school years long before Angus proposed marriage. The first bang on the door stopped her and she cowered, eyes wide, moving where Laura Ann's body shielded her from the sound. Just a fraction of a moment, a brief retreat, but it spoke dark secrets of her dread of Uncle Jack. She turned to embrace her aunt, but too late. Rose stood and walked to the door, stoic. A lamb headed to slaughter.

When his wife opened the door, Uncle Jack stepped into the home without a word, eyes on the prowl. Like he was searching for something, scouring every tidbit, leveraging for an angle. His way.

"Hello, Laura Ann," he said at last.

She nodded. "Merry Christmas, Uncle Jack." She stood and faced him, her quarry. He'd eluded her once today. Would he confess?

He didn't respond to her greeting but dusted snowflakes off his jacket, a brown outdoorsman thing like the ones that hung in rows at the hardware store. Not a stain on it, still stiff with factory sizing. He headed straight for the kitchen, avoiding Laura Ann's gaze.

"We'll get dinner set," Auntie Rose said. "We were just waiting for you." She moved quickly, but more like a robot on fast action than a woman proud of her kitchen skills. She made small talk, he responded. She ladled food, he sat down. She prayed, he bowed a head, then ate in silence. The spirit of Christmas died in the compress of their unspoken tension. Uncle Jack, the joy thief.

"Shoot anything?" Laura Ann asked, tired of hearing him chew.

"No. Why?"

"Saw your truck up on the rise earlier. With a gun in the rack."

Auntie Rose snapped her head up from its characteristic slump, her eyes pleading with Laura Ann "don't." No talk of guns or game laws—or wardens on the prowl.

Words burned on Laura Ann's tongue and she swallowed hot spite. "Ian stopped by earlier," she said, determined to make her point. "Mentioned he saw you this morning out near West Union."

"Might have," Uncle Jack responded, watching his plate.

"He said to tell you hello," she continued. "Comes by every Christmas to check for poachers." She watched for some response. He reached over the table to pull the pie in his direction.

"You don't have to head up to West Union to hunt, Uncle Jack," she continued, standing to gather up his plate and her own. Laura Ann could see Auntie Rose shaking as she lifted a hand to finish her last bite. "You're family. You can hunt here."

That comment got his eye. Uncle Jack regarded her for a long moment, then looked down to lift a wedge of pumpkin pie onto his plate. She headed for the sink, an ear inclined back toward the table.

"Thanks. I might do that Friday. Buck season's back in."

No one spoke while she cleaned up the dishes, set out coffee, and dashed some whipped cream on the pie. When at last she sat down, ready to enjoy her first dessert, Uncle Jack was finished, and for the first time in as long as she could remember, he smiled.

"I met a man today, Laura Ann," he said, his voice unnaturally pleasant. "Land buyer. Super opportunity."

"You told me you went hunting." Auntie Rose's voice rose in pitch, her fork of pie stopped halfway to her mouth.

"Today's Monday, Rose. It's a work day in my book."

"You had to work on Christmas?" Laura Ann asked.

He looked down at his pie, then over at Rose. "You should be glad." He turned back to face Laura Ann.

She held his gaze, counting the seconds in silence, waiting for him to look away. She learned the trick from Daddy, staring down bad dogs. The skill paid dividends, particularly with her uncle.

"Glad?" Laura Ann asked, pouring coffee but never breaking the lock with his eyes. She listened for the sound of the liquid, judging her filling of the cup by ear.

Uncle Jack got up from the table, coffee in hand, waving toward the window. "I found you a buyer, Laura Ann. A solution to your money problems. You're one lucky girl."

She set the coffee pot down hard on the table, jarring the dishes. Auntie Rose jerked when the pot hit the tablecloth, spilling some of the hot drink on her blouse. Laura Ann huffed, then crossed the kitchen for a wet rag.

"I've got it," Auntie Rose insisted, her eyes on her husband. Uncle Jack's faked smile never faded.

"What money problem?" Laura Ann asked, wiping her hands on her apron.

His chest swelled and he walked about the room in a slow circle, waving occasionally toward a window. "This. This problem. You can't afford the place, Laura Ann, but I've found a solution."

"I own it, Uncle Jack."

"No," he insisted, shaking his head, staring out the kitchen window toward the Middle Island Creek. "The bank owns this farm. You mortgaged it for all that medical care—a lot of good that did your dad. A mortgage you can't pay, by the way."

He turned from the window, pointing his coffee cup at Laura Ann. "The state wants to buy your place." He stopped his walk, sipping from the cup. "It's a good deal. You should take it."

Laura Ann shook her head. "I don't need your help—or the state's."

He chuckled, then let out a long breath. "Oh, yes, you do."

Laura Ann stiffened and crossed her arms, feet spread. Her fighting stance. "Why are you here on Christmas, anyway, Uncle Jack? Why not head out there tonight on the best holiday of the year and sell some more crop insurance? Or go shoot a buck out of season. You're pretty good at that."

"I'll pretend you didn't say that, young lady."

"I did say it. You don't care about Christmas, or this family, except what it gets for you. Don't pretend you're doing me some kind of favor. It's all about you. It always has been."

"I *am* doing you a favor, Laura Ann. I've got a buyer all queued up and ready to pay." His face went red like her truck, arteries swelling in his temples. "You need my help."

"No, I don't," she said, squaring her shoulders. "Don't need it, and don't want it."

"Stupid girl."

"Stupid *what*?"

"Girl. You're a kid, for crying out loud. Barely twenty, you don't have an education, and you've never held a job. No means of support. You'll be at the Social Security office begging for handouts inside a month." He waved the coffee cup like a lance, slicing her with his imaginary rapier.

Venom rose in her throat, hot words she'd heard from her daddy, ready to spew in Uncle Jack's face. Words about his broken marital vows with Daddy's sister, his tightfistedness, and his stream of lies. All words that would pierce Auntie Rose, words she dared not vent.

Uncle Jack took a step toward Laura Ann. Auntie Rose gasped, her knees buckling where she fell into a kitchen chair. Laura Ann set her stance and found her voice, all her pain pummeling him with one commanding word. "No!"

He stopped midstride and cast a puzzled look at her, then at Auntie Rose, who wrung her hands, eyes wide.

"I can and will run this farm, Uncle Jack. I've worked here my whole life and I'll make it pay. So clean that wax out of your ears and hear me. This farm is not for sale."

# CHAPTER 4

*Dear Daddy,*

*It's Christmas night and this is my first letter to you using the wonderful leather journal you gave me. I promise to write a letter every year. I miss you dearly. Being close to you, even with the cancer, was so much more joyful than the life I've lived since you left.*

*It's after midnight. My fourth try at this, and lots of tears on this page. I'm trying so hard to write you a letter, but these words are like sparks around gasoline. They ignite so many feelings, so many memories.*

*Your funeral was beautiful. Simple, just the way you wanted. Preacher said some nice things about you, and about Momma. He talked about reuniting with loved ones, and about the impact you made in our church. It was so cold. I wanted to throw a blanket over your casket to warm you up, but I knew you weren't there.*

*I thought that losing you would be the hardest thing I'd ever have to deal with. But it's not. Now I understand why you always protected me when Uncle Jack came to visit. He didn't wait long to show up. It was bad tonight. He's not a nice man, Daddy, and I wish he'd leave Auntie Rose alone. She and I cooked an amazing Christmas dinner together here at the house. Uncle Jack started arguing with her after dinner and tried to hit her when she was washing the dishes. When he swung at her, she raised the biscuit skillet out of the soapsuds to shield herself. He slammed his fist into cast iron, broke his hand, and then drove himself to the hospital, cursing. You'd be laughing, I guess, if you'd been here. Auntie Rose is spending the night at the farm. She's terrified to leave him—but scared to go home.*

*That's not all. Uncle Jack is pushing me to sell our land and somehow he stands to profit. I'm sure of it. You've only been gone a few days, and he's already had a man here taking pictures of the farm. The state wants to buy our property to extend the wildlife management area to the end of The Jug. He's promising enough money to pay off the mortgage and the medical bills. I told him, "No sale."*

*The cold snap hasn't broken yet, but the cows are fine. We have plenty of hay right now, but I might have to buy some more before February. It's wicked cold. I named one of the black cats "Lucky" because he's fortunate not to sleep in the barn in this weather. He comes in the house at night and sleeps with me on my bed.*

*Granny Apple is coming over tomorrow. She and I will take some of your things to the shelter to help them through this cold weather. She has been so nice, calling on the phone at least twice a day. We'll probably cook when she comes over.*

*I keep telling you boring stuff about my day because I don't want . . . can't seem to put my feelings on paper. Please forgive me. It might take me a while to be able to write about what I feel. Right now, it's all very raw.*

*There are two things I need to say. First, I promise I won't break the chain. I know how much the farm means to you, Daddy. How it came down from your family so many years ago. I wish I could give our family name to a son, but*

*I know you're happy that I am who I am. I won't let Uncle Jack or anyone pressure me. It won't be easy, getting by. But God will provide. He always has.*

*The other thing is much harder for me to tell you. I've done something you probably wouldn't approve of, and I hope you'll forgive me. When you were sick, I did something to make some money. A lot of money. Preacher would never approve of what I've done and I don't dare tell anyone around here. But my body paid for your medicine until we mortgaged the farm to pay the bills.*

*What's done is done. I can't bring myself to write about what I did. I know it sounds crazy, maybe like an unspoken prayer request or a secret sin. You told me once that a person can do the wrong thing for the right reason. I know what I did was wrong. I sold a piece of myself. But doing that kept you alive and that's the right reason. You raised me to make good decisions, Daddy. I decided that if my body could give you life, whatever I could do was worth the sacrifice. No matter what Preacher or Auntie Rose might say, I'd go through that humiliation and pain all over again, just to have you here with me again, even for a day.*

*I love you.*

## DECEMBER 26

"No welfare. Ever." Laura Ann rubbed her eyes, raw from her tearful night with the journal, a restless three hours of sleep, and an early feeding in the barn. Bent over the kitchen table, her head pounded with each blink. Life spiraled down and joy fled with it.

"It's not welfare, honey. It's help," Granny Apple said, a hand on Laura Ann's forearm. "Lots of people need assistance at some point in their lives."

Laura Ann shook her head. "Daddy would never want me to do that."

"Angus didn't want to leave this life so early, either," Auntie Rose said, gripping Laura Ann's hands hard and pulling them toward her. "He raised you to be a survivor, sweetheart. But that doesn't mean that you cheapen yourself to accept help when it's offered."

*Cheapen myself?* The words pierced her. She dared not tell her aunt why.

Laura Ann shook her head again. "I'll find a way to get through this."

Granny Apple smiled, crow's-feet wrinkling into a leathery landscape of skin that reminded Laura Ann of a plowed field. Little girls ran from Granny sometimes, scared of the "Wrinkled Lady." Laura Ann knew better. Every fold in that face was a book in her friend's encyclopedia of wisdom, years of experience ready to be unearthed over a glass of milk and a biscuit.

"It's not about you," Granny Apple said in a slow raspy voice. "So don't do this alone. Lean on us. And lean on Him."

Laura Ann nodded, glad for the support and the counsel from her mentor. A woman of the woods.

Auntie Rose took a deep breath and let it out slowly. For her, understanding took a little longer, the McGehee independence and courage beaten out of her after so many years.

Granny Apple touched the joined hands of Laura Ann and Auntie Rose, a heavenly huddle at the farm's kitchen table.

"Good thing you had that skillet, dear."

Auntie Rose shrugged.

"You can't go home, can you?" Granny Apple's grey-blue

eyes locked on Auntie Rose like a mountaineer microscope. She never missed a hint, a twitch of the mouth or a misty eye.

Rose shook her head, lowering her gaze, no doubt to avoid Granny Apple's knowing look. "It's worse than you know," she said, her voice cracking.

Granny Apple exhaled patience. No words, just a loving smile and a squeeze of Rose's forearm. Together, they waited for Auntie Rose to share more. She looked up at last, lip quivering when she spoke to Laura Ann.

"Jack wants more," Auntie Rose volunteered. "Not just the farm. He wants the tobacco too — the allotment. He demanded that I get it back."

Granny Apple nodded as if she could read minds, a gesture that seemed to say, "I could see this coming."

"I don't understand," Laura Ann said, their hands clasped tight together.

Auntie Rose took a deep breath, as though steeling herself for some pain she could not avoid. "He's got him a lawyer. Gonna sue for the allotment, if he has to."

"He can't. Not without your support," Laura Ann said, her pulse quickening.

Auntie Rose looked up, years of grief bound in wet eyes, her lips pursed tight. Words fought to release themselves, but she bit them back.

"I don't understand," Laura Ann said again, releasing her aunt's hands. She ran fingers through her hair, then propped her chin on laced hands.

"Daniel Whitt — the lawyer — is an old friend of your uncle Jack," Granny Apple said, patting Auntie Rose on the forearm. She stood and moved to the stove, picked up a coffee pot, then returned to the table. She freshened Rose's cup, and pointed to Laura Ann's water glass. "More?"

She shook her head. "I don't know him. Is Mr. Whitt local?"

"Yes," Granny Apple replied, replacing the pot on the stove. She returned to her seat. "He has an office over in Culloden. He and your uncle were friends in school." Her last words had an edge on them, as though the story they hid was still raw for her. Or for Auntie Rose, whose head hung, her face without expression.

"Your tobacco allotment must be farmed every year to keep it active," Granny Apple said, looking at Laura Ann.

"I know. And I told Uncle Jack last night that I had no intention to farm it. Tobacco killed Daddy and I'll never grow it again."

"I admire your pluck, sweetheart. But your uncle doesn't."

Auntie Rose smiled the briefest of grins and took another long breath, remaining silent.

"I heard about this some time ago," Granny Apple said, patting Auntie Rose on the forearm. "Jack knew you hated what tobacco did to your father, but he's determined to keep that allotment alive, no matter what. Word in the valley is that he'll sue for a review of your father's will and ensure that the allotment passes to his sibling. Your aunt."

"What difference would it make, Granny Apple? That allotment's not valid anywhere else. Whoever farms it has to grow the tobacco on my land. And I won't let that happen."

Granny Apple shrugged, raising an eyebrow. "That's why he has a lawyer, child."

Auntie Rose looked up. "He doesn't think he can win." These words came out different than any others that day. Words of defiance, of strength. "That's why he got me involved. He threatened me if I didn't get you to support the deal. But I don't want that allotment. I hate it. I hate what that horrible plant did to my brother, and now it's dividing our family."

Laura Ann shook her head and placed a hand on Auntie

Rose's. "Tobacco will not split us up." She put her best effort into a smile. The pain between her eyes screamed for relief. For sleep. Or aspirin.

"Jack will be tough to beat," Granny Apple said. "He's got experts."

"But I've got time." Laura Ann stiffened, then stood, and pointed out the window toward the barn and a fallow field beyond it.

"If a tobacco allotment isn't farmed every year then it expires. And you have to get the tobacco in the ground by June." She crossed her arms, staring out the window. "I only need to keep him off balance for six months. Then it's too late."

"That could work," Granny Apple said, picking up a pair of used plates from the table. "What did your daddy's will say?"

"Everything passes to me, except for some family mementos that go to Auntie Rose. Grandmother's things."

"Then you'd better stiffen your back, girl. Your uncle's coming after you with a vengeance. And he won't be easy to beat."

After Aunt Rose left, Granny Apple followed Laura Ann out to the barn to help with chores. "Thanks for coming over," Laura Ann said. "I'm worn to a frazzle and it's nice to have some company."

Granny Apple bent and broke open a bale of hay, tossing flakes to pregnant Angus mothers below. They stomped with heavy hooves on a manure-layered concrete floor, jostling for position as new hay fell into their feeding area. Feed the cows and shovel manure through the winter, then struggle through calving season in the spring. Turn them out the rest of the year and raise the crops to feed them. Never relax.

"There's a story you need to hear, Laura Ann. Something

that you need to understand." Both women exhaled clouds of fog in the frigid air, busting apart bale after bale to fuel the crunching jaws underneath them. "A story about your uncle. And your mom."

Laura Ann stopped her work, a hank of twine wrapped about her hand, one loop of hemp still holding the bale together. Flakes of hay sprang open as far as the cord would allow, creating a fan of dried grass.

Granny Apple never looked up, continuing her work. "Jack Harris loved Hope Sinclair. Your mom. He set his eyes on her in middle school, and she's all he ever talked about. I can remember that boy shoveling manure for me one winter and all he did was recite her name. Every time that shovel scraped concrete, he shouted out 'Hope!' I thought he was trying to motivate himself to move slop. I guess he was, in a way."

Laura Ann pushed her bale toward Granny Apple, and then sat on another to listen. The elder woman kept up the feeding process, happy, it seemed, to work and talk.

"Jack asked your momma to the prom every year throughout high school, and she turned him down every time. Hope only had eyes for Angus McGehee. Your mom and dad were courting from ninth grade on, and no surprise to most of us when your dad asked her to marry him after they graduated." Granny Apple stopped her labor and looked at Laura Ann, curled up on a pile of hay. "When they got engaged, Jack was devastated."

Granny Apple pushed the last flake down to the cows and took a broom to sweep the loose hay off the floor. "Jack decided to get revenge. Leastwise, that's the way I see it."

"How?" Laura Ann hung up the broom when Granny Apple finished sweeping, and together they walked to the stair.

"He took advantage of your father's sister."

"Auntie Rose?"

Granny Apple nodded and frowned, then headed down the stair to the corncrib. Together they shoveled cobs into the troughs, no words between them for minutes. Laura Ann waited, determined to match her mentor's patience.

"They had to get married, Laura Ann. Fast. We pretended to be happy for them, but I worried it might not last." She held a cob in her hands for a long time, studying it carefully. "It's a wonder they're still together." She tossed the cob to a waiting cow that crunched the end of the hard corn as soon as the grain hit the feeder.

"No, it's not."

"Pardon?"

"It's not a wonder they're together. That's because of Preacher," Laura Ann said, staring blankly at the tall pile of corn. Immense, like the unspoken burden she carried. "You don't have to listen to him every Sunday, Granny Apple. Preacher's put an incredible fear in her. She'll never leave Uncle Jack."

"She might."

"Not likely. She's convinced that the beatings are her fault." Laura Ann picked up an errant cob, turning it over in her hands through a long silence. "And Preacher confirms that every time they talk."

Granny Apple stopped a moment, staring beyond the cows, then started shoveling more corn. "And what about you?"

"I was raised in that church—"

"And you can leave it. Come worship with me. Or visit Pastor Culpeper's church in Pursley." She paused her shoveling, then added, "Now that your father's passed, no one's holding you back."

Laura Ann looked down, her eyes studying the worn concrete below her feet. It seemed a long time before she noticed that the scraping of Granny Apple's tin shovel had silenced.

"Your dad's holding you back, isn't he?"

Laura Ann tried to quell the quivering chin that gave her away. At last, she nodded.

"Five generations of McGehees are buried in that cemetery, child. I know how hard it is. When my Max died, it took everything I had to leave Alma and find a new place to worship. But I'm glad I did. Preacher's got his own gospel, and it's not good." She stooped to pick up a portion of a cob and tossed it to Laura Ann, motioning toward a hungry black mouth.

"What about Auntie Rose?" Laura Ann asked, anxious to change the subject. "What did Daddy say?" Uncle Jack was never allowed to touch her, not even to get close. It all made sense now.

"Your dad hated Jack for what he did to his sister, for ripping her away from the family and the farm," Granny Apple replied, shoveling harder than ever. Anger swelled in her voice. "Your aunt loved this place. Always has. When your grandparents died, Jack pulled a fast one and got her to sign over her half of the property to him. He sold it to the state, probably to the same fella who's trying to buy it now." She stopped shoveling, breathing hard in the cold. "Jack used that money to buy his way to influence around here." She wiped her face, knocking back cobwebs that drifted down from the dusty joists above.

"Jack took your Aunt Rose to bed — just to get back at your dad for marrying Hope. Then, when your mother died young, his anger flared. He blamed your dad for Hope's death. And that's when he started beating your aunt. Hope's gone, he's stuck with a bad decision, and your aunt's miserable. It's a sorry affair."

Granny plucked at a broken cob, ripping off individual kernels one at a time. "Part of me feels sorry for him."

"For Uncle Jack? Why?"

Granny Apple's lips formed a half-smile, half-frown. "Jack wanted kids. Rose lost her baby and couldn't conceive again. No idea why. I'll never condone what your uncle has done to your aunt, but there's this little part of him that I still remember when he was a boy, a cute young man with big eyes and bigger dreams, talking about growing up and having a large family. Maybe . . . ," she began, her voice breaking, "maybe if that family had happened, he'd a' settled down and wouldn't be what he is today. Frustrated dreams do that to people."

Granny Apple leaned on her grain shovel again, exhaling a deep breath, pain blown out with her next words. "And then there's you, child — the spitting image of your mother. The older you got, the more Jack saw her in your face. You rub salt in his wounds every time he looks at you." She paused, looking Laura Ann up and down, and smiled. "Especially now. You're tall just like Hope, with the same pretty figure. Even the eyes, one green and one blue." Her brief smile faded.

Granny Apple set her shovel aside and took a seat on a milking stool. "Need me one of these at home, something sturdy I can stand on." She adjusted herself on the wood seat and then let out a long sigh. Laura Ann waited, practicing the patience she learned every day from this remarkable woman.

"Rose lost her baby in the summer after they finished high school. A miscarriage. Barely seventeen at the time. Now you're all the family she's got." She looked at Laura Ann, tears flowing down deep creases.

"Don't trust your uncle," Granny Apple said at last, wiping at wet eyes. She picked up an ear of corn, bending it slowly with both hands until it snapped in the middle, then stared at the fresh break in the reddish-tan cob, surrounded by rows of yellow.

"Never be caught alone with him, Laura Ann," she added, her voice a raspy half-whisper.

She paused, then tossed the two halves to a drooling black mouth.

# CHAPTER 5

———⟡———

## DECEMBER 27

Laura Ann pared away oak in gentle curls, advancing her tool along the lathe rest as spinning wood contacted her sharp blade in a mesmerizing flow of shavings. She imagined Daddy with her here in the shop, a blank of poplar wood in his lathe, peeling away curls of greenish-grey to reveal yet another stair baluster for the custom woodwork company he supplied back east. Today, he stood nearby in her memory, guiding the razor-sharp gouge along a short section of red oak, shaping a stool leg for Granny Apple.

The delicious tang of oak filled the air, its aroma sharp like a wood version of cheddar cheese. Three stool legs stood ready to assemble, waiting on their last brother to become Granny's combination of a seat and step-up. Shifting to a new tool, Laura Ann slid a skew chisel against the left end of the round cylinder, her gentle pressure relieving a tiny "V" in the wood, shaping the first evidence of a decorative bead. With deeper and deeper cuts, she pared away three more grooves, rounded over by the flat of the skew blade into gentle semicircles. Ten minutes after she started the job, she sanded her work, fast but accurate on the old lathe that once defined her daddy's life each evening.

Oak dust settled on her like beige pollen, raining down as

she bored holes, then glued legs and stretcher dowels to form the frame of a stool. She'd watched Daddy assemble these a hundred times, frames he shipped to the Mennonites in Tennessee where someone wove an oak-splint seat and sold the product as "country made." She blew dust off the finished frame, adjusting her glue job to ensure it sat square on the top of Daddy's table saw. Laura Ann wrapped her arms about herself, imagining Daddy there behind her, hugging her while he admired her work. Years ago, as a middle schooler, she'd built her first stool. He never shipped it, but hung that oak stool from the rafters of the shop as a testament to his favorite helper. Layered in dust, it dangled from the ceiling above her.

The compressor sang its pressure song for a minute as she cleaned her shavings from the floor, sweeping up dust and curled oak into an ancient pan. At pressure, the motor shut off and the shop went silent. Stooping to scoop the sweepings, Laura Ann settled onto the smooth wood of the floor, worn shiny by years of Daddy's boots. She drew her knees into her chest, arms wrapped about them, and waited.

Christmas, now two days past, tugged at her as a bad memory. Auntie Rose had gone home that morning. Laura Ann's only companion, Lucky, nuzzled at her leg, his black fur tinged with dabs of sawdust. His purr sang tenor to the soprano whistle of cold wind against leaky windows. Her own heart measured the beat with a deep bass as she hung on, smelling Daddy in the oak. Eyes closed, she held on to him, dreaming of mornings long ago at his knee, and more recent nights at his side.

Daddy, her best friend.

"It's beautiful, child. How on earth did you do it?" Granny Apple asked, cradling the stool in her lap later that afternoon. Seated close together in the kitchen of her friend's tiny mountain home, Laura Ann watched with pride as she caressed the smooth oak, rubbed soft with a layer of finish that deepened the color of the veins and grain of red oak. She ran a finger along the warp and woof of a blue woven seat, where faded blue-scarred denim rose and fell in a patchwork of inch-wide squares. "Is this made from blue jeans?" Granny Apple asked, thumping the tight weave like a ripe watermelon.

Laura Ann put an arm around her friend and squeezed tight. "It's got part of Daddy in it." She traced the seat's tight weaving with a finger. "His overalls." Her voice cracked.

Granny Apple drew a deep breath. "It's such a beautiful gift, Laura Ann. But this has too much of your dad in it for me to accept. Do you understand?"

Laura Ann faced her, eyes wet. "No. Please. I want you to have this."

Granny Apple ran her hand across the top of the blue seat, her hand gentle on the fabric. "Angus McGehee lives in these threads, child." She smiled. "I'm honored. But you don't use any more of his clothes to make stools, you hear? Next one you weave, get some old jeans down at the thrift store. They bale the ones they can't use and send them to Cumberland to process into insulation. Mary Ellen Harper will give you some. You tell her I sent you."

Laura Ann set the stool on the floor. The aroma of fresh bread filled the room. Yellowed linoleum curled at the edges where it lay under white cabinet overhangs and blue gingham curtains shaded a sunlit window above the sink. With just enough room for a small table and two chairs, an old gas stove, and three feet of counter space, Granny's cooking area was adequate for one.

A blue and white crockery bowl sat on the far end of the counter, dusty with flour. Here her friend worked the dough as she baked her way into the hearts of families from Middlebourne to Frew on the Middle Island Creek. Times past, before Laura Ann took over farm chores, she would walk down the long Jug Road to the crossing, skip across the concrete, and climb the path to Granny Apple's house, tucked away in a hairpin curve on State Route 18. Together they baked and wrapped dozens of loaves. The years drew them apart, Laura Ann's responsibilities tugging her away from frequent visits.

Laura Ann walked to the counter and ran a finger about the rim of the crockery, the same bowl she'd mixed with a decade ago. She learned to cook here, mentored in kitchen ways by a woman who had no children, yet knew dozens who called her "Granny." She wiped her hand across a worn marble slab that sat on the counter, still slick with flour from the last loaf kneaded on its surface. Instinctively, Laura Ann opened the drawer below it, pulling out an apron. Like old times.

Granny Apple patted her on the shoulder and then moved to the oven. She handed off a pair of hot pads, then took two more herself and lifted the first of three blackened metal bins filled with browned loaves. Warm air filled the miniscule kitchen, drenched in the aroma of sourdough. She held one of the hot pans toward Laura Ann as though they had been cooking together all along. Six years had passed since she handed off the last loaf, but both women fell into old habits like no time had passed. In the silence born of close association, Laura Ann knocked the bread free and set each loaf on a cooling rack while Granny Apple tore off sheets of brown paper to wrap each one for gifts. A small sticker adorned the ends, holding the tucked wrapper in place for the next hungry recipient.

"Take these home." Granny Apple handed two loaves to Laura Ann. "But come back soon. We need each other. Now more than ever."

# CHAPTER 6

DECEMBER 28

"Got room?" a voice asked from behind Laura Ann. The quiet but familiar timbre stood out against a loud background of chatting lunch patrons at Auggie's Old Fashioned Pizza.

*Friend.*

She turned, drink in hand, to face Ian. Two slices of pizza pie, dripping with warm grease, flopped over the edge of a flimsy paper plate. A sausage and mushroom delicacy, hot from the oven.

"One of these is for you." Ian peeled a second plate from under the pile of warm crust. Balancing two plates like an expert, he shoved a huge wedge of Auggie's Old Fashioned Thick Crust in front of her and sat down. "You look hungry."

Laura Ann blushed. "Does it show?" She lifted her Coke and sipped from the straw, her eyes never leaving Ian—guardian of the outdoors, defender of the helpless, her game warden and best friend. His colors were the palate of the woods: green gabardine slacks and a starched beige shirt. A gold star topped his left pocket, the terminus of a crisp military crease. Ian paid attention to details, including clothing, poachers, regulations, and even her food needs. Since their kindergarten days, he'd always been close by, ever her protector.

Looking beyond him, she watched other patrons eye her new table partner, the only armed person in Auggie's. Just the sight of the pistol on Ian's hip sent diners pushing back in their chairs, as if each had some personal poaching story they were afraid he might read in their eyes. Ian confided in her once that most everyone in Middlebourne had been a poacher at some point in their lives, immersed in a country culture that condoned the taking of meat when people needed it. "I'm not here to take the dinner out of their pots," he'd told her. "I've got enough work just busting the ones who slaughter for fun."

Ian watched her eyes rove the audience. "See any bad guys?" he asked, chuckling. Laura Ann shook her head. More blood rushed to her cheeks.

"Don't worry about all the stares," he said in a low voice. "They're looking at the gun." He motioned with a nod of his head toward the weapon. "Happens all the time."

Laura Ann smiled, prodding at her pizza with a fork. "Thanks, Ian. This was kind of you."

"Least I can do. I remember a freshman girl who met me here a few years ago, sipping on a Coke and breathing in the pizza. Pretending she could eat it but too cheap to buy. A really pretty girl." He cleared his throat. "She looked just like you."

*Pretty?* Her heart leapt.

Laura Ann gripped her drink with both hands, lowering it to the table. Ian, comfortable as an old shoe, had never used that word with her as long as she'd known him.

*Pretty.* A term only Daddy used to describe her. Until now.

She stared at her pizza, unable to look up, fearful she'd reveal her joy.

A hand moved into her field of vision, pushing the pizza closer to her. "Hey," he said, reaching over to tap her on the forearm. "I'm sorry. Was that too bold?" He chuckled and she looked up. His wedge of cheese and dough, folded down the middle, was headed for a hungry mouth. "But it's the truth, McGehee," he said with a wink. "You're beautiful."

Ian smiled as he ate, his stare pulling a hot flush into her cheeks. For a long moment, watching him eat, she was years younger, a freshman girl drowning in a sea of teenage strangers. Tyler Consolidated High School threatened to overwhelm her, swimming in an ocean of students from all over the county. Fifteen years old and struggling with her self-image, she yearned for the privacy of pint-sized Boreman Elementary, only a mile from her home. Tyler Consolidated was too much to handle. She'd disappeared into Auggie's to find a safe place after the first day of her freshman year, to find those few friends she knew in tiny Middlebourne, a short three-mile walk from home. Like that day six years ago, she was back at Auggie's, drinking in the perfume of hot delicacies. And just like six years ago, here came Ian, walking into her life to bring her joy. But different this time — not just as a friend. Something more.

"Thank you," she said. Ian devoured half his slice during her daydream. He raised an eyebrow, his trademark "you're welcome," and kept munching.

"I mean, thanks for the compliment." She looked down and cut into her slice with the plastic fork and knife he'd deposited on her plate, trying to work the big wedge into a manageable size. Her stomach joined her heart's cries for attention, growling to be fed. "And thanks for the pizza," she added.

Ian knew her well. He'd never eaten a mushroom of any kind before that first day they spent together in Auggie's, his redemption of their first day of their freshman year. If the truth were told, he'd probably confess he still didn't like the topping. But he bought this selection to please her. Laura Ann's heart pounded louder as the first bites of warm pork sausage, mushrooms, and melted cheese met her tongue. A love gift.

"So," Ian said at last, wiping the last of tomato-tinged

grease from thin lips. "What brings you into town today?" He motioned toward the big plate window, salt-encrusted pickups pulled to the curb amidst mounds of dirty snow. "Did you walk? I didn't see your truck."

She tilted her head in the direction of a plastic sack on the floor. "I walked. Went to the thrift store," she said with a full mouth, raising one hand over her lips when she spoke. He smiled when she muttered the words behind the shade of her palm. Ian said once that she was the only girl he knew who was embarrassed to talk with her mouth full. He liked that.

"Jeans?" he asked. "Man, those things would fit Hoggy Pitts."

"Probably did, before he lost all that weight. I'm using these to make some new stool seats. Mrs. Harper at the thrift shop said she'd help me sell some in New Martinsville. Granny Apple's idea."

"I could use one. The stool, I mean." His wide smile faded and he leaned halfway over the table in her direction. "We need to talk," he said, his voice low. "Want a ride home?"

"Now?" she mumbled.

"Finish your meal. We can talk when we drive." He paused, looking around the room. "I've heard some things. Wanted to tell you what's up."

This time Laura Ann raised an eyebrow, her cue that she understood. As children at Boreman Elementary, they had facial codes for sharing thoughts across Mrs. Hawkins's third grade class. "Uncle Jack?" she asked in a whisper.

He nodded, looking around the room. Small towns have big ears. "That coyote's sniffing around, and he's got your scent."

She reached out and touched the top of Ian's hand. His hand tensed and his grey-blue eyes riveted on hers.

"Thank you," she said, her food ignored for the first time since he set it down. "For watching out for me."

Ian sat transfixed, his eyes on her fingers where they rested on the top of his left hand, poised above an empty ring finger.

His palm turned up in slow motion, the thin hair on the top of his hand sliding under her farm-calloused fingertips. She felt the roughness on the side of his palm as it rotated under her shaking fingers. She dared not withdraw.

He folded his hand about hers, lifting it barely off the table, then looked up.

"I have one fear, Laura Ann ..." He swallowed, his Adam's apple bobbing as he gathered his breath. Beads of perspiration dotted his forehead, matching the wet film that sprang from her palm.

She tried to speak, but words didn't come. He raised his other hand in a gentle "no" to silence her attempt, shaking his head.

"I need to say this. Please. It's on my mind all the time."

She smiled, taking his grip and holding tight. She placed her other hand under his, took a deep breath, and prayed for his next words, her heart pounding in a brutal fury.

"I worry that I won't be there, Laura Ann. Be there when you really need me."

His Adam's apple bobbed again and he held her hand in a strong grip. "I want to change that."


Bright yellow-gold reflected off sheets of hard snow in the bottomland of Middle Island Creek. The glaze shimmered, a mirror reflecting the glare of winter sun. Ian drove slowly on Route 18, but it didn't matter. Laura Ann was in no rush, anxious to spend every moment listening to his voice. Any crisis seemed manageable when she spent time with him.

"He's cunning," Ian said as he drove, his eyes focused on the road. "Your uncle reminds me of a poker champ — but he plays people, not cards."

Snow obscured soft shoulders and truck-busting drops into deep ditches on each side of the winding country lane. "I pulled the public records before I left my office this morning. Jack made a big campaign contribution to the state commissioner of agriculture — three years before his reelection. Then, *poof,* my boss the commissioner shows up taking pictures of your farm on Christmas Day."

"That was the state commissioner?"

"The same. He dropped in at the office for a surprise visit yesterday. I didn't connect him with your uncle until I met him." Ian waved at a passing pickup, then continued. "Jack's out to get you, Laura Ann. Or to get the farm. Whatever."

"They're one and the same, Ian," she said, her gaze focused somewhere far away. "But I'll get by."

"I admire your pluck, McGehee," Ian said as he slowed the truck, then looked over at her. Sun sparkled off the gold on his chest. "But you'll need more than optimism."

"I know that, Ian. Question is, how long do I have?" Despite the warm cab, she crossed her arms, shivering against an unknown chill. "I just lost Daddy. And now this."

Ian stared straight ahead as he passed The Jug Store, slowing to descend to the sixty-year-old low water crossing. "How long? No idea. Your uncle's moving a bunch of chess pieces we can't see. All you can do is wait for the attack." He shrugged. "Maybe he thinks that you'll run out of money and give up."

"My uncle doesn't know me very well."

"No," Ian replied with a smile and a quick glance. "You've got a point there."

"So — let's be brutally honest. You and me." Laura Ann waited, hesitating to say more. Her words had two meanings.

Ian slowed the truck and stopped in the middle of the

concrete crossing. He parked the vehicle and turned the heat up a notch, then turned to face her.

"Okay. Hit me, McGehee."

"Don't be silly."

"I'm serious," Ian snapped. "Lay it on me."

For a long moment, neither spoke. She could feel her cheeks flush red and turned, facing out the passenger window. She released the seat belt and pulled her feet up under her, then pivoted back to face him, rocking on folded legs.

"Okay. About the farm."

He deflated a little, something important left unsaid, then folded his arms, and turned toward her.

"I have enough money to get by. For a while. But I don't know how long that will last."

"Be specific."

"The bank was tough on us, Ian. They'd only lend a thousand dollars an acre."

"It's worth a bunch more than that."

"I know," Laura Ann replied, shaking her head. "But they were stern. Said times were tough and they had to limit their risk."

"In other words, they offered to lend you less money."

She nodded. "At a high interest rate, and not for very long."

"What do you owe?"

Laura Ann took a deep breath, voicing a debt bigger than she ever thought she'd deal with. "We borrowed one hundred seventeen thousand."

Ian whistled. She knew his pay, about thirteen dollars an hour for a new game warden just off a two years' associate's degree, and fresh in the job. Even for him, with a steady income bigger than she could make farming, those numbers were daunting.

"I have enough cash to hang on until spring."

"Excuse me for prying, but how?" Ian asked.

"Remember the burley we cut in August? We usually harvest ten thousand pounds. Probably a little more this year." She looked at her hands, memories of sticky tobacco sap and their August harvest still vivid, Daddy's last crop. "He was in lots of pain, but Daddy wanted to make sure I had the money."

"Burley prices are way down, Laura Ann. Less than a buck thirty a pound. Most farmers aren't making any profit this year."

"We've already paid our fertilizer and seed bills. I can keep all the cash."

"Thirteen thousand then, if the market holds," he said, drumming his left fingers on the wheel and staring out at the creek. He did math in his head faster than anyone she knew. "About six months on the mortgage, not counting any other needs."

"I figured five months. I'll need a little for staples and the power bill."

He stared out the window for several seconds. "You need twenty-eight thousand a year. Maybe thirty." He exhaled in a low whistle. "I make twenty-six. Before taxes."

"I can do it, Ian. But I need you to believe in me." She reached across the bench seat and put a hand on his shoulder. He tensed.

"I hate to be so bold, Laura Ann, but how? How will you do what other farmers around here can't?"

"I have a nest egg," she said, looking down, her voice subdued. For a moment, her gaze went to the top of her jeans, then she looked out the passenger window, removing her hand from his warmth.

No one spoke for a long time, Ian's heater blowing on high to keep them warm. Eventually, Ian broke the silence and put the truck in drive.

"If you say you can do it, McGehee, then I'm the last person on earth to doubt you." He drove off the low water crossing, up the hill, and into the forest, winding down Jug Road toward her farm. The naked grey of oaks and poplars passed in cold review as they followed the road along a ridgeback. The dirt road ran the length of lands once in the McGehee family, but sold as family died off, and converted piece by piece into a state hunting preserve. Ironically, once the home to McGehees, now Ian's work domain.

"I know you're stressed about this," he said a few minutes later. "You're the most determined woman I know. So, if you say you can do it, I'm right there with you."

Laura Ann turned to face him again. Her insides burned, like they did at the wrong time of the month, but worse. Painful memories gnawed at her, embarrassing reflections of those times she'd sold herself.

*Perhaps some secrets are better left unspoken.*

"Thank you," she said, clearing her throat, determined not to voice her pain — or her secret. "I want to succeed at this, Ian. And I — I want to do it with you."

Ian coughed. He slowed the truck as they crested the ridge, emerging from the wood where it looked out over her farm. Rolling pasture cascaded down toward fallow fields, and in the bottomland far away, the farmhouse, and barn.

He stopped the truck. "Do it with me?" he asked, turning to face her.

She swallowed hard. "I want to save this farm. With your support."

"I got that part. But how?"

She breathed a deep sigh. "Connect me with people who can help."

"Let *me* help," he said, moving a hand to her shoulder, an exclamation point on his words.

Ian's hand slid down the arm of her coat to her wrist, hesitated, and then coursed across the top of her hand. Laura Ann felt a crazy tingle in her spine when his skin connected with hers. His strong grip and gentle touch were like reuniting with a favorite glove, one she'd missed for a very long time.

"I'm in this with you, Laura Ann McGehee," he said, his fingers squeezed around her palm. She wiped at a tear with her free hand, and then slid across the seat, cradling her head on his shoulder. Ian pulled her close and she shut her eyes, focused on the warmth that embraced her. Laura Ann's heart thumped joy, caressing her insides with a comfort she'd only imagined in her dreams.

*I am not alone.*

"The bull got out early, huh?" Ian asked with a chuckle, prodding Laura Ann gently in the back.

She milked the teat of a cow corralled in a small stall near the back of the barn. Behind her, a frail calf lay on a bed of hay, curled into a circle. Pants of cold breath emerged from the tiny animal's nostrils. The mother stood, unmoving in Laura Ann's grip, as her milk was drawn for the newborn.

"Guess so. This one was a big surprise," Laura Ann said, squeezing her hands from top to bottom to drain life-giving fluid from the cow. Warm streams of milk made a *pssst* sound against the side of a plastic pail. Soon, milk covered the bottom in a frothing steamy white. "The herd is due March twenty-first. I'm not prepared for calving in this cold weather."

Like it could smell the nourishment, the baby calf stirred, working to stand on frail legs, then collapsed again in a pile. Ian went to the calf, scratching it behind the ears. The young one lowered its head to the ground, too exhausted to move.

"He needs the colostrum," Laura Ann said, squeezing the

teat one last time. She stood up, moving away from the cow, and went to the far side of the stall for a bottle and nipple, then poured the fresh milk for feeding. "Born yesterday, but the little guy hasn't taken to his momma yet. If he doesn't get some of this first milk, his body won't be able to absorb the antibodies."

Laura Ann nursed the calf through two bottles, then Ian set him aside. She stood and brushed off hay, then put away her feeding bottle and they left the stall. "This time tomorrow, he'll be on his feet. We'll probably have to feed him late tonight, and again in the morning."

"I like that word *we*," Ian said, then reached for her hand after she closed the stall.

Laura Ann felt the touch of his fingers as she threw the latch, and turned to face him. He reached up with his free hand and brushed at a piece of hay dangling from her bangs, then brushed more off the shoulder of her barn coat. She could feel his pulse in her fingers, his strong grip on her milk-wet hands.

"Got plans tomorrow?" she asked, pulling at the hand wrapped around hers. He moved closer.

"Sunday? I hoped you'd join me for church and dinner out."

She nodded in silence. Her free hand obeyed the passion of the pounding drum in her chest and she reached for the arm of his coat. She tilted her head up, eyes locked on his, pulling him close.

Ian's fingers came to her chin, caressing a line up to her cheek. She started to speak, a faint protest. His finger touched her lips and stopped the word, then he cradled the side of her face in his palm.

"Do you believe in the magic of coincidence?" he asked, a lilt in his voice.

She grinned, her spine tingling with each touch. "Daddy used to say that coincidence is when God chooses to remain anonymous."

"Or when we're too proud to admit it's part of His plan," Ian replied. He traced a finger along her temple, then ran his fingers through her hair, his hand alighting at the back of her head. He pulled her toward him.

"Is this part of God's plan?" she asked, breathless. Her own pulse beat against Ian's, his palm resting on her neck.

"I hope so." He bent over, forehead touching hers, warm breath on her cheek. "I've prayed for years that it might be."

# CHAPTER 7

DECEMBER 29

She smelled him.

Laura Ann tried to raise an arm to reach him, to hold him close, but he disappeared. A vapor. Her arm moved in a leaden way, unresponsive. Her voice froze in her throat. She thrashed against unseen forces holding her down, his smell — the one she despised — permeating her senses. He must be within reach.

"Daddy!" she screamed, forcing the words from her mouth.

She woke up.

But she could still smell him, his other scent, the acrid tang of burning tobacco that announced he'd entered the house, her smokeless sanctum. Daddy was home.

Laura Ann sat up in bed, groggy, yet fully aware. She smelled cigarettes. She fought to remember the last hours. Something in her heart tugged at other memories, of a passion she'd bottled up for years, waiting on the right time. Yet she sat here alone, that mysterious ardor unfulfilled.

The scent grew intense. She reached for her housecoat and slipped on night shoes to cross cold floors. Her nose led her, drawing her from the bedroom. None of it made sense. Snatches of memories returned as she passed her coat and jeans, tossed late last night on her bedroom chair. Feeding a calf. The barn. She stopped at the door, fingers to her lips, immersed in a fresh memory.

*Ian.*

But the smell? Laura Ann walked down the hall, daring to believe she'd lived a nightmare losing Daddy, yet desperate for proof that last night—Ian—had been real. She pursued the strong scent of cigarettes. Daddy home? Alive? In the house?

She exited the hall where it ran down the center of the house into the kitchen, glancing out the back window. Light flickered in a strange pulsing way, yellow illuminating the landscape of a snowy barnyard. She ran now, slippers slapping at cold oak. The light intensified with each stride as she exited onto the back porch, then set her dark-adjusted eyes suddenly ablaze.

The tobacco barn. In flames.

For the briefest of moments, Laura Ann froze in place, unsure which dream to trust. Daddy alive? Ian embracing her? Her farm on fire? In the drafty cold, she smelled her answer. Burning tobacco. Her only source of revenue. The lifeblood of this farm—and the death of Daddy.

She screamed.

Laura Ann dashed for the bedroom, ripping off her housecoat and shedding her nightgown while on the run. She skidded to a stop aside her bed, nearly naked, and jumped into her jeans and shirt. Socks and boots, laces pulled tight but untied. She threw on her barn coat and raced back to the kitchen, plans forming, and reforming plans.

She ripped the phone from its cradle and hit the light switch in the same movement. The bulb stayed dark. She flipped the switch twice more, same result. Above the phone, Ian's card beckoned her, wedged against the wall. She had to call him, but couldn't read in the dark. She punched 9-1-1, desperate for the ring, praying for a quick response. Kitchen clocks darkened, their LED lights snuffed out, she had no idea of the time. Five rings later, a gravelly voice answered.

"Please state your emergency." The operator sounded tired.

"Laura Ann McGehee. At The Jug. Our barn is on fire." She screamed the last words, desperate to go fight the blaze.

"Laur'Ann?" the voice replied. "What is it, child?"

"Mrs. Harper?"

"Your barn?"

"On fire! Call Ian Stewart!"

She hung up the phone, slung open the back door, and plunged into a river of icy air. Yellow and red blazes lit up the sky as the fire roared a hundred yards away, consuming more of the barn by the second. The main power pole, planted at the corner of the tobacco barn, spewed sparks from a burning transformer, the base of the pole wrapped in flames.

She ran, flakes of snow dusting her as they drifted down. Hot flakes. Not snow, but ash. The ash of ten thousand pounds of burning tobacco. A million cigarettes, ablaze at once. An unbearable stench.

Laura Ann's boots slapped at the ground, untied. She stopped briefly and whipped the laces about her ankles with a crude knot, then stood up to run again. Fifty yards away, at the corner of the tobacco field, Daddy's last crop roared in a brilliant inferno. Flames licked at the roof, bursting from the ends of the barn through the many openings built to air out the drying crop. Behind her, safe in the red dairy barn, yet somehow aware of looming disaster, her cows mooed.

"No!" she yelled, closing on the tobacco barn. In the distance, the edge of the wood flickered in ghostly ways, lit up by this roaring beacon. Short stubby stalks of summer's tobacco stumps stood in the frozen fields like a desiccated army, observing but not in the fight. She stopped a few yards away, repelled by the heat of the blaze. Her arms fell to her side, useless. There was no way to fight this. She could only watch.

Sticks of dried tobacco lit up like huge blazing cigars. Up to eight stalks of tobacco, pierced at their base and slid on each split oak stick, hung upside down in cascading rows from floor to ceiling. Through the brilliantly lit holes in the old log barn, Laura Ann could see stick after stick of bone-dry tobacco flare up. Flames engulfed each successive row and churned up the tinder of prime burley, flames rippling layer by layer toward the top of the barn. Licking tongues of fire poked at the rusty metal roof, caving it in as the support burned away.

She stood alone in the field, blistering in the heat of the huge fire. Red-hot sheets of rusty roof tin fell inward, plummeting to the bottom as pillars of fire shot out the top. Like a jet engine, the fire roared, sucking the air around her. A blazing yellow-red bolt licked at the sky fifty feet above.

Beyond the flame, she saw lights. The insane bouncing of a truck racing across their frozen dirt road, headed straight for her. In the distance, she could see the green of the truck in the dim light of her burning crop. Ian's work truck. He'd come.

Fear gripped her in the jaws of a brutal reality. She stood in the heat of a fire that consumed her only legitimate chance at saving the farm. A financial reprieve, to fulfill her promise to Daddy. She turned toward the house, strangely dark, and without power.

Ian's wild ride down the hill ran its course and his truck skidded to a stop. He jumped from the truck, running toward her.

"Laura Ann!" he yelled, arms outstretched.

She stood like a statue, turning her eyes back to the flames, one arm extended to him. He stopped at her side, then wrapped her in his arms. They watched together in silence.

One by one, logs cut by her great-great-great-grandfather fell inward, the top row of the barn drawn into the conflagration. History burned away before her. When at last a single flashing red light showed at the top of the hill, the barn was reduced to embers. The siren seemed distant, even the caress of Ian's hand on her head unfelt, while she watched the last of the flames consume the base of the old barn.

In the glow of the dying fire, she saw a chain. Links joined links, like hands of men at work together in an ancient fire brigade, leading beyond the fire into the dark of the forest, until they disappeared in an unknown history. The link closest to her melted in slow motion, smelted in the dull orange of the barn's smoldering foundation. It drooped, and then ran like hot metal into the red embers of her only cash crop.

The chain ended with her. She saw no future, no path beyond.

Ian waved his flashlight back and forth as they scoured the snow for footprints together. A fresh dusting of powder covered the fields, and new layers of thick snowflakes fell each minute. Walking a few feet to Ian's right, Laura Ann sighed, desperate for any clue. As good a tracker as he was, she knew that any possible traces of an arsonist would soon be obliterated by a blanket of white.

"I can barely make out the prints with this light," Ian said.

Deputy Sheriff Rodale shrugged, trudging along a few steps behind them, hands in his pockets.

"Someone approached the barn from over there." Ian stopped and pointed in the direction of the farm road. "They came and went in a single track, but once they reached the road the boot prints were wiped out by our vehicles. They probably anticipated that." He gestured to the top of the ridge and the direction of the intruder's path.

The deputy shook his head and muttered something that Laura Ann could not make out, then thanked Ian for his help and walked back to his cruiser. He left without even a word of condolence for Laura Ann. The firemen departed long ago, but at least they cared.

Ian brushed flakes of fresh snow off her jacket and put an arm about her. "Nothing we can do out here. Let's go clean you up." They both sported black from head to foot where they'd poked about the edges of the barn after the main fire died, searching for some clues. In the deputy's opinion, the transformer started it. No amount of evidence, whether visible footprints or Ian's game-tracker logic, could change the deputy's mind.

Laura Ann nodded at Ian's recommendation. "I smell like an ashtray." The first glimmer of predawn lit up the eastern sky. She tugged at Ian, leading him into the house. "You can shower here and change into some of Daddy's things."

"Thanks for the offer, but your power's out. Remember?"

Her shoulders slumped for a moment, then she brightened and pointed to the back door. "We can draw water at the hand pump in the barn. I'll heat you up a bath the old way." She gestured toward the gas stove.

Ian nodded. "I'll get the water. You rest a minute," he said, pulling a kitchen chair in her direction. On the way out he stopped at the back door and tested the lock but it spun free. "You still can't secure the house?" he asked, spinning it again.

"Never needed to. Until now."

Ian patted the doorjamb. "You sit tight. After we get cleaned up, I'll fix this door." He paused, watching her. "I think I should stay — if you don't mind."

Laura Ann smiled. "I don't mind at all," she said, pointing at the busted lock. "I was hoping you'd ask."

An hour later, Laura Ann lay curled up next to Ian on the sofa of her tiny living room. He wore a set of Daddy's overalls, freshly pressed. "I never expected to see these on anyone else."

She chuckled, pointing to the frayed knees. "Looks like you're ready to work, Officer Stewart."

Ian squeezed her shoulder, pulling her closer to him. He swallowed hard, gritting his teeth.

"What?" she asked.

"I am," he said, hesitating. "I mean, I *am* ready."

Laura Ann tilted her head to one side, raising an eyebrow. "Thank you, Ian. For everything."

"Rest up, Miss McGehee. I've got your back," he said with a playful pinch, then added, "and there's no place else I'd rather be."

Laura Ann let those words ring in her ears for a long moment, then repeated after him. "No place else?" She raised a hand to his face, her fingers lingering on the line of his jaw, his breath moist on her cheek.

"Nowhere — but here."

She felt his jaw move under the tips of her fingers. Laura Ann shut her eyes, in wonder. Floating in a dream. She imagined she could hear him breathe, his heart pounding in her ears.

As her eyes closed and heart raced, her lips parted of their own volition. A gentle warmth descended to meet her face, his lips brushing against hers, tentative, then pressing again with a tender confidence.

She melted into him.

Laura Ann padded into the kitchen a few minutes before ten, rubbing at the grit in her eyes. The world looked so different this time of morning. Most of her life she'd been awake before the sun. Not today. Ian greeted her from a seat at her breakfast table.

"Hello there, sleepyhead." He stood and grabbed a chair, pulling it out for her. Laura Ann couldn't remember the last person who did that. She yawned and plopped into the seat.

With two of the gas burners aflame on the old Tappan range, the kitchen was toasty warm. Ian opened the door of the old white gas oven, a pan of fresh biscuits browned and ready.

"You cooked these?" she asked, diving into the pan with the spatula that he offered. Ian set a jar of pear preserves on the table and brought over a pot of coffee. She waved off the drink.

"Suit yourself." He freshened up his own cup and sat down. "The calf is feeding," he said, sipping coffee and watching her across the lip of a steaming mug.

"You've been to the barn already?"

"I stayed up. I've got your back, remember? Went out at six to feed the cows. Checked on the little guy too. He was nursing hard when I got there. Latched on to his momma like a four-legged leech."

"Wow. I've never had help in the barn — other than Daddy. And he couldn't help with much of anything after November." Warm fuzzies walked up her back, easing the memory of last night's pain. She pushed the pan of biscuits across the table. "You didn't eat yet?"

"Nope. Waiting on you."

"You must be starved!"

"I am." Ian reached across the table, took both her hands, and offered a blessing. He scooped a pair of steaming biscuits out of the pan, then tapped the edge of her plate with his fork. "I have a recommendation. We stay here today. We'll do 'home church.'"

"I'd thought about that. I don't want to answer all the questions we'll get about the fire." She shook her head, recalling the suffocating drape of ash that engulfed her last night. "At least, not now."

"Agreed. So how about we spend the day together. You and me?" Ian's nose wrinkled with the suggestion, his Roman beak lending strength to high cheeks, a thin face, and a tall forehead.

Grey-blue eyes stared back at her from below bushy eyebrows, his trademark.

"I'd like that," she said with a grin. It felt good to smile again, to be around someone happy. He winked at her, spooned some pear preserves onto her plate, and then dove into his meal. Together they devoured half the pan of biscuits.

"I need to ask you something," Ian said later, slowing down after a third helping. "About the fire."

"Yes?"

"Think about it. How many tobacco barns burned up in all the years we've lived here?" He raised that eyebrow again.

"I don't know. A few?"

"This is the only tobacco fire I can ever remember, Laura Ann. While you were sleeping, I called the state emergency ops center in Charleston. They have a few fires on record, but all those were in fire-cured burley barns. Nothing air-cured has ever burned up in this county—or in the five counties around us." He bunched thin lips, looking up at the ceiling a moment, then added, "Until yours."

She shrugged. "First time for everything?"

"Nope. I don't buy it. And as for the deputy's view that the transformer 'just blew up,' that doesn't fit either. I called the power company to get the transformer replaced and they agree with me. There was no lightning or wind last night, and your place pulls almost no power load. Transformers don't spontaneously combust." Ian munched on half a biscuit topped with the last two spoons of pear preserves. He scooped out the dregs of the sweets and licked his spoon clean. "Even the insurance adjusters I called said that kind of fire was unheard of."

"So we're back to the footprints?" she asked, savoring her own last bite. Ian knew how to bake—another surprise.

"Someone set that fire, Laura Ann. Trouble is proving it. By the way, the fire department will be here late this afternoon to conduct an investigation. I called them too." He wiped his mouth and put the question on the table. "So—who'd do this?"

"It's a short list, Ian. About one person long."

"Your uncle Jack? Maybe. He's the easy choice. But I think he's too smart—no, make that 'cunning.'" He looked out the window in the direction of the black remains of the barn. "He'd send someone else." Ian took a deep breath, then added, "We'll have to hope the firemen find something."

Ian got up and moved his chair to sit next to her. He took her hand, pulling her gently toward him, and rested his elbow on the table. "How will you pay the bills, Laura Ann? Now that you've lost the tobacco?"

"I'll find a way." Her lip stiffened, her secret income source the first thing that came to mind when he asked. She hated that thought, battling to push it out of her mind.

"Put yourself in the banker's shoes. I need you to be specific. How do you pay?" He squeezed her hands.

"I don't know yet. But I won't let them take my farm. I promise you that."

Ian took another of his deep breaths, a sign he was forming hard words. "I admire your drive, Laura Ann. You've got guts, and—"

"That's all?" she asked. "Guts?"

"Okay. So gutsy is good, but it doesn't answer the mail for the banker or the real estate offer." He hesitated, then added, "I need hard numbers."

"I have a plan," she said with hesitation. "That's all I can say."

Ian huffed, shaking his head. "That answer won't cut it, either."

"So what do you want me to do?" she blurted out, her voice cracking. "I can't pull money out of thin air." Her eyes felt wet, a betrayal of the battle that raged inside. Self-esteem waged war with Daddy's memory. She hated herself for the moral compromise she'd already made to save this farm. Tears ran free down her cheek. She lowered her head, unable to let go of him, yet embarrassed to reveal her secret.

"I need you to listen, not act," he replied in a slow voice. "Drop the optimism for a minute and let's be pragmatic." He released her and lifted fingers to her cheek, wiping at the wet. "First of all, let me know who puts pressure on you. You call immediately, understand?" He pointed to the phone. "Memorize my number."

"This is my battle, Ian."

"No. It's not just about you, Laura Ann. I'm involved now, and this is *our* battle." His eyes bored through her. "But if we're going to function as a team, you have to share the game plan. You can't keep it to yourself." He paused a moment, his tone softer. "I know you pretty well and I get this sense there's something important you're not telling me."

She shrugged, silent.

Ian took a napkin from the table, cradling her chin in one hand and wiping gently at the little rivers on her face. "We'll get through this, I promise. Remember what you told me when I worried if I'd finish my associate's degree? And what you said so many times in those long months when I was looking for a game warden job?" His smile punctuated the questions as he daubed at the last dampness. He put a finger to the corner of her mouth, dragging it up into a forced grin, her hot cheeks rising under the caress of a tender hand.

"You remembered?" she asked, her voice barely a whisper, convicted now by her own words.

He nodded and pushed back an errant bang from her eyes while he waited for her answer.

"A daddy lesson," she said at last. Laura Ann's smile faded, her lips testifying to a terrible hypocrisy. "Trust God to provide."

She dropped her gaze, staring in humiliation at her hands.

Laura Ann tucked a quilt around the back of Ian's shoulders. His head sank into the down of the pillow she'd brought him only minutes earlier. She knelt by the sofa, her face close to his, the breath of his light snoring a damp warmth on her cheek.

The stubble of a day's beard roughened a face she'd never seen unshaven in their years together. A stickler for a fresh haircut and a smooth face, Ian's sudden vulnerability, his day without a razor, sent a strange warmth coursing through her. He'd come here — and stayed — just for her. She fought the temptation to caress his jaw, desperate to draw her finger across his chin like she used to touch Daddy, in wonder at the daily forest that sprang out of his skin.

Straight brown hair lay askew on the pillow, but the line of his hair against his neck was perfect. A weekly trip to Curt's Barber Shop always preceded his Saturday visit to The Jug. Daddy once commented that Ian cut his hair for Laura Ann, his habit of arriving freshly groomed every weekend to "check in." Perhaps Daddy saw more in Ian than she'd allowed herself to dream. Just a friend, dependable to the end, his Saturday visits meant fellowship and fun, a break in the predictable pattern of work at the farm. She saw the truth now — he'd come courting. After fifteen years of companionship, she'd been too preoccupied with him as a boy to notice the beau.

Laura Ann again fought the urge to touch him, then stood to adjust the quilt over his feet, and backed away. She lingered at the door to the living room, wishing she could crawl onto the sofa with him, curled at his side, and feel him breathe in his sleep. She wished he would wake and tell her just how to deal with her dilemma. Perhaps he could save her from the only financial option she had at her disposal. Laura Ann prayed that he would rise now, and deliver her from herself.

She backed away from the door, staring down the hall to her bedroom. At the end of the short passage, the bathroom beckoned, the yawning mouth of its narrow door ready to swallow her. Laura Ann's destiny, and the farm's one salvation, rested in a silver foil package in the medicine cabinet.

Like one giant hand of fate pushing her from the kitchen down the length of the hall, and another bony hand dragging her into the bath, twin forces pulled her from Ian to her next task. While he slept, she would take the first step, preparing her body for cold hands that would steal life from her one moment, but pay cash the next.

Her steps to the bath forgotten, she found herself staring in the mirror at a woman she knew, but had no desire to be. A blister pack of pills in one hand, she fingered the foil, pressing its malleable silver down on the hard bump below. The pink magic beneath her fingertip would soon transform her body in remarkable ways that could save this home. A daily pill that enabled her womanhood to put crucial money on the table, if only for a time. A regular pill she must take every day to catalyze changes in her body and gain her advantage—a financial buffer and the time she needed to save the farm.

She stared at the mirror. Long brown hair, pulled back into a ponytail, draped over her left shoulder—hair that screamed to be washed. Hair unkempt from fighting fires and sleeping in too late. Brown curly hair that defied control.

She stripped off the foil from this day's dose and perched a pink pill on her tongue, the doctor's elixir to alter her body for profit—for family, and for land.

*But at what price?*

One green eye, and one blue, blinked back with no answer.

Laura Ann made her choice. She shut her eyes and swallowed, drowning out the voice and its wisdom — Ian's repetition of her own words — a wisdom that fought to rip the pill from her throat.

*God will provide.*

# CHAPTER 8

APRIL 16

The sweet aroma of fresh-plowed earth wrapped itself around her like a cool blanket. Thick furrows of new soil lay to her left, winter's humus warming under a bright spring sun. Laura Ann rode the rumbling Case tractor sidesaddle, her left hand gripping the cherry-red lip of the fender while her right hand steered the powerful machine. She guided the belching diesel with a sixth sense for the slice of shiny blades behind her, a four-bottom plow spilling out long ribbons of deep red soil that laid over the green of a winter rye cover crop. April's sun bore into dirt that had never seen the light of day, drying into a light brown crust on exposed ground. A ruddy spring palate of red, brown, and green spread out behind her, ready to embrace seed and to bear new life.

Stabs of pain pulled her attention from the tractor, claws ripping at her insides from deep in her belly. "No. Not again," Laura Ann moaned, pulling her hand from the fender and shoving her fingers between jean and shirt.

The pressure of her fingers beneath the belt line of her pants did nothing for the stabbing pain. She buckled at the waist, bending over the steering wheel. The tractor veered and her left tire jammed into the soft soil of her last plow line. The Case lurched from its normal smooth roll in the track of the previous furrow. She hurried to shift the big machine into neutral.

Laura Ann pulled the throttle back to idle and slipped out of the seat, lowering herself gingerly to the ground. Behind her, straight lines of torn earth ended where she stood—earth ripped apart just like her insides. The hot stab of her latest attack stole her balance and she faltered, stumbling in fresh-turned soil.

Laura Ann steadied herself, leaning into the tractor's tire. Like waves crashing onshore, her cramps multiplied times over, swelling for their peak someplace deep inside her abdomen. She breathed deep, shutting her eyes and digging her hands into soft clods that stuck to the tires. Half a minute she clung to the big wheel, imagining a towering wave of torture that curled above, ready to smash her into oblivion.

"Some occasional mild cramping and nausea. Nothing more," the doctor promised, his head hidden somewhere beneath a sheet that draped over her bare legs while he probed with a long ultrasound wand and cold instruments. He told her it might hurt, but never apologized when she winced at the bite of the long needle deep inside her. He reminded her of an angler shrugging off the bloody worm that broke in two when he pulled it from the soil of his bait bucket. Dr. Katinakis claimed to care for his clients, but she felt more like a commodity than an object of concern. Feet strapped in cold stirrups, her body bared in the most private way to a man, she'd handed herself over to a team of strangers who'd suctioned out precious life.

The wave crashed again, pummeling that place he'd violated just yesterday. A place she'd exposed for her own gain.

Laura Ann crumpled, curling on her side against the embrace of cool earth, her knees drawn up to her side. The rumble of the idling Case faded into the background as images dashed through her head, hot waves building for their third collision on her shore.

A doctor with foot-long hypodermics and cream-colored wands, nurses with gentle voices whose pleading eyes cried out "why are you here?" Bright lights and pink linens, suction devices and latex gloves. And a pat on the back from a patronizing physician who reminded her that, after all that pain, "Everything will be just fine."

*I'm not fine.*

The wave crushed her. She moaned, her voice dying in the moist earth below her face, echoes drowned out by a rumbling diesel. She focused her attention on the dirt, the sweet cool smell of fresh soil. Dirt—her only sure solace and redemption. No more waves built within her. She sat up.

Laura Ann opened her eyes just a moment, glancing at her watch, an old Timex buffed to a satin patina from the scratches of hard work. Three contractions in the past ten minutes. She stood, pulling at handholds on the tire and tractor seat. Dizzy, she leaned back into the tire, then reached around the clay-caked wheel to fish out a small jug, her only refreshment. Lukewarm water wet her lips but her stomach revolted before she could swallow, a fourth wave of pain springing to life within her. The old quart milk container fell from her hands and she crumpled to her knees.

Her lunch came up.

Laura Ann wiped her mouth on the sleeve of her work shirt, then crawled a few feet away and lay down on unplowed earth, damp grass her bedding. The deep-throated rumble of the idling diesel thrummed inside her, the sound of new life vibrating through soft ground. She gritted her teeth again, shutting her eyes against yet another wave of cramps and nausea.

"No strenuous activity tomorrow. Just go shopping," the counselor joked only yesterday in Morgantown.

*Shopping?*

Every dollar she touched went into a Mason jar stashed at

the back of the refrigerator, its clear glass a window to her financial reality. There could be no stores, no expensive fun. And no relaxing. Tomorrow it would rain, perhaps the first of several days of storms. Today was her one chance to get the fields ready for planting. Cramps or not, strenuous or not, she had to plow and disc. Without fields, without planting, there could be no crops—and no mortgage payments. Far down the hill, in a cold container tucked behind mayonnaise, her next payment waited. A wad of lifeless bills counted into her hand by a man with no smiles, doling out thirty pieces of silver—her body traded for the farm's salvation.

*But not thirty pieces. Not even one.*

Seven hundred dollars. Not the twenty-five thousand she'd read about in the magazine. Not the ten thousand she read about on the website. Not even the four thousand dollars she'd brought home three times already. Just seven hundred dollars, barely enough for one week of mortgage, shelled out by the doctor like he'd parted with the last of his life savings.

"For your trouble," Dr. Katinakis said with a shrug, his fingers holding tight to that last bill lest Laura Ann snatch it from him. "This is the best I can do. You had what we call a 'dropped cycle.' I need you to try again."

She shuddered, recalling his prolonged wink and grin, that creepy informality when he laid his fingers on her forearm, lingering just a moment with the parting words, "I hope you'll come back."

Laura Ann gritted her teeth against the crescendo of suffering, all her attention focused on the sweet scent of grass and dandelion. Delicate yellow flowers tickled her cheek where she lay in a fertile green pasture.

*Green.*

Seven green bills joined others, saved like Daddy taught her, barely enough to make the next payment, and not a dollar to spare. As though the woman counselor who'd greeted her at the clinic knew just how much she'd need to survive. "You're tall, attractive, and physically fit," the woman said, looking her over like a cattle auctioneer. "Take all the medication as we prescribed. I'm sure you'll do better next time."

*Dropped cycle. Medications as prescribed. Better next time.*

Promises made. Promises broken.

Laura Ann snapped a dandelion free, the white milk of its sap sticky where it bled on her finger. She held the soft blossom to her cheek and closed her eyes, resting her head on cool grass and gritting against the next wave of pain.

"Behold, children are a heritage from the Lord, the fruit of the womb a reward."

*Womb.*

Pastor Culpeper's recitation of the Psalm in Sunday service pierced her, a dagger thrust into her bosom of guilt. "Like arrows in the hand of a warrior are the children of one's youth." He read on, preaching to the little Baptist church in Pursley where she'd worshipped since Daddy's passing. "Blessed is the man who fills his quiver with them! He shall not be put to shame when he speaks with his enemies in the gate."

*Quiver. Shame.*

"We always pay our bills, Peppermint," Daddy said many times, the memory of another lesson tumbling into the midst of her recollection of the pastor's sermon. Daddy's words and the Psalm tore at tender scabs deep inside her, godly wisdom picking in tandem at raw wounds.

She'd sold arrows from her quiver to escape the shame of debt.

*Have I lost the blessing?*

"Laura Ann?" a voice asked. She felt a hand beneath her head, warmth that spoke "Ian." She opened her eyes, squinting against the sun.

"Are you okay?"

She smiled, moving her hand from under her head, sliding her other hand beneath the belt line of her jeans to palm the pain that gripped her moments ago. Nothing. Only memories of hot pitchforks driving themselves deep into her belly. She smiled.

"Ian? I—I'm fine." She tried to push up off the ground, but he lifted her, arms under her back and legs, gathering her into his chest. Laura Ann gasped and threw an arm about his neck, sure she'd fall. Ian carried her a few steps to the tailgate of his pickup.

"What happened?" he asked, setting her gently on the truck. "I've been down at the house waving at you, looking for the tractor to move. Got tired of waiting and drove up to see if you were alright." He laughed, thumbing in the direction of the idling Case. "Taking a nap?"

Laura Ann shook her head in silence, running her fingers through her hair to knock out bits of weed. "I didn't plan it that way."

"Are you sick?"

She nodded. "Female stuff. You wouldn't understand."

"I might. Remember, I have two sisters. You sure you aren't sick?" he asked again, motioning toward a yellow pile of half-digested food.

"Really bad cramps, Ian. I threw up. Must have curled up in the grass for a minute."

"Not just for a minute. I thought you'd left the tractor in the field. Took me a while to figure out you weren't at the house but up here lying on the ground." He handed her his Thermos. "Something cold? Looks like you could use it."

Laura Ann nodded in silence and took a long draught of ice

water. She capped the Thermos and then slid toward the edge of the tailgate. "Thanks. I'm glad you're here."

Ian laughed again, shaking his head. "You forgot, didn't you?"

"What?" she asked, sliding off the truck. She brushed more weeds from her shirt and pants, headed for the tractor.

"Tonight?" he asked, pointing at the low sun. "Dinner and a movie, remember?"

Laura Ann stopped in her tracks, mentally rerunning the day, her one desperate opportunity to get the fields ready for planting. After yesterday's trip to Morgantown, and today's unbearable pain, she'd lost track.

*Date night.*

"Oh, no! Ian, I'm sorry. I—"

He put a finger to his lips, a big smile lighting up his bony face. Ian stepped forward and took her hand. "Gonna rain tomorrow, girl. We'd better be plowing." He tarried, as though searching in her eyes for some news she wouldn't share. "We'll catch a movie Saturday after I get off."

She started to protest, but Ian shook his head, dropping her hand to move past. With a foot on the bed of the tractor and a hand on the wheel, he launched himself into the seat. Moments later, before she could pull him back, he'd lifted the gang of four plows, put the big diesel in reverse, and backed out of the jam she'd created minutes ago.

"Take my truck and go get the other tractor," he yelled over the acceleration of the engine. "I already hooked up the disc. I'll finish this off and get the other disc when I'm done." And with that, he drove away, his blades spilling out four new ribbons of soil.

Ten minutes later, Laura Ann sat on the old blue Ford, a disc harrow hooked up behind her. With both of them working the field, the job could be finished by dark. He'd given up his favorite evening to plow. To be with her.

Laura Ann eased the tractor into the plowed field, setting her disc into soft rows of fresh dirt. Sharp silver wheels sliced through curled furrows, chopping soil into crumbles. Robins and boat-tailed grackles swooped in on the worm pie that spread out behind Laura Ann's tractor, a seedbed filled with a feast of night crawlers. The sun dipped into the tops of the poplars, now adorned in a brilliant life-green of new leaves. Pass after pass, working her way across the new field, she pummeled fresh plowing into new planting soil. The first cool of evening gripped her when Ian shifted from plow to harrow. His tractor worked the far half of the field, the two of them growing twelve feet closer each pass they made, closing the gap from opposite sides of the seedbed. The place deep inside that seared her minutes ago now glowed warm for him, their paths slowly winding across fresh dirt toward an eventual intersection.

The damp of the Middle Island Creek crept up from the valley, a misty fog in the moist April evening. Early night air blanketed the farm. Acres of freshly turned earth filled the air with the perfume of farming, faintly musty, faintly sweet. This was the aroma of life, like the fields after a rain.

Laura Ann raised her head high, capturing the musky fragrance of tilled earth, her mouth open as though she could drink it in and make it hers to remember every day. Something powerful about the smell of plowed soil made it amorous, even sensual. Acres of fertile dirt spread out before her, prepared by loving hands, ready to accept seed and spring forth with new life.

*Romantic.*

That was the word. God had inclined her nose—surely her entire body—to adore this bouquet.

Laura Ann finished her pass down the length of the field

and spun the tractor for her last line of disc work, one that would put her on an intersecting path with Ian. She determined to meet him midfield, then cook him a late dinner and wrap him in her arms to thank him — in a special way — for this sacrifice.

"I came over to the farm yesterday," Ian said after a long silence. They sat together on a porch swing watching the night fog roll over the valley and its acres of new fields. Laura Ann curled her head into his shoulder, her arms wrapped tight about his chest. The bony protrusions of his ribs were distinct washboards below his khaki shirt. "You didn't answer the house phone and I was worried."

She hesitated, her fingers caressing the stiff cotton of his official shirt.

"You got back late last night," he continued. His voice went high on the word *late*.

Laura Ann released her grip about his chest, pushing up in the seat to look him in the eye. "How did you know?"

He shrugged, avoiding her eye.

"Granny Apple called me," he offered at last. "She was fretting too. She called you several times, then heard you went to see a doctor."

Laura Ann stiffened, then responded. "I was. At a doctor in Morgantown."

"Are you okay?" he asked, moving his head to catch her gaze again. He took her hand and squeezed it.

"Yes. But I have to go back in three weeks." She paused, hoping he wouldn't ask more.

"What's the problem?" Ian asked, folding both her hands in his. "I want to be there for you, and to pray for you."

She shrugged. "It's not important."

"It is to me," he insisted. "More than you realize."

"This is embarrassing, Ian. Private. I'd rather not talk about it." She moved away from him and stood up, pushing the porch swing hard as she left it. Wiping at a tear in her eye, she faced away from him and stood at a porch post, staring into the night. Rising fog blanketed much of the low farmland near the Middle Island Creek, muffling sounds from the forest. The distinctive call of a night-feeding whip-poor-will echoed up from the creek bottom. Laura Ann counted each accented syllable of the call.

*Whip-poor-will.*

Ian moved from the swing to the far side of the steps, gazing out into the night. She hoped he'd stay there, and not move closer for a while.

"I've been practicing a long time for what I'd planned to say tonight," he said, clinging to a post, eyes focused somewhere in the distant dark. "But ..."

Laura Ann's heart leapt with his first words, then died in the silence that followed.

"You went to Morgantown in the middle of that insane snowstorm back in February. Remember? You told me then too that it was female stuff. I prayed all day, Laura Ann. Prayed for whatever it was that you felt you couldn't share with me, in hopes you'd be healed or cared for."

Ian never moved from his post. "We've walked through some hard times since Christmas, but we've been together every day, even if I had to work late. There was no doubt in my mind that we're right for each other — no doubt until today."

*Until today?*

Laura Ann's heart raced, every fiber straining for her to lift a hand, move a foot, or say something to stop his next words before he could utter them. She turned to face Ian. She moved too late.

"When I realized you were on the ground —" His voice

cracked and he turned away, drawing in another deep breath. "When I saw you there, I thought I'd lost you. I drove like a madman across the field to get to you." He wiped at his own eyes and walked away to the end of the porch.

Laura Ann followed, holding her distance. Wars raged inside her to run and wrap her arms about him.

Ian turned back to face her, welling tears reflecting in the dim light from the living room window. "I didn't plan to confront you with this, but the stranger you act, the more distant you become. This secret of yours—what you call 'female stuff'—is coming between us."

He drew in a deep breath and stepped toward her, raising a hand in her direction. "I love you, Laura Ann." He stood there, waiting for her response, then continued. "But I hate secrets." He coughed, and then added, "I have my reasons."

"Think, then speak," Daddy used to say. She measured her next words, desperate to scream them.

"I'm sorry, Ian—but it's my business."

"It's *our* business, Laura Ann. Whatever this is about. I've been here every day helping you to keep the farm afloat." He paused. "I thought we were a team."

"We are. We were—," she said, choking on the last word.

"Were?" he blurted out. His footsteps were the only sound in the silence that followed. He approached and put a hand on her shoulder, tugging at her to turn.

Laura Ann backed away, bumping into the porch rail. She could run no further, withering in the face of the first anger she'd seen from him in months.

"The farm—," she began.

Ian cut her off. "No! I've heard all about your dreams, and know just what problems we're facing. *We* are facing."

"I'd do anything—"

"Old news, Laura Ann. Tell me something I don't know.

You're going to the doctor, or at least you say you are. I want to know what ails you — and that's where I can't tolerate secrecy." He lowered his eyes a moment, and then looked back up. "I'm sorry. I just want to help."

Ian backed away from her, gritting teeth that clamped down on words she was sure he'd swallowed. "I've hidden nothing from you, Laura Ann. And I don't ever intend to." He gulped and looked away.

*Whip-poor-will.* The bird cried out, the echo of its song muffled in the fog. No bird called back. Solitary. Isolated. Alone.

She gripped the porch rail behind her, backed into a corner she could not escape. "I'm not exactly sick, Ian."

"Then?"

"A gynecologist in Morgantown has me on some strong medications to regulate my cycle."

"That's all?" he asked, a nervous laugh mixed in the question. He laid his hands on her shoulders, long gentle fingers clutching her with a familiar vigor. "Nothing else?"

She shook her head, tears flowing unchecked. Ian gripped her with the warm strength she'd yearned to feel. No money was worth losing him, not even the thousands she'd been promised if she'd return to the Morgantown clinic one last time. She buried her head in his shoulder, hiding her face as he wrapped his arms about her.

"No. That's all," she said, her voice cracking in a desperate mix of secrets, tears — and lies.

# CHAPTER 9

JUNE 21

"You need me, girl. With my help you can pay for this place."

"I'll manage—without you." Laura Ann watched Uncle Jack's every move where he stood at the edge of the drive, mindful of Granny Apple's warnings about him.

"You won't survive." Uncle Jack flipped a cigarette butt into the middle of her garden. "How much you got, anyway? A few thousand dollars? Paying the bank at twenty-three hundred a month? You're gonna crash. That is, if the bank doesn't call your note first."

"My bank account is none of your business. If my father were here," she continued, "he'd thrash you for talking to me this way."

"Is that so? Well, he's dead and gone, isn't he? But no matter." Her uncle kicked at the swinging gate on the picket that surrounded her herb garden, slamming it back hard. The entire fence shuddered under his ire.

"Let's hope the bank doesn't come calling with an audit of your worthless mortgage," he threatened, walking toward his blue pickup. "My offer might not be there when you come looking for help."

"Be assured, you're the last person I'd ask," she said, working to control the quivering in her voice.

"Stubborn girl. Like your old man."

"Thank you," she said, her grip tightened on the hoe handle at her side. "I'll take that as a compliment."

"Stupid too."

Uncle Jack lingered at the driver's door, as if his words might have stirred some special desire in Laura Ann to relent to his wishes. He watched her, a deep frown creasing his face. In her twenty years, she'd only seen him smile once. Every visit to the farm ended like this. On the best of days a honk summoned Auntie Rose to the car. Explosive visits—and there were many—always ended with Daddy standing in the drive, holding his ground as Uncle Jack slunk away. Her uncle's swearing would start soon.

"Better get that tobacco in the ground this month"—his hand gripped the lip of the door, white knuckles showing on thick fingers—"or it's over."

"It *is* over, Uncle Jack. There won't be any planting, and I won't sell the allotment. Not to anybody." She jammed her hoe handle into the dirt, an exclamation point on her determination. No matter what, Uncle Jack would never grow that noxious weed on this land.

"You're a fool. When the bank takes this place, I'll be standing on the curb laughing."

"I have no doubt of that."

Uncle Jack cocked his head to the side, and then shrugged. "Call me when you change your mind." He opened the door and started to slide into the seat, stopping to throw one more insult her way through the gap between the door and the frame.

"About time for another of those big deposits, isn't it?" He turned and spit, then looked back at her before he slid into the seat. "Tell your sugar daddy I'm watching him."

Uncle Jack slammed the door. He spun the big Ford's wheels in reverse, and rocks shot out when he kicked the truck into drive, some of them peppering the fence in front of her.

A middle-finger salute made his parting message quite clear.

Laura Ann's knees buckled and she sank to the ground in her herb garden, legs folded. She lowered the hoe with shaking hands, setting its sharp blade in the pea gravel of the garden path. Daddy's white picket fence surrounded a twenty-foot square plot, each pointed slat cut in the woodshop last year during his final summer.

Laura Ann leaned into the wooden form of a small raised garden bed, nine squares like a giant tic-tac-toe filled with spices for her kitchen. Anise sprung up behind her, serrated leaves and flat clusters of white flowers shooting up for salad garnish and the licorice-like flavoring in her Christmas cake. Narrow leathery shoots of rosemary fought for control of the soil in the same bed. Their fragrance filled the air, mixing with the scent of fresh earth where she'd been pulling weeds before Uncle Jack's uncivil visit.

*My "sugar daddy"?*

If Uncle Jack really knew what price she'd paid to make it this far, he'd crush her in the town's rumor mill. She leaned over, her head resting on the low wooden form. How much longer until she ran out of options? Barely hanging on, she determined to make this work — if at all possible — without the Morgantown doctor's money.

She reached into the herb bed absentmindedly, plucking at a few weeds she'd missed around the base of the rosemary. Moist black soil, her special mix of composted manure, leaf mulch, and river-bottom sand, released with a slight tug. She tossed each weed in the rock path, pretending each successive plant was a month.

The last of her savings—and a pittance from the clinic in Morgantown—got her through April. Twelve fat calves went to auction in May. June depended on her selling fifty stools to a buyer in New Martinsville. July and August? Sell more of Daddy's prized Angus at auction, if her stools didn't carry the day. September? Depend on harvest time, and perhaps find an extra source of income. If everything failed, break her secret promise, and return to the money tree that waited in Morgantown. A bright pink clinic, cold stirrups, and a sheet draped over splayed legs.

Her mind played games, imagining a worm in the dirt clod she'd pulled to be the doctor who probed her like a vet pulling a calf at birth. No concern for her as a person, simply another girl lying naked beneath a gown, ready to be harvested.

A harvest that kept her farm alive.

Laura Ann wondered about Auntie Rose, strangely silent in the months since Daddy died. Uncle Jack would make sure she stayed away, locking her up with a key, a tongue lashing—and a fist if necessary—to keep her from her childhood home. Laura Ann plucked another weed, wondering how hard it would be to jerk Auntie Rose from the clutches of her oppressor. Like Uncle Jack holding Auntie Rose hostage in town, she knotted the weeds tight in one hand. She pushed up from her place on the ground and wheeled a full barrow of weeds to the compost pile.

A June sun bore down with the full fury of today's summer solstice. Grasshoppers jumped from her path when she crossed the lawn, its withered blades burned a crunchy brown after weeks of drought. She tarried at the old compost pile. Salty rivulets worked their way down the middle of her back, under Daddy's old church shirt, tied in a knot across her belly.

She shaded her eyes against the glare. Ian's pickup appeared at the top of the ridge, billowing dust. She'd never seen him drive this fast. What new trouble raced her way?

Moments later, Ian's tires crunched on her drive. "Are you okay?" he asked when he leapt from the truck.

She nodded, wiping soiled fingers on her jeans, then took his hand when he ran up.

"I saw Jack when I drove in. He nearly ran me off the road." He gasped for breath. "I almost went after him, but needed to check on you first."

"I'm fine." Laura Ann squeezed his hand and placed her other hand on his arm. "He's trying every angle. Uncle Jack came out to squeeze me into selling—or leasing—the tobacco allotment."

"And?" Ian asked, wiping the sweat of his own brow with the back of his arm.

"Told him 'no.' He didn't take the news too well," she said with a grin.

Not looking her way, Ian picked up the hoe at her side. "Rumor mill's going full tilt."

"Whatever the story, Ian, I'm sure it has no basis."

"I hope so." He blushed. "I mean, I'm sure there's no basis."

She furrowed her brow, watching his eyes.

*Embarrassed? Or nervous?*

"What are you trying to say?" she asked.

"Word is ..." Ian coughed and started again, looking away when he spoke. "Folks are talking, Laura Ann. They say that you're accepting paying visitors at the farm." He bit his lip. "Male visitors."

She nodded toward the porch. "Do you see a red light?" She hoped for a laugh, but he frowned.

"What?" she asked. "You believe that stuff?"

"This affects me too, Laura Ann."

"Oh, really?" She crossed her arms. "And how's that?"

He paused, watching her for a long time, his eyes misting as he fought for the right words. "I'm the man they're talking about. The paying kind."

Laura Ann's hands went to her mouth. "How can people say that?" she asked. "Everyone knows we're friends."

"Just friends?" he asked, a faint smile wrinkling his cheeks.

"More than friends," she replied. "Much more."

"I'm getting lots of questions — at the office, and around town," he said, looking down again. "You know. Innuendo. 'The look.' Some snickers at Auggie's." He shook his head. "Not a good thing for a law enforcement officer."

She walked up to him, coaxing his right hand from his pocket. When she took it in her own, she felt a bandage and looked down. Flesh-colored tape covered three scraped knuckles. She pulled the hand to her lips and kissed his wound. "What happened?"

Ian raised an eyebrow and shrugged, looking at the taped hand. "I won a reprimand and a three-day vacation." He moved his hand to her shoulder to pull her closer.

"Truth is, I slugged our office manager." His face reddened, his pulse quickening in the throbbing beat of his neck. "Randy started spouting off about me 'shacking up at the McGehee place.' So I broke his nose." He smiled, ponds visible in his eyes. "Got a stiff reprimand and three days of administrative leave for my trouble." He took a deep breath and continued. "For what it's worth, my boss said he didn't blame me. Told me to chill out and go chop some wood."

Ian chuckled, then continued. "So — I've got three days off, gorgeous. You need any help?"

"Hanging out together, stacking hay and irrigating a parched corn field. My goodness, folks in town are gonna talk," Ian said with a laugh from his seat at her kitchen table. Sweat soaked his shirt with long white stains under his arms and down the center of his chest. A sunburn reddened his cheeks with a look of embarrassment. "You're a taskmaster, McGehee. It's eight o'clock, for crying out loud. Was this your idea of a date?"

Laura Ann laughed, tossing a freshly peeled carrot his direction. "Think fast, Game Warden." Ian caught the flying orange stick in midair and crunched loudly into the treat.

"Not a date," she said. "But how about a rain check?"

"Deal!" Ian walked up to her at the sink, wrapping his arms around her waist where she stood paring vegetables. He pulled her close, lowering his head over her shoulder.

His warmth fit into the small of her back, his chest rising and falling in a slow rhythm, pushing the wet fabric of her shirt against her skin. Ian's head tucked into the small of her neck, the stubble of a day-old beard scratching against her. She pulled her hands up to meet him, and leaned her head into his.

"I have a request for you," he whispered. "An invitation."

"Really?" she asked, twisting in his arms. Her face came close to his, brushing against the sandpaper of his chin.

"A romantic evening in Parkersburg. A splurge."

"No, Ian," she said, shaking her head. "Save the money. Please."

Ian pulled her tighter, squeezing strong arms about her in a mock punishment. "No can do. Got big plans."

"Where?" she asked, pretending to fight his grip and squirm toward the sink. He held her firm.

"The Blennerhassett," he replied, drawing out each syllable.

"That beautiful old place down by the court house?" she asked. "No. Too expensive." She prayed he'd resist. Daddy let her wander into the hotel years ago when he was filing some papers at the Wood County Courthouse. The memory never faded, the elegance of the hotel's reception area unlike anything she'd seen in her life, even more sophisticated than the Wells Inn in Sistersville. Walnut wainscot. Deep leather chairs. And amazing food, according to local lore. Her mouth watered.

"Not gonna hear it, McGehee. This will be a special night." He cleared his throat, looked away, then back at her. "Very special."

Laura Ann relaxed in his arms, lowering her hands to rest on his shoulders. "Very?"

He nodded. "Our six-month anniversary."

"Anniversary?" she asked, tracing the line of his ear with a finger.

"Since that first kiss. So ... I have reservations. A week from Friday."

"I can't stop you, then?" she asked with a grin, tapping his head with a freshly pared carrot.

He grinned, red wrinkles creasing his face. "Not a chance."

"Then it's a date. I accept."


On tiptoe, Laura Ann felt for a zippered container on the top shelf of her towel closet, then pulled it free. Seated on the toilet lid in her bathroom, she opened a padded pink makeup kit and, one by one, laid the contents in the freestanding porcelain sink to her left. Her hands shook as she touched each piece in the kit, a sorcerer's bag of genetic paraphernalia that transformed her body into money—four times—at a price.

Images of Daddy filled her mind when she reached into the tiny case. She saw him in her daydream, standing here at the sink morning after morning, the door always left ajar when he shaved. Many days she would watch him from the kitchen while she cooked and he scraped a stubbly black forest off his face.

Daddy's memory morphed into mental images of Ian, his tall frame hovering over this same sink hours ago, washing his face like Daddy used to do before dinner. She'd watched him from the kitchen too. Were Ian watching her now, he'd cry to see what she'd hidden from him in this package. Her little box of magic that helped service a debt she had no reliable means to repay. Daddy would cry for her sacrifice too, burdened that his self-inflicted disease led her to this place of desperation.

She removed two foil packs with rows of pink, yellow, and green pills, each medication labeled by the day, a different color for each week. She held two new packs, each waiting to smooth her way for three weeks into the first phase of her next body preparation process. She laid aside a small foil-topped bottle labeled "Pergonal," and its twin demon — a hypodermic syringe. She spread out the demon's claws, three dozen sharp silver needles, recoiling at the sight of the razor-sharp points. Packed at the bottom of her pink Pandora's box she retrieved a small spiral-bound notepad, filled with handwritten notes that recorded her days of oral supplements and self-administered injections. From the cover of the zippered pink box she pulled out a business card for Dr. Alexandros Katinakis. The doctor's picture in the upper left corner of the card made her cringe. The caress of his fingers in her hidden places would long remain a disturbing memory.

Laura Ann replaced the notebook, the card, and the paraphernalia, then zipped the case shut. Pink bag in hand, she stopped in the kitchen and took a box of matches from over the gas stove, then headed for the front door.

A small pile of wood waited at the edge of the drive, her little campfire prepared when Ian drove away long after midnight. The few sticks and tinder she'd gathered would burn quickly, but not hot enough to endanger the farm on a dry night. Horizon to horizon, the Milky Way blazed above her in a cloudless sky as she lit the tiny bonfire, encouraging flames with a few puffs. A gentle night breeze carried smoke away from the house, and the dry wood caught fire. Within moments, her blaze licked upwards, seeking more fuel.

Laura Ann set the pink zippered bag on top of the fire. Quickly, flames ate through the plastic, molten drips of burning pink falling into hot coals. Another burst of flame shot forth in a blaze of green and yellow—this time, the pill packs. A few moments later she heard a telltale hiss—the boiling of Pergonal in its bottle. More dripping balls of flame meant a melting hypodermic. Like an offering, she fueled a pyre with drugs, needles, and eight months of secrets and regrets. Venus suspended a waning crescent above her, heralding a new moon, a new month—and new life.

Laura Ann stood transfixed by the dying fire. Embers glowed with all that remained of her former days. Her funerary obliterated the options she'd chosen when she had no other choice. Gone were the catalysts of four nightmares where cold hands suctioned precious innocence from her womb.

Yet, somehow, her offering lacked closure.

*The drugs are gone, but my secret remains.*

# CHAPTER 10

JUNE 24

Lucky nuzzled against Laura Ann's leg in the woodshop, his jet-black fur speckled with shavings that spit from the edge of her blade. She pulled her tool off the lathe rest and nudged the cat aside with her foot, then moved the skew chisel back into a spinning oak cylinder, shaping the delicate surface of a decorative bead. For hours she'd turned lathe blanks, marking out cuts and shaping beads. Pungent reddish-beige oak dust covered her from shoulder to foot, and a pile of stool parts stood in the box at her side.

Lucky jumped up and curled on the stack of today's production. Fifty stools a month — two a day except Sundays — would match her income from the creep in Morgantown. With a barn full of Daddy's red oak lumber and a bale of old jeans from the thrift store, all she needed was glue, beeswax, linseed oil — and time. Thanks to Ian's last three days of help on the farm, she had time. Her heart picked up its pace when his image came to mind. Like a tall poplar, thin but majestic, Ian stood out in the crowd.

Tiny chips flew from the lathe as her skew chisel advanced into the cut, paring away the gentle curve of a quarter-inch semicircle, one of three on her latest stool leg. With the deft pivot of the chisel and gentle swing of her arm and shoulder, she shaped the bead in a single pass, transforming the wood into a decorative post. Two more cuts of the sharp blade, and she had her latest leg ready to remove from the lathe. Curls of oak sheared away above the parting tool when she forced it into her pencil mark, denoting the end of the leg. Smooth red-tinged wood spiraled off the lathe over the top of her hand, curling to the floor like long locks of a wooden Rapunzel. The spinning cylinder separated from the lathe and she grabbed it midair with her left hand. Daddy would be proud.

Fifty stools — two hundred legs — spun through the slicing bit of her chisel. She set the newest leg on the stack beside Lucky and turned off the machine, stepping back to admire her handiwork.

"You're sleeping on our next mortgage payment," she announced, nudging the cat. Accustomed to being bumped by cows and busy farm girls, he hardly moved. She stooped to pick him up, dusting off his temporary coat of oak dust. He didn't seem to care. "Run find someplace else to sleep. I have work to do." She carried him from the shop into the light of a hot June afternoon sun and lowered him to the ground.

Leaden with the threat of showers, grey clouds filled the western sky. She prayed rain would materialize soon. For five days she'd watched clouds pass by, headed to dump their load of life-giving water on the mountains at the east side of the state. Something about the Ohio River, twelve miles to the west, raised an invisible wall against moisture. Her parched ground thirsted for refreshment, the red clay scorched and cracked in the glare of an unrelenting sun. Even hay grasses wilted in this infernal torture. West Virginia could be the North Pole in January, but transform into a humid Death Valley five months later. Today it felt like Death Valley on steroids.

Laura Ann headed for the garden, a still-thriving mix of tall sweet corn, tomatoes, and sprawling vines of squash and cucumbers. For half an hour she knelt in the soil and pulled at weeds that defied heat and hoe. Orchard grass fought to make a home in the tomatoes, tall shoots sucking up the water she fed each day to her precious plants. She ran her fingers along the sticky vines of ripening tomatoes. Next week she'd be canning dozens of jars of the red fruit, stewed, whole, or pureed into soup. Vitamin C bottled up for bitter winters.

"Gonna rain."

Laura Ann jumped, surprised by the voice, but glad to hear it. Granny Apple's greeting brought her off her knees, tomatoes in hand, with a smile.

"Hi, Granny. Did you bring a basket?" She held forth a handful of her first Big Boy crop.

"Got all I can handle, child. Mine are making like there's no tomorrow. Been canning all morning." She took the tomatoes from Laura Ann's hands and helped her step over a vine heavy with cucumbers.

They walked together to the house, Laura Ann dusting off her clothes as they approached the porch. "I'll have fifty stools ready to ship at the end of the month. Ian said he'd help me truck them over to a buyer in New Martinsville."

Laura Ann shed her shoes at the door and held it open for Granny Apple. Her mentor wore her trademark summer outfit: white canvas tennis shoes, white knee-length jeans, and a button-up white cotton shirt. Fanning herself with her hand, Granny entered and set the tomatoes on the kitchen table. Laura Ann shut the door and flipped on the window air conditioner.

"Rain's comin'," Granny said, then took a seat at the kitchen table. "Tomorrow. Maybe tonight."

"I sure hope so." Laura Ann joined her at the table, freshly washed tomatoes on a plate. She carved the red juicy fruit into thick slices and set them before Granny along with a pair of forks and some salt.

"Feel it in my bones, child. Never wrong."

"Ian helped me water the pumpkin field last night," Laura Ann said in between bites of thick juicy red. "Trying to save the crop."

"Didn't need to," Granny said, wiping at a dribble of red juice on her own chin. "Gonna get real wet."

She pushed her second slice of tomato around on the plate, not looking up. Laura Ann watched her with the fascination of her childhood days, always amazed at this country woman who knew so much, but never revealed how she learned it.

"Ian left late." Granny Apple offered the statement as a simple matter of fact. Her eyes met Laura Ann's, a wide smile growing on her wrinkled face. "He's the one," she announced at last. "Your dad liked that boy. He's right for you."

"Thanks." Laura Ann stifled a chuckle. "I'm glad you approve."

"I do. Question is, will he?"

Laura Ann cocked her head. "Excuse me?"

"Secrets, Laura Ann. They don't become you."

Her heart skipped, then began its futile race. The way it did when Ian came to visit, or when she was up against Uncle Jack all by herself. "Secrets?" Laura Ann asked, looking down at the plate. She sat naked across the table from a woman who knew everything.

Granny Apple picked up the used plates and forks. She took dishes to the sink in silence, washed the tomato juice off, and set the plates in the drainer. Laura Ann joined her, wiping the plates dry. Granny turned and extended a thin wrinkled hand, taking the drying towel and gripping Laura Ann's hand for a moment.

"You kept that allotment out of Jack's hands until it was too late to plant burley. You won, honey. And he knows it." She paused, then added, "It's over."

Laura Ann nodded, willing her shaking hand to be still, but failed.

"You didn't sit around hoping for a way out." She squeezed Laura Ann's hand, the firm grasp of strong aged fingers and calloused palm. "Whatever you did to beat him, dear, it was courageous."

Laura Ann nodded, unable to look up.

"But now it's done, hear? It's behind you, sweetheart. So learn from it—and don't keep secrets." Granny Apple released her hands, turned back to the sink, and washed away the last of the tomato juice from the basin.

She dried her hands. Heading for the door, she offered one last warning. "Keep a good eye out. Jack won't ever give up."


Laura Ann stood at the door to the front porch for a long time, staring at her friend in white who ambled across the field along their two-track dirt path, crossing the pasture on her way to the highway.

Heavy black clouds massed to the west, like Granny Apple had predicted. A metallic aroma of approaching rain filled the air, carried by gusts that blew out of the west, across the Middle Island Creek. After weeks with no rain, anything that might fall today would shed off the hard clay and head straight for the creek. She prayed for a gentle soaking drizzle, but gathering clouds threatened otherwise. Dust devils kicked up across the farmyard, spiraling eddies of red dirt that whipped across trampled ground and disappeared into the distance beyond the barn.

Her cows sensed the coming storm, all of them lying down

in the pasture, noses into the wind. She was glad for the weather change, a temporary end to roasting temperatures that stressed her black-skinned herd. Even Lucky hunkered down, curled in a chair on the porch.

Laura Ann sat down with the cat, lifting him into her lap to watch the weather. The shop and her stools could wait. Daddy would pull her out of her chores at a time like this, determined to watch storms and enjoy the cool. Unless, of course, they were pitching hay in the field—and then he would be racing to escape the death bolts that incinerated men who stood on hay wagons.

Daddy. How fast six months had passed, half a year of living alone—despite the visits from Granny, or the rare opportunity to call on Auntie Rose. Half a year running the farm with help from Ian. Surviving calving season with all its stresses. Plowing, planting, and coaxing crops from the ground. Half a year of lonely nights, except those wonderful evenings when Ian kept her company. Always a gentleman, he never pressed to stay the night. Honor defined him.

Fire and anvil. Rays of pink and orange shot through the cloud layers, slicing a ceiling of grey. The metallic odor of rain faded as the gusts died into a quiet lull. Humidity clamped her in its jaws again as she watched the storm head to her right, away from the farm. The cows lay still in the pasture, noses to the west. Daddy would chide her for trying to guess the weather from watching them. "Cows lie down because they're full," he told her once. "And they lie down before it rains to get a dry patch of ground." He laughed every time he said it, like repeating a farmer's joke he'd heard once. She hoped they kept their dry spot, praying that rain would soon find her farm.

Lucky's purr box rattled while Laura Ann rocked. "Learn to rest," Daddy said once. She'd done that so rarely these last months. Even Ian commented she'd become obsessed with getting things done and encouraged her every day to slow down.

It felt good to sit now and watch life go by, like she used to do with Daddy.

Grasshoppers rubbed their legs together, filling the afternoon with a summer serenade. Shimmers of heat rose in the still air. "Listen to your little voice," Daddy said once when she asked him about making a decision. "That's what I do. I pray about how I should proceed, and then I listen."

"What do you hear?" she'd asked, leaning at his knee where he rocked one summer night.

"A second sense. A feeling. I call it my 'little voice.'"

"What does it say?" She wondered that a man so strong would depend on something so small and invisible as an inner voice.

"No words, Peppermint," he said, his hand stroking her hair as he rocked. He stopped the motion and pointed at the base of the rocker. "Would you put your finger under there when I'm rocking?"

"No," she exclaimed, moving back from the chair and the reach of his hand.

"Why?"

"It would hurt!"

"And what tells you that?"

"I can already imagine what it would feel like, Daddy. That's not funny."

He motioned to her to move close, his face a sign of trust. She pulled near but careful to avoid the soiled white curve of the rocker.

"What you feel inside, that sense of the pain you'd experience, is sort of like that small voice I'm talking about. It's giving you a feeling of what's about to happen, a sense of the direction God wants you to go."

She nodded under the weight of his hand on her head, and then laid her cheek on his knee.

"Listen to your little voice," she said, repeating Daddy's words while she stood, watching the distant ridge.

A glint caught her eye, the reflection of a car. A silver SUV crept down the farm road, easing through ruts in the pasture. No danger of any mud this day, yet it moved with deliberate slowness, like a lost traveler scanning a street for the correct address.

Laura Ann moved off the porch to the picket fence as the vehicle passed the remains of the old tobacco barn. She recognized the ornament on the front of the car. A Lexus. The tinted windows of the fancy car hid the driver. Another emissary from her uncle? Standing alone, Laura Ann stiffened, determined to hold her ground. Soon, she hoped, she could stand side by side with Ian to weather the blistering ire of her uncle.

A woman stepped out of the car.

"Pumps?" Laura Ann exclaimed with a small laugh, too quiet to be heard. A thin woman in a skirt and loose top took an unsteady step away from the automobile as she tried to shut the door. She wobbled in the slag on her short heels, glanced at Laura Ann with a brief smile, and then grabbed for balance with a look of desperation.

Laura Ann let out a chuckle and stepped through the gate. "Need a hand?"

"Sorry," the woman replied, embarrassed. She got her balance, then gingerly pushed the door closed and stepped in Laura Ann's direction. "Guess I should have worn sandals."

Laura Ann smiled. "Don't apologize. Most folks from out of town expect a driveway or something."

The woman stopped, her head cocked. "You know I'm from out of town?" she asked, a hint of concern in her voice.

Laura Ann pointed at the vehicle and smiled as she walked toward her. "Fancy car," she said with a shrug. "It's a small town."

The visitor stood Laura Ann's height, her skin a deeper

brown than she'd seen in a long time. Black wavy hair flowed over her shoulders, framing a broad smile and modern glasses shaped like little rectangles. Her nose was a little larger than she deserved, leading down into thin lips made deep red by a fresh application of lipstick. A printed top draped loose over her upper body, matching a tight pastel skirt. Saturday afternoon in the mountains, but this woman dressed like she'd planned on a nice dinner or church. She took an unsteady step in Laura Ann's direction, extending a hand as her smile grew.

"I'm Sophia. Sophia McQuistion."

She didn't look like a McQuistion. Mexican maybe, but certainly not Scottish or Viking. The visitor closed the gap between them, wobbling in her pumps on the rough drive. "Are you Laura?"

Everyone knew her name was Laura Ann. Like when people came calling and asked for James McGehee. Everyone knew Daddy went by his middle name, Angus. She stiffened again. Uncle Jack sent a woman to do his dirty work.

"My name is Laura Ann. Laura Ann McGehee. Can I help you?"

The thin woman hid something, her loose-fitting top pressed back against her tummy by a sudden breeze. A maternity top. Uncle Jack sent a *pregnant* woman, hoping to win her over with sympathy. Laura Ann stopped, lowering her hand.

"I'm sorry," Sophia replied, pumping her hand out again. "Laura Ann. It's a beautiful name."

Laura Ann raised her hand slowly and took the woman's grip.

Her little voice screamed.

Like connecting with a lost sister, her entire body tingled when they touched, something about this woman strangely familiar. She held the grip, struggling to understand why it affected her so. Like meeting her twin, lost since birth.

The lady brought her other hand to the embrace, steadying herself with her grip. "I'm so glad to find you at last."

Laura Ann's skin crawled, bumps rising on her arms under beads of sweat. "Find me?" she asked.

Sophia nodded. "It took a few months." She nodded toward the Lexus, adding, "And a few miles."

"Have we met?" Laura Ann asked, something inside her shrieking "run!" and another part, the curious girl, holding on to the woman's hands to prolong the connection, to absorb some mysterious part of her that had been strangely reunited this hot day.

The woman's eyes filled with tears in an instant. "I've been searching for you for a long time."

Laura Ann pulled at the grip, nodding in the direction of the house. "I'm sorry. Forgive me. Would you like to come in?"

Sophia nodded. "Yes. I would. Is that okay?"

"Sure. I guess," she said, steadying Sophia at the edge of the rocky drive. "But I don't know why you'd come looking for me." Concerns about Uncle Jack niggled at the back of her mind. Surely, no one this nice would do business with him.

Once on the brick sidewalk, Sophia regained her balance, and she used her free hands to wipe at tears coursing down her cheeks. "Please, forgive me for being so emotional. It's just—it's just that I've dreamt of this day for a very long time."

Laura Ann glanced at Sophia as she led the way up the steps. At the screen door she stopped, then faced Sophia, one hand on the tarnished brass handle. "Did my uncle Jack send you?" she blurted out. If Sophia was one of his minions, she'd have to go. There could be no welcome.

Sophia shook her head, the smile reemerging. "No. I don't know him." She laid a hand on Laura Ann's where it rested on the screen door. "I come as a friend."

"Then?"

"I'm here to thank you, Laura Ann." More tears welled up, and she did nothing to stem their flow. "To thank you for what you've done for me. For *us*," she added, her free hand moving to her belly.

Sophia paused a long moment, taking a deep breath. "I'm carrying a baby, Laura Ann. A child I've wanted for so long." Her voice trembled with a choked sob, her chin quivering as she forced out the next words.

"*Our* baby, Laura Ann. An amazing gift. Through your eggs, you gave me a child."

# CHAPTER 11

Laura Ann's heart pounded with a desperate frenzy. Her left hand came up to her abdomen, as if to feel that painful place and search for the part of her that she'd sold and lost forever. Her heart stuck in her throat and she fought to breathe, the screen door behind her forgotten.

It wasn't supposed to work out this way. "Discreet donations by girls age nineteen to thirty." "Generous compensation." "Privacy guaranteed."

The promises on the radio? All gone wrong.

"How?" she asked, her voice cracking and knees weak. Laura Ann released the door handle and sank into a rocking chair on the porch, never losing sight of the bump below Sophia's loose top. "How did you find me?"

Sophia pulled her hand back, her fingers covering her mouth. The broad smile disappeared. "Oh, no."

Laura Ann sat in a daze, unable to draw her eyes from the woman's midriff as every one of her four trips to Morgantown replayed in her mind. Memories of the money she'd been paid tugged at her stomach, acid churning in synch with her pounding heart. Nausea overwhelmed her.

"Totally private," the counselor had assured her during the first clinic visit last November. Mounds of paperwork followed the fast-talking woman's effusive assurances, papers Laura Ann read page by page but did not fully understand. "Select your preferences for contact with the prospective client." She checked all the right boxes, sure she'd requested maximum privacy. But something had gone terribly wrong.

Sophia bent over, turning away from Laura Ann. She stumbled to the edge of the porch, steadying herself at the old white post. "I'm so sorry," she said, choking on her words. "I never should have come."

"No." Laura Ann's heart broke free of the vise grip she'd placed on her emotions and it jerked her out of the rocker. No matter how much it hurt, she would not let this moment pass. "Please, Mrs. McQuistion. Don't go."

Sophia turned, taking a deep breath. "I don't understand."

"Please stay." Laura Ann approached her, willing her heart and stomach to settle a bit. "I want to know more."

Sophia sniffled, then put a hand to her belly, looking down. Both of their gazes went to her cantaloupe-sized swelling. Without a word, Laura Ann stood up and stepped toward Sophia. The visitor alternately looked at Laura Ann, then down at her own hands, moving them slowly over the cloth that covered her pregnancy. Sophia's chin quivered, but she stood her ground, the post to her back.

Laura Ann moved closer, no words shared between them. She extended shaking fingers toward the loose cotton print. She stopped short of touching the woman, looking up at her in silence. Their eyes met, Sophia forced a smile, then nodded.

"It's a boy," Sophia said after a long silence. "He's seven months."

Laura Ann nodded, whispering the words again, tasting their magic as they passed her own lips. "A boy. Seven months."

A breeze blew, gusting cool. Dust swirled off the farmyard into their midst. The cold of a second gust rustled Sophia's top, her belly rising when she inhaled. A life suspended in this gentle hammock of another woman's body, moving up and down in synch with the wind of a mother's lungs.

Laura Ann looked away from Sophia to her left and the source of the gusts. A mighty cauldron of weather tore in from the west, roiling clouds grey-green and wet with fury. The storms were headed straight for her farm. Laura Ann gasped in wonder at the sudden emergence of this squall, blowing in hard.

The hair on her arms stood on end. Before she could react, lightning split the air and struck at a tall spire on the barn. White light burst from the rooftop as thunder hit with a resounding *boom*. The jolt knocked Laura Ann off balance and she fell forward, her palms pressed hard against the swell of baby, Sophia blocked by the white porch post behind her. Beneath the firm press of Laura Ann's fingers, she felt it.

Jolted by the thunder and her fall, the baby kicked.

Beyond the screen, Laura Ann heard the phone ring, its tone nearly drowned out in the moan of a hard wind. No time for talk. She jumped to her feet and shoved Sophia inside, then slammed the front door shut behind them. Echoes of thunder rumbled through the valley, vibrations she could feel in her gut.

"Are you okay?" she asked. Sophia stood close to the door, eyes wide.

"Wait here," Laura Ann said, then turned to the living room window. Through it she could barely see the cows, hunkered down against the onslaught. The advancing storm obscured them, a dense grey veil draped across the pasture. Water gushed from the heavens, a well-defined wall of grey headed straight for the house.

Laura Ann pushed away and ran to the kitchen, desperate to check the barn. Through the window over the sink she could see the shattered pinnacle of her barn roof where Daddy's lightning rod once stood on the peak of the white ventilator. It hung over at an odd angle, still attached, but less sturdy after the lightning strike. She watched a long moment for signs of smoke or fire erupting from the end of the barn. The barn looked an ugly brown, its bright red mixing with the ochre-hazel fusion of whirling dust, and the queer grey-green light of the storm.

Sophia joined her. "How can I help?"

"Watch for a fire or smoke," Laura Ann said, pointing at the barn. "I need to check on the doors and windows." She turned to head down the hall to the bedroom when she heard the phone ring again over the tempest's howl.

"Hello?" she gasped, grabbing at the wall phone, mounted in the hall. She pulled the cord around the corner to watch Sophia, and past her the barn, through windows now wet with the first spatters of driven rain.

"Laura Ann!" Ian exclaimed. "Are you okay?"

"Barely. Someone came to visit," she said, just then remembering what transpired only moments earlier. Her past confronted her in a way she'd never anticipated. "We were—we were talking, and the storm blew in fast. Lightning hit the barn."

"Sit tight!" Ian yelled into the phone. She could barely hear him. His voice drowned in the pummeling of heavy rain, and walls that creaked against a fierce west wind. Ten thousand liquid marbles dropped on their metal roof when the wall of water hit the farmhouse.

She heard little of Ian's voice, but two words caught her ear. Words that wrenched at her gut. Words that every West Virginian feared.

"Flash flood!"

She screamed over the tin-pounding torrent. "Where?"

"Middle Island ... a few minutes ..." The phone went dead, then she heard a high-pitched squeal. Moments later, Ian's voice returned. Her heart skipped in anticipation of losing him. "—careful. I love you."

No matter the roar of the storm, she heard those last three words clearly, words he'd shared three nights ago, standing at the edge of the porch under the blaze of stars. His prolonged good-bye, as if working up the courage to say something he'd felt for a very long time. Words that set her on the path to the bonfire, and a new future.

Yet Laura Ann's past haunted her now more than ever. She watched Sophia, staring out the window at the barn.

"Ian?" She spoke over the maelstrom. "Please, say it again."

"Okay. Heard it on the scanner. Don't—"

The line went dead.

Night battled day.

The grey-green of the approaching storm collapsed to near black when the deluge consumed the farmhouse. Phone in hand, Laura Ann reached around the corner of the kitchen to flip on a light. No response. She stood with the phone to her ear, strain-ing against the pummeling of rain on metal above her, in hopes Ian's voice would return. She flipped the light switch again with the same result.

Leaning over the sink, Sophia strained to see out the win-dow. The barn disappeared behind a curtain of wet black.

Seconds after she tried the light, the room was aglow in a bluish-white, the flashbulb of another lightning strike, but far-ther away, down toward the Middle Island Creek. Moving east. Wind whipped over the top of the house and created a mad turbulence beyond the kitchen window, rain lit up by distant flashes, their only source of light.

Lightning struck again, somewhere across the creek, brief flashes that lit Sophia's face. Her brown eyes reflected nature's flashbulbs, staring out at a scene Laura Ann sensed this woman had never experienced. She pulled at Sophia, pointing down the hall toward the living room.

They walked the length of the narrow farmhouse to gaze out front windows drenched by a horizontal blast of rain. Water leaked in under the bottom of the wooden frames, their seals overcome by the wind's force. Laura Ann retreated to the kitchen for some dish towels, and together the women set out a cotton dike across the front of the house.

Pointing out across the pasture, Laura Ann pulled Sophia close and spoke above the din. "My friend called. To warn me about a flash flood."

"Flood?"

Laura Ann nodded, gesturing again in the direction that Sophia had come. "The low water crossing's the only way out. Very dangerous. You need to stay here."

"How long?"

Laura Ann shrugged, staring into the wet blackness, unable to see beyond the drive.

"I don't know."

Laura Ann poured a second glass of iced tea for Sophia, and then set the pitcher in the refrigerator. The room was damp but cool, the window at the sink opened to let in some fresh air. Rain fell in a constant stream, the sound like hundreds of pebbles dropping into baking tins. Beyond the window, a mini-waterfall cascaded off the metal roof into the farmyard below. Laura Ann imagined it must have been like this the first night Noah entered the ark. The firmament of heaven divided above Tyler County this afternoon and entire lakes fell from the sky.

Rivers of runoff water swirled away from the home, its foundation set a hundred years ago high above the turbulence.

Beyond the barn, toward the wooded edge of the Middle Island Creek, water rose into the lower fields, brown swirling muddy torrents cresting far above their banks and pushing high into the hayfields. The rain and woods obscured her view of the creek, but she could well imagine what transpired in the bottomland.

A flood of this magnitude would devastate trees and lowland buildings in its path, sweeping them downstream with incredible force. Logjams would stack up in tight places and sharp bends, dangerous dams forcing water into thundering haystacks of roiling brown water, millions of gallons on a determined path to reach the Ohio River. The low water crossing would be many feet underwater by now. It could be days before the water subsided if the rain didn't let up soon. Like the strainer at the bottom of a tub, The Jug and her farm sat in the lower half of a huge drainage, America's longest creek. Every drop that fell upstream must eventually pass her farm.

"You're worried," Sophia said. Laura Ann turned to face her at the kitchen table, a cold glass cupped in her hands. Sophia's iPhone lay silent on a blue-checkered tablecloth. Cellular service never reached the farm, even in the best of weather.

Laura Ann nodded. "Not worried ... but concerned," she replied, pointing toward the rising creek. "The water's up into the fields."

"Can it reach us?"

Laura Ann shook her head. "No. Unless Noah floats by, we're safe. So are the cows. But the longer this keeps up," she said, pointing toward the roof, "the longer you'll need to stay."

Sophia lowered her drink and waved at Laura Ann to join her at the table. "Please sit down," she said. "I want to tell you my story."

Laura Ann wiped her hands on a dish towel, hung it over the sink lip, and joined her at the table.

"I'm sorry I intruded in your life," Sophia offered.

"It's okay," Laura Ann replied. "I must have signed the wrong form at the clinic. Don't blame yourself."

Sophia stared at her tea in silence. At last, she said, "I struggled a long time with the decision to look for you." She poked at the mint leaf with a spoon, her gaze focused on the tea. "But you weren't the first."

"First?"

"I found the father before I looked for you."

"Father?" Laura Ann asked. She looked at Sophia's hand, a large oval diamond on a simple gold band. "I assumed—"

"That I was married?" She shook her head. "No. I *was* married. For a while." She looked back down at the cold tea sweating in the glass. Neither woman spoke, the staccato *ting ting ting* of water on the roof a percussive backdrop to their silence.

"James died three years ago."

Laura Ann's heart skipped. "My daddy was a James. We called him Angus, his middle name. Granddaddy was a James too." She paused. "They've both passed on."

Sophia nodded, but didn't speak right away, her lower lip trembling. "James and I wanted children so much, but it never worked out. When he died, I spent a long time missing him, too scared—or too raw—to meet someone new. Then I decided it was time to move on, to try to make the family we'd both wanted. But our infertility turned out to be *my* problem."

"That's why you needed a donor?"

"Yes. I wanted a child with Hispanic roots, but the Morgantown clinic didn't have any donor eggs from women like me. So I chose a Hispanic dad." She picked up the iPhone and ran her thumb along the edge of the silent device. "He was easy to find."

"How did he react? When he met you."

"Really strange, like he was proud or something. He bragged about getting me pregnant and about the quality of his 'samples.' And about how many children he'd fathered. He didn't care anything for the baby—or for me. It really creeped me out."

She paused, resting a hand on her stomach. "You know, I think he wanted to be found. I was very lonely—maybe even a little desperate for a man in my life." She raised an eyebrow. "It probably showed."

"And?"

Her eyes got wide and she took a deep breath. "I wish I'd never gone looking." The roll of her eyes spoke volumes.

"So. Why me?" Laura Ann asked. "Weren't you afraid?"

"Afraid to try again? Sure." She stood up, walking to the sink to place her empty glass in the basin. She stared out for a long look at the rain, and the swelling flood in the pasture below. "The experience with the father nearly ruined it for me," she said. "But I determined to press on."

Sophia turned and faced the table, leaning back into the edge of the sink. She moved a hand to lay it atop her stomach, looking down as she moved her fingers along the cotton print from the top to the bottom of her belly. "The first time he kicked," she said, her hand pausing at a spot on the right side of her belly button, "that's what got me moving again." She shrugged. "And something about your donor profile—your picture—kept coming to mind. The one of you in that beautiful print dress."

Laura Ann looked down at the table again.

*What would Daddy say now?*

"There's only three things you can lose that you'll never get back," Daddy shared with her one winter, bundled up against the cold during an early morning feeding. "Your life, your credibility—and your virginity." His words shocked her then at age fourteen, direct words meant to help her deal with the challenges of teenage life. His lecture mixed in a tangled way with Preacher's many angry sermons on purity, pointed words that tore at her now. She'd lost something like that. Something pure. Something virginal. She'd sold something precious that she could never get back.

Sophia spoke. "You were courageous. You gave me life."

The rumble of distant thunder distracted Laura Ann for a moment and she looked left to the living room, through the window into the distance. The few Angus she could see in the rain lay where they'd been all morning, noses into the storm.

*Courageous?*

Pushed against a financial wall, desperate to save her daddy's most valued belonging, she'd sold her body. Despite her success, she felt nothing but guilt—and fear. She could have sold all the cattle, leased the tobacco allotment to Uncle Jack, even sold part of the farm and kept most of the property intact. But instead she'd turned to her body for cash and a quick way out. A solution that kept every facet of life at the farm intact. But at what price?

Pastor Culpeper's words tugged at her, unforgettable wisdom from her last visit to his church. "Let go and let God," he'd said, the words clinging to her like flypaper. Her story, of taking total control, was the antithesis of the faithful surrender he'd encouraged.

Sophia's hand moved in a slow circle about her stomach, as if massaging the baby, the fruit of a man and woman who'd never met, joined inside her to create a child that Sophia—and Laura Ann—had always dreamt of.

A baby—Laura Ann's baby—one she might never meet.

For the second time that day, her heart stuck in her throat, her breath stolen away.

She'd sold a child that might have been her own.

# CHAPTER 12

Drenched by the rain, Laura Ann reached across the truck's bench seat and offered a hand to Sophia, pulling her to a semblance of safety in the dusty cab. She needed to assess the flood damage, no matter how bad the weather. Sophia may as well come along. Laura Ann wished she'd swept out the dried mud and bits of hay that littered the interior, but her guest hardly seemed to notice.

"Donating eggs isn't as simple as they make it sound," Laura Ann said. She engaged the four-wheel drive and pointed her truck out of the barnyard. Lakes of standing water surrounded them, pelted by the constant downpour. "I saw an ad for donors on a bulletin board at the hospital. I heard another on the radio. But they don't tell you much about the dark side."

Sophia gripped the seat and the door handle with iron fists as the truck weaved up a slick clay slope toward the ridge, all four tires spinning.

"It hurts. A lot," Laura Ann said as she drove, indifferent to the mud. "Cramps. Nausea. Bleeding. And sometimes they don't pay what they promised." She shuddered at the memory. "Not at all like giving blood."

Sophia sat in silence for a long time while Laura Ann shared her story of four trips to Morgantown. When the road leveled out, her arms relaxed, and she turned to face Laura Ann, eyes glistening. "Thank you," she said, her voice cracking. "For that sacrifice."

"Sacrifice," Laura Ann said with a nod, recalling the shower of sparks that drifted up from her little pyre three days ago, mixing with the nighttime blaze of a hundred billion stars. "That's a good word for it."

Laura Ann looked to her right for a moment, slowing down. The truck guided itself in water-filled ruts as they wound through the wood.

"We'll park the truck here," Laura Ann said, waving her hand toward a grassy spot. The narrow winding road led through tall oaks and sweetgums in the state's Wildlife Management Area, property that stood between her farm and the low water crossing. But the water no longer ran low.

From the grassy knoll, Laura Ann saw what she'd feared all afternoon. Grey sheets of rain and a dense mist in the creek bottom mixed in a fearsome way, obscuring roiling red-brown water that tore the earth apart before them. Fifty feet below the truck, a massive logjam sent water jetting thirty feet into the air, scouring away at the low-water crossing where the flood pounded down with a mighty roar.

Trees lay in a jumbled pile where the creek normally made its acute twist back to the left, flowing downstream about the jug-shaped island that was her home. Any other day, water would meander up against the dam formed by the low water crossing, in a sharp turn at the neck of The Jug, then cut hard left to make its seven-mile clockwise jaunt around an island of pastures and trees. Today, however, logs careened into that tight turn at the dam and stuck, grabbing at every heavy floating thing that came their way. In the mix of brown and grey logs, Laura Ann could see parts of rooftops, a swing set, plastic kids' riding toys — and the hood of a car. Wedged deep in the pile, it was probably one of the many old vehicles abandoned in low-lying fields upstream.

Laura Ann looked beyond the logjam, searching for the power and telephone wires that broke hours ago. Two lines lay limp on the muddy bank, disappearing into the turbulence. There would be no power or phone service for a long time.

Water shot in boiling haystacks over the wall of logs, crashing down into the creek bottom on top of the sixty-year-old concrete causeway and dam built to correct the ugly land cut made by predecessors who'd burrowed through a narrow ridge to bring water to grist mills. Water blasted at the old concrete, scouring away its foundation. The roar of water pummeled them with a low frequency vibration that worked its tendrils into her gut.

"I need to get closer," Laura Ann said. "Stay in the truck. I'll be back in a minute."

"It's raining," Sophia protested. "And dangerous."

"I'll be careful."

Sophia nodded and waved her on, her eyes riveted on the watery drama unfolding before them. Laura Ann closed the truck door and began her trek down a slope of slick red clay, rivers of water tearing away at the ruts. Everywhere, red-brown water cascaded to its salty end a thousand miles away. The deafening roar of water thrummed deep in her abdomen. Were the sight not so awesome, the sensation would be nauseating.

Laura Ann drew closer to the concrete causeway. In drier weather, the crossing provided a man-made diversion at the upper curve of the creek, thirteen feet higher than the lower curve on the opposite side, ensuring that nature came into balance after her predecessors destroyed the creek-diverting ridge to build a ragged sluice to feed the first mill. Their plan for a water mill, positioned at a unique point of geography separating two levels of flowing water, created the scar that would soon destroy her creek. Without the man-made causeway no water could flow in a grand clockwise circle about the farm. Without the causeway dam, the waters of the Middle Island Creek would shoot straight through this ragged sluice in the neck of The Jug and pass her by.

The first deep rumble in the earth made her knees weak, rock below her giving way in the dim light. She looked around for a falling tree or mudslide, sure she stood in the path of something about to career into the water. Vibrating earth moved under her feet again, the moan of rock about to give way.

Suddenly the old cofferdam and causeway broke in two. The jet of water spewing over the logjam scoured so deep, and with such power, that the middle of the causeway cracked and lifted in the water. She felt the demise long before she saw the roadway buckle, then watched in horror as a monster slab of grey concrete jacked upwards, a feather in the hands of its liquid destroyer. Pushed hard by the waterfall that freed it, the slab crunched into the creek bottom downstream, upended in a strange way, then wedged against a muddy bank with nowhere left to go.

Angry water piled up on either side of the new hole, pushing on ragged edges of a broken crossing. Another deep rumble worked its way through her legs, and Laura Ann watched the ends of the causeway, now mortally wounded, lift like pancakes and flip downstream. In the span of less than a minute, her only route across the neck of The Jug piled up like stone carrion into the creek bank.

She knew what would happen next, the destruction of the only road to town. The jumbled concrete at once became a funnel, shooting a jet of water up against the raw red of an eroding mountainside. State Route 18, perched on a perilous cut above the creek, would not survive long. Furious water tore at red dirt, ripping away clay that held the road in place. Soon, the only passage from West Union to Middlebourne would be swept into the maelstrom.

Watching the bank disappear, she spied a figure in yellow and white. A yellow raincoat perched on the road above. Waving.

*Granny Apple!*

Her home just a few hundred feet upriver from the crossing, tucked safe against the hill, Granny Apple had come to watch the end of an era, the destruction of the old dam and causeway. Perhaps she felt that impending loss in her bones, like she felt the weather. Or like Laura Ann had felt it, in her feet and her gut. Laura Ann waved back to get her friend's attention. Granny would tell Ian. She'd let him know everything was okay.

She could imagine Granny Apple's words, were she within earshot. "Get inside, child. Nothing you can do out here." And she'd be right. The figure in yellow and white waved one last time, then walked back in the direction of her hillside home. She'd communicated in the most elemental of ways. Both knew the other was fine. And Ian would soon find out.

She turned and headed back to the truck. Would that Granny were the one stuck with her on the farm instead of this new person, someone who dug up recent graves, a stranger who pulled the ashes of past mistakes from her tiny bonfire. She trudged through the rain, wading in red torrents that cascaded down the mountain road. Five minutes later she sat in the truck, soaked to the skin.

"I saw you waving. Who did you see?" Sophia asked.

Laura Ann sat behind the wheel, wiping a sheet of water from her face with soaked hands. "A neighbor," she said. "She'll tell everyone we're okay."

Darkness consumed them, daylight snuffed out by a curtain of wet grey. "No one knows I'm here," Sophia said after a long pause. "Just you."

Laura Ann started the truck, rechecking the four-wheel drive before she navigated treacherous mud on the downhill return to the farm. She backed the truck through a three-point turn and headed along the rutted track to home.

"What else did you see?" Sophia asked after a long silence.

Towering oaks and poplars lined their path through the hunting preserve as they descended to the farm.

Laura Ann shook her head, dreading this forced union with a single pregnant woman who bore the fruit of Laura Ann's womb like a badge of honor.

"The crossing is gone," Laura Ann stated, matter-of-fact. "No one will drive out of here — or come to see us — for a very long time."

She let those words hang on the air for a moment, expecting some reaction, but heard none. Laura Ann looked to her right at Sophia, her back ramrod straight, hands clenching the dash and the door as the car slid down the slope on mud slick as ice. When she looked back a second time, Sophia's jaw was clenched, sign of the steely determination that led her to this place, to this day. No cries of remorse, no worries of a departure. And no words of comfort.

Mental images of Ian came to mind as Laura Ann guided the truck. Daydreams of an evening together at the Blennerhassett, of a romantic dinner and, perhaps, a diamond ring. Nightmares tore at her, the dread of secrets revealed, of stools unsold, and a mortgage left unpaid. She set her face toward home, determined to speak no more.

With her face soaking wet, tears would never show.

Laura Ann watched her guest in the dim light of a kerosene lamp, one burning in each room of the farmhouse. Long after nine o'clock, and past time for bed, the dark meant comfort.

Sophia looked up, her thin face drawn tight over sharp cheekbones and chin. Kerosene shadows flickered on her face, a surreal brown with deep eyes that hid stories untold. Laura Ann couldn't remember the last time a woman other than Auntie Rose spent the night at her home.

"I have a bed ready," Laura Ann said at last. "I fixed up Daddy's room for you. I hope it's okay." Laura Ann pointed down the hall, in hopes Sophia would leave her alone and go to sleep. The constant pounding of rain on tin and caring for her stranded visitor set Laura Ann's nerves on edge. Most of all she feared Sophia's probing. She preferred to conceal her motivations and bottle up a disgraceful past.

Sophia smoothed her hair and stood, approaching Laura Ann. "I'm sorry," she offered, her hand extended. "For putting you through this."

*Does she read minds?*

"Really," Laura Ann insisted, "it's okay."

Sophia moved toward her, perhaps too close. She laid a hand on Laura Ann's forearm. "You're just being nice, but for that I thank you." She backed up, her eyes glistening in the soft yellow glow of the lantern. "I'd like to know more. Tomorrow. When you're ready."

"More?" Laura Ann asked, her voice a squeak.

"Yes, more about you. About *why* you gave me this gift." She patted her stomach, the hand lingering on the ledge of her belly.

"I didn't give you anything," Laura Ann insisted. "I sold myself to save our farm." She took a deep breath and continued. "At best, call it altruism." She paused again. "But certainly not a gift."

Sophia moved closer. "Altruism? Maybe. But I think it was more than a concern for the welfare of someone in my situation. You sacrificed so much to make this possible, Laura Ann. That's courageous."

*That word again. Courageous.*

"How?" Laura Ann asked. "How is it courageous for me to hide something I did for fear I'll be branded a slut? Courage would have been to stand up and fight for the farm without selling my eggs." More words bubbled up, desperate to be released. "Courage would have been to trust God for the outcome."

"A slut? I don't know what you're covering up, Laura Ann, or why you're feeling so—I don't know—ashamed? Maybe that's not the word."

"*Ashamed* is a good word. But *regretful* is better."

Sophia stiffened. "That hurts."

"I'm sorry, Mrs. McQuistion. But you've made me face some hard realities today."

"Call me Sophia. Please." She made a basket shape with her hands, framing her question. "What kind of realities?"

"I've cheapened myself. I put a price on something precious. No matter how much it helped you, that doesn't make it right."

"How can you say that you cheapened yourself?" she asked, her voice rising. "You're wrong, and you insult me to say it."

Laura Ann moved away, walking to the front door where it stood open to the cool humid night, rain pouring from the heavens. She looked out at the dark, no sign of a star or a light in the distance. Pitch black, like her mood.

"Is that really the way you see it?" Sophia asked. "Like you're some kind of prostitute?"

At the word *prostitute* Laura Ann gripped the doorjamb, struggling to keep herself together. The dark spot inside that she'd tried so hard to hide welled up like vomit. She could hold it no longer. Laura Ann dashed through the screen door onto the porch.

She moved to the post by the steps and wrapped her arms about the wet white pillar, spatters of rain drizzling in her face. The cool of the wet mixed with her tears in a salty damp. So many tears. Tears for Daddy. Tears for terrible pain each trip to Morgantown. And now this, confronting a past she'd tried so hard to burn away and forget.

Sophia called from behind, standing in the portal. Her voice lost its edge. "Can we talk?"

Laura Ann circled her arms about the post, determined not

to be pried away. Peering into the dark, she considered running into the pasture, finding one of those dry spots with the Angus, and lying down. Life had to be better out there.

"Please?"

Laura Ann forced a nod.

"Can I tell you a story?" Sophia asked from behind her. Laura Ann remained silent.

"I was born in Mexico." Sophia moved to the post at the opposite side of the steps. She clung to it, one hand on the thick round pillar, another resting on her belly. "I grew up in Nuevo Laredo. Not a great place.

"My parents were poor. My father was a police officer, one of the few good ones. We had little to support us because he wouldn't accept bribes." Sophia's voice cracked as she told her story, staring with Laura Ann into the black.

"When I turned sixteen, I took a job as a waitress in Cancun. I know what it means to sell yourself, Laura Ann. I made a terrible mistake a few months after I moved there, determined to help my family." She paused and took a deep wheezing breath. "You did the honorable thing. I did not."

Laura Ann turned at last to watch her, long black hair frizzing in the damp. The profile of her high cheeks and nose were barely visible in the light of the house lamps. Despite her thin frame, she radiated strength.

"I made a decision, Laura Ann. I prostituted myself on the pretense that I did it to help my family. I pursued money, but not honor. That phase of my life didn't last long—but long enough." She took another deep breath and leaned her head into the post.

"I came down with a bad case of chlamydia. I'd been with lots of men—college boys on the cruise ships, business travelers, even the police. I thought it was a yeast infection and went to a doctor. He diagnosed the real problem—the STD—but the medication he gave me didn't work. On a positive note, that disease scared me off the streets and I got better. I found some housekeeping work at a hotel. I couldn't send much money home, but I felt better about what I earned. And felt better about myself."

She backed up and took a seat in the rocker. Laura Ann watched her, then released her own post and followed her toward the chair. As Sophia sat down, Laura Ann curled her legs under her and sat on the wet porch at her side. "Years of untreated disease scarred my ovaries, Laura Ann. I couldn't have children. Unlike you, I did sell myself. I compromised my morals to raise my standard of living—and to help my family. What you did to give me life, and what I did to make a life, are two polar opposites. Please," she said, placing a hand on Laura Ann's shoulder, "don't for a minute think you're in my shoes."

Sophia's hand lay for a long time on Laura Ann's shoulder. "I slept with men so that I could buy dresses and shoes, and send some occasional pesos to my family. I lived a lie because I wanted to enjoy the fruits of my labor." A sob broke free and she coughed. "You can't undo a harm. Look what it cost me."

Wet eyes met wet eyes. Sophia moved her hand to Laura Ann's head, the gentle touch of a mother, stroking her hair. "You were a donor, Laura Ann McGehee. You took a courageous step—innovative even—to save your farm. You probably went against the grain in your community, maybe your church. But I can tell that what you did bothers you so much that you've bottled it up inside like some kind of deadly sin. You're scared to death that my presence here will expose you to everyone you love, and in doing that, you'll lose them."

Laura Ann raised her head, her chin quivering with unspoken regret. She strained to find the right words. "I hoped—even prayed that what I did might help someone," she said, determined not to cry again today.

"And it did. To your credit. Not your shame."

"People talk, Sophia. They won't see my actions as some kind of sacrifice. Just a sale." She choked back tears and continued. "The worst part? I can handle the ridicule, but the last thing I want to do is hurt Daddy's good name." She swallowed hard. "Preacher says a woman's womb is opened—and closed—by God. If that's the case, I had no business contributing to another woman's mistake."

"I've lived those arguments. A thousand times," Sophia said. "Many of my friends said what I did was unethical. But they *had* kids." Her voice squeaked, trying hard to form painful words. "They have no idea how much it hurts, to want children yet be told 'no' in every prayer. My priest said what I did was adulterous. A single woman, taking matters into her own hands."

"We both did that. Took control," Laura Ann said. She imagined Pastor Culpeper reciting another of his wise morsels. "My pastor says that when we shortcut God we learn nothing, and lose everything."

Sophia reached toward her and put a finger to Laura Ann's cheek, wiping her thumb slowly across a streak of wet.

"Do you think we did that? Shortcut God?"

Laura Ann nodded. "I do."

Both women sat in the cool embrace of the summer rain, wrapped in silence. Sophia spoke at last. "Perhaps I'm here for a reason."

The words struck hard. Daddy, in this rocker, his hand on her hair only months ago. Deep coughs dragging horrible stuff from his lungs, while he said goodbye in his own way.

"Maybe I'm here for a reason," he'd said to her. "And that reason, I'll wager, is to get you a flying start on life, Laura Ann." He patted her head with bony fingers devoid of strength. "Even if I'm only here to launch you into the world—I can be happy with that."

Sophia turned in the rocker, her hand cupping Laura Ann's cheek like Daddy's hand had months ago. What did he say about the "little voice," the sense of something to come? She bit her lip, determined to listen to her heart. This must be what he told her it would feel like, this sense that God had some special word, some amazing plan, and it could only be revealed if she listened and trusted. "Faith at work, trusting in little things, and gentle voices." Those were Daddy's words.

"Here for a reason," Sophia had said. Laura Ann reached up and took her hand. She didn't resist the touch, a small smile on her lips as Laura Ann made contact. Their connection shot tingles down her arm, a sense that there was something special about this moment. Daddy would want her to open her heart and listen with every fiber of her being. "Listen and love." That's what Daddy would say.

She pulled Sophia's palm close. "Maybe . . . ," Laura Ann began, her heart finally slipping free of bonds that gripped it for months, "maybe we're both here for a reason." She smiled, her pulse throbbing with a new vigor, a clear understanding of this message that God placed in her heart—at this moment. Pastor Culpeper's reading fell into place like the last piece in a spiritual jigsaw puzzle, her "little voice" reciting Scripture.

*My grace is sufficient for you, for my power is made perfect in weakness.*

No little voice, the message overwhelmed her like a warm shower, wetting a parched soul where there had, for too long, been no refreshment.

Sophia's hand trembled in Laura Ann's grip, her own body vibrating with unspoken joy. From her kneeling place beside Sophia's rocker, her face inches from the maternity top, she peered in wonder at the life that hid beneath the cloth. Light poured into Laura Ann's heart with a second message, one she determined to share aloud.

"Whatever we've done, Sophia, God hasn't given up on us. Something tells me we're here for each other," she said, gesturing toward Sophia's swelling with a nod of her head, "and *both* of us are here for *him*."

# CHAPTER 13

---

JUNE 25

Laura Ann awoke, her hand to her face, wet drips on her forehead.

*Plop.*

A drip landed in the softness of her pillow. She reached under the bed, pulling out a pan she'd stored there long ago. Replacing her pillow with the blue and white antique basin, she pulled back her sheets and waited for the next drip.

*Ting.*

Almost five in the morning. The wristwatch at her bedside heralded the beginning of a soggy new day. Laura Ann tried the light switch on her lamp with no success. She'd hoped this nightmare would be over when she woke, an end to the flood. But nothing had changed.

She felt her way across a braid rug with her bare feet, toes as eyes in the dim light of an early morn. Only a few feet across the room, she remembered what she missed. Rain. What became of the metallic symphony of water on roof tin that lulled her to sleep last night? Silence wrapped the little farmhouse in a noiseless embrace.

Laura Ann pushed printed curtains aside to look north toward the ridge. In the grey light of a wet predawn, low fingers of cloud drifted over the farm, damp claws that sliced through trees. A low overcast darkened the landscape.

Minutes later in the kitchen, a dented aluminum percolator received yet another charge of Folgers and water, then set to work. Laura Ann placed the pot on the gas stove to brew, her old reliable drip coffee maker defiant in the face of no power. Grandmother's kitchen gift to Daddy and Momma before she was born. It brewed perhaps thirty thousand cups of coffee for her father. She hated the stuff, but Sophia would want some when she woke.

The screen door squeaked as she stepped out the back of the house. Armored against bands of drenching rain in knee-high rubber boots and a rain slick, she waded through a miniature lake that ran from the house to the barn. Distant rumbles of thunder to the west announced the advance of the next wave of wet misery.

"Tired of this weather?" she asked drenched Angus cows that stood milling about in the feeding area of the barn. "I don't blame you." Laura Ann bent over and scratched Lucky where he nuzzled against her boot, purring and mewing for food. "Later, fella. We have to shovel some corn."

Laura Ann's presence set the cows moving, following her down the length of the barn. She moved along one side of a long feed stall, separated from the herd by an old board fence and oak wood troughs. The Angus pushed against one another to match her stride.

"Hungry bunch," she commented, moving cobs of corn from the crib. Mice scattered in the dim light at her first scoop of a wide grain shovel. Lucky pounced from behind her, pawing at a grey ball of fur with a long white tail. It disappeared into the maze of cobs before he could get claws into the treat.

"You're getting slow in your old age," Laura Ann said with a laugh. She shoveled scoops of hard yellow cobs into the troughs, feeding black muzzles that pushed into the path of the breakfast food. Thick black heads, like elongated triangles, bobbed up and down between the grey slats of the railing. Long pink tongues, spotted with black, curled around cobs and pulled them into waiting mouths, dense teeth crunching a golden meal. Tongues licked at wet noses, like fingers emerging from hot mouths to gather a meal and clean up, all at once.

Laura Ann filled the trough for the two dozen Angus and set the scoop aside. "You ladies got awful wet," she said, pushing her fingers deep into the thick fur on the front of a cow's head. The crushing impact of teeth on cob vibrated through her fingers, so much power from such a gentle animal. The heifer raised her hard forehead into Laura Ann's fingers, begging for more attention when she stopped scratching.

The breath of cows, their body heat steaming up the barn, made the air so moist she could swim in it. The pungent aroma of manure filled the air. Not the acrid feces of chickens, but a rich earthy smell. Daddy used to call it "the smell of money" when they shoveled the barn—a rainy day task, and today seemed as good a day as any. Without electricity, there'd be no work in the woodshop. She patted another Angus on the head and moved toward the front of the barn, grabbing at a set of gloves.

"You guys thirsty?" Laura Ann asked, putting her shoulder into the first push on a pitcher pump at the far end of a deep watering tank. Water from a shallow well gushed from the old cast-iron spigot as she pumped, providing a little for the herd to wash down the corn, not enough to quench their thirst for over ten gallons a day. Plenty of water waited in the fields to meet that need.

Low in the fields along the banks of the Middle Island Creek, brown water and floating debris swirled high, extending far into fenced pastures. Like a lakefront, pasture grass grew down to the edge of the water, fence posts disappearing into brown muck. No wonder the cows came into the barn. In the dim light of dawn she could see all manner of debris scattered in the field. The flood rose high during the night, depositing a line of junk along the highest water level. White objects — house trash from upstream — lay scattered across the pasture. Sticks, logs, and grass clung to barbed wire along the fence, and trees bowed low in the rushing floodwaters.

Laura Ann lifted Lucky and stroked him, his purr box on full roar. Sheltered from the humid breeze of the storm she stood inside the open barn door and plucked bits of hay and cobwebs from black fur.

"Did you stay dry last night, fella?"

Lucky looked up at her with wide yellow and black eyes, like he may have understood. She'd last seen him just before the big blow. So much had transpired since she watched the passage of storms in the garden on a hot afternoon. Her own storm blew in yesterday, but she had a peace now that wiped away all the concerns she'd carried for so many weeks. Lucky nuzzled in close to her breast, seeking another scratch on the ears.

"Hungry?"

Laura Ann turned in surprise, unaccustomed to another voice in the barn since Daddy passed on. Sophia stood in the side door, peering in. "Breakfast is ready!" She wore a huge smile, like she too felt an immense burden lifted since their talk last night. Despite the torrential rain, this day dawned anew.

"I'm starved," Laura Ann replied, setting Lucky on the ground.

"Your good luck charm?" Sophia asked, pointing at the cat. He nuzzled at Laura Ann's boot again, unwilling to be ignored.

"Daddy used to say there's no such thing as luck," Laura Ann replied. "Said you make your own destiny. I named him 'Lucky' as a joke. To prove that luck really existed." She pointed at the cat.

"I agree with your dad. That reminds me of a story I want to share with you. About my James." She gestured toward the house. "Come eat."

Laura Ann cut into another bite of Sophia's Western omelet. Years of biscuits, gravy, and bacon had not prepared her for the delight of fresh vegetables and cheese on eggs. A devoted fan of breakfast and the early morning, she savored the omelet like it might be her last meal.

"I didn't know you were up," she told Sophia. "I'd have stayed in to get something ready for you."

"The smell of coffee woke me, but I'm glad you didn't cook. I needed this." She waved a hand about the kitchen. "A chance to get 'normal' again. When I found the tomatoes and peppers, an omelet seemed like a perfect way to start the day." She pointed at the refrigerator. "But I don't think your freezer will last with the power out."

"No problem," Laura Ann said with a smile. "It runs on natural gas."

Sophia nodded. She set her fork down and pushed the plate away. "So. I had this story to tell you. I couldn't do it last night. Too emotional."

"About?" Laura Ann asked with a partial mouth of food.

"James. My husband."

"I wanted to ask," Laura Ann began, then wiped her mouth, "how a girl from Mexico ended up with a Scottish name."

"Through the best of luck," she replied with a grin. "I met James when I was working at the hotel in Cancun. I'd just turned twenty, and he'd flown down on a trip that he won for being the best salesman at his company." She chuckled. "He didn't fit in with the crowds at all. Not a drinker. No suntan. I don't think he enjoyed it much. Until we met."

"How'd you meet?" Laura Ann asked, sipping on cold milk.

Sophia blushed, her deep brown face burnished a sudden scarlet. "I had an accident in his room, and he helped me."

"Accident?"

"I stumbled while making his bed and fell through a plate glass door onto his patio deck," she said. "I was rushing to get his room finished. It's a good thing he was there. He picked me up, set me on the bed, and cleaned my wounds, then he called the front desk for help. By the time the paramedics arrived he'd patched me up, even bandaged the worst cuts. I didn't want to leave."

Sophia cradled her hands about the mug, staring into it again like she did last night. "James spoke Spanish. It amazed me because so few Americans did. He was so tender, like my mistake had been his fault." She paused. "That comment you made, about luck and destiny?"

Laura Ann nodded.

"James used to say something like that. He looked me up the next day at the hotel and asked me out. In fact, he asked me out every night he was in town. He came back once a month for the next year, and proposed on the first anniversary of my fall. And that's how, a few months later, I came to have a Scottish name."

Laura Ann took a long breath, then pursed her lips while she tried to think of a way to ask her next question. Sophia watched her with an intense focus, like she had some innate ability to see into Laura Ann's heart, to know what words would slip from her lips.

"I lost him three and a half years ago," Sophia said, guessing her question. "He passed away suddenly. A stroke." She wiped at a tear, her head lowered. "One day we were shopping for Christmas gifts, the next he was gone."

"I'm sorry —"

Sophia reached across the table and touched her hand. "I'm glad that we had a chance to meet, Laura Ann. James would have enjoyed getting to know you." She chuckled. "He loved machines. He'd be right at home on your tractor."

Laura Ann nodded. She understood that about men. Daddy commented once that Ian came to the farm every Saturday just to drive the equipment. She agreed with him then, but preferred now to think that he'd been courting her all those Saturdays. The memory of Ian stole her smile and she lowered her head, staring into her glass of milk.

"Are you okay?" Sophia asked, touching her hand again.

Laura Ann nodded. "I'm missing something. Something big. And it hurts."

"What?"

"I have a friend—"

"Just a friend?" Sophia asked.

Laura Ann looked up to see her smile again. She shook her head. "More than a friend. Much more."

"What are you missing?"

"Actually, I haven't missed it yet. Dinner. On Friday. At a fancy restaurant in Parkersburg, but—"

Sophia nodded. "Surely we'll be able to get out by then ..."

Laura Ann felt her own eyes go wet. "Something will work out. It has to."

"Planning a special evening?"

Laura Ann nodded, then looked down at her empty ring finger. "Very special."

"We have power!" Sophia exclaimed from the living room, pushing a button on the front of the television. "And TV!"

Laura Ann smiled, amazed at the impact of something as simple as electricity. Daddy's emergency generator came in handy on occasion, and she confessed, bringing the well pump back on line was nice too. No more hand pumping their water out in the barn.

Laura Ann dropped a bag of old jeans on the floor where Sophia sat scanning for a news broadcast. "I'm cutting denim today. For my stools." She held a pair of scissors in her visitor's direction. "Want to help?"

"Stools?" Sophia asked, picking a torn pair of jeans out of the sack.

"My mortgage. Fifty stools a month to feed the bank. Fifty dollars each. I cut the denim into strips and weave a seat."

"Then hand me those scissors and let's get going," Sophia replied. She dove into the bag and pulled out a pair of worker's jeans, covered in white paint. "These too?"

Laura Ann shook her head. "Don't bother. They're junk."

An hour and six pairs of jeans later, the pile of inch-wide strips on the floor grew sizable, a sure sign of progress. Sophia held up the last of her most recent pair, portions of the belt loops and zipper unusable in the process. "Another one down. And a blister on my right hand."

Laura Ann laughed, pointing her toward the sewing machine in the corner. "If you'd like a break, we have to stitch these together into a single strip."

"I have no idea how to use one of those things," Sophia said with a laugh while pointing at the antique electric Singer. "You are one talented woman."

"Because I can sew?"

"That and more. Look at this," she said, moving to the front window and pointing out at the pasture. Cows made their way across lush green grass in the downpour. "You run an entire farm, build furniture, and inside" — she said, pointing at shelves of classic novels — "you run a small library." She crossed the room to pat Laura Ann on the back. "Any man who catches you is one lucky fellow."

Laura Ann sat up at that last comment, dropping the cuttings in her lap. She stared out the window in the direction of the cows, and the ridge in the distance.

"What? I said something I shouldn't have?" Sophia asked, her ebullient spirit diminished for a moment. Her hand rested on Laura Ann's tense shoulder.

"Oh, nothing."

"I might have been raised in another country, " she said, walking around Laura Ann to sit cross-legged in front of her, "but I'm still a woman." A white cotton top billowed over her jeans like an upside-down lily when she settled to the floor. "There's a man standing out in that field. And you're looking right at him."

"How do you do that?" Laura Ann asked with a chuckle, turning back to face her.

"ESP. I'm psychic."

Laura Ann frowned, setting her shoulders square and cocking her head a bit.

"Just kidding. But I do sense things about people." She tapped Laura Ann on the knee and smiled a broad toothy grin. "Part of you is growing inside me, girlfriend. I'm sure that has something to do with our connection."

Laura Ann nodded and her frown relented. "Maybe."

"No 'maybes' about it." Her smile stole away fear.

"Alright." Laura Ann's turn to blush. "His name is Ian. He's the game warden. We've known each other since kindergarten."

Sophia's silence and inviting eyes demanded more.

"He came to visit every Saturday for the past six years. Checking in — that's what Daddy called it. All through high school and after we graduated. He'd get a haircut every weekend and come here next. Know what I used to associate with his visits?" Laura Ann asked, loosing a giggle.

"I'm all ears."

"Wildroot Cream Oil. An old barber hair tonic. I'll always remember that smell, like it announces that Ian's in the room." She paused, looking out the window in the direction of the man she dreamed would land on her porch this moment. "I don't smell it on him much anymore. New barber, I guess." She paused, then added, "I wish he'd use it again."

"Where is he now?"

Laura Ann shrugged, her eyes misting. She bit her lip and tilted her head in the direction of the window. "He'd be here if there was any way. I know it."

Red, orange, yellow. Green, blue, violet. Bands of translucent color, blended together in a pair of brilliant crescents, arced across the western horizon. Beyond the dazzling double rainbow, the bases of clouds burned with color. Splashes of purple and pink colored the low evening sky, reaching to the blazing ball of red that descended behind a distant western ridge. In all her days gazing at sunsets with Daddy, many of them while working in the fields, Laura Ann had never seen God's handiwork arrayed in such awesome splendor. She stood on the porch with Sophia, the two of them transfixed, watching the distant red ball sink and draw a dark shade across the base of the clouds. With each minute, the rainbow faded, its sun source sinking beyond sight.

Moments after the red disappeared the sky blazed a black-purple, like the deep violet juice of a ripe muscadine grape dripping from the bases of fleeing clouds. A blaze of indigo retreated into the west and towed the dark of night behind it. Half an hour later only a dull purple remained where the sun set moments ago.

The last vestige of the day.

And the end of the storm.

# CHAPTER 14

JUNE 26

"Good morning, sweetheart."

A hand brushed against her cheek. Somewhere in the fairyland between dreams and waking, she could smell him. That cloves-sweet scent, fresh from the barber. A hand warmed her cheek. Rough fingers. Wet. Laura Ann fought the dream, struggling to reach out to the fragrance she knew so well in her heart, but could not verbalize.

"Time to wake up."

The voice was deep bass, smooth, and commanding. It called to a warm spot deep inside. She felt the sure grip of a hand that once held hers. And a kiss. The scent of cloves and lanolin pulled at her with the strength of a ship's hawser, towing her to consciousness. Lips touched hers a second time. Warmth against her warmth.

Her eyes opened. Ian hung in the air, suspended above her, his breath on her cheek, the moist of his kiss still fresh on her mouth. He smiled.

"Still dreaming?" he asked. He squeezed her hand again, a reassuring hold she'd not felt for days.

Laura Ann smiled, opening her eyes fully. She grabbed at her sheet and pulled it up to her neck, returning his grip with her other hand. "Tell me you're real. I need to hear that."

He bent over again in the dim light of early morn and kissed her a third time, a long embrace, kneeling at her side in the dark bedroom.

Laura Ann raised her free hand and placed it on his face, stroking the smooth skin of a fresh shave, marveling at his lines in the early light. Her fingers ran across sharp cheekbones down to a prominent chin. They crossed thin lips that curled when her caress tickled them. He reached up and took her hand.

"Surprised?" he asked, pulling her toward the edge of the bed, her face close to his. He whispered, as if he knew she had visitors.

"Yes!"

"Thought you would be. Didn't know you had company." He laid a hand on her side to tickle her. "Who is he?"

"Ian! You know better."

"Just kidding." He pointed at the window near her bed. "I thought about tapping on it to wake you up when I saw the Lexus. But the door was unlocked, so I let myself in. Couldn't resist the temptation to wake you. I'm surprised you're not in the barn already."

"No need. Rain's stopped, cows will be out. I decided to sleep in."

"I'm glad. Do you wonder how I got here?"

"Just about to ask," she said, putting a finger to his mouth. "But don't tell me yet. Meet me in the kitchen. Now shoo!"

"Yes, ma'am." Ian rose and squeezed her hand once more, then bent and kissed her again. She put a hand to his face, holding him in place for a long time, desperate to pull him tighter, but worried she might be found out. Of all the days ...

Five minutes later, freshened from the bathroom, she joined Ian in the kitchen. She wrapped her night coat about her and pulled the belt tight, then threw her arms about him. Ian lifted her off her feet, twirling her in the kitchen, his head nuzzled into the base of her neck and shoulder. "I missed you," he said, squeezing her tight.

Laura Ann sniffled, her joy pouring out of her eyes after two days of pain, weather, worry—and remarkable revelations. Mental images of Sophia came to mind and she stiffened, dragging her feet on the floor to slow his twirl. She pushed away.

"What is it?" he asked.

She glanced down the hall, then put a finger to her lips. "*Shhh.* She might wake."

Ian stopped, then crossed his arms. "She who?"

"A friend."

"You can do better than that, Laura Ann. I can read you like a book. What's her name?"

Laura Ann grimaced, glancing down the hall a second time, then moved toward him, pushing toward the back stoop. "Let's talk outside."

"No." Ian was emphatic and pulled a chair from the table, guiding her into it. His grip was gentle, but firm. "We need to talk. Something's not right. I braved a raging river to reach my damsel and now she's acting all mysterious." Ian's countenance soured, and he added, "So, who is he?"

Laura Ann wilted, her face in her hands. "No one you know. And it's a woman. A friend."

"Her name is?"

"Sophia. Sophia McQuistion. From Pittsburgh."

"Okay. But you've never mentioned her. Why's she here?"

"Twenty questions?" Laura Ann asked, her voice squeaking. She looked up into his eyes, a strange distrust there that she'd not seen before. He moved back from her.

"It's a valid question. A Lexus in Tyler County? On your farm, spending the night?"

"She was locked in when the low water crossing washed out."

"I can buy that. The causeway's a goner."

Laura Ann took a deep breath, then placed a hand on his knee. He tensed. "Can we start over? Somewhere around that last kiss in my bedroom?"

"I'd like that."

"Her name is Sophia. She's a woman I helped once in Morgantown, and she dropped in unannounced to thank me. She intended to just stop in and say 'hi,' then head over to the Wells Inn for the night. But it started raining, and—"

"Great. So why the secrecy?"

"I'm sorry, okay? I'm just surprised—pleasantly surprised—that you're here."

"I'm not convinced, but I'll believe you. So, want to know how I did it?"

"I have an idea. But I don't think you swam," she said with a chuckle.

"That logjam's a doozy. I scoped it out yesterday, then waited for the water to recede. It's not down much, though. Put in above the logs with my canoe, and pulled it out below the farmhouse. I was able to paddle all the way up through the pasture. Got a little wet wading the last bit to the house, though. It's a mess out there."

"Did Granny Apple tell you I was okay?" she asked, pressing her hands into his.

"She did. Called me right after you waved at her. That was a relief." He let go of her hand and ran his fingers through her hair, still tangled from sleep.

"What about you?" she asked. "How is it in town?"

Ian shook his head in silence, his jaw clenched.

"Middlebourne?" she asked.

"The Middle Island crested thirty-one feet above flood stage, Laura Ann. It wiped out West Union. The west side of

Middlebourne is under water, lots of homes completely covered. Main Street is high and dry, but Route 18 is cut off in a couple of places. Entire homes went down the creek. It's lots worse than the 1950 flood. Much worse." He paused. "But you don't seem much worse for wear." His gaze lacked the usual openness, even the warm touch she'd seen when she opened her eyes in the bed. He seemed distant.

"Granny Apple?"

"She's fine. Couldn't hurt that woman. She's been helping folks up and down the creek through all this. Your aunt Rose and uncle Jack are fine too. Water just missed 'em."

"And your place?"

"My house is okay. Soggy but solid." He looked down the hall, then back at Laura Ann. "So, do I get to meet her?"

She tarried a moment, then took his hands. "Yes."

"Great. I have to be at work by ten. I called and told them I'd be late. All the county officials are on emergency duty, but they know I'm out here checking on you. The only other way is to drop in with a helicopter, but all the birds are busy."

"Are you serious?"

"Serious as a heart attack. I tried hard to get a chopper to fly in last night, but all of the assets were on rescue duty. We pulled up the flood maps and figured you'd be dry. But I'd have come swooping down in a whirlybird if I'd had my way."

She pressed his hands, pulling him forward. She stood and tugged him into an embrace. "I'm sorry. I just worry—"

Ian held her tight, but not the usual way. "No, Laura Ann. You never worry. That's what's got me so confused. This lady must be a piece of work."

"She is." A voice spoke from behind her. Laura Ann flinched, tensing in his arms and trying to spin about.

"I'm Sophia McQuistion. You must be Ian."

Laura Ann looked up at Ian, his face a bright red. He released her but held her hand. His grip seemed almost forced, like he wanted Sophia to see them connecting. That warmed her, and she pulled tight to him.

"Yes, ma'am. I hope that Laura Ann told you something about me." He looked down at her, then back at Sophia.

"Not just told," Sophia replied. "More like 'gushed.'" She smiled. "I'm sorry I interrupted. I heard voices."

Laura Ann stared at her, in desperate hope that Sophia would get this point: "Don't tell." A moment later, Sophia winked, then nodded and opened her arms toward Ian.

"We need to get you some breakfast. You must have worked hard to get here this time of day." She looked at Laura Ann, then back to Ian. "What time is it?"

"Six fifteen, ma'am."

"Please. Call me Sophia. I'm certainly not old enough to be your mother."

"Yes, ma'am." Ian smiled. "Not much power 'round here. Want me to fire up the generator?" He tugged at Laura Ann for an answer.

She nodded, then put a hand to his shoulder and stood on tiptoe, putting her lips to his. "Thank you."

After Ian departed the kitchen, Sophia padded across the floor closer to Laura Ann. "I'm sorry," she said. "I was concerned. Chalk it up to pregnant nerves."

Laura Ann forced a smile, then spoke. "He can't know."

Lights flickered, then came on in the kitchen. Ian would be back soon. Sophia nodded, then added, "Secrets won't help, Laura Ann. Remember, you did a courageous thing."

"Thank you. But I need to tell him in my own way. Okay?"

She nodded. "What does Ian like for breakfast?"

Laura Ann smiled, her first sense of relief since Ian's waking kiss. She gave Sophia a hug. "Biscuits and sausage," she said, releasing her and pointing to the refrigerator. "But now that we

have some power for the blender, some salsa and a breakfast bur-
rito would be a nice surprise."

"I don't understand your uncle Jack," Ian said, driving the farm
truck with Laura Ann in the middle and Sophia seated by the
door. "Everyone in town is on a wartime footing while they fight
this flood, and none of them are happy. But you'd think he'd
won the lottery. He's so happy he's delirious. It's weird."

"My uncle is a weird man," Laura Ann replied. "And mean."

"Why's that?" Sophia asked.

"Long story. Three-course dinner," Ian said. "But I'll take a
rain check," he added, patting his stomach.

"My uncle lives by the belief that 'It's all about me,'" Laura
Ann said, tapping Ian on the knee. "I'll cook that dinner and
we'll tell her all about our experiences. Including barn fires."

"Sounds fascinating."

"It is. Now check this out," Ian said, reaching the end of the
ridge road just before it descended to the old low water crossing.
He pointed fifty feet downslope at the logjam, the detritus of
a massive drainage piled upstream of the crossing. Ian put the
truck in park and went around to open the door for Sophia,
extending a hand as she exited.

"When's the baby due?" he asked, helping her down from
the truck.

Sophia looked back at Laura Ann first, then answered, hesitating. "I—I'm seven months. Another ten weeks, I hope."

"Great. A summer baby. The best time for birthday parties."
Ian gave his hand to Laura Ann and helped her scoot across the
truck bench. "I was a Christmas baby. Terrible timing."

Laura Ann and Sophia walked down the slope with Ian. The
hard rain carved deep ruts down the embankment to the creek,

ravines too deep to navigate. Even if the crossing were usable, Laura Ann realized she could never drive down this slope. Her truck would bottom out, and so would the Lexus. She'd have to wait for dry weather and doze dirt into the ruts with the tractor. Or hope the state came to fix the crossing and the road.

At the bottom of the slick descent, she could see the magnitude of the destruction upstream. Ian was quiet, as if in mourning for those above this dam who'd lost so much.

"Delmer Keith," he said, pointing at the roof of a house jammed into the immense jumble of flood trash. Parts of two houses were visible in the logjam, and now she could see signs of three cars. Fence material, wire, playground equipment, a church sign, the side of what looked like a barn, and dozens of round hay bales—all jammed into a broad dam across the creek. Upstream, the water stood nearly twenty feet above its normal level, the flood trash an impenetrable levee.

"Delmer and his kids were hunkered down in that place. His wife was driving home." He waved a hand toward the jumble of house parts and the roof pointing out of the pile. "She watched a wall of water come toward the house and sweep it off its foundation. To hear her tell the story, it must have been pretty funny. But it's not. Everything they own is wedged in that mess."

Sophia gasped. "Are they okay?"

"Yes. Mrs. Keith told me that she saw the boys jumping out the windows, and Mr. Keith head out the door, falling flat on his face in the water. The house slid off the foundation but didn't go anywhere. At least, not 'til the next night. Then all heck broke loose with that long bout of rain. Must have been something to see. This house floated half a mile to get here."

Laura Ann marveled at the destruction. The demolished causeway seemed a small thing when she thought about losing a home. So many had lost so much.

Sophia waited while Ian led Laura Ann farther down the

slope. Where once a concrete passing had stood for decades, all evidence of the causeway had disappeared. A channel of water flowed through what once had been concrete and rock. To the right, above the bank where remnants of the old crossing now rested, Route 18 slid off the mountain. Slabs of asphalt hung limp above a jagged scar in the clay bank. The road was destroyed.

"No easy way from Middlebourne to West Union. Have to go up Muddy Creek Road to Gorrell's Run to get over there. Could be a long time before this gets fixed." He pointed at the remains of the causeway. "Even if they get your crossing repaired—and they won't soon—you can't drive direct to town. The road's nearly washed out in two other places, not just here."

Laura Ann's heart sank, drowned by images of bankers demanding payment, fifty stools waiting to be shipped—and a corn crop no doubt decimated by the rain. She reached out and took Ian's hand, leaning her head against his shoulder, drawing on his strength.

Ian put his arm about her and held her tight. "I've got your back," he said, staring with her at the destruction. "Somehow we'll dig out of this."

"The baby's kicking." Sophia lay on the sofa in the living room after dinner and a bath. Her nightgown draped across her belly, she rested her hand on the bump like a ledge. "This drum gets pulled tighter every day."

Laura Ann moved across the room and squatted at her side. Her heart thumped hard in anticipation. "May I?" she asked, extending a hand toward Sophia's stomach. Her friend nodded, guiding her hand to a hard prominence.

"Push here," Sophia said. "It might be his foot."

Laura Ann pressed her fingers gingerly into Sophia's warm stomach. The baby lay just beyond her touch.

"Push a little harder. I won't break," she said with a laugh.

Laura Ann smiled and put both hands to Sophia's gown, pressing down on the prominence, massaging it about. In response to her pressure, the baby pushed back with a tiny kick. Laura Ann jerked her hands away. The kick shocked her, movement that confirmed the life Sophia carried—Laura Ann's egg become a child.

"It's okay. He's just getting comfy." She pulled Laura Ann's hands back to the round melon of her belly beneath a cotton gown. "Talk to him," she encouraged. "Get close."

Something magic pulsed through Laura Ann, her hands following Sophia's guide, the caress of soft cotton warmed by her friend's skin. The baby moved again, strange bumps moving across the landscape of body and nightclothes.

*What should I say?*

Sophia released her palms and massaged about her belly, moving the baby into a new position. Laura Ann placed her face close to her own hands and spoke. "Anyone home?"

Sophia smiled, closing her eyes and laying her head back on the sofa, as if relaxing every muscle to make a way for Laura Ann to reach her baby. Two women, one child, all connected. One flesh.

"I know something about you," Laura Ann said, chuckling to herself. Her face close to Sophia in a private way, she felt her friend laugh with her, their shared secret of the baby's parentage.

"Tell him what's on your heart," Sophia said, lying trancelike.

Laura Ann shut her eyes, trying to imagine the baby just below her hands. She moved the foot a bit, then laid her cheek on Sophia's stomach, reveling in the warmth of her friend and this home for a child that shared her blood. Like a human pillow,

Laura Ann cradled Sophia and the baby, whispering three words over and over.

Sophia laid her hands in a gentle rest on Laura Ann's head, pulling her closer to the child, her touch a comforting affirmation. Without embarrassment, she clung to Sophia and the incredible life that thrived within her.

Her words resonated in Sophia's womb. "I love you."

# CHAPTER 15

———⚬———

## JUNE 27

Sophia stood on the back stoop, staring toward the barn and flooded fields. She'd been on the washing porch for a long time after breakfast, frozen in one place like a pole. Time wasted away, but Laura Ann resisted the temptation to start the day without her new friend.

"The water's a little lower ... but not much," she said, joining Sophia on the old sloping stoop that joined the back of the kitchen. Great-grandmother did her wash here decades ago, laboring over a wooden tub contraption complete with big rollers to squeeze water out of the clothes. The first washing machine, or what looked like it. The old Maytag stood in the corner behind Sophia, a monument to women long past, and unused for the last fifty years.

Her visitor let out a long breath — some unspoken frustration — then pulled her iPhone out of a pocket and rechecked for service. Laura Ann knew the result before Sophia looked at it. No cell phones worked on The Jug. Too many hills in the way. Uncle Jack continued to complain about that every time he visited, but the mountains never moved.

"I'm working in the woodshop today," Laura Ann offered,

dusting her hands like it was time to get to work. "Care to join me? Lots to do—and your help would make it twice as fast."

Sophia nodded, but did not turn. She cleared her throat, then spoke. "Is there any way I can get to town to rent a car?" she asked, then coughed again. "Today?"

Laura Ann chuckled. Surely Sophia could see the problem. Cars would never cross that flood at the neck of The Jug, even with the low-water crossing intact. "We could swim, but I wouldn't recommend it." She turned and headed for the door. "Seriously, if you're up for it, I can use a second set of hands. We've cut all the jeans. When we do get out to town, I'll need to pick up some more."

"I *am* serious," Sophia replied, her voice stern. She turned to face Laura Ann, taking a step toward the kitchen door. "I need to leave, to head back home. Today. What are our options?"

"Is someone waiting to hear from you?" Laura Ann asked. "We could have asked Ian to make some calls. He offered, remember?"

"I know. I was too polite and I should have taken him up on it. I need to get back home, Laura Ann. I'm not worried about the car. I know it will be fine here for a while—if you don't mind."

"Of course not. But you're welcome to stay too—as long as you need." Laura Ann thought back on their time together last night. She hoped this need to leave would soon pass. "I could get you out in a few days on the canoe. It would be fun to have you here in the meantime."

"Thank you, Laura Ann. I'd like to take you up on that offer. But I really do need to leave today. To make some calls, to check in with the office." She took a deep breath and continued. "And to settle some important legal paperwork." She gestured toward the flood. "Is there any possible way?"

The first thing that came to mind? The mortgage. Not the

rushing creek or the potential for disaster canoeing with a pregnant woman. Laura Ann's thoughts went straight to the challenge of finishing fifty stools in the next seven days, how to drive them to New Martinsville without a creek crossing—and the twenty-five hundred dollars she needed to cover her next bank payment.

Sophia waited for an answer, her head cocked and eyebrows furrowed.

"Sure," Laura Ann volunteered with a loud huff. "We can tow your suitcase across a roaring gulch." She shrugged. "Certain death. Or—we can try to canoe out. I've never done it with this much water."

"Ian canoed in just yesterday, then back out again. And you told me you've traveled this creek a hundred times."

"Yes, but never at flood stage. Very dangerous."

"Dangerous, or very dangerous? There's a difference."

"Is there?" Laura Ann asked, crossing her arms. "Like the difference between drowned and very drowned?"

"That bad?" Sophia asked, the harsh look on her face fading in a flash. "Is this life-threatening—or just difficult?"

"For a pregnant woman? Possibly threatening to the baby." Laura Ann felt funny using those words.

*Baby? It's my son.*

"Have you ever canoed?" Laura Ann asked, struggling to take her mind off the child and last night's intimate connection.

"No. But I can learn."

"I don't want to tell you what Ian would say." Laura Ann shook her head.

Sophia cut her off quickly. "But what do *you* say?"

She remained silent, watching the face of her visitor. Determination like none she'd ever seen was painted across Sophia's face.

"It's that bad?" Laura Ann asked after a long pause. "You

can't spend a few more days and wait for the water to subside? We might even be able to wade across within a week."

Sophia shook her head. "I have a client who's working a thorny child custody issue, Laura Ann. I'm key to her arguments. A child's well-being hangs in the balance ... as well as the mom's."

"I guess you can relate." Laura Ann gestured toward Sophia's hand that rested on her bump.

"Yes, I can. I'm very close to this custody issue — considering." She took another deep breath, as though trying to calm some inner struggle. "Just presume that this is an emergency, and you're the mom." Her eyes pleaded. "Could we make it? In the canoe?"

"I know *I* can ..." She paused, staring at Sophia's eyes. Daddy said you can see truth in a man's eyes, and hear trouble in his voice. She picked up on both. "It's you I'm not so sure about."

"I'm very capable."

"This is crazy." Laura Ann threw up her hands. "You'll die if we don't get out today?"

Sophia didn't answer right away. She looked down at the floor, then turned to face fields covered in muddy brown water. She seemed to count every risk before answering, then spoke with a quiet forcefulness, a fierce determination — and something more, a tone that Laura Ann couldn't quite read.

"I understand the risks, Laura Ann. I can be packed in a few minutes. We need to go."

In her twenty years, Laura Ann had never witnessed this kind of devastation. Her sixteen-foot canoe sliced through roiling brown, and eddies of milk chocolate with white latte froth, carrying with it every imaginable floating scrap of humanity. She guided the canoe through the tops of short trees, pushing debris out of branches that slapped at the canoe, clearing the way for Sophia who sat a few feet behind her. Canoeing between treetops was an experience all its own, the creek still twenty feet above its banks, yet almost ten feet lower than where it crested two nights ago.

An occasional dead animal lay rotting where the cresting flood pinned it in a tree above her reach. A few forest animals were caught up in the maelstrom, along with two dogs, and in the crotch of a half-submerged tree, the swollen and mud-matted carcass of a calf. Water bottles, plastic toys, firewood, and round bales of hay littered the creek. Years would pass before this carnage could be cleaned away, or was consumed by nature. The water moved in a swift whispering current, desperate in its race toward lower elevations, on a terminal trip to the Ohio River, and eventually, the Gulf of Mexico.

Laura Ann dipped her paddle to keep the canoe headed in the proper direction, preferring to steer from the front. Here, she could watch for eddies, avoiding the trouble spots that she knew held submerged hazards. But she'd never been prepared for this. She could only keep the canoe on a rough course down what appeared to be the middle of the creek. Familiar landmarks lay twenty feet beneath her, invisible.

"Hold on," she warned Sophia, a quick turn of her head to check her passenger, buttoned up tight in a life preserver. Sophia's white-knuckled hands gripped the gunnels of the boat, near an unused paddle. Laura Ann faced ahead, deft in her maneuver to send the boat around a massive tree, its trunk swept over by the flood. She would take no chances today.

She pushed hard on the paddle to control the boat from the front, frustrated with the sluggishness of the heavy canoe carrying two adults and a suitcase wrapped in a trash bag. Any other time, riding alone, she sped along lightning fast and maneuverable. Not so today.

"Look," Sophia called out, taking her hand off the gunnel to gesture to the right. Laura Ann shot a glance back, caught the point, and followed it. They were a mile into the journey, past the boundary of the farm. Lodged into the trees, a portable toilet bobbed upright in the current. Downstream of the toilet, what looked like a small shed lay stuck in another tree, water cascading over the remains of a roof, the kind of turbulence Laura Ann feared most today. That the toilet escaped being sucked into the logjam was remarkable. The force of the night flood exceeded anything she could imagine.

"We're a couple of miles from the takeout," Laura Ann said with a loud voice to avoid turning her head, yet be heard. "We'll pull the canoe out downstream of the crossing, on the right bank."

She steered around another tree, and continued. "The water will come at us fast and furious from the right when we enter a big pool. That's where the creek meets itself at the neck of The Jug. Ian said the pool is navigable, but we don't want to take any chances."

For the next two miles, Laura Ann showed Sophia some different paddle moves, coaching her how to dig her paddle in on the right to pitch the canoe to the right, the top priority when they met the swirling confluence at the whirlpool. As they traversed a long straight section of the creek where it made its last mile around The Jug, fewer items were lodged in the trees, most of the upstream trash sucked out by the limbs behind her. "Can you hear it?" Laura Ann asked half an hour later.

"Sounds like a waterfall," Sophia responded, dipping her paddle at opportune times to help steer.

"That's the logjam. The water will come rushing in from the right. Think right, always right. We have to cross that flow and get to the far bank."

"But couldn't we stay on the creek all the way to town?"

"We could, but I'd have no way to get back home."

"Long walk," Sophia replied, and then added with a point of her paddle, "and here it comes."

Fifty yards ahead of them, Laura Ann saw it too. On the bluff above the big pool sat The Jug Store, looking over the confluence where waters scoured away rock and clay during the century since her ancestor tunneled through the ridge in the late 1700s. She could see a few people gathered at The Jug Store parking lot, watching the creek below. A quarter mile beyond them, Route 18 collapsed into the water. The last stop at the end of a busted highway, The Jug Store would serve as a gathering place for months to come.

"When we pass the big sycamore, listen for my yell," Laura Ann hollered, her voice straining above the roaring water. "Unless I say otherwise, paddle right. But don't let us get pointed into the current. Got it?"

"Ready!" she heard in reply.

In less than a minute, they would pop out under the store. Sixty seconds from a rude dunk in the water, or a proud landing on the downstream bank. The creek flowed wide at this point, covering farmlands for half a mile to the left, but the chocolate brown water hid a multitude of deadly hazards. She glanced back at Sophia, guiding the boat well, her oar in the water.

*Sisters.*

The word popped into her mind, watching the last of the trees pass, the rumble of the waterfall vibrating like a timpani inside her.

She'd always dreamed of a sister. Another girl to share those things that Daddy, much as she loved him, could not understand or should not hear. She'd grown up with a hoe or a paddle in her hands, with hard work her first priority over malls and boys.

Laura Ann took one last look back at Sophia, her tight pink T-shirt under the orange life jacket a contrast in cultures.

*Sister.*

Laura Ann counted the seconds after she passed the big syca-more before she dug her paddle in on the right side. Pulling it toward the canoe, the bow jerked right toward the oncoming rush of water that poured over the logjam at the neck of The Jug. Her throat tightened, gooseflesh rising on her arms. This was more than she'd gambled for. No time to check Sophia, she dug in again, fighting the onslaught that hit the canoe like a mini-tidal wave.

The boat pitched and, behind her, Laura Ann could feel Sophia lean into the wave just like she'd taught her. The boat shot left, headed for the trees on the downstream side of the pool below The Jug Store. Any other day, that bank offered a gentle beach, rest, and protection. Today, it represented death.

Water sluiced through the trees on her left like seawater through a whale's baleen, a rushing tide of foaming brown that slammed into trunks submerged twenty feet underwater. She could never navigate that minefield, sure to hit a tree sideways, flip, and spill them both into the torrent. The smack of a head against wood, or a baby crushed against a limb, and a life would end there.

Acid jumped into her throat as she dug in on the right side again, yelling, "Right! Right!"

Behind her, Sophia jammed her paddle in the water, forc-ing the boat toward the current with a hard stroke, then pulled with the paddle once more. Laura Ann caught a quick glimpse of people gathered at the store, pointing down. She lowered her eyes back to the water, her tormenter — and her grave, if she did this wrong.

"Don't try anything stupid," Ian warned her when he visited yesterday. "I can handle things for you in town."

"If I do need to go, I can do it myself."

"Don't be stubborn, Laura Ann."

"I'm not stubborn. I'm independent."

*I'm going to eat those words.*

Dirty foam splashed over them as the canoe crossed the swirling pool, bucked by the current that rushed toward them on the right. She caught a brief glance of the towering logjam, through the ridge cut, and shivered.

"Straight ahead!" Laura Ann yelled, digging her oar in to haul the boat forward. Like swimming at an angle across a rip tide, their next move would take them across the current, to the safety of the far bank. Laura Ann dug her paddle in deep and pulled with her back and legs, desperate to propel the boat forward out of this misery. Working together, they pushed the boat across the center of the current and toward less turbulent waters near the far bank.

"Left!" Laura Ann screamed, realizing too late that their combined heaves were more powerful than she'd needed, the boat darting across the water to impale itself in a vertical bank. She flipped her paddle to the left, pulling toward the bow. Behind her, Sophia matched her moves. The boat spun on its axis, assisted by a strong upstream current. Half a minute after they entered the whirlpool, they shot downstream, caught in the flow toward Middlebourne. They were through.

Guiding the craft to the right, along the bank below the edge of Route 18, Laura Ann heard horns. One honk, then many, from cars and trucks blaring away up at The Jug Store. For the first time that day, she allowed herself a grin. The old men at the bar in The Jug Store would chew on that story for a few years. A girl, and some woman wearing a pink top, shot the rapids at The Jug whirlpool during the worst flood on record. And they lived to tell about it.

It was a stupid move. She should have refused Sophia's request, no matter how dire her situation. Her heart pounding, she chided herself for letting stubborn pride get in the way, silently sure she could do this. Chiding herself for endangering Sophia—and the baby. Nevertheless, facing heavy odds, they'd won. She turned and flashed a smile to her newbie canoe partner. She and her sister had won.

*Chew on that, Uncle Jack.*

"I mean it, Keester," Laura Ann said, wishing he'd move on. "We like to walk."

"No can do," the older man said, wiping his brow. "Got that canoe out of the creek for you, little lady, and I'm a' gonna get you to town. Right thing to do."

Giving up, Laura Ann extended a hand. "Thank you. For asking the guys to help us."

"'Tweren't no trouble, Miss McGehee. Five of us, it took, but she's outta there, and the suitcase too. We'll set 'er upstream of the jam and she'll be awaitin' when you comes back."

"All right. We'll take you up on that ride," she said, gripping Keester's hand with all the strength she could muster. "But only as far as Main Street." She turned to her left. "This is my friend, Sophia. She came to visit but her car is stuck at my place." She nodded in the direction of the truck bed. "Her suitcase. We're going to get her headed home today."

Keester tipped his hat, a John Deere ball cap with a dark

stain of hair oil about the headband. "Pleasure. Reckon you wouldn't be drivin' outta there anytime soon."

"I reckon," Sophia replied.

Laura Ann smiled, suppressing a laugh. Country lingo sounded funny in Sophia's city mouth.

"Alrighty then. Hop in, little ladies, and we're off."

Keester Bays loved Red Man. Empty pouches of the famed chewing tobacco littered his truck, and a baseball-size wad of tobacco distended Keester's right cheek. Only Keester could stuff an entire pack of Red Man into his mouth at one time. The sickly sweet odor of tobacco spit blew through the truck while they drove with the windows down, headed a couple of miles into town.

"So, Keester, what's got you and all those boys up at the store so early this morning?" Laura Ann shouted over the wind noise.

"Road's out," he answered, turning his head to spit.

"Road's gonna be out a long time, Keester," she said, squeezing Sophia's shoulder. "Are those guys at The Jug Store going somewhere, or just hanging out?"

"Hangin' out." He said it like "hangin' out" during a major disaster was all in a day's work.

"From out of town, huh?" Keester asked, leaning in Sophia's direction. "What brings you to these parts?"

"My late husband, bless his soul," Sophia said, slipping back into her country role. "He loved these parts. Miss McGehee did us a big favor once. My James passed more than three years ago, and I got mighty lonely. So I came to pay a visit."

"Sorry to hear that, Miss."

Laura Ann choked, squeezing back another laugh. She ducked her head, then turned to face out the open window and feigned a cough.

*Well done.*

"We're getting off at the bank, Keester. Thanks for the ride," Laura Ann said, glad they'd made it to town without a severe grilling. Or a proposal.

The truck slowed and pulled into a parking place. Laura Ann clambered out, followed by Sophia. "Gotta run, Keester. Say hi to Mrs. Bays."

"Aren't you forgettin' somethin'?" Keester asked, looking back at the suitcase in the truckbed.

"Nope. I've got it," Laura Ann replied. Before Keester could unlatch his seat belt, she'd placed a foot on the bumper and launched herself into the bed. She handed the travel case over the side to Sophia, then leapt out.

"Bye now," Laura Ann said, careful not to touch the driver's side of the truck, draped in a windblown covering of dried brown spit. "Thanks again for the ride."

Keester shrugged, then touched the bill of his hat in a sort of mountaineer salute, and drove away.

Laura Ann waved, glad she'd escaped without more questions, then turned to Sophia. "I need to go in the bank for a while. To make a deposit and check on the mortgage."

"Is there a problem?" Sophia asked, rummaging through her purse for her phone.

"The flood. Fifty stools are due in New Martinsville in seven days. I can't drive them out." She took a deep breath, trying to swallow her stress on the steps of the one place that could sink her. "No stools means no money."

Sophia put out a hand toward Laura Ann. "I understand."

"Anyway. I came to find out what the bank's grace period can do for me. I'll be about ten minutes." She looked down at Sophia's phone as its screen sprang to life. "I know you have some calls to make. Try the Enterprise dealer in New Martinsville. That's the only car rental in the county. We can get you a taxi that far."

Sophia nodded, a strange resignation in her eyes. "Thanks. I'll stay out here and watch the bag." She looked down at her phone. "Got a signal!" she said, smiling.

At the top of the steps, Laura Ann looked back. Sophia stood on the sidewalk, the phone to her ear. Moments later, Sophia buckled at the knees, sinking down to sit on a low brick wall that flanked the bank's steps. One hand on her belly, the other to her ear, she bent over in a strange pose of concentration.

Or perhaps some unspoken pain.

"Your mortgage is due on the first, Laura Ann. In four days. Beyond that, the bank has the option — but is under no obligation — to extend you a grace period."

Matt Parker, a persnickety loan officer prone to the repetition of simple facts, sat behind a broad desk without a single sheet of paper on it. Just a computer screen and keyboard. In all her days working with this bank, the only one in town, she'd never seen him handle a piece of paper.

"I know it's due on the first, Mr. Parker. What I'm here to ask is when does the grace period end? When is the last day that I can pay without penalty? Thanks to the flood, I can't get my stools to New Martinsville. I'm here to do some advance planning so that I pay on time."

"That's distressing to hear, Laura Ann." He turned to his computer. "But it confirms our analysis."

"Distressing?"

"Yes. All of our loans are subject to federal audit. With your father's death — I'm sorry, of course —"

"I'm sure."

"Yes. Well, with his passing, we're very concerned about your ability to pay. Surely you can understand."

"I appreciate your sympathy, Mr. Parker. But let's get to the point."

"Point? Certainly. We've rated your loan recently and it's been downgraded to what the banking industry terms 'doubtful.'" He stared at the screen like it was some kind of friend, never making eye contact with her. "We've recently been required to put up a financial reserve as collateral against your debt, Laura Ann. If you miss a payment, we may have to call the loan."

"On what grounds?" The voice came from behind her. Familiar strength.

*Sister.*

Laura Ann turned, Sophia pulling a bag as she settled into the chair next to her. She took the seat as Mr. Parker looked up. She had her smile back. The woman who deflated on the bank steps had fled, the old Sophia returned.

"I beg your pardon?" Mr. Parker said, his eyes darting between the two women. "Have we met?"

"No." Sophia unzipped her purse, rummaged for a moment, and produced a business card. "My name is Sophia McQuistion. I'm a tax attorney from Pittsburgh. And a friend of Laura Ann's."

*Attorney?*

Laura Ann's mouth fell open, but she felt the touch of a hand on her knee as Sophia shot her a quick wink.

Sophia gave him just a heartbeat to review the card, then launched the question again. "On what grounds has your auditor downgraded this loan?"

"I'm sorry Mrs. — Mrs. McQuistion. We're not authorized to discuss that with outside parties."

"Fine. I know the game, Mr. Parker. So, let's speak in the hypothetical. A 'doubtful' loan is rated an '8' on the auditor scale, and represents debts for which the bank has demonstrable evidence that there will not be repayment. Sixty to ninety days of past-due accounts, or loss of revenue to repay." She paused, watching him. "Am I correct?"

He shrugged in silence.

"Has Ms. McGehee missed a payment?"

"That's not in question."

"Yes, it is. You put the issue in play with that comment about the 'doubtful' rating. I repeat, Mr. Parker. Has my client missed any payments?"

"Your client?" Mr. Parker stiffened, his face sour. "No. She has not."

"So. If she's not delinquent, one of the two key provisions for this rating, then I conclude that you have downgraded her account for reasons of questionable revenue. But you'd have to show proof of that to an auditor, wouldn't you? Proof, it seems, you may have fabricated." She looked at Laura Ann, then continued. "When is the next payment on this note due?"

Mr. Parker took a long breath, then turned to the computer screen. "Due in four days. On the first." He exhaled a long breath, then added, "Overdue on the fifteenth. About three weeks."

While he searched his screen, Sophia reached into her purse and pulled out her checkbook.

Laura Ann's heart skipped. "No," she said, reaching across the gap between them to lay a hand on Sophia's check. "I can do this. Please."

"I know you can," Sophia said. "This is not a loan. I'm buying your stools." She turned toward Mr. Parker. "Let's be double-sure that some overzealous bankers don't arbitrarily downgrade a reliable loan." She held Mr. Parker's eye with her last comment, and he winced.

In the silence between Laura Ann's amazement and Mr. Parker's discomfort, she filled out the check and signed it with a flourish, then handed the paper to the banker. He refused to touch the check. Sophia laid it in front of him, then stood, pulling on Laura Ann while stuffing her checkbook in her purse.

"Deposit it, Mr. Parker. To the credit of Laura Ann McGehee's mortgage. Consider it an advance payment—and a sign of her reliable income stream." She turned, grabbing the suitcase, and gestured with a move of her head for Laura Ann to leave. Sophia stared Mr. Parker down for a long moment.

"We'll return in one hour for the receipt."

# CHAPTER 16

"That lawyer lady bailed her out."

"Drug money?"

"Not drugs. Men. The paying kind."

Her ears tuned to the loud conversation of two patrons at the pizza parlor, Laura Ann shoveled in another bite of Auggie's Old Fashioned sausage and mushroom. The little restaurant was packed for lunch, most of the people showing the effects of the flood. Muddy clothes, water stains on their pants, or knee-high rubber boots — coping with a tragedy that decimated the lower half of town.

Laura Ann dabbed at some pizza sauce on her chin and rolled her eyes.

"What?" Sophia asked in between bites.

Laura Ann nodded her head in the direction of the window, an older woman seated with a man about the same age, both of them outfitted in waders. The woman droned on in a voice loud enough to hear across the crowded room.

Laura Ann whispered, "Don't you hear what they're saying about us?" She wagged her head in the direction of the rude lady at the window.

"Every word," Sophia replied.

Laura Ann smiled, cocking her head to one side. "You don't show it."

Sophia shrugged. "I'm an attorney. And a good poker player too." She shook her head. "Don't let it bother you. They're just jealous."

"Jealous?" Laura Ann asked, polishing off the last bite of her pizza.

"No one's talking about them," she said with a big smile. "So they yap about other people just to get noticed."

"That's sad," Laura Ann replied. The pizza, mixed with a stomach full of stress, soured in her gut. She waited for Sophia to finish her last bite, then gathered her things and stood to go.

Main Street of Middlebourne resembled the hybrid of a gold rush town and a national disaster area. Heavy equipment moved into town on lowboys towed behind big tractor rigs, all of them funneling in from the direction of Sistersville on the only passable section of Route 18. State emergency vehicles, news vans, and a Salvation Army food truck belched exhaust as they clogged the town's main artery. Mud tracked everywhere ... red clay slinging off tires and flat chunks of mud squashed on the pavement like earthen cow pies. Up and down Main Street, people moved fast, a hive of bees determined to shovel out of yet another flood. A community knit together by dogged West Virginia determination.

"Does it bother you?" Sophia asked after lunch when both were out of earshot of Auggie's. "All that talk?" The two wove their way down the crowded sidewalk, loaded with groceries, two bags of jeans—and a receipt from the bank. A three-quarter mile walk lay ahead of them, headed out of town to the Par-Mar gas station, and the cab stand for the town's part-time taxi.

"Sure it bothers me," Laura Ann replied. "Especially now. With Daddy gone."

"Is that typical? These rumors?"

"Folks gossip. You're a new face and they probably wonder

what you're up to, spreading business cards around town and all."

"We saw a banker, Laura Ann. That's hardly newsworthy."

"It's big news for some. Uncle Jack's friends love salacious rumors. They'll probably label you as loose money from out of town." She chuckled. "Maybe a brothel madam who runs her business out of local farmhouses." She moved aside as a loud truck rumbled by. "Other than my uncle's friends, most people will simply wonder why you're here. Distrust runs high after a flood. Real estate deals, rip-offs, carpetbaggers. Uncle Jack will be busy trying to scam something in this, you can be sure."

"You've mentioned him a couple of times. Never positive."

"Nothing good to say."

A diesel pickup zoomed past headed through town, then screeched on the brakes. The driver slammed the mud-spattered red truck in reverse and zoomed back, weaving and erratic.

"Hey there, L.A.! Need a ride?" A young man in a soiled green Marshall University ball cap pulled alongside her. He matched their stride, driving in reverse, his huge muffler belching black and loud.

Laura Ann cringed, shaking her head while she pressed forward. "No thanks, Tommy."

"Long walk home, babe."

"We're headed to the Par-Mar for a taxi. We're fine."

"Shouldn't pass this up." He waved a hand in Sophia's direction, his eyes evaluating her head to toe. "Hey, who's the pink and pregnant lady?"

Sophia kept her gaze set straight ahead, matching Laura Ann's stride.

"A friend, Tommy. And we don't need a lift."

"Suit yourself." The young man hit the brake, stomped the diesel into drive, and roared away.

Laura Ann frowned and kept moving. "I liked him—a few years ago," she said. "But he had a problem controlling his hands. He has a nasty temper when he's denied."

Passing the bank for the third time that day, Sophia slowed, out of breath. "I need to stop a minute," she said, panting. Her face red with exertion and wet with sweat, she set her bags down and plopped on a mud-covered bench at Bridgeway Road. The bridge behind them—the half of it still intact—stood resolute against a frothing torrent. Sitting on this bench thirty-six hours ago, she'd have been ten feet under water.

"I need to make one more call." Sophia panted. She fished out the phone and leaned back into the mud-caked bench. Laura Ann set her bags aside, and then wandered over to a road barrier at the washed-out crossing, providing a little privacy.

Sophia's hands described something during an animated call that Laura Ann couldn't hear. She waited at the edge of the bridge, rebuilt not long ago, marveling at the power of the water that severed it for the third time in her twenty years.

To her left, Route 18 resembled a two-mile-long mud pie. As far as she could see, everything at eye level was a reddish shade of taupe. A coat of mud—earth paint—covered grass, road, and homes. The pastel red-brown of drying mud caked phone poles, trees, and barns at a constant level. Chalky brown desolation.

Sophia waved at her and Laura Ann headed back to the bench.

"I've found a dear friend," she heard when she got closer. "I'll need another week here, but I'm fine." Sophia touched the screen and dropped the phone into her purse.

Laura Ann cocked her head to one side as she approached. "Everything okay?" Laura Ann asked. "Sorry to eavesdrop, but ..."

"Fine. My employees can manage without me." She took a long breath, sweat dripping from her forehead. "I've changed my mind."

"I don't understand. I thought—"

Sophia shrugged. "Sorry. I shouldn't have put you through this, Laura Ann. But when I met that rude banker, it got me thinking. You're up against some stiff opposition if the bank wants to recode your loan. I can't leave you hanging. The least I can do is to stay and help you get those stools ready." She smiled. "I mean—if you don't mind. Who knows? I might even get my car out."

Laura Ann felt her face go flush, aggravations over the dangerous canoe trip mixing with the memory of the miraculous bailout at the bank. How could she refuse?

Sophia pointed up the road. "We've got company."

A pickup rolled in their direction, a familiar face leaning out the window.

"Word travels fast," Laura Ann replied. "I guess he got your voice mail."

The truck came to a stop and Ian threw open the door. A beige coat of wet mud caked the sides of the vehicle. When Ian stepped out of the pickup, Laura Ann threw her arms around his neck. He stood tall, a stalk of corn.

"You couldn't wait." He chided her with a squeeze. "Just had to climb in that stupid canoe and come to town."

She let go of his neck. Unshaven, he had a salty line about his brow where sweat gathered under the game warden ball cap. His eyes were red, like he'd been up long hours, and she caught a familiar whiff of hair tonic. "I heard you were in town when I dropped in at Auggie's for a bite. That's when I checked the voice mail. Sorry I didn't find you earlier."

"Did you manage to get some lunch?" she asked, pinching his side.

"Are you kidding? I jumped in the truck and headed this way soon as I listened to your message." He pinched her in return. "Had to hurry. I saw Tommy's truck over at the Exxon. Thought he might get to you first."

Ian waved toward Sophia. "Forget the taxi. I'd be glad to take you over to New Martinsville myself." He patted the hood of the truck. "Boss said it's okay, what with the flood and all."

Sophia stood and picked up the grocery bags. "I'd love a lift, but—"

"She's staying with me a while longer, Ian," Laura Ann said, cutting her off. "But a ride back to The Jug would be super."

Ian glanced at Sophia, then back at Laura Ann, and shrugged. "You're sure you don't need a ride to the rental place? Really. It's not a bother."

"No," Sophia said in unison with Laura Ann. They both laughed.

"We're headed back to the canoe." Laura Ann let go of Ian to take the sacks from Sophia. She set them in the bed of the truck. "And for the record," she declared with a playful pinch at Ian's bony ribs, "Tommy Sovine never had a chance."

Half an hour later, Ian held the bow of the canoe above the log-jam, bracing the craft against the high water that rushed past. "You're sure about this?" he asked, wagging his head.

Laura Ann tapped his cap with a paddle. "I was born in a canoe," she replied, determined not to show her concern.

"That's a stretch," he replied. "I don't know … two women? On their own?" he asked, wagging his head, his smile broad. "Better get across fast and hug that far bank. Hold on to the trees if you need to while you round the bend. I don't want to have to pry you out of that log jam."

"Yes sir, Officer Ian. Now, let us go. Gotta get home and get started on a meal. You'll come for dinner. Promise?"

Ian nodded. "Gonna have to sleep on the couch, though. I'm not canoeing out of The Jug at night during a flood."

"That's the way I want it," Laura Ann responded, then reached forward to touch his hand. "We'll be fine. Pork chops, beans and potatoes, fried okra, and a cobbler. Don't be late." With that, she put her oar in the water and pushed out of his grip.

The Middle Island Creek raced to its doom, swollen muddy torrents overflowing their banks, but not the ravaging liquid monster that tore through the valley three days ago. Laura Ann called out directions to Sophia but didn't need to watch her. They were a team now. The canoe shot across the creek and Laura Ann guided them along the brushy edge, pointed downstream toward the logjam.

She raised her oar in a wave goodbye, and Ian signaled back. Tall like a tree, shoulders and arms his branches, he stood anchored on the far bank, his eyes locked with hers. Warm tingles rippled down her back. She waved once more, and then set her eyes on the deadly dam.

"Hug the left bank," Laura Ann hollered, making herself heard above the water's roar. No longer the wicked waterfall that she'd witnessed below, water sliced through the logjam, a wooden strainer sifting a brown torrent. A canoe would stand no chance once smashed up against the jumble of trees, cars, and houses. A minute later, Laura Ann cut sharp left only twenty feet from the dam to join the natural flow of the creek in its seven-mile loop about their jug-shaped spit of land.

Three miles downstream, Laura Ann guided the boat to a rest, pointed into a broad bank. Every trip when she glided to a stop below the farmhouse, she wondered in amazement at a waterway that enabled her to canoe with the current yet always find her way back home.

"If you'd told me we could do this, I'd have never believed it," Sophia said, helping to pull the canoe and its load of food through sticky mud into clean grass. "It's like an Escher painting. You finish where you start."

"A what?" Laura Ann asked.

"An artist named Escher. He did a lithograph of stairs that spiraled back on themselves. Like this creek."

"That's why my relatives settled here," Laura Ann replied, grabbing a handful of plastic sacks. "Imagine how they appreciated it, before there were any roads."

"Let me have some," Sophia said, taking two sacks from Laura Ann. "I'm not as fast—but I'll get there." She motioned with a loaded hand in the direction of the house. "I know it was a lot of trouble, but thanks for taking me to town. And for your hospitality. I think the stay will do me good."

"It's the least I can do." Laura Ann toted her load alongside Sophia, starting the quarter mile uphill slog to the house through verdant fields lush with timothy and clover. "Thank you for that help at the bank."

"You're welcome. I got the best end of the deal, by the way. Now I have Christmas presents for everyone at the office."

Together they waded upslope through deep soggy grass. Like a green sauna, the air above the pasture lay thick with humidity. Sophia stopped frequently to wipe at her brow, pushing back matted black hair. Laura Ann's T-shirt clung to her chest and back, soaked through by the time she'd walked halfway to the house.

"Whew!" Sophia exclaimed, setting her bags down for the fourth time. "Out of shape."

"Maybe not," Laura Ann said, waiting at her side, yet anxious to be on her way. The cool of the woodshop beckoned her. "Remember, you're expecting, Sophia. Take it slow."

"Perhaps. But this shouldn't be so hard."

"The humidity makes it worse. Let me take two of those." Laura Ann reached over and took the sacks. Sophia did not resist.

"How did they cut this grass before tractors?" Sophia asked once they were underway again.

"By hand. They used a big blade. A scythe."

"This entire field?" Sophia wheezed. "Cut by hand?"

"They had all summer," Laura Ann replied, smiling. She remembered Daddy's favorite joke. "If we're not working," he'd asked with a laugh, "what else is there to do?" Hard work, the essence of a good life.

Breaking a path through tall grass, two-thirds the way up the slope, Laura Ann looked back at Sophia.

She'd disappeared.

Laura Ann dropped the sacks and dashed back down the trail of bent grass. Thirty feet back, she found her friend, lying on her side in the pasture, motionless. "Sophia!" she cried out, dropping to her knees. No response.

Laura Ann put a hand to Sophia's face. Sweat sheeted off her skin, yet she felt cool. The arteries in her temples flared, throbbing in a rapid beat. Laura Ann could barely feel a pulse at her throat. She panted in shallow rapid breaths.

"Sophia!" Laura Ann cried again.

She had little time. Sophia needed to cool off fast. Laura Ann pulled her T-shirt off and raced back down their path toward the creek. Clad in a sports bra and jeans, she plunged headlong through the hayfield, headed for water. Half a minute later she bounded up the grassy trail, clutching a soaked shirt.

"Can you hear me?" Laura Ann asked as she squeezed a pint of mud-tinged water on Sophia's throat, and then draped the damp T-shirt on her forehead. She patted her on the cheek, then took Sophia's cool clammy hands in her own and massaged them, desperate for some response.

Sophia didn't move.

# CHAPTER 17

Relaxing on the front porch in the late evening, Laura Ann slowed her rocker to match Sophia's cadence. "I don't remember any of it," Sophia said. "We were talking about cutting the field by hand, and the idea of all that manual labor in this heat made me sick. I went from nauseous to dizzy in a heartbeat, then lost my balance. I woke up here, lying on the porch."

Ian sat on the front steps, his back to one of the white posts, whittling on a stick while the women talked. "Sounds just like heat exhaustion. You don't remember the tractor ride?" he asked, holding up the point on the stick to get a better view of his handiwork.

"No. How did you get me up on the porch, Laura Ann?"

"After you woke, I ran to the barn and got the big tractor. It has a front-end loader. I sort of rolled you into the bucket and drove you up here, then rolled you back out at the steps." She pointed to tractor tracks in the front lawn.

"Just like that?" Sophia asked with a laugh. "Cooled me down with a bunch of sweaty flood water, scooped me up in a dirty tractor bucket, and dumped me on the porch?"

"It worked," Ian said. Then he added, with a chuckle, "By the way, I used that loader to move manure last week."

Sophia's jaw dropped and her eyes went wide. "Cow manure?" she asked, dusting off the back of her arms like there might still be some on her.

"Don't worry," Laura Ann said. "It was dry."

The three sat in a comfortable silence, watching the sun set in a clear summer sky. Ian reached across the porch with his stick to tap Laura Ann's sandal.

"Great dinner. Loved those pork chops."

"You outdid yourself," Sophia said. "I adore your kitchen, by the way. It's been years since I cooked with gas."

"Don't need much electricity out here," Laura Ann replied. "Gas stove, gas heat, gas refrigerator, gas freezer, gas hot water, gas generator. And all the natural gas is free. The oil well's on our property—up there," she said, pointing toward the ridge.

"That, and some batteries for the radio," Ian interjected. "By the way, I brought you one of my walkie talkies, Laura Ann. If you two ever need to reach me." He picked up another piece of wood and began to whittle again. "The radio is in my bag."

"I appreciate that," Sophia said, her tone more somber than it had been all night. "We might need it."

Sophia bit her upper lip, and then folded her hands, fingers interlaced. She looked down at her stomach. "Something's not right. With me."

"What do you mean?" Ian asked. He dropped his new piece of wood and turned to face her.

"Ian's an EMT, Sophia. He carries his medical bag with him everywhere."

"Always," he replied. "So what's the problem? Besides the heat stress, I mean."

Sophia took a long deep breath, and then continued. "I've never been this dizzy before, even on hot days. Today when I stopped to sit on that bench and call my office, I couldn't stand up a moment longer."

"How often does this happen?" Ian asked.

"It hasn't. At least, never like this. I'd get a little woozy once in a while, and I chalked it up to the pregnancy. I walk about a mile every day back home—but never on a day like today."

"I'm guessing it's the heat and the humidity, but let's see what we can find out," Ian said, springing up to go in the house. A minute later, he emerged with a long gray tote bag lined with red piping, red handles, and a large red cross.

"You weren't kidding," Sophia said, her mouth agape.

"Game wardens draw gunfire sometimes," Ian remarked. "It pays to be prepared. And I enjoy it."

"You're one handy man to have around," Sophia said.

A few minutes later, after poring through a medical manual in his bag, Ian stood next to Sophia and spoke in a serious tone. "Your blood pressure's pretty high. One fifty over a hundred. That puts you at a greater risk of heat exhaustion."

"I've never had high blood pressure. Always low. Could it be the pregnancy?"

"That's possible. You might have gestational hypertension. It's not uncommon in some pregnant women … although you don't fit the profile. You're young and thin, with no previous history of high blood pressure. Or, it could be something a little more complicated, a problem your doctor would need to evaluate." He put the blood pressure cuff back in his bag. "You could see a doctor in Sistersville. We have a hospital here."

"Could this affect the baby?" Laura Ann asked.

Ian picked up his EMT manual, thumbing through it. "Perhaps. The book says to watch for toxemia or preeclampsia. Those can affect the child, and might result in a premature birth or a low birth weight. Worst case? They can lead to seizures."

Everyone grew quiet with his last word.

After a long pause, Sophia drew in another long breath, then asked, "What other symptoms does it talk about?"

Ian raised an eyebrow. "Persistent headaches, blurred vision, sensitivity to light. And pain in your abdomen." He paused. "Any of those bothering you?"

She nodded, lowering her head to massage her temples. "Not before. But now? A splitting headache. I thought it might be from dehydration." She lifted up a half-finished glass of water.

"Might be." Ian looked at Laura Ann for a long moment, then back at Sophia. "But if it's not, we could leave right now. It's getting dark, but I could have you at the hospital in ninety minutes."

"On the canoe?" Laura Ann exclaimed.

Sophia waved him off. "No. That's okay. I mean, it's just a headache."

Laura Ann left her chair and sat at the foot of Sophia's rocker, her hand on her friend's forearm. "Falling out in the field might be more than a headache, Sophia. We don't have to wait. Ian can get you out this minute."

She patted Laura Ann on the hand and shook her head. "I'm too stubborn," she said with a smile. "Let's sleep on it. I'll probably feel lots better after some rest. Besides, if we do have to make that trip again, I'd rather cross the whirlpool in daylight."

Ian nodded and repacked his bag.

"I'll be up early," Laura Ann said. "First light."

"Not me," Sophia replied, standing up. She wobbled a bit once erect. "But don't eat right away. I want to cook breakfast. My gift to you both."

Ian beamed. "You're on!"

Yellow shafts of light danced with the flicker of a kerosene lamp, a gentle golden glow illuminating the living room and the world beyond it. Another lantern in Laura Ann's bedroom cast a yellow pool of light on the end of the porch.

"He's snoring." Laura Ann pointed through the window at

Ian, stretched out on the sofa, too long to fit, but too tired to notice. "He stayed up all last night to help people dig out in Middlebourne. No wonder he's exhausted."

The flicker of flames made the pickets of the porch railing appear to move in the dim golden light, and faint shadows shifted on the grass beyond. Laura Ann stood with Sophia at the rail and gazed out into a humid June evening. The end of day gathered both women in its arms as beetles buzzed in dark air, alighting on the screens.

"How long has your family been here?" Sophia asked, turning to sit on the rail of the porch. Her features were a gentle brown in the lamplight, her hair a dark skein in the dim glow of the distant flame.

"We've lived on The Jug since 1796. My great-grandfather George Gregg—five greats—built the mill at The Jug handle where the crossing washed out. He's the one who cut through a low ridge to build a mill at the bend. He sold The Jug to his sons at ninety cents an acre. His grandson Thomas bought up most of the property, including the acreage we farm today. The property passed down through family, and most of them eventually sold their shares to the state for a Wildlife Management Area." She waved her hand toward the dark. "Our farm is all that's left of the original homestead. A hundred-seventeen acres."

Sophia stared out into the night. Tree frogs chirped in the limbs of walnuts and sweetgums that surrounded the sides of the house, a gentle background to the night's peace.

"I have no idea about my family history," Sophia said, her voice subdued. "We just were. I had grandparents, but don't know anything about them. My father didn't talk about relatives much, and my mother was an orphan." She clung to peeling paint, her fingers tracing some invisible figure in their touch on the old rail. After a time she asked, "Did your dad talk about his family?"

"All the time." Laura Ann moved a step closer to Sophia. "We'd recite our ancestry for fun. It became a game."

"Ancestry?" Sophia asked with a chuckle. "How far back can you go?"

Something warm swelled inside her. Maybe that's the way Daddy felt when she'd asked him about his family. "We go back to 1403," she said. "Daddy was named for Angus Dubh Mackay, a fierce chief of his clan. His name meant 'Black Angus' in Gaelic. The Mackays were descended from Picts, the ancient tribes of the north. The McGehees spring from the Mackay line, and became cattle herders in the northernmost lochs of Scotland. They used to battle the Sinclairs — Momma's clan — until everyone sort of settled down during the seventeenth century."

"Keep going. Please. I need to hear this."

"Honor was strong in our clan and it bred tough warriors. Our family never backed down. The Mackay motto is *manu forti*, or 'with a strong hand.'" She hesitated, and then added, "An old Gaelic proverb says, 'Better a swift death in battle than a slow one in bed.' Daddy repeated that saying every morning at breakfast." She sighed, adding, "Angus Dubh died of an arrow wound in the Battle of the Sutherlands."

Laura Ann took a long look at the dark, her eyes imagining boundaries for their property beyond the limit of her vision. "In 1792 our Scottish relatives were kicked out of their homes in a horrible land grab called 'The Clearances.' My relatives emigrated to the United States and settled here, in mountain lands. McGehees, Mackays — and Sinclairs, Momma's family. They married into the family lines of Scots who'd come over a hundred years earlier, like the Greggs from the southern highlands, who came with William Penn in 1682."

"Tell me more, so that I can make it mine." She put her hand to her belly. "And make it his."

"Daddy and I used to sing our ancestry." Laura Ann hummed

the tune to herself for a moment, tears welling in her eyes. Not since Daddy's last days had she recited their family tree. It percolated up from deep inside, like a nursery rhyme she'd learned and could never forget. Salty joy ran from her eyes into the corners of her mouth as she recited her legacy, the eight generations who had farmed this land.

> *Laura Ann, of Angus and Hope, son of James and Joy.*
> *Son of Justus and Andrea, son of Alice and Roy.*
> *Alice Marie the only child of Mary and Thomas Gregg.*
> *Thomas a son of Mary and George, the settlers of The Jug.*
> *George Jr. from Virginia, son of Sarah and George,*
> *Quaker son of William and Alice, co-founders of P.A.*
> *Greggs of Glen Orchy, McGehee of Loch Hope,*
> *Highlanders for 'aye,*
> *From Scotland to the farm at The Jug.*
> *McGehees of Clan Mackay.*

Laura Ann wiped her eyes on the back of her hand, reliving fond memories of Daddy singing to her on the old Ford tractor when she was a little girl, sharing his roots with her. Deep taproots that now took hold in the womb of another woman.

Sophia reached to her left and pulled Laura Ann into a hug. They stood, united in arms, swaying to the evening song of tree frogs. "Would you ever leave?" Sophia asked, her voice a sweet harmony to the night's sounds.

"No. This is what I was raised to do," Laura Ann replied. "To be. And to be here. To move the farm forward another generation. And to raise a family." She looked back, Ian asleep behind her. Her gaze lingered on his long frame, legs dangling over the edge of the couch. She wanted to give him a bed. She would, in time.

"Did your dad ever think of leaving, of breaking the chain?"

She pondered her friend's words, Sophia unaware of Laura

Ann's history, of her father's last wish. More tears welled up, but she set her jaw, breathing deep. How to explain this?

Laura Ann pulled at Sophia's elbow, tugging her gently to turn about on the porch. She pointed up to the beaded board ceiling. A mud nest snuggled into the corner, five yellow-white beaks visible over the edge of the cup-shaped nest. To their left, two adult birds rested on a ledge.

"Do you see those barn swallows?" she asked, pointing to the adults. "They return to that spot every year, building a mud nest in the spring. Every year they lay eggs, every year they raise chicks. Every year they leave. But they always return, to that very corner. Not to the other end of the porch, not to the eaves. Just to that corner."

She pulled at Sophia's arm once more, moving closer to the sleeping adults. "Every fall they migrate six thousand miles to South America. They fly hundreds of miles a day to lands I can only dream of. But they always come back. To this home, and to that very spot, to raise their family."

In the dim light of the kerosene lamp, she could see their colors. Perhaps she saw them in her mind, mixing with the partial shades visible in the lamplight. Orange-brown throats, a sharp black bill, pointy black tails that spread to reveal a beautiful fan of white markings underneath. Darting birds that raced from point to point above the yard, gathering bugs for food. Food that fed pink-orange furry throats peeping for attention, bugs that spilled out of tiny yellow-white bills clamoring for yet another insect morsel.

"I am that swallow," Laura Ann said, taking Sophia by the hand in the dim light. She squeezed for emphasis. The words panged her, sparking an irresistible desire to place her fingers on Sophia's stomach, to reconnect with a part of her that she'd lost forever.

Her very first chick, alive in the womb of another woman.

"No matter how far I roam," she said, her gaze shifting to Ian asleep on the couch, "I will always come back. This is my home."

She looked back at the gentle outline of Sophia's swelling belly under a crisp cotton top. "One day, a time will come when I am but a memory. Then one of my swallows will carry on."

"Laura Ann?" Sophia called out from her bedroom half an hour after her turn in the bath, washing up from a brutally hot day.

"Yes?" Laura Ann said from her bed. Like in the old days with Daddy home, speaking to each other at night after the lights were out, she answered her friend in Daddy's old room.

"The baby's moving again," Sophia said, her voice cracking. "Would you like to come feel it?"

Laura Ann hesitated to respond. This, the very answer to her prayer that night, yet it seemed so dangerous, so personal. She might connect for good and never let Sophia go. Like a last kiss before saying goodbye forever to someone you love, perhaps it was best not to kiss at all.

She lay there for a long moment in silence.

Sophia called out again. "Laura Ann, I understand if you don't want to. But it would mean a lot to me."

She could wait no longer, every fiber screaming to jump up and run to Sophia, to lay her face on her friend's gown and cry for the baby she might only see once. To hold it, even if only through the soft fabric of Sophia's skin, to cuddle the life that she'd given away to save a farm she'd vowed to protect. She'd sold her chick to buy the nest.

Laura Ann rose, like a spirit under the control of another, drifting from her room to the bed next door. Sophia sat propped up, pillows under her back, her legs splayed, the outline of her belly visible under her nightgown. Starlight their only illumination, Sophia was a dim form on the sheets. Yet, like seeing with infrared vision, and with a mother's sense, Laura Ann could discern the form of the baby as it moved under the cotton covering of Sophia's nightclothes.

A tiny life bumped and stretched inside this woman. A life that began inside her own body. Laura Ann's heart leapt for that life to be inside *her*, to move and announce its coming to *her* family. She knelt at the side of the bed, but Sophia patted the top of the mattress. Laura Ann took a seat beside her, Sophia's hands guiding hers to the correct place. A knee poked up, a foot rubbed across the inside of the womb, tiny motions seeking some temporary relief in the tight confines of Sophia's athletic frame.

Laura Ann's heart slammed inside her, a question begging to be answered, a request screaming to be made known. Her hands shook under the guiding caress of Sophia's fingers. Her mouth dry, Laura Ann spoke the words that had lingered on her lips for days. No more time. She had to ask now.

"Can I see him after he's born?"

Sophia lifted her hand from Laura Ann's and put it to the girl's forehead, like the gentle touch of a mother Laura Ann could scarce remember.

"Yes. I hoped you'd ask." She made a sound, like cooing at a baby, then added, "I promise. I'll bring this little swallow home."

Laura Ann shook, as from a fever or a deep chill. She wanted so to see the child, to hear his name when he lay in her arms, something to give meaning to her sacrifice and to her family's roots. She yearned for Sophia to draw on the child's history, to honor treasured family names, in a way that remembered those who'd come before. The way Daddy would have wanted.

Sophia spoke again, her hand resting in its place on Laura Ann's head, perhaps sensing the unspoken need. "Like my late husband, a man he can never know . . . and his grandfather who passed along proud blood through you," she said, "I want him to be called 'James.'"

Laura Ann's heart broke, that name so precious when spoken in this bed.

Sophia lowered her hand to rest on Laura Ann's, where together they palpated a prominence just beyond the reach of their fingers. Sophia squeezed her hand, willing the shaking to stop. Laura Ann looked up, her sister's wet eyes twinkling in the starlight.

"We'll teach him his ancestry, Laura Ann. And his middle name will be 'McGehee.'"

# CHAPTER 18

JUNE 28

Fog invaded every crevice, a suffocating cloud that blanketed the bottomland. It stole sound and dampened the morning call of birds and the crow of roosters. Even her voice felt sucked from her throat when Laura Ann tried to yell back to Ian from the barn. Like a giant muffle, it lay over her, spiriting voices away into the vacuum of an invisible sunrise.

Distance disappeared, no sense of depth to the barnyard. Buildings emerged from the dense covering as she approached them, eerie structures transforming with each step forward. She crept along ground she knew well enough to cross blind. But blind might have been better. This goo robbed her senses of direction and perspective.

In the barn, Laura Ann started the tractor and headed for the front of the house. A ride through the pasture to his canoe would save Ian — and her — a long walk through tall dripping-wet grass.

Ian bounded off the porch, grabbed the tractor's roll bar, and swung himself up on the big Case. He took a seat on the fender aside Laura Ann. "You ready?" he asked quietly, wiping condensation off his brow. The wet blanket of cloud seemed to invite whispers, as if sound offended nature itself.

"Ready to be left alone? No." Laura Ann wondered at other possible meanings of his question. Would she share her burden with him? Not yet.

"Secrets don't become you," Granny Apple said once. Here sat a man she cared about more than anything on Earth, yet she kept him in a fog of her own, a dense blanket of secrecy wrapped around her relationship with Sophia.

"I'm worried about her. I wish you could stay," she said in a furtive attempt to keep the focus on Sophia, not herself.

"If it's heat stress, she'll shake it off with rest and liquids," he offered. "But she needs to see a doctor about that blood pressure when she gets home." He laid a hand on her shoulder. "Question is, will *you* be okay?"

"Yes. But I plan to keep that radio of yours close by."

"Just a minute," Sophia called out, rushing onto the porch. "Don't leave! I packed some leftover breakfast pastries for you to take with you."

Ian smiled, raising his hands in mock resignation. "If you insist. Those sugar horns were great."

"*Cuernos de azucar.*" Sophia repeated in Spanish.

"Whatever."

"Hang on a minute. I think there's a couple of *marranitos* left too."

"Yeah. Love those ginger-pigs."

"Ginger*bread* pigs, Ian," Laura Ann chided.

Fifteen minutes later, Ian sat in his canoe, his gear stowed and ready to push off into the pea soup that hid the Middle Island Creek. The tractor sat a few yards away, idling at the upper limit of the flood line. Any other day, the growl of the throaty diesel would echo off nearby ridges. Today, fog muffled the engine to a low rumble.

"You be careful," Laura Ann said, pushing his small green canoe backward into dingy water. Ian pulled with his paddle and spun the canoe about once he hit deeper water and cleared the grip of the grass.

"No problem. Call on the radio if anything pops up." He tarried before pushing through thick branches to join the river on the other side of the tree line. He pointed his paddle at Laura Ann. "You're my rock. You know that, right?"

"I'm a rock?" she asked with a laugh.

"No," Ian said. "You heard me. I'm proud as punch about how you manage everything. Especially now." He tipped his green game warden ball cap in a mock salute. "You always manage to find a way, Miss McGehee."

His words pierced her, his trust untarnished by any knowledge of her darkest secret. She bit her lip and raised her hand in a silent wave.

Ian eased the boat forward, slipping into the fog. His last words were clear, though he quickly faded from sight.

"I love you, Laura Ann. Always have. Always will."


"Ian raved about that breakfast," Laura Ann said, hanging a dish towel on the oven's handle. "He'll nurse the leftover pastries and make them last for a couple of days."

"More where those came from," Sophia replied. "Just get him back here to try them out."

"He'll probably stop in tomorrow morning. But now we can call him any time we want with the radio." She shook her head. "Somehow he keeps his job and his trips out here in balance." Laura Ann looked at Sophia, remembering too well yesterday's fainting in the pasture. "How about you. Any better?"

"Good as new," she said with a smile. "No headache. No

wooziness. No problem. So … how about a tour of the place?
It's supposed to be dry today once the fog lifts. And I need to
get out." She smiled and wagged a finger. "But no long walks.
Maybe we can take the truck?"

Laura Ann nodded, leading her to the back door. "I need
to get out too. We'll start with the woodshop, and your stools.
Then I'll show you the barn," she said with a wave. "Something
very special out there. Up in the hay loft."

Sophia followed and for the next hour the women wove their
way through her father's shop. It was a slow trek, handling stools,
smelling fresh-cut wood, and walking through a history punctuated by spoken memories of Daddy. From the shop, she led
Sophia to the barn, Laura Ann explaining how to care for the
cows in the winter, describing how to put up hay, and extolling
the virtues of dried corn, barn cats, and clover.

"Come upstairs for a minute," Laura Ann said, gesturing up
a short flight of stairs to the loft. Sophia fell in line behind her.
"When my great-grandmother was little, she carved her initials
and the date in one of the beams. I did too when I was six. I'll
show you."

Cobwebs of long-dead spiders hung from the corners of
the stairwell, draped with flecks of hay that drifted down from
above. The sweet perfume of dried grass grew stronger with each
step up the old rough-cut boards of the staircase, worn smooth
by more than a century of use. Laura Ann put her hand to the
doorjamb at the top of the climb, pushing open a small board-
and-batten door.

"Her initials are over here," Laura Ann said pointing ahead
to a dim corner of the barn where the steep pitch of the roof
approached the floor. "She carved them in 1906, when she was
seven years old."

Laura Ann knelt down, running her fingers along the shallow engraving of two ragged letters in the face of a thick beam. "N.M. 1906." "Novella McGehee 1906," she said, turning back to face Sophia.

But Laura Ann knelt alone.

"Sophia?" She dashed back to the stairwell. Two steps from the door where her hands had lingered moments ago, she heard a gasp. Sophia's hand extended out the door onto the worn oak flooring of the barn's second floor, her fingers balled into a fist. She moaned as Laura Ann went to her knees at the top of the stairs.

Sophia lay prostrate, her cheek bloodied where it hit a hay-littered step, arms outstretched and grabbing at air, as if clawing her way up the stairs. Her chest rose and fell in a series of raspy breaths.

"No!" Laura Ann exclaimed, slamming the door back at the top of the steps and grabbing Sophia's extended arm. Miraculously, she'd not fallen off the precarious staircase, or slid to the bottom. Laura Ann felt for Ian's radio in her pocket. She'd left it in the kitchen.

"Sophia!" she screamed, gingerly stepping over her friend and onto the stairwell. She struggled to find a way down without crushing Sophia's torso, a chest that fought to get the semblance of a breath.

Moments later, she cradled Sophia's bloodied face in her hands, fast shallow pants of air coming from her mouth. Her eyes shut, she recognized Laura Ann's touch, barely nodding, but not forming any words.

"Relax. I've got a good hold. You won't fall," Laura Ann reassured her. "Try to take a deep breath. Slow."

Sophia shook her head, too weak to talk, her mouth wide open to snatch every possible puff of air.

"I'm taking you down," Laura Ann said, then threw an arm

about Sophia's waist. With another arm cradled under her friend's head, she worked her way down the stairs, dragging her over each step on a controlled slide over slick oak and tall risers.

Near the bottom of the steps, she lowered Sophia's head to the wood, desperate to speak with Ian, yet unable to tear herself away to run for the radio. The choppy breaths continued, little wheezing pants that Laura Ann knew would not fill the lungs of an expectant mother. She put a finger to Sophia's throat, frustrated that she couldn't find a pulse. Sophia's heart raced like the intense flutter of a hummingbird, with no defined beat.

"I've got to get the radio!" She squeezed Sophia's shoulder. "I promise. I'll be back."

Sophia's panting grew more ragged, but she managed to raise a hand, as if waving Laura Ann away.

On the horns of a dilemma, she let go of Sophia and ran.

Laura Ann's heart leapt when Ian replied minutes later to her radio call, his voice scratchy, but readable.

"Say it again and slow down."

"Sophia's collapsed. She was climbing the stairs in the barn. She's wheezing, like she can't get a breath. She can't move."

"Can you get a pulse?"

"I tried. It's racing. I can't count it."

"She is breathing, right?" he asked. She could tell he was moving fast, struggling to talk. Probably helping someone in town and trying to talk at the same time. His own dilemma.

"Panting hard. And panicked."

"We've got to get her out, Laura Ann. Can you move her?"

"I can't carry her ... but I might be able to stand her up."

"Can you get her into the truck?"

"And go where?"

Ian didn't reply right away, like he was forming a thought. She waited, praying for his voice, for his reassurance. For some word on how to save Sophia, from so far away.

"Buckle her in tight," he said, the signal stronger than before. "I'm leaving town now."

"Okay. But—"

He hadn't stopped talking, and her transmission stepped on his.

"—at the crossing."

"Ian! Say it again."

"I said, I'll meet you at the crossing. Understand?"

"Take her to the causeway?"

"It's our only choice. Lock her in tight and drive to the neck of The Jug, Laura Ann. Somehow, you've got to get that truck to the bottom of the hill. It's the only way to get her out." He paused, then added, "Watch her close. If she stops panting . . ."

"What?"

"Call me. Then start CPR."


Laura Ann screamed at the rain-rutted road and her slow pace. Seated on the truck's bench seat, Sophia leaned into her shoulder, micro-breaths barely moving her chest, breathing like a dog that had run too far and too fast. She prayed for Sophia's survival. A mile to go to the crossing. Much too far.

*Why this, Jesus? Please save Sophia. And baby James.*

The road smoothed out as she topped the ridge, layers of leaves on the forest road softening the ride. Sophia's chest continued to heave in valiant attempts to get one solid breath. Laura Ann gunned the truck, moving it through the wood as fast as she dared.

"I'm there!" a voice said on the radio, Ian's first call in minutes. "At the crossing."

"I'm in the Management Area," she called back. "What does the hill look like?"

He hesitated, no answer. Laura Ann's back tingled with a premonition of his next words.

"You don't have any choice, Laura Ann. You *have* to get down that slope. We can't save her if you don't."

Minutes later, she slowed the four-wheel drive to a crawl, sneaking up on the tortuous descent down to the Middle Island Creek. She'd loved driving this hill in her younger days, but never like this. Deep gullies, worn raw where water coursed down the road, yawned like canyons the entire length of the short grade. Steep wet clay, with no way to reach the bottom if the truck bottomed out, and slick as ice. Ian stood on the far bank, his truck nosed up to the stream, a rope in hand. He needed her truck on the other side, something to tie off to.

Laura Ann rechecked the four-wheel lock, scanning left and right of the gullies. To her right, she'd tumble off the edge of the road, rolling the truck all the way to the bottom. To her left, a muddy bank of ugly red clay rose up steep.

Only one choice.

Her left wheel riding up as high on the clay bank as she could grab, and the right tire riding the middle of the rutted road down low, she plunged into the descent, both hands welded to the steering wheel. She felt Sophia's hands seek her knee, a feeble hold as the cab lurched. Momentum and speed were her twin friends, the only way to power through the yawning jaws of truck-sucking trenches.

The left front wheel slung mud in a furious torrent as she gunned the engine, climbing as far up the red bank as her nerves would allow. The truck tilted precariously, weaving down the road, one tire low between the ruts, the other four feet higher and spinning on clay that had never seen a vehicle's tread. She raced pell-mell for the creek bottom, slamming at last into piles of rocks that littered the bottom when she leveled out near the water.

Across the swollen creek, Ian pumped a fist in the air. He made a circle sign with his hand, his direction for her to spin the truck around. She let herself breathe at last, looking to her right to check on Sophia.

Her head cradled into Laura Ann's shoulder, her fingers clutching her knee, Sophia let out a short breath, and three short words.

"We made it."

Laura Ann backed the truck up to the edge of the floodwaters, her hands cramping in their grip on the wheel. Ian called again on the radio from his place on the far bank, sixty feet away, a coil of rope in his hand.

"Check her respiration and pulse."

Laura Ann nodded, disconnected her safety belt, and turned in the seat. "Sophia?" she asked, praying for some sign of improvement. No response.

"Slower breathing, a little more regular," she spoke into the radio after seeking a pulse. "Her heart's still racing." She ran to the other side to open the door and unstrapped her passenger.

"Watch out," he called on the radio, then heaved a light line to her, a rock tied to the end. It clattered to the shore a few feet away.

"Pull it over," she heard him say in the next transmission, his words partially drowned out by the roar of water that spilled over the log dam a few feet to her right. She grabbed the line and tugged, hauling a heavier rope, and behind it, a cable from the front of his truck's winch. Less than a minute later, a towrope in hand, he called again. "Hook the rope to your hitch. I'll take a strain."

Like towing the truck out of a bog after a heavy rain, she whipped the rope and hook about the ball on her hitch, then raised her hand, thumb extended. Ian took up the slack immediately with his cable winch, the rope popping up taut, tugging hard on her vehicle.

Laura Ann returned to check on Sophia in the cab. She wiped the sweat from her friend's brow. "Breathe for James," she said.

When she turned around, Ian had waded deep into the water, a second rope wrapped about his waist and slung over the towing hawser, with a harness of some sort and two life jackets threaded over one arm. To his left, barely visible in the fog, The Jug Store sat on the crest of the cliff overlooking their rescue, the men inside no doubt unaware of lives that hung in the balance below them.

Ian forded the stream, water over his shoulders as he clung to the tight rope, unable to keep a footing on the rocky bottom, so swift ran the deep brown current. Sixty feet of frothing water drenched him, but he crossed it far faster than she thought possible, working hand over hand along the heavy line. She ran to him at the shore, pulling him close as he waded out of the current, soaked with cool brown.

Ian thrust the harness into her hands. "From my tree stand," he said, wiping his wet face with a free hand. "Help me get the life jacket on her first. Then the harness." Together they moved Sophia out of the truck, then dressed her in the flotation and the camouflaged halter. The jacket and harness swallowed her like a child. Ian cinched them as tight as he could, then untied the rope he'd wrapped about his own waist.

Without a word, Laura Ann understood his intention. He threw his waist rope over the cable, hitched a loop about it, then threaded the bitter end through the belt of her jeans. "Guide yourself along the high line. Gotta pull your way across." She nodded.

He whipped another hitch in the line a few feet ahead of Laura Ann, and used it to tether her with a carabineer clip to his belt, then gathered Sophia into his arms as easily as lifting a pillow. Sophia draped across one shoulder, he clipped a carabineer from her harness over the high line and stepped into the flood.

Together they waded into the maelstrom. Sophia's only salvation, a ride to the hospital, waited twenty deadly yards away.

When they reached the other side safely, Ian unclipped Laura Ann. "Passenger side. Backseat." Laura Ann ran for the truck door. He slipped Sophia off his shoulder into his arms, her shivering body cradled tight against his chest, then slid his patient, dripping wet, across the backseat.

Her face pallid and eyes shut, Sophia lay panting in tiny breaths, her arms clutched tight about her chest. No more of the ragged struggling-to-breathe pants; she seemed to be slipping away.

"Might go into shock. You'd better drive," he said to Laura Ann, unbuckling the harness and jacket and tossing it into the passenger seat. Laura Ann slid the seat forward, giving Ian room to kneel in the back with his patient. Ian handed her a knife. She ran to the front of the truck to slice the high line free of the winch cable and reel in the slack. A few moments later, she stood at Ian's side, passing him the medical pouch he always stored behind the driver's seat.

They said little. Laura Ann didn't hesitate, slamming doors shut once his feet pulled in. Seconds later she had the truck started and in gear. Backing out of the creek bottom with a three-point turn, she raced up the muddy slope, spinning tires until the truck gripped the firm asphalt of Route 18.

She would follow the creek all the way past Middlebourne,

and with it the dense fog. What posed problems for Ian's canoe meant a nightmare for driving, fog lamps no match for the dense mist. Once past The Jug Store, she crept forward at ten, then fifteen miles an hour, feeling for the edges of the roadway. A road that washed away in many places just days ago.

"The truck radio," Ian barked. She jerked a microphone from its holder and passed it back. Middlebourne lay two miles away down this soupy highway.

"Ten-Thirty-Three. Ten-Thirty-Three," Ian yelled into the mike. "Unit seven inbound Middlebourne, Route 18, destination Sistersville ER. Request medical assist. Over."

Laura Ann gunned the engine when a patch of clear road emerged, whizzing past small white houses and the occasional barn. The lifting fog wouldn't last long; the road moved close to the creek again in half a mile. She prayed for people to stay off the highway early on this morning.

"Unit seven, this is base. Copy your ten-thirty-three. Interrogative ten-twenty, over?"

"A mile out of Middlebourne," he replied.

"Unit seven, base, is the patient in your truck?"

"Ten-four. You ready to copy?"

"Go ahead, seven. We'll relay to Sistersville."

"White female, early thirties, seven months pregnant. Unconscious. Pulse weak."

"Got it. Watch those roads, Ian. Lots of fog."

"Copy. Request an emergency unit meet us en route."

"Working it. No guarantees." The voice paused, then added, "Better keep moving."

Laura Ann slowed for a bank of fog that blanketed the road just before her entrance into town. It wouldn't last long. Past town, she'd cross the river one more time and, Lord willing, the roads would open up. They were fifteen minutes and fifteen miles from the ER on the best of days.

AUSTIN BOYD / 205

"Ian?" Laura Ann asked.

"Yeah?" He ripped open a blood pressure cuff and strapped it around Sophia's arm.

"How bad is it?" she asked, turning hard right to zip down Main Street. Minutes later she rolled over the last bridge. Ahead lay a dozen miles of twisting blacktop to reach Sistersville.

Ian didn't answer for a long time, his hands busy pumping the blood pressure bulb. At last he spoke up, his voice subdued. "It's serious, Laura Ann. Might be preeclampsia." He paused to take the numbers. "With this blood pressure, they're both in danger."

"Be more specific," she demanded, stomping on the accelerator when the road straightened. "How bad?"

Ian cleared his throat, pumping the blood pressure bulb again. He took a long deep breath, then answered.

"Just pray."

Vinyl and linoleum. The pervasive odor of plastic overwhelmed her. Alone in the guest area of Sistersville's tiny emergency room, Laura Ann huddled in a green molded chair, forcing back nightmares of too many days in rooms just like this, only a year ago. The beginning of Daddy's quick slide from life.

"She's stable." Ian dropped into the chair next to her.

Laura Ann grabbed at Ian's arm. Before she could speak, he answered her question. "Sophia's conscious, but it's more complicated than preeclampsia. The doctors improved her blood pressure with medication and they're getting some more tests now."

His clenched jaw said more than his words. "Preeclampsia is a serious complication, Laura Ann. If her kidney function stabilizes, and they can keep her blood pressure down, she'll come through it fine. Untreated, it leads to serious trouble for her and the baby."

Her eyes grew wet with more questions.

"Possibly—a premature birth." He bit his lip, looking away for a moment. "There's an expert in Wheeling. They'll transfer her there soon."

Laura Ann nodded, crossing her arms against the chill of the room and wet clothes. Like a human blanket, Ian wrapped his arms around her.

Her shivers became his.

# CHAPTER 19

JUNE 29

"Insurance card and identification," an attendant said the next morning, with a brief glance to acknowledge Laura Ann's presence. The woman slid a pile of papers into a double-pocketed folder labeled "Wheeling General Hospital" and pushed it under the glass divider in Laura Ann's direction. Her second hospital in as many days. A clear wall separated them, the woman on one side alive in a world of databases and bills. The patient's representative on the other, wading through the pain of life.

"It's not for me. I mean . . . ," Laura Ann said, handing across Sophia's driver's license and an insurance card she'd fished out of her friend's purse. "Sophia lives in Pittsburgh."

The administrative assistant nodded, typing in data she gleaned from the cards. "Anyone to sign for her?" she asked a few minutes later. "Any family?"

*Family?*

Laura Ann froze, unsure how to respond. Her flesh and blood grew inside Sophia, yet no one could know. Sophia was family, but how to describe it?

"We're sisters," Laura Ann said at last, looking down. Was it a lie? A falsehood would telegraph itself across her face like white

207

chalk on a black slate. She looked away. More than sisters, they were bound by the same blood shared across the tenuous border of a womb, Laura Ann's DNA circulating inside her friend's body.

Sisters in a strange and yet wonderful way.

"Sign here. And here." And in another six places, signatures promising money from Sophia, bills that Laura Ann could never pay. Copies of papers just like those she'd signed for Daddy in his first visit to Sistersville's ER, the genesis of the iron shackles that bound her in a seven-year mortgage. Steps on the path that brought her to this very day.

Hours later Laura Ann trembled in the chill of air conditioning. Attendants and nurses scurried about clad in long sleeves, some in sweaters. Outside, the world sweltered.

She shut her eyes against brilliant lights and dog-eared magazines. A soap opera droned on across the room. A motley group of parents and children surrounded her, old and young, heavy and thin, all dressed like they'd quit something mundane to run to the ER with a loved one. People here were dressed for living, not for going out.

Her hands twitched, desperate to be at work, or to cradle a book. She yearned for something to fill the time while Sophia slept. Minutes here melted into hours, bound together by the fabric of whispered prayers. She stood up at last, determined to escape.

"I'm here with Sophia McQuistion," she said to a nurse at the front desk. "I need to step out for a moment. To knock off the chill. If there's any news ..."

The nurse nodded and smiled. "You go on. I'll have someone

come get you. And after you deal with those goose bumps, come see me. I'll get you something warm."

Sunshine beckoned, beaming through the automatic doors of the exit. Outside, she strode fast to the other side of the parking lot, reveling in the warmth and fresh air, welcoming the clutches of a humid day.

At the end of the lot, a rapid *tat tat da tat* drew her attention. Ian wheeled his truck around the curve of the emergency entrance and tapped on the horn one more time in response to her wave. A special delight on this bitter day, Granny Apple sat in the seat beside him. She'd come!

"Heard you needed some help," Granny Apple said a minute later when Laura Ann met the truck in the lot. She gathered Laura Ann in the wiry grip of thin arms. "Any word?" she asked as she pulled away.

"More tests," Laura Ann said. "The doctors promised some answers, but I've been here what—four hours?"

Ian squeezed her hand. "It takes time. She's in good hands. Her doctor's the best obstetrician in the valley."

"All the same, I'd like to find out more about her. And the baby."

At that last word, Granny Apple's brow scrunched down a bit, her grey eyes peering deep into Laura Ann's words with a keen insight. Laura Ann spoke the word like a mother would, a nuance Ian might have missed, but one that scarce escaped Granny Apple. Her friend could read an entire story into those two syllables.

*Baby.*

Granny Apple touched her on the arm just above the elbow, and then smiled. "Let's go get some news." Together they headed back into the waiting room.

While Ian went to the desk to get news and borrow a wrap

for Laura Ann, she sat with Granny Apple as far as possible from the incessant drone of television.

"She's the woman I saw in your truck the day of the flood?" Granny Apple asked, probing around the edges of Laura Ann's story. She prodded gently, but with a sure stick.

Laura Ann nodded. "Her name is Sophia McQuistion. She's from Pittsburgh." She hesitated, fearful that her mentor would eventually pry the story free — but determined that she would not. "Sophia couldn't leave because of the crossing."

Granny Apple laid a hand on Laura Ann's and squeezed it. "She must be a dear friend," she said with emphasis, squeezing a second time. "You're going to need a little help if you'll be staying up here a spell."

Laura Ann turned to face her, greeted by an accepting smile and a knowing nod. A woman with the gift of helps. "I came with Ian to let you know that we'll take care of the farm. If it don't rain, water will be low enough in another couple of days to wade across at the old causeway. I'll wander over and check on things every day." Decked out in white button-up shirt, white jeans, and white cotton shoes, she reminded Laura Ann of an angel with wrinkles. She patted her on the knee. "Ian went to the farm, by the way. Got some of your things. Just in case."

"Thank you. I don't know how long this will take."

"Yes, you do." Her visage darkened. "From what Ian told me, this sounds real serious. Sophia needs to rest and hold that little bun in her oven. She's what . . . seven months?"

Laura Ann nodded.

"It's too early. We need her to get to thirty-one weeks. More is better. And it's too early to be fighting toxemia. Later in her pregnancy, perhaps, but not now."

Granny Apple knew mothers. A midwife in her early years, she'd counseled many young women on the brink of motherhood. Some guessed she'd delivered two hundred babies in her day. Others said twice that many. Every family on the Middle

Island Creek had at least one relative who met their first day arriving in her hands.

"I — I don't know how I can stay here that long," Laura Ann objected. "The bank ..."

Granny Apple squeezed again. "Don't worry about the money, child. Ian and I have a plan."

"A plan?" Laura Ann stammered.

Granny Apple nodded in silence. A smile played at the corner of her lips. "I'll let Ian tell you about it."

"I don't know how to thank you — "

"Don't have to. Just get your friend well and come back home. In the meantime, you'll need a place to stay. How about your cousin? Stefany."

Mental images of Stefany on the television came to mind. Eight years older and working in a career wildly divergent from Laura Ann's, her third cousin lived in another world. Flashy red hair, a professional wardrobe, and an apartment in the city. Worlds away from the farm and their little valley.

"Ian got ahold of her. She left us a key. She's out of town reporting on the flood and not in her apartment much. Said it would be a big favor to have someone come and house-sit."

Granny Apple stood, pulling at Laura Ann's hands. "Ian told me that Sophia doesn't have any kin. You need to be here for her, Laura Ann ... and for her baby." Her voice lowered in a special way like a momma's would, a tone that sang of her deep empathy for the maternal bond.

"Stay here for all your sakes, child. We'll care for things. As long as it takes."

"This is Dr. Murphy," Ian said, introducing a middle-aged man in green surgical scrubs when he entered the waiting area. Laura Ann's eyes went immediately to the tiny splatters of red that stained the front of his operating outfit. Tufts of brown and grey poked out from under a tight cotton cap, and a wrinkled mask hung about his neck. He wore green pull-on shoe-covers, like he'd just emerged an operation.

"My pleasure. Ms. McQuistion mentioned that you're sisters?" he said, extending a hand. His eyes wandered up and down Laura Ann, the keen eye of a physician on the hunt for trouble. Her lie had found her out.

Ian cocked his head, an eyebrow raised. Laura Ann looked from the doctor to Granny Apple, expecting more inquisitive looks. Yet, with the knowing gaze of a woman who'd already heard every story a troubled girl could invent, she smiled, a wrinkled explosion of warm comfort. Granny Apple nodded, as if to say, "Go on. It will be fine."

"We're *like* sisters," Laura Ann protested, taking the doctor's grip in hers. She shook hard, determined to show strength.

Dr. Murphy shrugged. "That's funny. She was quite adamant about the family part. Anyway, I'm sorry to have been tied up in surgery. After I met with Ms. McQuistion, I was called away on emergency. Just now catching up."

"How is she? Do you know what's wrong?" Laura Ann asked. The doctor launched into an explanation that she understood most of, but not all. Ian nodded as he listened, his frown deepening with each successive bit of news. At the words *heart disease* Laura Ann's own heart skipped a beat.

"Her heart damage is severe. It's a grave condition for any pregnant mother. Maternal mortality is high in these cases, usually around five to eight percent."

Laura Ann watched Ian while she listened to the doctor. The color washed from Ian's face with that last comment. Confirmation of the doctor's message.

"I work with many mothers like Ms. McQuistion. We'll watch her closely. She has a mild impairment of exercise tolerance, which is why she 'fell out,' as she said, when walking or climbing stairs. Her history of chlamydia, combined with severe hypertension—high blood pressure—makes a premature birth and postpartum hemorrhage very likely."

Granny Apple's eyes were affixed on the doctor, dissecting every word. Her own frown deepened with the words about premature birth. Like two bellwethers, Ian and Granny gave image to the criticality of Dr. Murphy's words. Laura Ann missed some of his prognosis, but caught the next words.

"... valvular lesions, mitral stenosis, and insufficiency. Her heart cannot pump enough blood for the two of them. We spoke at length about this. Ms. McQuistion was concerned about why her heart murmur hadn't been noticed in visits to her obstetrician. I explained that it's not unusual to have a murmur, and then lose it, during the course of the pregnancy. Shortness of breath is also not uncommon. A third of women with heart disease won't discover it until they're nearing term in a pregnancy. That's what's happened here."

Words came and went, Laura Ann caught in a whirlwind of emotions, surrounded by the conversations that flowed between Ian, the doctor, and Granny Apple. Premature birth. Danger to the mother.

*Morbidity.* A word she'd heard all too often in consultations with Daddy's oncologist.

"Yes. A caesarean section may be justified," Dr. Murphy said to Granny Apple in response to her question. "Where there is significant heart disease—and where a long or difficult labor is expected—we'll do a caesarean to lessen the risk to the baby and the mother."

"When?" Laura blurted the word, her only foothold in the technical discourse between the doctor and her close friends. "What about the baby?"

The doctor tilted his head a bit and seemed to shrug. "She's very much preterm. A premature birth at this point is probably out of the question. Lung problems, low birth weight. But my main concern is with the mother, of course. Her well-being comes first," he said, then added, "before the fetus."

*Fetus?*

Laura Ann heard the rushing *whoosh* of blood in her ears, the pounding of her heart thrumming inside her head. She'd spent enough time in hospitals, and read enough articles in the paper, to decipher the unspoken message in his last word.

"I beg your pardon?" Laura Ann exclaimed, clenching her fists. The doctor clipped his next words.

"Women with her extent of heart disease, complicated by extreme hypertension, run a high risk of delivering a defective child born with a heart malfunction or other significant abnormality. One in ten mothers like her will die if not delivered soon. If I can save the life of one of them—the mother or the child—I am committed to save the mother first."

"Surely there's some hope," Ian blurted out. "What hope for the baby?"

"I'm sorry, sir. I'm a pragmatist." Dr. Murphy took a deep breath, forming his words. "In cases like this one, where the heart disease and complications are so severe, there is *some* hope for the mother. But for *both*?" He shook his head, his eyes cast down. "The chances are very slim."

The doctor left, and Laura Ann turned to Ian. "Let the baby die?" she cried out.

"That's not what the doctor said," Ian insisted. "He's trying to save Sophia's life."

"It *is* what he said. He told us the baby might have some kind of birth defect and there's little hope for him."

"That might be what you heard, Laura Ann, but I'm sure it's not what he meant."

"Now you're talking like an EMT, Ian. Why are we debating saving one or the other? What happened to saving both of them?"

"What Dr. Murphy said was that if we can save only one life—then it should be your friend. But remember, that's her decision." He withdrew his hand. "Not our decision—and not yours."

"Ian," Granny Apple said, laying a hand on his shoulder. "Could you leave us alone for a while?"

He sighed and nodded. "Maybe you can explain it better." He spun and left the room.

Granny Apple extended a hand to Laura Ann. "Let's talk." Her hands resembled twigs with skin, but her grip was one of enormous strength, a sure hold that said "I understand." "This baby has a special meaning to you, doesn't it?"

Granny Apple's question was neither condemning nor inquisitive. More like a statement. No judgment, no precondition. A simple matter of fact.

Laura Ann nodded, unable to speak.

"I've never met Sophia. She must be a strong woman to do what she did."

Laura Ann nodded again, eyes wide in amazement.

*Does she know?*

"You sold something precious, Laura Ann. Now you're connected to her in a special way. To her—and to the child."

Laura Ann bent over, her face cradled in her hands, determined not to cry. She moved her head up and down, not much, but a sure gesture in the arms of her mentor. She dared not look up, too ashamed to put a word to what she'd done. Her sin had found her out.

"Do you remember what I said to you the morning of the flood?"

She moved her head up and down again.

"Secrets don't become you." Granny Apple drew in a deep wheezing breath, sighing out the weight of some unspoken disappointment. "Preacher would agree with me on this one. And

Lord knows, he and I don't agree on much." She sighed again, a long exhale of exasperation.

"Did you know her beforehand?"

Laura Ann shook her head.

"And that's how you paid for the farm all those months? Kept the property in your family, covered most of Angus's medical treatments, and still managed to put food on the table?" She cradled Laura Ann in a tight grip.

"I never could have done that," she said with a lilt in her voice. "I'm way too old."

Laura Ann let go a little chuckle.

"How many times?" she asked, stroking Laura Ann's hair like Momma used to do.

"Four," Laura Ann replied, forcing the words while shutting out memories of the excruciating pain. "It was horrible."

Granny Apple held her for a long time, fingers running through her hair. Laura Ann ached for words of comfort, but knew her friend would share words of wisdom. Words that sprang from tough love.

"You bought your dad some time. Some dignity too. And— probably brought a gift of life to many women in the process." She paused. "But for all the good you did for them, I can't say it's something I would have done. Or recommended." She held Laura Ann tight. "I know those are hard words. But something permanent's been done here—a decision you can't undo."

Laura Ann looked up, her heart in her throat.

"You've got a decision to make, child. Whether to move on and accept that you can't control the outcome of your actions— or to try to hang on to something you shouldn't. Even though it sprang from your body, the baby in that woman is not yours. And her health is not yours to decide. I want a happy outcome for both of them." Granny Apple shivered. "But that might not be possible."

Laura Ann buried her head in Granny Apple's shoulder. Her white shirt was smooth, a gentle cotton that matched her wise heart. The fragrance of cinnamon and spice, possibly a pie she'd been baking when Ian came for her, embedded itself in the fabric.

"Pray for wisdom, child. These are trying times."

# CHAPTER 20

## JUNE 30

Sophia's skin took on a pale cast under the purple-white glare of fluorescent lights, the room's shades drawn closed against the bright rays of sunrise. Dressed only in a faded gown, slit ingloriously down the back, she lay in the bed, connected to a maze of tubes, monitors, and a drip application of intravenous fluid. Above her sat a digital monitor, reporting her blood pressure, respiration, and heart rate. An inflatable cuff, pumped up every few minutes by the computer, lay strapped about her left arm. Another line ran to her right index finger, a red light glowing where it measured her oxygen uptake. The impeccably dressed Hispanic woman in heels who'd first landed on a rock driveway at The Jug could be found no more, yet her eyes, those brown spheres of warmth that sparkled at their reuniting, drew Laura Ann toward her. Sophia beckoned her sit beside her.

Dr. Murphy tarried at the foot of the bed, her room his first stop on morning rounds.

"I understand your reluctance, but we have to act soon, Ms. McQuistion." The doctor looked down, his stylus ticking off some unseen checklist on a digital chart. "I'll do my best to support your wishes, whichever path you choose. But you must understand, you're in a tough spot here. We'll do everything we can for you and your child. But it's time to face some brutal realities. There's a chance we'll have to take the baby before term, in order to save you. And there's a chance — a significant probability — that a baby delivered that early won't survive."

He looked up at last, adding, "But I assure you. We'll make every effort to save your child."

He watched Sophia for a brief moment, and then continued.

"The medication we're using is targeted at reducing the swelling around your heart, damage due to your rheumatic fever. If we were only dealing with the heart disease, yours would be a fairly straightforward treatment." The faintest of shrugs accompanied his next words. "That's serious, but manageable. However, your pregnancy significantly complicates matters."

The doctor looked up and made direct eye contact. Like two card players putting their best hands on the table, Sophia and Dr. Murphy locked eyes, each with their cards face up. "Should you slip into an early labor, Ms. McQuistion — one that is instigated by your prior infection from chlamydia, or by the preeclampsia slipping out of our control — then you risk complications such as atrial fibrillation. The upper chambers of your damaged heart will begin to contract at an excessively high rate, in an irregular way. Blood flow will slow dramatically, and, in the worst case, you will experience heart failure."

He bit his lip, his jaw clenched, but never took his eyes off her. "At that point, we might save the baby with an emergency caesarean. But — it would be difficult to save you both."

Sophia smiled. It was a forced raising of the corner of her lips, testament to some incredible inner strength that defied understanding. A woman who'd overcome so much to reach this day would not be deterred. She reached out to Laura Ann at the bedside and took her hand, then responded to the doctor's challenge.

"Thank you for your candor, Dr. Murphy. I understand the prognosis." She gripped Laura Ann's hand in a tight embrace and spoke with renewed vigor. "I overcame terrible odds fifteen years ago, odds that I'd wind up on the streets despite my upbringing. A medical crisis — the chlamydia — pushed me out of a destructive lifestyle and saved my life. Infertility, my second crisis, brought me to West Virginia."

Like a woman climbing a long set of stairs under an immense load, Sophia stopped, gathering her breath to tackle the next flight. "The probability I'd make it through those crises, each offering a very small chance for success, says that I've already beaten tough odds to arrive here in your excellent care. I'm a fighter, Dr. Murphy. I overcame poverty, prostitution, language barriers, racism, and infertility. I'm not afraid to tackle this."

He shrugged, looked down at the tablet for a moment, and then lowered the tiny device and its stylus into a pocket of his physician's coat.

"I admire your pluck. I'm here to serve your medical needs — whichever direction you decide to go. But I do not consider it prudent to continue a pregnancy as high risk as yours."

"No pregnancy is without risk — or liability."

That comment chilled the room and Dr. Murphy stood silent, then crossed his arms. "I'm aware you're an attorney, Ms. McQuistion. Quite a good one, according to a colleague I consulted in Pittsburgh. Considering your success in corporate litigation, you can understand my reticence to push the boundaries with regard to your care."

"I understand, Dr. Murphy. I don't blame you for your concern, and I thank you for your emphasis on my healing. But I am dealing with many issues in this pregnancy, only one being my health."

"It's the *top* priority," he said, moving closer to her bed.

"Dr. Murphy, this metaphor is a poor one but it will have to do. I'm an attorney and I love my job. I did not endure the struggle to get an education, pass the bar, and become a lawyer simply to say I was an attorney. I did it to practice tax law, to win. To win cases, to make people whole, to defend companies, to right injustice. You may have competed to reach this point in your medical practice with similar aspirations."

He nodded, just inches from the end of the bed, his gaze locked with hers.

A beeping alarm interrupted them. Blood pressure on the rise. She took in a deep breath and closed her eyes for a moment. Dr. Murphy moved to the monitor, silenced the alarm, then motioned with his hand for her to continue.

"In the same way," she said, her voice quieter and speaking at a slower pace, "I would consider it a failure to quit now, struggling as I did to become a mother. In fact, I'm a mother already. A child is growing within me. I will not abandon my quest at the threshold of childbirth and spend the rest of my life wondering 'what if?'"

"If you slip into labor at this point, there's a reasonable probability you won't have a life left to spend in wonder," he replied, his hand on the foot of the hospital bed.

"That's true. I understand the implications of my decision, Doctor. But I will not consent to allow you or anyone else to take my baby's life in order to save mine." She choked, gasping for breath. "Call me stubborn — determined — or crazy, depending on your point of view. But that is my decision."

He raised an eyebrow, regarding her for a long moment. At last, he began a slow nod, his lips pursed. "Remind me not to argue against you in court, Barrister." He smiled and put a reassuring hand on her foot where it lay covered by a sheet. "I will do my level best to ensure that you — and your child — emerge from this crisis in the best possible condition." His eyes connected with hers through a long pause. Then he turned and headed for the door. At the exit, he turned to face her.

"Were I a woman, Ms. McQuistion, knowing what I do about your disease and this pregnancy, I would probably choose a different path. But I confess I wish I had more patients like you. Rational people, unswayed by crisis, committed to a certain course of action." He tapped the side of the door.

"I'm honored to be part of your team, Counselor. We will endeavor to win."

After the doctor left, Sophia started to shake. She turned, leaning her head into Laura Ann's arm, the best she could do for a consoling hug considering the entanglement of tubes and wires in a hospital bed. Laura Ann put a hand to Sophia's head and smoothed black bangs in desperate need of a brush. The two women clung to each other for a long time, no words between them. Stories passed in the tightness of their grip, two challenged women clinging to each other for comfort.

"I never knew"—Sophia said at last, a crack in her voice testament to her pain—"about the rheumatic fever."

Laura Ann held on, stroking more dark bangs into submission.

Sophia's brown irises focused on some distant place, her mind's eye set on a time many years ago. "I had a bad sore throat when I was nine or ten," Sophia said. "I couldn't eat or drink for days. I got some bed rest, and some remedies that my mother learned from her mother, tonics that soothed the hurt. It was just a sore throat, after all."

She took a deep breath, her pulse quickening in Laura Ann's hand.

"Strep throat, Dr. Murphy said. It caused my rheumatic fever. And I'm not alone. Lots of women have it but don't find out until too late. In pregnancy."

Questions fought to be released from their dungeon, but Laura Ann bottled them up.

Sophia turned her head to look at Laura Ann. "I don't regret my decision," she said, emphasizing her point with a squeeze. "Without this baby, we'd have never met. And I'd have been the poorer for it."

Sophia spoke to the longings of Laura Ann's heart, sharing a kinship they both felt. Baby or no, this new sister had enriched her life when Laura Ann needed love most. The drip of a tear onto Sophia's arm was her only—and best—reply.

"I have a bad case of heart disease, Laura Ann," she continued. "I never knew it. They're trying to do their best for me." She squeezed again. "But I need your help. A promise—if you're willing."

Laura Ann nodded slowly, her chin quivering. She put a finger to Sophia's cheek, wiping away pools that rolled over smooth skin, cascading like salty waterfalls to the white sheets below.

"If I can't be there for our baby, will you take care of him?"

Another tear broke loose when Laura Ann dipped her head. "Yes. I promise."

*Our baby. Take care of him.*

One moment, she imagined the child in her arms. The next, she saw Ian.

*Can I have both?* she wondered, gripped by the brutal reality of her pledge.

After a long silence, Sophia reached over to her bedside stand and fished out a paper, handing it to Laura Ann.

"What's this?" Laura Ann asked, looking over a long list of names.

"Your first product mailing list," Sophia replied. She took a deep breath. "I wrote it up after our visit to town."

"Mailing list?"

"For the stools. I insist on paying for the shipping too. There are fifty people on that list, and I'll probably have some more. For Christmas gifts."

"It's too early for Christmas. Besides, you don't have to do this." Laura Ann's breath stole away, the idea that Sophia would buy even more stools—to help her. So many friends, doing so much.

"I buy early. And no, I don't have to do this. But I want to. For them." She smiled again. "And for you." She patted the bed. "This is fun."

Laura Ann moved toward the end of the bed, laying the list at Sophia's feet. "You have so many friends. I don't even know that many people."

The smile disappeared, and Sophia's hand came to her lips. She turned her head for a long moment, shaking it in silence.

"Sophia?"

Her friend looked back at her, a strained smile, and eyes red. "No." She shook her head with the word. "It's not what you think."

"I'm sorry—"

"Don't. Don't be sorry." She looked away again. "You don't know me very well. Yet."

Laura Ann paused, struggling for the right words, then spoke what came to her mind. "I'd like to. To know you better."

Sophia looked back and the smile returned. "Really? The unvarnished me?"

Laura Ann nodded, wishing she'd been "unvarnished" with Ian long ago. "All of it. We're sisters, remember?"

They laughed. Sophia scooted closer to her in the bed. "Okay. The people on the list? They're acquaintances. Clients. Coworkers. But not friends. At least, not a close friend like you."

"I don't understand."

"We work together. Or live near each other, even party or shop together. But there's no one ..." Her eyes got red again, her lips taut. "No one who'd do what you've done for me. You're putting your farm on the line to be here, giving up everything you have."

"I'll manage. Daddy always said I needed to trust more."

"Speaking of your father, I want you to go home. At least for a while."

"I'll be okay. Ian and Granny took a huge load off me, just like you did. They put their savings together and paid another two months' mortgage, in advance." She thought back to the moment when he'd told her of their plan, recalling the elation, the incredible sense of peace that washed over her. Ian and Granny Apple, dedicated to helping her, despite her secrets. Despite a broken trust Ian knew nothing of.

She pasted on a smile, determined to move forward, to be honest with him at last. "Daddy was right. God provides when you least expect it." She patted Sophia on the shin, a reassuring touch through the sheets.

"See? That's my point. You trust with such a simple faith, and you're here with me no matter what the cost — that's real friendship." Sophia shrugged. "I don't have friends like you back home." Her chin bunched up in a strange mottled way. She squeaked her next words. "I'm so lonely ..." After another deep breath, she added, "Except when I'm with you."

Laura Ann dipped her head in a faint acknowledgment. She understood. It was like that with Ian. She had friends, but none fulfilled her. Except him.

"Is that why—"

"Why I came here?" Sophia interrupted, regaining her control. She nodded. "I hoped—I prayed that you might be someone I could connect with." She smiled again, her stress draining away. "And that prayer was answered."

"How?"

"You liked me for who I am, Laura Ann. Back home, I carry

lots of baggage. My old 'career' in Mexico. My job as a tax attorney, my late husband. I could show you many splinters that have festered after climbing a rough social ladder. I know lots of busy people, but no one who'd slow to a crawl for a lonely heart like me. Until we met. You accepted me for who I am, not for my income, or because of what I drive." She tilted her head, regarding Laura Ann for a long moment. "You may be the first true friend I've had since James died."

Sophia pulled her sheets up to her neck, her arms bunched tight in front of her chest, eyes focused on some distant point beyond the room. "Loneliness is like being chased down a cold dark alley, Laura Ann. With no way out." Her voice trembled. "But with you, I finally found a door to a safe warm place."

When Ian showed up after work, Laura Ann hugged him quickly, then led him by the hand from the room, leaving Sophia behind to nap. Determined to answer the voice inside her that screamed for action, she pulled him through the hospital. She dared not lose her nerve, dared not even one brief glance into his accepting face. If she walked fast, perhaps he wouldn't see her eyes.

"Whoa! Slow it down, McGehee! What's the rush?"

She didn't reply but whisked through the double doors at the main entrance and headed into the familiar embrace of the summer's late afternoon heat. She would not open her heart to him inside, surrounded by the smells and colors of her nightmare. She turned right and pulled him into a grassy area, then collapsed on the ground, her legs folded under her. She patted the grass at her side.

Ian settled beside her with a little space between. She stared away for a long time, praying for the strength. Praying for the wisdom that Granny spoke of. Praying for Sophia and for James. After a long silence, she cleared her throat, and put her hand out, seeking him.

"Daddy was right," she began.

"How's that?" Ian asked, his reassuring squeeze of her hand an encouragement to continue.

She wanted to look at him, to see his face. But his disappointment would crush her. She could not watch.

"He used to tell me — especially back in middle school — he'd say, 'Peppermint, admit it when you're wrong.'"

Ian was quiet, a gentle finger stroking the top of her hand. He had Daddy's patience.

"So. There's this thing," she began, covering her mouth with her free hand when she coughed. "This thing you need to know." She bent her head, determined to forge on, her fingers gripping her chin until they cramped.

"About Sophia?"

She nodded, unable to form the words.

"I understand, Laura Ann. I spoke with the doctors. I probably understand better than most."

"No," she blurted out, shaking her head, bent at the shoulders. She choked back a sob, determined to be strong. Like Daddy.

"What then?"

Laura Ann took a deep breath, then let the secret fly. "I'm going to be a mother."

Ian released her hand. He sighed, a deep mournful sound she'd never heard from him. Mr. Positive no more.

"When?" he asked, his voice firm. She could sense him moving away, pulling his knees up in front of him.

"Soon," she said. "But not like you think."

Somewhere deep inside her, perhaps spurred by the genes of

her Scottish forefathers who kept living when their homes were seized, she found the strength to turn. She looked up into his eyes, red eyes that bled betrayal and broken trust.

She reached out for his hand, but he pulled it back, his turn to look away. Laura Ann took another deep breath and pushed on.

"Sophia is pregnant with my egg," she said, waiting for the words to sink in before she continued. They had little effect. "I sold my eggs, Ian. Four times. To make money so that I could pay the mortgage."

An earthquake inside her threatened to spill itself out, but she clamped her mouth shut, her chin and chest cramping with the effort. She locked her eyes on Ian, her only source of strength. No ... her *second* source of strength. Somewhere deep inside, that little voice spoke, that gentle Spirit that Daddy used to tell her about so often.

*Love is patient. Love is kind. Love rejoices in truth.*

A moment later, Ian looked up, his jaw clenched. "I could have helped," he said, forcing the words. "But you never asked."

"I'm sorry." She reached for his hand a second time, and he pulled away again.

"When?" he asked, facing the entrance.

"The first time? I went to a clinic in Morgantown last fall when Daddy was in chemo." The tears finally burst. The memory of that first day tore at her, the doctor's leering way, the lingering touch of his fingers, the bite of the needle ... all nightmares she'd buried so deep. She bent at the waist, unable to say more.

Somewhere, a bird called. Here in the middle of the city, surrounded by acres of paved land and towering buildings, a mockingbird sang. Its varied tone parodied her own behavior, pretending to be someone she was not. She should have told Ian long ago. Before the first kiss. Before Sophia. She stared at the grass beneath her through a long silence, her vision dulled by tears.

"How many?" he asked at last, an answer to her prayer that he not shut her out forever.

"Four times," she said, wiping at her eyes with a hand, but unable to look up.

"No. That's not what I meant." He paused, his long exhale a sign he was trying to make a point. "How many eggs did you sell?"

The question pierced her. The one truth she'd never dared to voice. "Dozens," she said, then came clean, determined to find closure in this confession. "Sixty-eight eggs."

Ian stood up, moving farther away. He leaned into a tree beside her, facing the entrance. "How many more Sophias?" he wondered aloud. "How many more children?" He sighed again, then added, "*Your* children."

His words trumpeted her deepest fear, a mystery that would haunt her for years to come. "I don't know, Ian. And I don't think I ever will."

# CHAPTER 21

---

## JULY 3

"It could be a week ... or a month. There's no way to know," Laura Ann said, stepping out of Ian's truck near The Jug Store. It felt good to be back on home turf after five trying days at the hospital. "She's got a lawyer friend coming down today from Pittsburgh. Said she had some important papers to sign. This is a good time for me to get out, to take care of things at the farm, and get some clothes. You should take some time off and enjoy the holiday tomorrow, Ian. I plan to stay with Sophia." She watched him for some reaction, then added, "For as long as it takes."

*Will he understand?*

Ian stood on the far side of the vehicle, looking at her across the hood. His face showed neither smile nor frown, his lips a straight line of pragmatism. He spoke up at last. "Stay until the baby's born?"

"If that's what it takes."

They regarded each other from opposite sides, her hands resting on the fender. The ride down from Wheeling had been horribly quiet, so many unspoken words between them. "Give him time," Granny Apple had counseled her. "You wounded his trust ... and his pride. He wants, more than anything, to protect you and provide for you."

Laura Ann waited on the other side of the truck, hoping for some words, for some of the spark to return. Suddenly transformed, Ian's face made a funny expression, one eyebrow up, his lips contorted in a half frown, half smile. He raised his hands in the direction of the creek. "Then lead on, McGehee. Let's get you home and get packed."

*Home.*

The word sunk in for the first time when she turned from Ian and faced the Middle Island Creek. Five days in Wheeling with one change of clothes, five days in the frigid overlit world of the hospital where night never came, where rest was fleeting, and no wind ever blew. Standing on the roadside near The Jug Store, she could feel home, taste it on the hot damp air.

Summer wrapped itself about her. July's sun scorched the earth, the flood a distant memory for the baking clay beneath her feet. The sweet aroma of clover floated on the breeze. More than a week after the flood, hayfields would be thriving, swollen with sugar and ready for harvest. Hot and dry, it was a perfect day for mowing.

For the first time since her confession, Ian took her hand. "Come see your new crossing." The touch of his skin shot sparks of new energy through her. A rejuvenating hope.

She followed him down the slope from the store, holding him tight. A trickle of water ran out the base of the logjam, a stark contrast to the roaring waters of last week. In front of her a silver cable ran from a nearby tree to a post on the far bank. A pair of harnesses hung from the tight wire, dangling just beyond her reach.

Ian released her, his hand to the harnesses, admiring his handiwork. "Pretty neat contraption, huh?" He pulled on the line and slid it along the taut wire. "When the water's up, we can strap this baby on and wade across," he said. "I towed your truck to the top of the hill, by the way. The key's under the mat."

Laura Ann's mouth fell open. "When did you have time?" she asked. "You were with us in Wheeling yesterday until five or six."

Ian smiled, rubbing his eyes with mock fists. "Took us a couple of late nights. Some guys helped." He held a small line attached to the harnesses. "You can pull these back across the creek when someone leaves them on the other side. You're gonna get your feet and legs wet, but at least you can cross safely." He offered her a harness. "Ready?"

Five minutes later, she and Ian climbed into her farm truck at the top of the rise. On the slope behind them, two sets of tracks narrowly avoided ruts worn deep by heavy rain. She marveled how he'd driven the truck back up this hill.

Laura Ann sat in silence for most of the ride home while Ian drove. She ran her hand across the nap of the cloth seat, stained with bits of dark oil and umber clay from workdays in the field. The cab smelled of diesel, the sweet heavy scent of tractors, the fragrance of good times. Outside, poplars and sweetgums burst forth with new green after the deep watering of the rain, lining the road with fresh growth. Blackberries sprouted verdant brambles, and brave weeds fought for a foothold in the tire tracks of an unused road.

Topping the ridge, the truck emerged from the wood and home beckoned. Laura Ann wondered what Sophia might have thought when she followed this path. What did she feel when she drove out of this dark forest tunnel into the light? When she saw the white farmhouse, red barn, and undulating green pastures filled with black cows? Dr. Murphy filled her mind's eye for a moment, his dire predictions ripping a hole in Laura Ann's heart.

She put a hand on Ian's arm. "Stop for a minute."

He pulled over at the top of the pasture and she stepped out of the truck to sit at the cattle guard, looking downhill toward home. Ian followed, curling up in some tall grass at her side. She leaned back against a rusty metal post, wrapped her arms about damp jeans, and rested her chin on her knees, in wonder.

*I have three loves.*

Her lifeblood sprang from these fields, from the forest behind her, and from the house beyond — her first love. Ian captured her heart — her second love, if he would have her. Yet, in Wheeling lay a third love — in the bosom of her new friend. A sister from another culture, from another country, years older, tied to her by a powerful maternal bond she would not sever. Much as she missed this place, much as she longed to fall into Ian's arms this moment, some part of her yearned to be back on the bedside with Sophia. She leaned left a bit, her head resting tentatively on Ian's shoulder. His arm circled about her but he felt distant. Not the firm grip of days gone by.

"Something's different," she said, at a loss for the right words. Like a tiny thread run through her heart, she felt the tug to race back to Wheeling, fifty miles north. Her heart tore, pulled in three directions.

"Different? Maybe," Ian replied. "But some things have never changed."

She fed the silence, inviting an explanation.

"I cancelled our reservation at the Blennerhassett," he said at last. He pulled her closer in a reassuring hold. "But that didn't change my reason for inviting you."

Her heart leapt and she looked up at him. "Aye," she replied in the mock brogue of her daddy's people. "And what might that reason be?"

Ian's eyes twinkled with the sparkle of a secret he could barely contain. She let go of her knees, and leaned into his chest, her ear to his heart.

Ian's hand found its way to her head. Like a human brush,

he ran his fingers through brown tresses, sweeping them slowly back over her shoulder. Each pass, with his fingertips starting at her forehead, she tingled. She matched his rhythm, breath for breath, his chest rising and falling with hers.

Ian's hand rested on her head at last, the brushing stopped. His hand quivered, the faintest of a shake in his arm. He inhaled deeply, and then spoke, his voice cracking just a bit. "There's something I've waited a long time to ask you." He paused. "But maybe now's not the time."

Laura Ann sat up, pulling away to look at him. "Ask me *now*," she implored, desperate to bury the past and move on.

"Okay." Ian reached in his shirt pocket and pulled out what looked like a house key, with a small leather tab bound to the key ring, three letters embossed in brown. It read "L. A. S."

Her heart skipped.

"I changed the locks on the house … since you're going to be away for a while. Here's the new key." He rubbed his thumb across the embossed letters. "I took some liberties with the monogram."

Laura Ann sat up and spun around, grabbing both of his hands, her eyes wide with surprise. He released one hand and reached up to touch her, the first caress of his fingers on her face like touching a high-voltage line, sending jolts of joy down her spine.

"I don't bring much to this relationship except a pickup truck and a small savings account, Laura Ann—"

"No! You do—"

He shook his head, interrupting her. "And I still don't know exactly how to deal with all the things you told me. But I do know *you*—we've been friends for too long to let it end here. Whatever led you down the path to that fertility clinic in Morgantown, whatever motivated you to keep it such a secret, I know that you did it to honor your dad and your family. It was the wrong thing, in my opinion, but you made that sacrifice for the right reason."

A million words rose in her throat, the first one his name, but Ian put a finger to her lips to quiet her. He pulled on her one hand to get up from a sit and knelt before her. He palmed the leather key fob and held it up. "L. A. S.," he read, with a smile. "Laura Ann Stewart." He took a deep breath, and then continued. "I think it has a nice ring to it."

"I love it," she said, her voice cracking.

*Ask me now!*

Ian held her left hand with his right, his fingers encasing her palm, and then shoved his other hand in a pants pocket.

"Laura Ann McGehee, you're the best friend I've ever had. My one true friend." He cleared his throat, the beating of his heart telegraphing itself in his temples. "But I don't want to be just friends."

He opened the other palm, revealing a small diamond ring, a tiny stone in a Tiffany setting. Sunlight danced off the facets of the little gem, glimmering in his hand.

Her heart racing, she launched a silent prayer of thanks.

"I didn't really change the locks," he said with a little laugh. "That's the key to my heart, Laura Ann. It's always been yours, tucked away, right here," he said, touching his chest. "If you'll have it." With a shaking hand, Ian slipped the diamond onto her ring finger, then looked up, his eyes misting.

"Will you marry me?"

"She kissed me first."

Daddy's words arose from nowhere, the first he'd spoken in half an hour of tending trotlines in the Middle Island Creek. Wading in green-tinged summer water up to her waist, twelve-year-old Laura Ann tended her own line, some twenty feet upstream from him. Bare feet feeling her way across a muddy bottom, she listened as she worked.

Like her, Daddy followed his own line, a stout cord strung between trees on opposite banks, suspending a series of shorter lines that descended into the slow waters of summer. Like her, he pulled chicken livers from a pouch at his waist, threading them one at a time on sharp treble hooks. Livers that would beckon dinners from the creek's lazy pools. Catfish.

Daddy moved through the deepest water, baiting his line of hooks, not looking up when he spoke. He wandered through the water, lost in another world, in daydreams of a time years ago.

"I was thirteen," Daddy said, speaking to the water. "She was twelve. Your age." He laughed, pausing in the memory. "I thought I was all growed up, schooled to seventh grade in one room. Headed off to the big middle school in town."

Daddy slid dark crimson livers expertly onto each hook, sinking razor-sharp barbs into bloody flesh. Three silver tips, hidden in wait for their prey. He moved at one with the water, Daddy, the master of the fish.

"She was a bonnie lass." Standing still, Daddy's eyes focused on some distant mirage. "I asked her to meet me at the Valentine's dance."

Daddy peered down at the deep red of the next bait as though into a crystal ball, somehow connecting with a life that had been torn from him far too early. Ripped from him like a fish tearing the liver from this treble hook, a gash that would never heal.

"Your granddaddy took us home that night. He pushed me out the car door when we dropped her off at the Sinclair place."

Daddy threaded the next liver and dropped it in the creek, the weighted line forming a brief hole in the water. Like this memory, it dropped out of sight of the present, yet waited to be retrieved by the simple tug of an invisible thread.

"Not a word she spoke on that porch," Daddy said a bit later. "Just those eyes. The green and blue emeralds of Hope, staring up at me."

He wiped the back of his hand across his mouth, staring at the line where it dropped into the green-black of the creek. His wet hand tarried at his lips, connecting mysteriously with a woman she barely remembered.

"She kissed me first."

Laura Ann moved to his side, submerged to her armpits in wet life.

"Aye, Peppermint. Never another. She was the only one for me."

# CHAPTER 22

Rectilinear. The entire room screamed, "Square."

In the harsh purple glare of artificial light, Laura Ann's eyes wandered foot by foot from the familiar view of Sophia's bed to the walls, floor, and ceiling, every surface made up of right angles. Sophia, the only curve in the room, lay fast asleep, snared in a web of medical plastic that connected her to machines, monitors, and life-giving fluid. The hospital spider spun a cocoon about her, locking her to the bed, her home for the past month.

Standing at the one narrow window, Laura Ann rubbed sleep out of her eyes. To the east, the first rays of a rising sun broke over the ridge and the old gravestones of Greenwood Cemetery, a penetrating glare that beat back the recliner aches of a night's fitful sleep. It seemed just moments ago she'd been with Ian, seated at Sophia's bedside, the three of them talking late into the night. Where had he gone? How late did he leave?

Below her window, employees exited cars, headed for an early morning hospital shift. Most of them clad in blue or green, some in the brown garb of this floor's medical smocks, they ignored the lone girl above, a soul desperate to feel sun, to taste wind, and hear the outside world.

Nurses clamored in the hall, bustling with the first sounds of a new day. The cutlery on breakfast carts clanged, announcing the arrival of another bland meal. New voices replaced old ones, women conferring in muffled tones about patients, the high pitch of their voices echoing against a background of electronic chirps. Beeps for Sophia's respiration if it went too low. Beeps for her blood pressure if too high. Every heartbeat announced with a digital tone, in synch to the metronome of the Staples World Clock, ticking the seconds away behind her. Two million seconds spent in this room, and counting.

Green. She starved for grass, for trees, and for the color of life. Laura Ann turned back to the room, its only green a single metal port for oxygen, situated above Sophia's bed. Life green, it poked out of the off-white wall, a valve unused. She moved to the bed, her hand to Sophia's shoulder, rising up and down with her friend's shallow breaths. Laura Ann, starving for the outside world, stood guard, while inside Sophia another life grew.

She marveled at the ring on her finger, then glanced back at the clock, another six hundred seconds since she arose to capture the sunrise at half-past five. Every second precious for this baby, yet every one an eternity. She swallowed her pain and prayed for Sophia — for her child — and for six more weeks.


"Laura Ann?"

The voice tugged at her, a fist pounding on the door of her dream.

"Laura Ann?" The voice begged again, higher in tone, almost raspy. She awoke.

Sophia panted in her bed, her head turned to the side, an IV-punctured arm and hand thrust Laura Ann's way. Beneath crusty lids, in the dimmed light of the nighttime hospital room, Laura Ann saw fear in her friend's eyes.

"Laura —," she gasped. "I — I can't breathe!"

Laura Ann shot straight up, her eyes diverted first to the clock. A few minutes before nine p.m. Then to the monitors above the bed. Her oxygen saturation, blood pressure, EKG, fluid drip rates — terms and metrics she'd learned fast as Sophia's hospital companion. Bright lights warned of trouble on every display, one glowing red with a fearsome pronouncement: "Hypoxia." Red lights mirrored the panic in her friend's eyes.

Sophia gasped again, her fingers clutching at something in the air. "I — I can't catch — my breath," she wheezed, struggling against some unseen monster on her chest, her face flush with desperation. Before the next pant, a brown-clad nurse burst through the half-open door, headed straight to the bed.

"Saturation's way down," Laura Ann said, forcing her voice to sound calm. She squeezed her friend's hand. "She can't get a breath."

"Heart rate's up. Look at that flutter," the nurse said, a finger to the EKG display. She pushed a button on the call panel above the bed, summoning another nurse. "Page Dr. Murphy. Possible A-fib in 44B."

All business, the nurse turned to Sophia. Her friend's confused eyes darted back and forth between them, from Laura Ann to the woman in brown. Her mouth wide open, she gulped at air. Moments later, her eyes rolled back, a bare whisper escaping her lips. "I'm so — so weak." Her right hand moved over her chest, dragging the oxygen saturation sensor with it.

"Hurts. Here." Sophia's fingers rested over her heart, and her eyes closed. Moments later, they shot open, and she lifted out of the bed, her hands jerking tubes with them as her fingers sought her belly. She nearly tipped over two poles of IV fluid, pulling a web of tubing when she bolted upright.

"Oh!" she screamed, her voice cut short by a lack of air, her hands to her abdomen.

Another monitor beeped, the spike of a first contraction displayed, like watching a wave pile into a Hawaiian beach, growing fast from a low swell into a towering wall. She screamed again, a short burst wheezing into a sad whine. No air in her lungs to complain, Sophia fell back on the bed.

The nurse stabbed at a blue button on the call panel again. "Code Blue! Cardio in 44B. On-call OB to 44B. Stat!"

Hands flew across the bed, the nurse moving with an urgency Laura Ann had not seen in weeks. For a brief moment, the nurse caught Laura Ann's eye, her words laced with fear. "She's in labor." Another nurse dashed in the room, medical terms shared between them that Laura Ann could not understand, but whose implication she could not mistake.

*Sophia's life — and James's — hung in the balance.*


Dr. Murphy stood at the door of Labor and Delivery, draped in a surgical gown, a mask over his face. "She's asking for you, Ms. McGehee."

Laura Ann jumped up from her plastic seat and headed for the swinging doors behind the doctor. Inside the Delivery Suite, another nurse stood at the gateway to a room where gowned nurses and technicians bustled in and out. Ushered away from Sophia an hour ago, Laura Ann had waited in desperate prayer.

The nurse waved her in, pointing toward a bed where three nurses attended to various monitors and another swabbed cleanser on Sophia's belly. The dark orange of the antiseptic confirmed her fears. Caesarean birth.

Sophia's gaze caught Laura Ann's, and a weak smile lifted her pale cheeks. She extended a frail hand and Laura Ann took it.

"I can breathe better now." Sophia's limp squeeze belied brave words.

"Rest. It won't be long," Laura Ann replied. "There's a baby on the way." She forced a smile, some sign of the joy they both wanted to share at this incredible moment. But she felt no joy.

Sophia pulled at her hand, a sideways nod of her head urging her to move closer, to some place private. The nurse to Laura Ann's left, swabbing at a bare belly, caught a glimpse of Sophia's eyes, then set down her antiseptic and motioned to the other nurses. "Give them a moment," she said, shooing her coworkers out the door. She smiled in Laura Ann's direction as the team left the room.

Laura Ann wrapped both her hands about Sophia's, leaning close. She felt breath on her cheek, shallow regular pants, not the zesty life of the vibrant woman who landed on her drive a month ago.

Sophia's fingers tightened with the quiver of her chin, lips drawn tight. "It's time," she said at last, words whispered in a shaky voice.

Laura Ann fell upon her, burying her face in the pillow next to Sophia's head, her arm seeking some hold of her friend. Below her, she could feel the timid heave of Sophia's weak chest, each breath a struggle, fed by too little air and a desperately weak heart.

Cotton and pine. Laura Ann breathed freely of the scent of fresh-pressed sheets and the aroma of Sophia's hair, washed just yesterday when Laura Ann tended to her. The soft tresses of her friend's black locks lay like scattered weeds between Laura Ann's face and the pillow. She pulled Sophia as tight to her as she dared, seeking to absorb her into her bosom and pour into her the strength her friend craved.

"I am blessed," Sophia said. Neither woman moved, their minds tracking like those of identical twins. Sophia nudged her and Laura Ann rose up. She lifted her hand to place her forefinger over Laura Ann's lips, tarrying for a moment, drawing in the deepest breath she could muster. "I'm blessed to be the mother of this baby—no matter how long that lasts."

Sophia's hand moved behind Laura Ann's neck. She pulled her face close, wet cheek to wet cheek, mingling tears like their mixed blood in Sophia's womb. "Our son," she said, emphasizing her words with a gentle squeeze of the nape of Laura Ann's neck.

Sophia relaxed her grip and circled Laura Ann's neck in a feeble hug. She kissed Laura Ann on the cheek as they drew close, then whispered, the warmth of her breath gentle on Laura Ann's ear.

"I love you."

The touch of a hand on her shoulder roused Laura Ann from prayer. Dr. Murphy stood above her in the waiting room, his smile stretching from ear to ear. Wet clumps of short hair poked out from under a tight disposable surgeon's cap and splotches of blood stained his surgical gown, Sophia's life spilled on his chest.

"It's a boy," he said, pointing toward the delivery suites. "You can see them now."

Seconds later Laura Ann burst through the door of Sophia's recovery room. Brilliant white lights lit the area where green-garbed nurses bustled about Sophia's bed. They parted to make room for Laura Ann.

Her old smile was back. Someone had returned her glasses, gentle black rectangles framing her eyes, perched on a broad nose. Her eyes cast down, then back up to see if her friend witnessed the miracle that lay wrapped on her chest. A wrinkled red face peeked out above a tiny blanket.

Laura Ann stopped short of the bed. For all the weeks that

she'd dreamed of seeing the fruit of her own body, she was unprepared for this. She bit her lip, desperate to hold this child, yet terrified by the impact of what she'd done.

Sophia beckoned her with a nod of her head. Frail arms cradled a tiny life on her bosom. She pulled him close, her lips resting on the child's forehead. After a gentle kiss, she looked up, her smile drawing Laura Ann toward her.

Beneath the thick white blanket the baby wore a fluffy blue knitted outfit. Closed eyes and swollen lids hid tiny black lashes. The baby lay still, asleep in her arms, wisps of angelic black hair spilling out from under a tiny blue knit cap. Sophia's nose snuggled against his head. Her own eyes closed in some unspoken comfort as she drew in the baby's new smell.

Laura Ann stood at her side, in awe of the life that lay in Sophia's arms. Her friend lifted the tiny package a bit and offered the child in Laura Ann's direction.

"James," she said, her voice weak but determined. "Our baby boy."

So tiny and light. Laura Ann feared she'd drop the newborn when the nurse passed him into her arms. James's five pounds felt no heavier than a bag of feathers.

Laura Ann pulled him close, his face against her chin, whisper-thin strands of black hair tickling her when she kissed his forehead. Soft like a calf's nose, his warmth met her lips for the first time. She held him close. His sweet new-baby smell poured a soothing balm over months of pain.

A lifetime of Bible lessons and nighttime readings with Daddy stirred her deep inside, warm memories of passages that spoke about the blessings of children, mixing that very moment with her own dream of motherhood. She held the bundled blessing tight to her cheek. James's warmth and tiny breath bound him to her heart. Another link in the family chain.

She looked to the side to catch Sophia's eye. Her friend's eyes were closed but her mouth hung open in a strange way.

"Sophia?" Like a cue for the heart rate monitor, the very moment she spoke that name the equipment screeched a warbling alarm. "VT" burned cherry-red on the front panel over her head.

James flinched in her arms.

"Code Blue!" a nurse yelled, her voice echoing down the hall. All eyes turned from the final cleanup of Sophia's caesarian wound to the monitor, which displayed a trace like an undulating roller coaster, not the sharp peaks and valleys of her normal rhythm. Sophia's heart, to judge from the crisis erupting around her, was headed for a shutdown.

"Crash cart!" a voice yelled. Bodies parted for a silver table on wheels, loaded with equipment and wires.

"Give me the baby. Now," another nurse commanded in a stern voice. Before Laura Ann could respond, the sure hands of an older woman wrapped about the tiny child. Laura Ann backed away from the bed.

Eyes closed, Sophia gulped for air, her right hand jerking against a gaggle of tubes and wires as she sought to reach something on her chest. Exhaling with a moaning wheeze, she bent upwards out of the bed. Her eyes never opened.

"Sustained ventricular tachycardia," a nurse announced in a clinical voice devoid of emotion.

Dr. Murphy whisked past the doorjamb. "Stable?"

"Some pulse," the nurse replied. Behind her, another nurse stood by, clipboard in hand and her eye on the clock. Measuring Sophia's time.

Laura Ann heard the queer whine of a defibrillator on the cart, its tone increasing in quick steps with the building charge. Nurses prepared equipment, slung wires, and forced hypodermics of unpronounceable drugs into Sophia's IV line. The

246 / NOBODY'S CHILD

women worked as one with Dr. Murphy, the captain at the helm of their mercy ship.

"Losing her pulse. Got something, but not much."

"Cardioversion," Dr. Murphy ordered, reaching out to take two paddles from the nurse. "Clear," he announced, checking left and right as he lowered the devices to her bare chest and squeezed a trigger. Jolts of electricity coursed through Sophia's body, her back arching off the bed as her muscles reacted to the intense shock.

"Heart rate, one sixty-five," someone announced.

"Two hundred joules," Dr. Murphy called out, not lifting the paddles from her skin.

"Charging."

"Clear!" He pulled the trigger again. Her body lurched a second time. The instant her back settled into the bed, the bare hands of one nurse began compressing Sophia's chest, yet another nurse forcing a muff over her face and squeezing air into failing lungs.

"Losing that pulse," the first nurse said. She looked up, her eyes searching for some better prognosis on the monitors. Her gaze dropped back to Sophia, the rhythmic cycle of the two CPR nurses, and Dr. Murphy's steady hands.

"Three hundred joules." Dr. Murphy waited a moment for the CPR team to withdraw, then blasted electricity into Sophia's torso a third time.

Bared from the waist up, her chest rising in failed gasps, Sophia hovered somewhere between consciousness and the beyond. Nurses pumped air into her lungs, others shot mystery drugs into her veins, each a desperate attempt to bring the heart into rhythm. For the next minute the doctor took over the CPR, his forearms quivering when he stood over her, jamming her ribs down to coax blood from a failing heart.

Between chest compressions Dr. Murphy turned to a nurse

at his side, lowering his head for a fraction of a second, the first sign of surrender Laura Ann had ever seen in him. He motioned for the nurses to remove the bag from her face and lowered his cheek to Sophia's mouth, feeling for her breath.

"Her heart's nearly gone," Dr. Murphy said when he stood up. "There's not much more we can do. Another bolus of amiodarone in three minutes." He motioned to the lead nurse. "Then we'll try the paddles once more."

"You don't have long," he said to Laura Ann, holding the defibrillator above Sophia. Laura Ann prayed for a miracle—for Sophia to open her eyes and her heart to reclaim its rhythm with a normal beat. A rustle of her eyelids was the only response. She whispered a prayer in her friend's ear and squeezed her palm, kneading it with her fingers. The hand lay flaccid in hers, life draining out by the second.

At last Dr. Murphy edged Laura Ann out of the way, nodding toward the device in his hands.

"Clear," he called out, minus the tense energy he'd shown minutes ago. He set down the twin electrodes, one device on her breast, the other on the side of her chest, and pulled the trigger once more. Sophia never moved.

Dr. Murphy took over the compressions, three more manly heaves on her chest to bring her back. Moments later, shedding sweat, he half-leaned into the bed, a hand on either side of Sophia, his head drooping like an old sunflower, wagging slowly side to side.

"Call the code," he said, his voice weak.

"Time of—"

"Sophia!" Laura Ann exclaimed.

"—death, three twenty-one."

"No!" Laura Ann's balance fled from her. Scared fingers sliced through the air as her knees gave way and the world went black.

———————

Laura Ann held Daddy's hand, reaching as high as she could stretch to touch his fingers. He knelt down, grabbing her about the waist, then slung his arm under her bottom and hoisted her high. The evergreen aroma of cedar enveloped him, his black suit hung away from moths in the cedar closet, ready for Sundays or other special events. And for unhappy events—like today.

She lay her head on his shoulder, unable to watch. The scratchy wool of Daddy's coat was coarse under her cheek, but it smelled like the forest, or the bedding he put in her hamster's cage, or his shop when he built blanket chests. She breathed deep, trying to forget the scene behind her.

Momma didn't move. She just lay there, a strange white to her face like someone dumped flour on her and blew it off. Her hands were folded in an unnatural way on her chest, her feet pointed straight up. She looked like she was sleeping, but her eyes hadn't opened for three days. Daddy said she was dead.

People brought flowers, too many flowers. An assault on Laura Ann's senses, all kinds of smells filled the tiny one-room church in Alma. Flowers were lashed to big round wooden "O's," stapled to crosses, or crammed in baskets. Most of them were sweet-smelling blooms that didn't grow in the field or the forest, flowers she'd never seen before. Many of them carnations. Whites and pinks, and some of them tinted purple or blue. Momma didn't like carnations. She called them "funeral flowers," but she never said what a funeral was. Maybe this was it. A man stood behind Momma and spoke from a thick black book. He talked for a long time and it made Daddy cry. Daddy didn't like to stand still for a long time. He said it hurt his back. But he held on to Laura Ann, hugging her tight, squeezing each time she heard people say "Amen."

Momma left too soon.

Clinging to Daddy, she decided to shut her eyes, to never

look back. But what if Momma woke up? Maybe, if she looked back once more, Momma would open her eyes. Laura Ann turned in Daddy's grip to get a peek. She hoped for things just the way he'd taught her. He called it "prayer," talking to God about making Momma well. If God could make the disease go away, maybe He could wake her up too.

Momma lay asleep, stiff amidst the flowers, her hands filled with a small bouquet. A man stood next to her and shoved flowers into her grip. That seemed mean. Momma knew how to pick them. She loved red blooms, not pink. Laura Ann hoped for her to wake up, repeating the prayers like Daddy taught her, but nothing happened. Momma didn't stir.

Laura Ann opened her eyes, the cutting stench of smelling salts burning her nose. She saw green, the rumpled cotton of a surgical gown standing above her. She brushed away the hand that held a tiny vial near her upper lip, her hand seeking her forehead.

"Laura?" someone asked.

Laura Ann looked up into a bright light, dimly aware of the voice, searching for Daddy. In front of her lay a bed, a green-garbed man standing between her and the beyond. She wished for him to move, something beckoning her to stand up and to rush to the mattress. To cling to its special occupant.

*Momma?*

She pushed up from the floor, her balance unsteady.

The man in green moved, revealing a woman lying on a bed behind him.

*Not Momma.*

Her eyes closed, she lay still under a white sheet, her hands folded on her chest the same way as Momma's. She would not wake up. No matter how much Laura Ann hoped or prayed. Her skin seemed ashy, a cold pallor she'd not seen since the night Daddy flew away.

But there was color. One red rose, plucked from a hospital vase, lay neatly tucked between her palms. Brilliant red, like her lips, the first time they met.

*Sophia.*

# CHAPTER 23

## JULY 31

Ian stood tall in the hot afternoon sun, his frame stronger looking for the suit he wore. She reached over and squeezed his arm, then let her hand fall. She had no desire to show affection in this crowd. Much as she loved some of them, many of these people did not love her. She would not give gossips the satisfaction of spreading more lies.

Sophia's casket lay on a green-carpeted contraption that would soon lower her into the ground. Much fancier than Daddy's, a shiny black lacquered box, ordered by someone in Pittsburgh. Cicadas sang in the trees surrounding the cemetery. Two funerals in less than a year, two cemeteries, Daddy and a dear friend laid to rest within a few miles of each other. The locusts didn't care, their mating calls a constant buzz in the background of a scorching heat.

"Preacher wouldn't bury her in Alma," a voice said, drifting out of the small crowd behind her. A whisper meant to be heard. "You know. A single woman and all, with a baby but no husband."

"So?" another voice asked. "Laura Ann needs love right now. Not a lecture."

Ian reached over and took her hand, Preacher's last words echoing in her head. "Jezebel," he'd whispered just loud enough to be heard after he told her to find a cemetery plot somewhere else. The family church would have nothing to do with "strangers from out of town." Whether Laura Ann was the Jezebel he referred to, or Sophia, didn't matter. She dashed out of the Alma chapel two days ago, determined never to return, except to visit Daddy's grave.

Pastor Culpeper saw it differently. The voice of grace on her porch months ago when Daddy passed away, he'd embraced her yet again. Pamela, the pastor's wife and Daddy's hospice angel, drew her to this cemetery, sure they could find a spot for a woman with no kin.

Pastor approached the grave and spoke a few words, a short story about Sophia and where she came from, her family and departed husband, and her intense desire to be a mom. It was a nice eulogy, a friendly pastor, and a welcoming congregation, perched on the side of Route 18 in the tiny hamlet of Pursley. Her new church home. Daddy, resting in the historic family plot at Alma, would have to understand. She could never worship there again.

Pastor Culpeper paused a moment, then shared a few more words, every one a balm to her wounded soul. "God is always beckoning people to Himself with love and grace," the young pastor said. "Our task—a task for all of you here today—is to help people open up to recognize God's great love. Not to prove that love, or to answer all the possible questions about God. Just to open up every day, and help people see the hand of the Lord in what's happening in their lives."

He looked across the mourners, sweeping a hand toward the gathering, most of them attending out of respect for Angus McGehee. If his daughter grieved, they grieved with her.

"If we exclude someone who's different from us and don't

share that love of God," he said, looking straight at Laura Ann, "because of some rumored sin, or because she's a stranger," he added, glancing at the casket, "that exclusion erodes our witness on many levels. Every time we fail to love, we do serious damage to the heart of the gospel."

*Love.*

"Tell them you love everyone," Daddy told her once. Daddy, a man who understood the gospel. A man who lived it.

Pastor Culpeper looked her way, his smile the signal that it was her time. She prayed for peace as she stepped forward and began to speak. "Sophia McQuistion was my friend. She always wanted to be a mom, but she had a disease she didn't know about until she was seven months pregnant. She fought a good fight to make it to eight months and deliver a baby boy. A baby who sleeps right now in Wheeling, maybe wondering where his momma went. I can relate. I've lived that life."

Laura Ann took a deep breath and charged on.

"Sophia came here to say 'thanks' to a friend. That's all. We have a lot to learn from her. She lived with a heart filled with gratitude and always took time to say 'thanks.' So now I say it too. Thank you, Sophia, for what you taught me."

*Love.*

Half an hour later, most of the mourners had exchanged a few pleasantries, expressed their regrets to Laura Ann, and headed home. She tarried at the casket, her hands on the slick black of the wood that held her friend. Granny Apple moved alongside her. They stood in silence for a long time.

"Hard times demand tough choices," she said in her mentoring voice. "I'm glad we were blessed to know her, even if for a while."

"What is it with hard times, Granny Apple? Why so many?" Laura Ann asked, not looking her way. Too much death. Too many disappointments.

"Part of living, I reckon. God didn't promise it would be easy, child. Just that He'd be there for us every step along the way."

## AUGUST 2

"Ms. McGehee?"

An hour after she'd returned from lunch, a short man dressed in a grey suit stood at the door of the neonatal intensive care unit. Not a young man, but younger than Daddy, pudgy and wearing a broad smile. A lone cheery face in a world of busy professionals draped in green and blue scrubs. Laura Ann turned from her seat in the waiting area and set down her twice-read leather-bound copy of The Lord of the Rings.

"Yes?" she replied. The word drained her, the last spark of energy she could muster after a week of shuttling back and forth from Middlebourne to Wheeling, from church, home, and graveside to hospital, so that she might settle Sophia's affairs and still be close to infant James.

"My name is Joseph Brewer." He stepped forward, a business card extended, held by thick hairy fingers. "From Pittsburgh. I'm a colleague of Sophia's." He paused, swallowing hard. "And the executor of her estate." He struggled with words, then added, "Thank you. I'm sorry I couldn't get here sooner."

Laura Ann's heart skipped a beat. "I'm sorry for your loss, Mr. Brewer. For all of us. Have you seen the baby?" she asked, pointing back toward the closed doors.

"No. But thank you. I think it might be too hard for me right now." He bit his lip, looked down, then continued. "Before she passed away, Sophia asked me to make this visit. In person. I appreciate that you're at the hospital today near James. That's just what Sophia would have hoped for."

"I've been here every day, sir."

"I know."

"How? I mean, how could you?" She looked about, in wonder at who would transmit her whereabouts to an attorney fifty miles north.

"It's not important how I know, Laura Ann. But I do." His tone changed, more official than before. "I understand that the child may be released from neonatal ICU in a few days, and after some time in the preemie ward, James will be allowed to go home."

*Where is home?*

Laura Ann considered that thought for a long moment. Home is where love is. Where Daddy was. Where Ian is.

"What you said about James is correct," she replied, not sure what more she should say.

"I presume that you know Sophia had no family." His voice sank again. "I appreciate what you did to find her a resting place, by the way." He let that comment stand for a moment. "You were her only support during dark days. Thank you."

"I wish I'd known her longer."

"Me too."

Mr. Brewer paused, clearing his throat. "Sophia gave me some very specific directions about her child, should she not survive to care for him," he said. "She understood the risks and took all the proper legal precautions in the event of her death." His voice cracked and he cleared his throat again. "I'm sorry. This is quite hard for me. She was a valued colleague. And my boss."

"I understand."

"Nevertheless, Laura Ann, her direction was that — in the untimely event of her death — you be named the guardian of the boy."

He hesitated, as if waiting for her response, then added, "She set aside most of her estate to create a monthly stipend to support the child. We intend to probate the will after the baby leaves the hospital. I'll be in touch with you on the details of the guardianship—presuming you agree, of course—and I'll share information about the stipend. Sophia was adamant that you not suffer any financial hardship caring for her son."

Mr. Brewer wiped at his forehead with a handkerchief, shaking his head a bit. "I'm sorry. As soon as Sophia called me to the hospital four weeks ago, I've been dreading this day. But—but I'm happy for James. And for you." He put the handkerchief away and reached into his briefcase for some papers.

"Sophia made one more stipulation in the will. It's a wish, not directive in nature, but one she wanted me to convey if she was unable to share it with you personally." He took a deep breath.

"She asked that, if you and your fiancé are willing, you adopt the child as your own. She hoped he might grow up with your name, and as part of your family. With you as his mom."

At nearly nine o'clock, the night shift settled into their routine at the neonatal ICU. Laura Ann stood at the window looking into the care area. Ian stood by her side, his warmth palpable in the cool of the hospital. They watched a nurse check on James, one of three children still under a critical watch. Soon, perhaps, he would leave for the preemie ward, and then, home.

Laura Ann crossed her arms against the chill, willing her heart to slow its tortuous beat. Forming the words that must come out, determined to never hide secrets again, she took a long breath, ready to speak the desire of her heart—one that might destroy her relationship with Ian.

"A lawyer came to see me today," she began. "Mr. Brewer. A friend ... an employee of Sophia."

"And?"

"He came to tell me that he's probating her will." She paused, facing Ian at the window. "Sophia named me as legal guardian for James." She watched his face for a reaction, but he seemed strangely calm. "He said there would be a monthly stipend to help with the care."

Ian raised a hand, leaning into the cold glass. "You figured that was coming, right? The guardian part, at least." He watched something inside the care area for a long time, then added, "I've been wondering when we'd learn about her wishes. Officially, that is."

"I never wanted it to turn out this way, Ian. But yes — if Sophia's gone, I want to care for this baby." She swallowed some words, and then added, "I don't want to simply be his guardian."

He turned and looked down at her. "I don't understand."

"I'm his biological mother. I want to be more than his caretaker." She took a deep breath. "I want to be his *mom*."

"Laura Ann?" Ian asked, lowering his hand to tug at her elbow.

Her chin quivered while she watched him, hopeful he'd share the words she dreamed of.

He took her hands, unfolding her crossed arms. "We'll get through this. I'll be there right by you, and — "

Laura Ann couldn't hold back anymore, throwing her arms around him, her face planted into that strong place below his shoulder, the beat of his heart strong against her cheek. "Do you mean that?" she asked, sniffling. "You're okay with an instant family?"

"Yes, but I'm not finished," he said with a laugh, adding, "You interrupt a lot." He hugged her, lifting her off the floor. "It's all happening pretty fast, you know? But I've always wanted a son."

"Really?" she exclaimed, sort of a half-cry, half-laugh. "Mr.

Brewer said that Sophia asked us to adopt him. *Both* of us. And the lactation nurse said I could learn to breast feed with the help of some simple exercises and medication. And Granny Apple has lots of baby clothes she could loan us, and —"

Ian lowered her to the floor and reached up to cup her face in his hands, a thumb across her lips, another thumb wiping a tear from her cheek. "I think those are all great ideas, Miss McGehee. But that means we'd better hurry up and get married, right?" He winked. "After all, what's holding us up?"

"Yes, soon," she said, her smile so wide her that cheeks cramped. "I'd like that." She reached up to touch the long hands that cradled her. The gentle touch of a man who'd always been there for her, long before she'd noticed that he cared. Ian glanced back through the window, and she followed his gaze.

"Gotta tie the knot, Laura Ann. 'Cause pretty soon that boy's gonna need a dad."

# CHAPTER 24

Heat shimmered in translucent waves where it rose off the baked clay of August corn fields, mature stalks browning for a September harvest. Tired leaves drooped from towering poplars, faint streaks of yellow the first hint of the approaching fall. Dog days wrapped the mountains in their sweltering embrace. Under the relative cool of a shaded porch, Laura Ann rocked into the late afternoon of a summer Friday.

James's eyes stared up at Laura Ann, cradled in her arms. A month old today, the child gripped her finger with his tiny hand while he nursed. Laura Ann's gaze never left the infant, in wonder at this gift of life. She marveled how, each time James latched on to her, she felt a strange tingling, a warm, relaxed feeling she'd never experienced before.

"Your mother was beautiful," Laura Ann said in a quiet voice. A metal air chime tinkled at the edge of the porch, the wind carrying the hot smell of dry pastures and damp whiffs of the muddy creek bottom. "She loved it here," Laura Ann continued. "There's so much to tell you."

James blinked as though perhaps he knew something of his mother, knew of the struggle she endured to bring him into the world. His hand closed on Laura Ann's finger, the lines of his tiny palm etched into soft pink flesh. Satin black hair drifted weightless when he moved in her arms, seeking a new position as he drank. Her milk artificially induced with drugs and stimulation regimens, induced like the fertile eggs she'd shed months ago, Laura Ann wet-nursed her son. An adoptive single mother, and a bride-to-be.

James's eyes fell closed, pulling at Laura Ann for the last of his fourth feeding that day. A few minutes later, his mouth relaxed and he let go, his lips moist and curled in a slight smile. She watched him, her sole focus, asleep in her arms. Her toes pushed against porch boards to move the rocker in synch with the chirp of cicadas that sang in the sweltering heat.

Granny Apple stepped out of the house, a glass of ice water in hand. "Drink up, child."

Laura Ann took the glass, resting it on the broad wooden arm of the chair. Granny Apple settled into a rocker next to her. In silence, they watched the farm evaporate into cloudless skies. Oak rockers rumbled back and forth over uneven boards, a gentle percussion accompaniment to the perpetual buzz of insects.

"The state plans to repair the low water crossing 'round the end of this month. To get ready for hunting season."

"That's a relief," Laura Ann said, looking up at the vehicles in the drive. Since June, with no way to leave the farm by automobile, she'd been wading back and forth across the Middle Island Creek, a tiresome chore. Albeit, there were some advantages; drunks didn't choose the forest above the farm for their late-night hangouts.

"You two need to set a date." Granny Apple threw the comment out like a challenge. "The way people talk, and all."

"We have," she said. "It will be soon." Laura Ann knew they couldn't wait much longer for the wedding, nor did they plan to. No shotgun wedding, and no long engagement. Something in between. Since Ian's proposal at the top of the ridge, she'd been reminded each day how much he cared for her. His daily trips to see her these past weeks affirmed what she already knew—that he wanted to be with her all the time, not just wading across the Middle Island to spend every evening working the farm while she mothered a new infant.

Granny Apple stood up out of the rocker and approached, her arms extended. "I'll put James down. You can take a walk."

Laura Ann nodded and raised James into Granny Apple's waiting arms. As the screen door shut behind her adopted grandma, she looked up to see two men and a woman walking down the road toward the farmhouse. A flash of light reflected gold off the chest of one man dressed in khaki, his head topped with a frame cap.

*The police?*

"Are you Laura Ann McGehee?" Deputy Rodale asked a few minutes later, staring at some folded papers in his hand. Sweat poured off the man where he stood at the foot of the porch, a line of white chalking an arc under his armpits.

"What? You've known me since middle school, Brian."

He never looked up but studied the papers in front of him, then turned to the man at his right, scanning his face for some clue how to proceed.

"Brian Rodale!" Granny Apple exclaimed through the screen door, moving onto the porch to join Laura Ann. "Who's this with you and what in the dickens are you doing out here on a day like this?" She laughed and extended a hand to the stranger.

Black-haired and brown as Sophia, the man ignored her proffered hand, never taking his eye off Laura Ann. He neither smiled nor frowned, the expression of a bored observer ready to move on to the next activity. Not breaking his gaze at Laura Ann, he reached left and forced the papers into Deputy Rodale's soggy chest. "Get it over with," he said, clipping his words, his accent nothing like that of a mountain person. He crossed his arms, looked left at the deputy, then back at Laura Ann.

Deputy Rodale shrugged and turned to a thin woman who hid behind his girth.

"Phyllis?" Granny Apple exclaimed. "What's this all about?"

"Child Protective Services sent us out to see you," Phyllis said. A short greying woman of about fifty, and thin as a willow, she'd easily disappeared behind the officer. She held forth a second folded set of papers, bound in blue. "Brian is here to escort us on some difficult business. May we come in?"

"No." Laura Ann backed up in front of Granny Apple. "We can talk on the porch."

"Suit yourself," the stranger said, his accent a touch Hispanic. "Let's get this over with." He motioned to the woman.

Phyllis stepped up on the porch and handed forth the package of folded papers. "This is difficult for all of us, so please — let's do this the easy way. May we sit down?"

Laura Ann's pulse quickened, something in Phyllis's tone a reminder of her uncle Jack. "If this is an official visit," Laura Ann said, "I'd prefer to stand."

"It's official," Deputy Rodale replied, holding his set of papers forward like he couldn't wait to get rid of them. Granny Apple's hand snagged the package.

Laura Ann never took her eyes off the officer. "What do you want, Brian?"

The deputy bit his lip, looking left and right for support but finding none. He blurted out his words. "We're here to serve notice about the child."

Laura Ann clenched her fists, backing up a step, she and Granny guarding the door.

Granny Apple snapped, "Phyllis Macintosh. What do you think you're doing?" She threw the papers back at the grey-haired woman. "You will not take James from this house."

"What?" Laura Ann exclaimed, her eyes following the ruffled papers to the floor, then to the stranger at Deputy Rodale's right. The Hispanic man stepped forward, headed straight for her.

"Get this over with," he said. "Where's my son?"

"No!" Laura Ann screamed as the stranger stepped forward. She stuck out her arm.

Deputy Rodale put a hand to the man's shoulder, moving up the steps to restrain him. "Please, Mr. Mendoza. Not here. Not yet."

"Not ever!" Laura Ann quipped, her heart pounding double-time. She stood side by side with Granny Apple, her chin quivering, palms sweaty.

"Laura Ann," Phyllis said, stepping up on the porch with her companions. "I'm here representing the state. Mr. Mendoza filed suit for custody of Sophia McQuistion's child on the basis that he is the biological father and has parental rights to the child."

"No!" Laura Ann shot back. "Sophia named me as his guardian. We probated the will, and I have proof. He's my son. And the adoption papers have been filed."

"That's partially true. But he's not your son unless you adopt him in accordance with *all* of the laws of the state." Phyllis looked to the right for support from Deputy Rodale. He offered none. "The problem, Laura Ann, is that when Ms. McQuistion named you as guardian, the state was unaware of a biological father who made claim to the child. Mr. Mendoza has documentation to prove that he is the father." She moved closer, picking up the papers off the porch. "Her will has been contested."

"Not possible!" Laura Ann said. "Sophia used a sperm donor."

"I was the donor," the stranger replied, a mean smile breaking where boredom showed before. "That kid is mine, and she came to Cincinnati to thank me for it." He licked his lips. "She found me right after I got her pregnant."

"Is this true?" Granny Apple asked Phyllis. Her hand sought Laura Ann's forearm as if to say "let me lead."

Phyllis nodded, refolding the papers. "He filed these documents in county court, Granny. They're yours while we sort out this mess. He can prove that the clinic Ms. McQuistion visited used his sperm for the in vitro fertilization. She did in fact look him up and thank him for his role in the process. All the evidence shows that he's the biological father. Until we can determine which person has legal rights to raise the child — the biological parent or the named guardian — then the baby becomes a ward of the state of West Virginia." She paused, her eyes showing the first sign of empathy that day. "That's why I'm here, Laura Ann. James will go to a foster home while we work this through the courts."

"No!" Laura Ann yelled. "Not a chance. I've been there for this child every day since before he was born. You don't just waltz up here with some court papers and expect me to send my baby off to live with strangers."

"Yes, we do," the Hispanic man said. "Bring the kid out here. Now."

Deputy Rodale put a hand on the man's shoulder again, holding him back.

Granny Apple put an arm in front of Laura Ann, her voice its most severe. "Phyllis, you waded across a creek and walked a mile to get here. Just how do you intend to take the infant home?"

"She's not taking James —," Laura Ann said.

"*Shhh.* Phyllis? I asked you a question."

"Same way we walked in, Granny. I guess we'd carry him out."

"You're going to wade across that creek with a baby?"

"Not right now," Deputy Rodale said. "We're simply serving papers related to the suit. Laura Ann is responsible for bringing the child in. Unless—"

"Unless?"

"Unless the sheriff deems her to be a flight risk," Phyllis said, "or I observe some endangerment of the child."

"Endangerment? Really, Phyllis. Who put you up to this?"

"These are official papers, ma'am, and they've been properly filed in a court of law," Deputy Rodale said, taking the package from Phyllis's hands. "But we didn't come to see you. So please stand aside."

"I will not," Granny said, linking an arm with Laura Ann. "And you know my name, boy."

The Hispanic man pushed forward toward Laura Ann, swearing aloud as he swept Deputy Rodale's hand from his shoulder. "No more talk."

Daddy steadied her and faced Laura Ann, his hand on her shoulder. "Put your knee here," he said, pointing down with his other hand. "Then bring your fist up like this." He bent over and pulled her clenched fist into his face. "Use all the strength you've got."

He stood straight up. "If that fails, use those fingers. Claw his eyes out. Whatever it takes, go down fighting. You won't get a second chance."

Laura Ann watched Daddy a moment in the silence of the kitchen, then asked, "Why would someone want to hurt me?"

Mr. Mendoza threw his hand up, trying to sweep Laura Ann out of the way.

"No!" Phyllis commanded. "Stop him, Brian." Mendoza broke away from the deputy before Phyllis's words died in her mouth.

Laura Ann stood her ground. When his left arm connected with her, thrown across her as though he expected her to topple like a pile of apples, Laura Ann grabbed him above his left elbow, her squeeze iron-tight from years of milking. She wrenched his arm backward with a sharp twist meant to tear it from his shoulder. Wide-eyed, he bent toward her, and she turned Daddy's lesson into action. Lifting his arm high with the wrenching motion, she jerked her left knee in a powerful upward thrust into his crotch. Mendoza screamed, his arm rent backwards, and any future as a sperm donor put in jeopardy.

He doubled over, a guttural cough erupting from him. As his head came down in reaction to the pain, Laura Ann let go the arm and swung both hands in, her palms cupped. She slammed them about his head, boxing his ears, every intention to rupture both eardrums.

Mendoza screamed a second time, expelling the last of his deflated breath. Hands to his ears, his head below his waist, she laced her fingers in a double fist and slammed it down on his back, just below the base of his neck.

Mendoza sank into a writhing, moaning heap at her feet.

## AUGUST 28

"Admit it when you're wrong."

She could see Daddy now, standing over her where she sat on the toilet of their only bathroom, whiling away the day, too stubborn to confess her faults.

"Sometimes you do the wrong thing for the right reason,

young lady. We all do at some point in our lives. But if what you do is wrong, even if it's for a cause you can defend, it's still *wrong*." He said it with that painful emphasis that spilled a foul stench on a perfectly good word. Daddy always drew a strict boundary between right and wrong. Good and evil. His lines of demarcation were strong.

Daddy's words rang in her ears while she watched Ian approach, his lanky form a welcome sight after a sleepless Friday night in the Tyler County jail. No one befriended her in this dreary place, a mother ripped from her home and separated from her infant because of a dubious allegation of assault. The sperm donor charged into her, not the other way around.

She tried to read something in Ian's face, news about James and Granny, some hope she'd leave this place today. Deadpan, he revealed nothing. He followed the sheriff, a man her daddy rarely spoke to: Uncle Jack's younger and meaner brother, Jeremy.

"You posted her bond," Sheriff Harris said, not making eye contact with Laura Ann or Ian. "So she's all yours." The sheriff opened the jail door adding, "I don't know what you see in this little witch."

Ian jammed a hand between Sheriff Harris and the jail bars, staring him down for a long moment. Harris started to protest, then thought better of it.

"Whatever," Harris said. "Just get her outta here."

Ian extended his hand to Laura Ann with an encouraging wink. She needed no coaxing. A step ahead of her all the way, decked out in his official jacket and tie with a warden's badge on his chest, Ian led her out of the county jail. At the main door he pointed in silence toward his old farm truck waiting at the curb.

Yearning for some sign of affection, she turned and got in the pickup, not a word between them. She sat still, headed out of town across the bridge toward Sistersville, the wrong way if they were to return to the farm and to baby James. He took the first left, onto a country road that led to the tiny community of Next, then pulled off the lane to park beyond the sight of Route 18. When the truck stopped, he shifted on the bench seat to face her and his stern face melted, tears in his eyes.

"James is fine, Laura Ann. A little hungry, but doing well. I took some bottles of formula to the foster home half an hour ago."

"Foster home?" Laura Ann collapsed, her head in her hands. Ian freed the seat belt and pulled her into his arms.

"Somebody's watching us," Ian said after a time. "That's why we didn't return to the farm." She could feel him shake his head. "I'd have never guessed Jack would pull something like this."

"Uncle Jack?" she asked, sitting up straight to face him. She wiped at her eyes with a sleeve, until Ian produced a fresh napkin.

He nodded. "You were headed to the jail before I found out about the assault."

"It wasn't assault. They trumped that up."

"I know. But remind me not to cross you," he said, throwing a playful punch her way. "One of guys at the jail gave me a holler on the radio, but Jeremy wouldn't let me in to see you. So I took the rest of the afternoon off and headed for the farm. As soon as Rodale hauled you off the porch and brought you to town, Phyllis ran back to her office and filed a motion with Child Protective Services claiming endangerment. Granny was with James when I got there. Wasn't long before Phyllis showed up to get him, backed up by two deputies." He chuckled. "I don't think they wanted to tangle with Granny Apple. And they didn't count on me being there."

"But why?"

"Hold on. So, Granny and I gave 'em a hard time. Wouldn't let Phyllis touch the baby until after we'd carried him across the creek. I followed her all the way to town, then to the foster care home, and finally back to her office. That's when I saw him."

"Uncle Jack?" she asked, images of her uncle with his hands on James.

"She met him at her office after hours. I watched them through the window at the front of her building. They shook hands, Jack handed her some kind of envelope, and then he left." Ian shrugged. "I'd bet my badge he's behind that parental rights suit and that he paid Phyllis to file the petition of endangerment."

Laura Ann leaned toward him, about to say something, but Ian cut her off.

"There's more. I dug around in state records with the office computer last night. Turns out, Phyllis used to work for your uncle, as a clerk and notary for his crop insurance business. She got a job with Child Protective Services last December." For the first time, he smiled.

"When you search for her name and Jack's in the state records, you find lots of insurance claims. *Lots* of claims. But when you search for her name and yours together, there's only one entry — and it might interest you."

"Nothing about Uncle Jack interests me."

"This will. Seems that your dad bought a federal tobacco crop insurance policy in August — notarized by Phyllis."

"Daddy never bought crop insurance." She raised an eyebrow. "We couldn't afford it."

Ian smiled again. "That's what I thought, but it's got your dad's signature on it. Looks legit. And that's not all."

Laura Ann tilted her head.

"Someone filed a tobacco claim after the barn burned. And it was paid. To you."

"But I never did that!" she gasped.

"Precisely. They're running a scam, Laura Ann. Insurance fraud. So if they try to take baby James from you, we have just the ammunition we need to bring them down."

He gripped her left hand for a long quiet spell, twisting the diamond ring about her finger. He patted her knee after a time and spoke up. "We need to fight this as a couple. Mr. and Mrs. Ian Stewart."

"You won't hear any objections from me," she replied, a lump in her throat.

"Didn't think so. We have an appointment with Granny Apple, Pastor Culpeper, and his wife in Pursley." His smile grew from ear to ear. "Three weeks from today. At five." He motioned to the backseat of his truck, pulling a blanket free from atop a surprise. "I think you'll need this."

Laura Ann turned her head, spying a long deep white box tied with a pink ribbon. She'd never noticed the blanket in the back when they left the jail.

Ian lifted the big box over the seat and set it in her lap, so long it barely fit. "I picked it up this morning."

She pulled at the bow and lifted the top of the box free. Eyes wide, she brought her hand to her mouth with a gasp, then looked up in shock.

Ian nodded with an impish wink.

"Momma's wedding dress!"

"I picked it up from Mrs. Harper before I came to get you. She'd finished the adjustments. Now all I need is a bride."

"And here I am," Laura Ann said, leaning across the gown to kiss him.

Three weeks from tonight he would call the farm his home.

# CHAPTER 25

"I found five bottles and a dozen packages of formula," Ian said, strapping on a backpack. "Was that all?"

"I pumped what I could. The bottles and formula will be more than enough to get James through Saturday morning," Laura Ann replied from her seat on the steps of the porch. The same place she last saw her son a week ago.

"I'll hike these out to the foster family and see you tomorrow evening," he continued, pulling his pack straps tight. "You get some sleep, okay?" Ian towered over her, clad in jeans and a T-shirt, his boots muddied from the trip in. He looked up at an angry sky, the evening gone dark with the threat of more thunderstorms. Her eyes followed his to low clouds blowing fast over the ridge, wisps of grey torn from their parents and flying on the wind to some unknown place. Like James.

Laura Ann nodded, no words in response. Every minute she imagined the baby in her arms, the pain of her son's absence growing more intense with each passing hour. She stood and took Ian in a tight hug. "Love on him for me," she said. Ian nodded, but she knew the truth. He'd struck a deal just to drop off her mother's milk. He'd never be allowed to see the child.

After a light kiss, he struck off up the hill, headed on a mile-long walk out to Route 18, then a short drive into town. Some trustworthy family, vetted by the state, watched over tiny James. No one would tell her where he lay, a secret Ian kept to fulfill his part of a covert deal. At least she knew that the parents who watched her baby also felt her pain.

Laura Ann watched him hike out, arriving just an hour after his work day, slogging through fresh red mud to get the food for James's next day. Job, farm, baby. Job, farm, baby. He made the rounds each afternoon without complaint. Laura Ann turned the engagement ring on her finger, squeezing diamond points into her flesh as a reminder of Ian's commitment ... and their wedding two weeks from Saturday.

Half an hour after his departure, fluffy bases of a ragged storm gathered, dark and foreboding. Ragged wisps of clouds clumped together and moved in a slow march toward the farm. The Angus lay down with their noses into the approaching rain.

Without warning, a shattering crash of thunder split the sky. Jolted from her place on the steps, Laura Ann jumped up and dashed through the screen door, latching it behind her.

Like a knife plunged into a bag of water, the sky opened, inundating the barnyard with rain. The storm swept over the house and immersed Laura Ann in darkness. She huddled on the floor in the middle of the living room, arms wrapped about her legs, flashes of lightning her only illumination.

Laura Ann lowered her chin to her knees, the shock of successive bolts rattling windows, rain pelting glass. She prayed for Ian, for his safe passage to the truck. She prayed for James, to be fed, and to be loved.

Thor, the Norse god of thunder, raged his most furious outside her home, determined to torment her. She imagined each blast of light and sound to be a battle in her war. Daddy's sickness. Four trips to the fertility clinic. Fire. Flood. Sophia's surprise visit. The death of her friend. The mortgage. And now, losing James.

Another bolt crossed the sky, rumbling the valley like a monster timpani. Windows rattled and the door shook in response to the invisible force somewhere above her in the cloud.

Invisible power, but no less real.

"Your momma had a saying," Daddy whispered, holding Laura Ann in his arms. Together, they huddled in the living room, lightning flashing all about one hot summer's eve.

"What?" Laura Ann whispered in reply, afraid the storm could hear her. Above the house, thunder rolled in dark clouds, and rain pelted the windows like so many pebbles.

"She said that if lightning ever strikes twice, the Thunder Hag is about."

"Thunder Hag?" Laura Ann's eyes were wide with wonder, staring out at the flashes in the dark, brilliant bolts that momentarily lit the room bright as a camera flash, then plunged the two of them into an even deeper dark.

"Aye. The Thunder Hag. One bright day midsummer, when all the highlands were washed in a brilliant warm and the seas were made to sleep, she flew over Scotland in a pitch-black chariot, drawn by horrible red hounds, and flanked by dark heavy clouds."

Laura Ann's heart beat fast, sure she'd seen this hag headed toward the farm earlier that evening when the first bolts struck up on the ridge.

"Blackness swallowed the land and her chariot wheels rattled fearsome. She rode sea to sea, hurtling fireballs into forests of fir

and silver birch, setting Scotland ablaze from highland to moor."
Daddy squeezed her in his arms, holding her in a protective hug
safe from the onslaught of the terrible witch.

"And then Angus, King of Summer, called for the great hero,
Conall. Said Conall, 'I may slay her on the morrow.'"

Laura Ann trembled in Daddy's arms as the next bolt show-
ered them in a pool of light.

"Did Conall kill the hag?" she asked.

"Nay, but he drove her away for a season. Conall stood on
a grassy knoll and with a might heave cast his trusty spear into
her side. No swallow may dart as fast as his spear fled into her
horrible belly. Wounded, she screamed and threw double bolts at
heroic Conall, then fled the wrath of his mighty arm. Her wheels
cut the dark storm clouds a'twain, showering Scotland with a
torrent of rain, and quenching the fires of her rage. Scotland was
saved, springing up green as an emerald. And Conall stands up
there today — on our ridge — guarding against the fury of the
terrible witch."

Laura Ann stared with wonder out the dark window, another
bolt high in the sky lighting up the distant line of poplars on the
ridge. Somewhere in that forest waited a tall man, her hero, hurtling spears to protect her from a fearsome enemy who came to
steal and destroy.

## SEPTEMBER 3

"Felix Mendoza is the sperm donor," her fiancé said. "James's
biological father."

Laura Ann squirmed as the words left his mouth. She and
Granny Apple sat in the living room on Friday night with Ian,
listening to the news he'd gleaned this past week. Like a bard,

Ian roamed far afield, bringing back tidbits from the neighboring village of Middlebourne.

"Mendoza first learned about the pregnancy when Sophia visited him in Cincinnati," Ian said, perusing some notes on a small pad of paper. "She told me about this in the hospital, Laura Ann. The night you fell asleep while we talked. She was real lonely—and probably depressed. For whatever reason, she thought there might be some special connection with this guy when they met." He rolled his eyes. "Maybe it was her hormones talking. I don't know."

"She wanted a child with Hispanic blood," Laura Ann said. "And she wanted someone to share news of the baby with."

"How does a woman do that?" Ian asked. "I mean, why him?"

"She picked him off a website," Granny Apple said with a knowing glance in Laura Ann's direction. "Online baby shopping."

"It's a little more complex than that," Laura Ann replied, hanging her head. "But that's the essence of it."

"So how did he find out about Sophia's death? And locate James?" Granny Apple asked, her hands busied with some knitting.

"This is where it gets interesting," Ian said, his eyes averted from Laura Ann. "It was your uncle Jack."

Laura Ann's head snapped up, her mouth wide open. "Him again?"

"Hard to believe, but here's what I found out from the guys at the sheriff's office. Your uncle Jeremy's been shooting off his mouth." He winked at Laura Ann. "And I've done some sleuthing of my own."

"Go on."

"When you brought the baby home, and Jack learned about it, he apparently did some snooping around Wheeling General. He sweet-talked a nurse and learned that Sophia conceived through IVF. That's where a contact in Child Protective Services came in handy. Phyllis—his prior employee—placed an 'official call' and submitted paperwork claiming to research a parental rights suit, then found out about Mendoza."

He paused. "Laura Ann sealed her clinic records right after she met Sophia, so it's unlikely he learned anything about her. But it was no problem learning about Sophia. She's all over the Internet, the founding partner of a successful law firm." He coughed, and then added, "Or she was."

Ian put a hand on Laura Ann's shoulder, some quiet solace, and then continued his story. "Jeremy got liquored up at the VFW on Wednesday night and told a friend that Jack was working a deal to share in some kind of big win. Maybe he thinks that stipend from Sophia is worth a bunch of money and he's got an arrangement with Mendoza to split it. But that guess is a long shot."

"Or maybe he's just plain mean and wants to ruin Laura Ann's life," Granny Apple said, jabbing an imaginary Jack with her knitting needle.

"I could believe that," Laura Ann chimed in.

"Or," Ian said, "he figures that if he makes you miserable you'll fold like Rose did, and he'll get his fingers on yet another share of your dad's inheritance."

"That makes no sense. I own the farm."

"No. Technically, the bank owns it. You make payments on a debt that they secure with this land."

"He thinks he can run me out of town bawling? I fail to pay, and then the bank repossesses the land?" She shook her head, a deep scowl crossing her face. "He can't be that stupid."

"He doesn't know you as well as he should, but he does know business, Laura Ann. If you bail out of the mortgage, the bank gets to set the sale price and they write off any loss. He takes a short-term loan and buys the farm, flips it for his profit, and he's in the money."

"But he only wins," Laura Ann said, "if I give up."

Ian flashed a thumbs-up and added, "Close. He only wins if *we* give up."

## SEPTEMBER 4

"How do we beat someone like my uncle?" Laura Ann asked the next morning, scraping a skillet clean at the kitchen sink. "He's got the sheriff, Child Protective Services, and who-knows-what-else in his back pocket."

Hungry from a Saturday morning's work, Ian shoveled in another helping of fried ham, his mouth too full to answer her. He nodded like he had something to say, swigging the eggs and meat down with a bolt of hot coffee before he responded.

"You don't fight him," he said, wiping his mouth. "You keep him off-balance. Outsmart him." He picked up another slice of fresh-baked bread and smothered it with some of Laura Ann's fresh raspberry jam. Ready to gobble the sweet, he stopped, holding the bread midair, his mouth open in surprise.

"Listen," he said, turning his head toward the hall and the living room. "D'you hear that?"

"What?" she asked, setting down the pan.

"We left the TV on after you checked the weather. Stefany's show is coming on next. I just heard them announce it."

"So?"

"We need to watch. Not because of her, but the report she's doing. Come on." He dropped the bread, pushed away from the table, and sprinted down the hall toward the drone of the television set. Laura Ann folded a dish towel and followed at a slower pace. Since little James left, every movement taxed her.

"In a repeat of our weekly Special Report segment, investigative journalist Stefany Lukeman continues her series on the abuse of government insurance programs in the northwest counties hit hard by June floods."

Laura Ann joined Ian at the couch, a rare day when the television played. Perhaps it came with having a man in her house. Two weeks from tonight, this would become *his* house. Their home.

Stefany appeared on screen, the same cousin who'd sheltered her for five weeks in Wheeling. Nearly every day they were together, she'd shared some new tidbit she'd gleaned in her world of reporting that proved conspiracies to affect consumer pricing, to cut people out of work, or to move jobs. A woman who loved life, energetic in the extreme, she also had a passion for the little guy. Like a top spinning at high speed, she careened about the community as an investigative reporter, bouncing off one injustice after another.

Her cousin's green eyes and red hair set her apart from the other newscasters, a rebel in her dress and her color. Freckles, prominent cheekbones, and a strong jaw framed her most visible feature—full lips always drawn back in a smile. Her introduction filled the screen until she cut to a special report about Tyler County, their home.

"The impact of the June floods continues in the northwest corner of our state. Cleanup operations have been underway for weeks, and just now communities like Middlebourne, West Union, and Saint Mary's are recovering from what has been termed the worst flooding in this state in a century. But for all the stories of recovery and endurance, there's a dark side to federal and state flood relief programs. Massive fraud, perpetrated by a few, has crept into relief and subsidy efforts. From crop programs to federal flood insurance, 'entrepreneurs' are cashing in on what some say is easy money. Too easy."

Ian touched Laura Ann's knee, pointing in silence at the television. Her cousin rarely frowned. Today, Stefany's lips were full, pursed in concern.

"In Tyler County alone, more than four hundred farms reported losses in the June storm. But in our analysis of the flood, we found there were less than three hundred fifty farms located in the flood plain of the Middle Island and its tributaries. So why the discrepancy? Here's another problem. If you total up the flood-related crop losses for farms in our region, it exceeds the total value of any year's agricultural statistics for the past fifty years. To read between the lines, this would have been a banner year for agriculture in our corner of the state. Yet, you might recall, we suffered a devastating four weeks of drought just before the flood. So, which was it? A banner year for crops? Or fraud?"

Stefany held a sheet of paper in front of the camera, waving it and then pointing over her shoulder. "I'm standing at the site of a total loss — or so we're told. Located in the creek bottom behind me there once rested an extensive worm farm, over an acre in size according to insurance records I've obtained in the past week. Now, it's gone, all those worms washed downstream to the Gulf of Mexico, or to some lucky farmer's field. Yet," she intoned, pointing to the muddy area behind her, "no neighbors ever remember hearing anything about a worm business. It's a business that seems, to this reporter, to have sprung up overnight." She smirked, then added, "Night crawlers or shady operators? You decide."

Images of farms destroyed by the flood filled the screen, some of them places Laura Ann had visited. Piles of logs jammed up against bridges, houses washed from their foundations, and mud-covered fields scrolled by while Stefany described the losses. Ian tapped Laura Ann on the knee once more.

"These relief programs were meant to help the needy,"

Stefany said. "If you know of an insurance fraud related to the June disaster, contact me at the number below or let your local agriculture representative know. Help our government by policing our programs. That way everyone wins. I'm Stefany Lukeman for Eyewitness Reports. Live and local, Channel Seven."

Ian punched the television off, then stood up, pacing. "Here's the deal." He crossed his arms, a finger to his chin while he spoke. "Stefany found fraud in Tyler County. Jack sells crop insurance in Tyler County. We're pretty sure Jack is behind this deal with Mendoza. So, before we take this problem to the authorities — a group that includes Jack's brother — we keep your uncle on the ropes for a while, so to speak. We ask Stefany to focus more of her investigation on Middlebourne, and make dear old Uncle Jack sweat for a while." He shrugged with a half smile, half wink. "Who knows? We might uncover something we can use to win this case."

Laura Ann nodded. "You have a point. Uncle Jack's not as clever as he pretends to be."

"No. And if we're lucky, he's just dumb enough to leave some tracks." Ian made a pretend pistol with his thumb and forefinger, pointing at the set, and then added, "It's time for us to be on the hunt."

SEPTEMBER 5

"I'd be glad to help."

Stefany's words formed a second ray of hope, Ian's brainstorm the first. Late on a Sunday afternoon, she sat lotus style on the living room couch, kinky red-orange hair spilling over her shoulders. Dressed in jeans and a tight camisole top, she reminded Laura Ann of a college co-ed ... except for the steno pad in her hands, her pen flying in a furious trail across multiple sheets. For an hour, Stefany ate up every word of Laura Ann's story.

"There's more," Laura Ann said, hesitating. "Everyone knows by now that Sophia gave me guardianship when she died. What they don't know is about James's real mother."

Stefany tipped her head. "How many mothers can a baby have?" she asked with a laugh.

"In this case, two."

"Two?" Stefany's smile faded for a moment.

Laura Ann swallowed hard, determined to slay her secrets. "I am the biological mother."

Stefany dropped her pad, her mouth agape. "No way."

Laura Ann shrugged and managed a small smile. "I was an egg donor."

Stefany brightened. "Wow! Way to go, girlfriend. That is so great."

"You're serious?"

"Are you kidding? I mean, that's the bravest thing I've heard in a long time. You know how hard it is to do that? To donate?"

Laura Ann pulled her knees together in an involuntary reflex. She remembered all too well.

"Yeah. I guess you do understand. So, how many times? I mean, did you do it more than once? How many eggs?"

Laura Ann nodded, a sheepish hand lifting up four fingers. "Four times. Sixty-eight eggs."

Stefany whistled, then bent over to pick up her pad. "Does anyone else know?"

She shook her head. "Other than Ian and Granny Apple? No. At least, we don't think so. If Uncle Jack did, he probably wouldn't be helping this Mendoza guy sue for parental rights."

"Good point." Sitting in her lotus position, Stefany bent forward, her elbows on her knees. After a moment she sprang from the couch and bounced barefoot on her toes. "I've got it," she exclaimed. "'Pittsburgh mother bears child thanks to donor parents. Sperm donor fights for custody.'" She shook her head. "Hmmm. Won't work. Too long."

More bounces, more turns of phrases, then she stopped again, a finger to her lips. "'Inalienable rights of biological parents. Sperm donor sues for custody.'" She shook her head. "No. Still too long."

She paced back and forth, head bent, thinking. "I've got it," she exclaimed at last and scribbled furiously on her steno. "'Nobody's child.'"

"What?"

"See? You don't like it."

"No. I didn't say I didn't like it. I just don't understand it."

"*Nobody's child.* How does the law apply when two unmarried adults donate their DNA to make a baby that's grown in another woman's womb, and then she passes away? Who claims parental rights?"

"That's the crux of the problem. But James is not a 'nobody.'"

"Nobody's *child.* There's a difference, Laura Ann. Three adults have a legal interest in this child, if you follow our old way of thinking. And now the state takes an interest. Four of you. But when you look at this from another perspective, the authorities should be locked up for taking that baby from you. He's your flesh and blood, and you're the legal guardian of record. Go figure."

"He's my baby."

"And that's what we're going to help you prove. Just do me one favor."

Laura Ann nodded.

"Hold on to that little secret of yours for a while. Tell Granny Apple and Ian to keep it under their hats too. I have a plan." She tapped her teeth again with the pen, and then dashed down another note. "Though the evidence is pretty damning, we're not going after the insurance fraud just yet," she said.

Laura Ann furrowed her brow, unsure what she meant.

"We're gonna outflank these guys, cousin. Go for the jugular. Mendoza won't know what hit him—until it's too late."

# CHAPTER 26

Judge Dennis O'Dell sat behind an antique walnut desk, the walls of his office lined with leather-bound law journals. Three diplomas from West Virginia University hung on the wall behind Laura Ann. The county judge was hometown material, born and bred. She'd been lucky to get an appointment with him so soon on a Monday morning.

Judge O'Dell loved eagles. Brass eagles created a miniature flock on his desk, and more versions took ownership of their own shelves above the tan spines of *West Virginia Legal Code*. The judge sat in thought, papers in his hand, his reading glasses perched on a long Ichabod Crane nose.

"To be honest, Laura Ann," he said in a low voice, "I'm mystified about why Child Protective Services claimed endangerment and placed your son in foster care. And I can't understand why this suit was filed in Tyler County and not in Pennsylvania or Ohio." He scanned through more of the paperwork, shaking his head. "I'd say more, but there's a remote chance I'll be sitting on this case."

"I understand, Judge."

"Of course … if you agree that I can share whatever we talk about with the plaintiff and his counsel — then we're fine."

"I only came for one bit of advice, Judge O'Dell. We can't afford a lawyer." She shrugged. "And I don't care if they know that."

He looked up. "We?"

"My fiancé, Ian Stewart, and I."

"You're the only one named in the lawsuit, Laura Ann."

"I know. But we'll be married in twelve days. And we're in this together."

"Admirable. So, no attorney?"

"Every dime goes to pay off my mortgage, sir. It's all I can do."

"Angus would be proud of what you've accomplished, Laura Ann," he said, pointing a pencil her direction. "Very proud."

"Thank you, sir." She folded her hands in her lap. "So, can I win this without a lawyer?"

Judge O'Dell crossed his arms and leaned back in a tall brown leather chair. "No. And yes."

"Excuse me?"

He cleared his throat and thumbed through the papers for a moment. "Child support is a contentious issue in West Virginia family law. The Uniform Parentage Act hasn't been passed here, which makes things a bit more complex. You really do need a child support attorney with experience in adoption and surrogacy, or failing that, a civil attorney. But," he said, rocking back and forth in his chair, "it sounds like you don't have that option. Nevertheless, you need to know that money will figure into the child support discussion." He paused, then added, "Money, and marital status."

"Money? How?"

"Your income, for starters. And what Mr. Mendoza earns.

In other words, can either of you afford to support the child? Can you afford it after you're married? Those questions." He looked at her a long time. "But above all—your age is an issue. At twenty, you're old enough to be a mother, of course, but for custody battles it would be a negative to be young."

He leaned forward, arms on the desk. "You'll have to do your homework, Laura Ann. You understand?"

"I'm ready."

"Okay. Remember, everything I learn here and that I say here goes to both parties." He tapped his pencil on the paperwork. "This is an unusual lawsuit. Normally we consider the child's wishes—but we can't in this case. The alleged father's preferences figure prominently, which is difficult because the gestational mother is deceased and we don't have any way to corroborate his story. On top of that, he's suing the legal guardian for parental rights."

He looked at her for some comment.

*How much does he know? I'm James's mother.*

"Gestational agreements, sperm donor contracts, and probated wills are important, and you have the weight of law in your favor. The court will consider the best interests of the child, including the regularity of prior contact with the alleged father and the guardian. Finally, there's this difficult issue of relocation. He wants to take the child back to his domicile in Cincinnati. You want to stay here. The child really doesn't know the difference, one place or the other."

"He will."

"Perhaps. But not now, and that's all that matters." He smiled. "It's complex, Laura Ann. You really do need a lawyer." Judge O'Dell waved his hand over the papers. "Does any of this help?"

She nodded. "When does the case come up for review, Judge?" Laura Ann forced a smile, burying words that threatened to burst out, berating a legal system that put her through bureaucratic hell. "My child was nursing the day they stole him. Every day he stays in foster care is a day lost bonding with his momma. That's me."

Judge O'Dell spun around to a computer behind him and called up a caseload docket. He shook his head, and then turned back to face her.

"The sixteenth. A week from Thursday." He blinked twice in the silence between them. "Don't give up on a search for someone to represent you. It could make all the difference."

She stood. "Thank you for your advice, sir. We'll be ready."

Laura Ann stepped out of the Tyler County Courthouse into a bright afternoon sun. Like a fresh look at life, something in her stirred. She'd felt it before, what Daddy called his "little voice, the moving of the Spirit." Her spine tingled with anticipation, and something in her felt poised to strike. It made no sense. She was at her most vulnerable, yet somehow she felt a renewed courage, a new optimism that she could beat this challenge. With help.

*With help?*

A black pay phone beckoned her from across the street. She could never pay for his services, but perhaps there was a man who could help. Perhaps he'd do it for Sophia and for James. Laura Ann dashed across Main Street, fondling the few bills in her pocket. With a handful of quarters, she might have a fighting chance. Mr. Brewer, Sophia's executor in Pittsburgh, was only a phone call away.

SEPTEMBER 9

"How much did you know about her?" Stefany asked, stirring

her strawberry milkshake at lunch. Unashamed of her remarkable color, she always had her finger into something red.

Laura Ann looked around Murph's Restaurant for prying eyes. Twelve miles from Middlebourne, Uncle Jack's arm still reached a long way into some parts of Tyler County, perhaps even into Sistersville, Stefany's hometown.

"Everything I shared about Sophia, I learned from her." Laura Ann picked at a hamburger, more interested in Stefany's findings than in her meal.

Stefany raised a red eyebrow. She wiped her mouth and leaned over the table, whispering. "Did you know about her estate?"

Laura Ann shook her head with a shrug of her shoulders. "No. Mr. Brewer said there would be a monthly stipend, but he never said how much. Any little bit helps."

"There's probably a reason he didn't tell," Stefany said with a roll of her eyes, "the same reason Mendoza wants your baby."

"What?"

"I couldn't dig very deep in my few hours in Pittsburgh, but I learned that Sophia sold her interest in the law practice last year, a million-dollar business. Not huge, but significant."

"I'm not after the money, Stef."

"I know. And I'm glad. I also followed some leads in Morgantown and checked out that fertility clinic you used." She dipped her head to take another sip of milkshake, raising an eyebrow. "It's a shady place, honey."

"Why?"

"Did you know they lost their license?"

"No. I mean, how would I?" Laura Ann tried to visualize her paperwork with the clinic, the people she met, and the advertisement she read at the hospital. Nothing stood out.

"I'm sure it's not like keeping a health rating posted at a restaurant," Stefany said. "But I do know this. In the state of

Pennsylvania, where she was a legal resident, there's been a court decision that says any insemination done by an unlicensed facility will not be considered 'artificial insemination.' That means," she said, tapping the side of the glass, "that the sperm donor is automatically considered the legal father of the child."

Laura Ann's mouth fell open. "Wouldn't that also mean —"

"Mean that the egg donor is automatically the mother? Maybe. It's fuzzy. Pennsylvania law rules that a donor has all the accorded rights and responsibilities of a parent. Mendoza could even be forced to pay child support, if you win."

"Wow."

"What I don't figure is why Mendoza didn't file the suit in Pennsylvania. I'm guessing your uncle is pulling the strings, and he's not the brightest light in the lot."

"Don't underestimate him."

"He's cunning," Stefany said, pausing to suck on her straw. "But he's not what you'd call 'book smart.'"

"That's a pretty good assessment," Laura Ann said, sampling a potato chip.

"There's more. I pulled some strings. You didn't sign your privacy agreement at the IVF clinic until after you met Sophia. Why was that?"

"I had so many forms to deal with, Stefany. I didn't know it wasn't signed. But when I met Sophia, and learned how she'd found me, I called the clinic the first chance I had after the flood. They faxed papers to the hospital when we were at Wheeling General. I signed them and sent the package right back." She frowned. "My picture and personal data had been on their website for months advertising eggs from a full-blooded Scot with long brown hair. Even my picture, for crying out loud." She shook her head. "It was horrible. But it's gone now. I made them remove it."

"You might have made your data private but Mendoza sure

290 / NOBODY'S CHILD

didn't. I did a web search on his name. The guy likes being the center of attention. Seems the creep really enjoys being a sperm donor too. He keeps a tally of all the kids he's fathered. It's freaky." She shoved a sheet of paper across the table. "Read this."

Laura Ann took the printout and its words turned her stomach.

> 38-year-old full-blooded Hispanic seeks fertile partners who don't want to mess with the trouble of artificial insemination. 5'9", 165 lb, athletic (runner), well groomed, black hair, brown eyes, physically fit. Attended a military academy, with prior military service, residing in Cincinnati. Laid-back and relaxed, musically inclined. IQ 160. Prefers to help women conceive through natural insemination. Strong credentials as an IVF sperm donor, but enjoys the conception event more than the end result. Will provide services at my place or yours. No emotional or legal baggage. Email address below.

Laura Ann lowered the paper, her eyes wet. "Women turn to men like him to have a baby?"

Stefany reached across the table and laid a hand on hers. "The sad thing is, this weirdo is one of hundreds, Laura Ann. All of them advertising on the web."

She shivered. "That's disgusting."


"I've looked the papers over, Laura Ann. Count us in," Mr. Brewer said an hour later, his voice loud but scratchy on the speaker of her cousin's cell phone. Stefany bounced in the driver's seat of the car while she drove, punching the air with a fist as she rounded a curve on Route 18. In their rearview mirror,

Laura Ann watched the Ohio River fade out of sight as she and Stefany headed toward Middlebourne and the farm.

"Mr. Brewer?"

"Yes?"

"This is Laura Ann's cousin, Stefany. In Pittsburgh I learned that Mendoza has parental rights — because the clinic lost its license before Sophia became pregnant."

The phone went silent for a long moment. "Yes. That's correct."

"Did Sophia know about this before she started the in vitro process?" Stefany asked, driving like she had one eye on the road, the other on the phone that Laura Ann held between them.

"I can't say what she knew and when. But you're right. Pennsylvania is firm on this parental rights issue. That doesn't explain why James was placed in foster care, though."

"We know why," Stefany whispered as she drove.

"Excuse me? I didn't hear all of that."

"My uncle Jack has some strong ties with Child Protective Services." Laura Ann cleared her throat. "Friendship. Maybe money."

"Understatement," Stefany said, her index finger piercing the air like a rapier.

"Well, the good news is that Mendoza filed his suit in West Virginia. I'm licensed with the Bar there, and I'd be glad to support your case." Mr. Brewer spoke to someone in the background at his office, and then asked, "Have you discussed what evidence you're willing to present in court?"

"Yes," Laura Ann replied. "If it's possible, I'd like to win this without revealing that I'm the biological mother. Rumors spread fast here, and I'd rather be remembered as James's adoptive mother. For the baby's sake, for Ian's . . . and for mine."

"I can't promise that strategy will work," Mr. Brewer said.

"Are you willing to prove your parentage if we have to use it to win?"

Laura Ann paused a moment before answering, "Absolutely."

"Good!" Stefany exclaimed, whipping her car around a slow-moving truck. "Let's nail this thing."

Laura Ann looked to the right at Pastor Culpeper's little Baptist church as they passed through the tiny hamlet of Pursley. The chapel's faded white clapboard fried in the midday sun, the green trim of the steeple flaking off like wads of dried moss. Sophia's limestone marker stood stark white against a field of greying stones. The fresh-piled dirt of her grave dried to a burnt umber.

She closed her eyes.

"Of course, my first recommendation would be to lead off with proof of your maternity, Laura Ann, but I understand your concern." Mr. Brewer's voice pulled her back to the present, dashing painful memories of a burial in that churchyard. "I'll help you however I can. The entire staff will—for Sophia and James's sake. And for yours."

# CHAPTER 27

SEPTEMBER 16

Laura Ann's heart raced as she approached the historic Tyler County Courthouse in Middlebourne on Thursday morning. Like the warm Judge O'Dell, something about the 150-year-old place gave her a sense of hope. A steeple rose from the center of the two-story brick and limestone building, its four faces announcing the time in every cardinal direction. A copper wind vane on a green copper roof pointed to the west. The direction of storms.

Ian laid a hand on an old artillery piece as they strode up the courthouse steps, patting it on the side. "We have the ammunition now, Laura Ann," he said, his fist like a gavel on the grey paint of the retired gun.

"Got that right," Stefany replied. "Remember, act natural and pretend you don't see it coming. The Department of Agriculture will have a welcoming committee waiting inside. Federal agents will question your uncle Jack about irregularities with his crop insurance policies. I told them there was a good chance they'd find him here this morning."

"That ought to keep him off-balance," Mr. Brewer said, offering an arm to Stefany when they reached the door. Ian steadied Granny Apple as he held the door open for her and for Laura Ann.

Inside the foyer of the courthouse, Laura Ann spied Uncle Jack, hunkered in a corner, talking to a gathering of friends. Someone whispered *"shhh"* and Uncle Jack's group turned, mouths agape. Perhaps he'd expected one or two people, but Laura Ann strode in with a team of five. He ducked her glance— her uncle the rat.

Halfway across the foyer, their footfalls echoing in the old stone building, she saw his welcoming committee: Stefany's friends from Agriculture and the IRS. Dressed in suits, two men surprised her uncle from behind, one flashing a badge, the other motioning him toward the main door with a firm grip on Uncle Jack's elbow. All attention went from Laura Ann and her team to the agents. The crowd watched her red-faced uncle escorted ingloriously to the door.

Tingles ran down Laura Ann's spine. Someone else watched her. She turned and, to their left, Mr. Mendoza stood with Deputy Rodale. Mendoza's eyes were wide, glancing between her team of five and Uncle Jack headed out of the courthouse with an official escort.

A scant two or three minutes after arriving with Ian, she found her seat in the courtroom, Mr. Brewer and Ian flanking her at an aged oak desk. Stefany and Granny Apple sat behind her on benches that reminded her of church pews. Perched in the equivalent of a choir loft, Laura Ann felt like she was on display.

They'd arrived early. A few people found seats behind her, most of them folks she recognized, no doubt all of them friends of Uncle Jack—and most of them whispering, probably about him. A deputy arranged papers on the judge's bench, preparing for the day's case. Laura Ann said a quiet prayer for James.

"Do you know him?" Mr. Brewer asked, pointing with a

discrete finger in the direction of the lawyer who accompanied Mr. Mendoza into the courtroom.

"No," Laura Ann replied. "Granny Apple said his name is Daniel Whitt."

"I heard he's local," Brewer said. "May have been hired by your uncle, if Stefany's instincts prove correct."

"They usually do," Ian said with a quiet chuckle. "Prove to be correct, I mean. Her cousin's a young Granny Apple." Laura Ann saw him look back. Stefany winked, her red pen raised in a mock salute.

"Ten o'clock." Mr. Brewer looked down at his watch, then back at the gallery. "No crowds. That's good."

"All rise," a deputy bellowed as the judge sauntered through a door at the far left. The room rustled with moving chairs and the *whoosh* of padded seats, then went quiet.

"Judge Dennis O'Dell."

"He wasn't supposed to sit on this case," Laura Ann whispered. "I talked to him at length. Will it be okay?"

"No problem," Mr. Brewer replied. "This may work out well for us."

Judge O'Dell took his seat and motioned everyone to sit down. He conferred for a long time with his deputy, and with a clerk at his right. She ran out, brought back more papers, ran out a second time, and at last, he addressed the courtroom.

"Mr. Mendoza and Mr. Whitt?" he asked, waving in the direction of the oak desk to her right.

"Yes, Your Honor," replied the man next to Mendoza, a medium-height attorney with a starched white shirt. He stood to address the judge.

Judge O'Dell nodded in Laura Ann's direction and rattled off three names. "Mr. Brewer, Ms. McGehee, and Mr. Stewart?"

"Yes, Your Honor," Mr. Brewer replied, standing at their desk.

Judge O'Dell waved his hand again in the direction of the assembled teams. "Counselors, please approach the bench."

Mr. Brewer smiled and pushed back from the table, touching Laura Ann on the forearm. "Here we go. Keep praying."

Both lawyers approached the judge, leaning into a tall wooden bench adorned with carvings on both ends and a thick walnut top. She'd seen this scene on television—but it went nothing like TV. She could hear every word. Perhaps Judge O'Dell wanted it that way.

"Alright, gentlemen. I know you expected Judge Spencer on this case, but Roger's out of circulation for a while. Health issues. I've prepared a summary of the conversations I had with both of your clients over the past week, to keep everything aboveboard." He handed a sheet of paper to each attorney, and then continued. "I think we're clear on any conflict of interest." He looked at both for a response.

"No complaints? Very well. So, let's get right to it." Judge O'Dell leaned forward over the bench. "Mr. Whitt, I've reviewed this case and find that your client has failed to provide evidentiary proof of his alleged parenthood. Do you have state-certified documentation that proves the putative father is in fact the donor in the assisted reproduction of James McGehee McQuistion?"

The lawyer fumbled with some papers, then replied. "Yes, Your Honor. We submitted that as part of the initial filing."

Judge O'Dell pursed his lips. "I see documents from a fertility clinic in Morgantown that state Mr. Mendoza donated his sperm, and more documents from the gestational agreement that affirm Ms. McQuistion requested to be inseminated with the same. But no sperm donor contract in this filing, and nothing that proves he is the true biological father."

"Your Honor, this filing is very clear," Mendoza's lawyer argued. "Clinic records show that Sophia McQuistion chose the plaintiff, Felix Mendoza, as her sperm donor. The physician at the clinic used a fresh semen sample that traced directly back to Mr. Mendoza. She became pregnant through the process of in vitro fertilization, and—"

"I can read, Mr. Whitt," Judge O'Dell quipped. "I don't need a lecture on insemination, thank you."

"I'm sorry, Your Honor," the attorney replied. "Nevertheless, we have solid evidence, as you see, that Ms. McQuistion visited Mr. Mendoza to thank him for his role in her pregnancy. She sought him out as the father of her child."

Judge O'Dell waved his head from side to side. "Do you watch television, Mr. Whitt?" he asked, setting the papers down.

The attorney ran a finger under his collar. "Yes, sir. On occasion."

"Well, let me give you some down-home advice, from a man who loves his recliner and a good TV show. Every day I see this ad for a genetics company out in Utah. It sickens me, to tell you the truth. They offer paternity testing, as if a woman needs a test to tell her who the father of her baby is. But I guess that's where our country is headed. Men and women sleeping around so much they don't know who the baby's daddy is." He stopped, looking out at the audience, then lowered his voice. Even in his quiet tone, Laura Ann could understand him.

"So, you ask, where am I going with this little rant? I'll tell you, Mr. Whitt. You and your client worked some unexplainable magic with our county's social services and ripped a child away from a nursing mother. She'd been in that house caring for that child, not bothering anyone, for a long time before you showed up. I disagree completely with the county's decision to remove the child. Unfortunately, that's their domain, not mine." He frowned, bushy eyebrows furrowed over his glasses. "But your case *is* my domain, and I'm trying to tell you that it's incomplete."

He waved at Mr. Mendoza, and then toward Laura Ann.

"I'm ordering a state DNA test for Mr. Mendoza. You can buy a paternity test over at Prunty's Pharmacy, a block down the street, for a hundred and fifty bucks. I couldn't have accepted it as evidence, but you might have at least tried for some kind of solid proof. You've had plenty of time to prepare your case, and you can't even come to my court ready to argue it?"

He stared at Mr. Whitt, the red of the attorney's neck deepening.

"Yes, Your Honor. We can do that. But we — we'll also need access to the child."

"Agreed. The court orders a state-administered DNA test for the child in foster care, James McGehee McQuistion. The court will coordinate a cheek swab test for the infant. Now, do you think you can come prepared next time?" Judge O'Dell stared down the gun barrel of his nose for a long pause, waiting on the sweating attorney to answer.

Mr. Whitt turned around, glancing toward Mendoza, who shrugged, a bored frown crossing his face. Mr. Whitt turned back to Judge O'Dell. "Yes, sir. We'll need a few weeks."

Judge O'Dell looked back to the papers and started to stack them, then handed the pile of materials to his clerk. He never looked back at Whitt. "No, you won't. I made a trip to the drugstore to read the instructions on the paternity test myself. Doesn't take weeks. Not at the pharmacy and not in my court. Easy as pie, Mr. Whitt, and ninety-nine point nine nine percent accurate. If Mr. Mendoza is the father." His emphasis on the word *if* was impossible to miss.

Judge O'Dell looked up, and then stood in front of the attorneys. "You have one week." He raised a gavel and slammed it into the wooden base on his desk. "Court's in recess until this time next Thursday." He lowered the gavel to the desk and bent over toward Mr. Whitt.

"Don't be late."

SEPTEMBER 17

"You'll never win." Uncle Jack wagged his head, a frown his only expression. "It's Mendoza's kid, so you may as well save your pennies and quit."

Laura Ann sighed. Just her luck to run into her uncle at the Witschey's Market parking lot a day after the scene at the courthouse. Auntie Rose huddled in the front passenger seat of his pickup, hands folded in her lap. Uncle Jack wouldn't let his wife speak, so deep ran his emotional abuse. In the two weeks that James spent at the farm, she'd never heard from her aunt. Not a call, not a visit. "Good or bad, he's my husband, and Jack's the boss," she'd said once. His wishes always came first.

"What makes you think you'll beat me?" Laura Ann asked, moving toward him. An occasional pickup circled past them in the parking lot. With Ian back at work the day before their wedding, and she afoot with bags of groceries in her arms, she battled her uncle alone.

"Beat *me*?" Uncle Jack asked with a laugh. "It's not about me. That suit was filed by the Mendoza guy."

"Everything's about you," Laura Ann shot back. "I know how Mendoza found out about Sophia. You located him and brought him here. You bribed the child protection office to take my son away. You're in this paternity suit up to your ears."

Uncle Jack fidgeted. "You have no proof."

"Proof? I have witnesses, Uncle Jack. You were at the hospital in Wheeling, digging around to find some dirt to give you leverage." She gripped her bags tighter. "The nurses told us."

"This is a waste of time. Just remember who offered you a way out of that mortgage." He put the truck in gear, leering at her, his face flushed. "You snooze, you lose."

Laura Ann shifted the grocery load in her arms again, sweaty palms threatening her grip on the paper bags. "Then you'd better not sleep, Uncle Jack. 'Cause I'm on to you."

He hesitated just a moment, but she could see it in his darting eyes: the squint. His dread that she really did know of his role and would make it public.

But that wasn't what she meant.

Proof of her maternity would trump Mendoza. Question was, could she muster the courage to share it?

# CHAPTER 28

"Forget it, lover boy," Stefany said, pushing Ian through the doors of the church. "You're not supposed to see the bride before she enters." Laura Ann stifled a laugh, watching through a space in the door that led out the side of the reception area at the front of Pastor Culpeper's church. She kept the door barely cracked, sure that her game-tracking soon-to-be husband would find her out. Stefany pulled his attention in the opposite direction, and gave him another shove toward the chapel.

"Come on, Stef. Don't get superstitious on me," Ian objected, dragging his feet while Stefany prodded him into the church. "Laura Ann and I were going to walk down the aisle together."

She laughed, and made one more valiant attempt to get him through the double doors at the front of the little Baptist church in Pursley. Ian complied, and when he turned his back, Stefany threw a wink in Laura Ann's direction. "No can do," she said. "Get up there with Pastor Culpeper. Mrs. C is going to play the piano and I'll follow your lovely bride with the flowers. Now scram!"

Ian saluted Laura Ann's redheaded tempest of a cousin, and marched through the doors. Stefany gave a thumbs-up sign.

Laura Ann dashed in the side entrance, peering through narrow windows in the main doors to watch him stride down the aisle. Granny Apple, Pastor Culpeper, and his wife Pamela waited at the front of the church, a standing ovation of three. One witness, Granny. One pastor. And one pianist. Just enough, and not a day too soon. Clad in his new suit, Ian reached the front of the church, beaming.

"Good job!" Laura Ann said with a high-five to Stefany, her redheaded relative decked out in the prettiest dress Laura Ann could remember seeing. Except for what she had on ... her Momma's wedding gown.

"No problem. He may be a lawman, but he's still just a guy. You ready?"

"I've been ready, Stefany. For a very long time," Laura Ann said, touching her cousin's forearm.

"No regrets?" Stefany asked, a hand on the door.

"None."

Stefany wiped at her eyes, releasing the door just a moment to arrange something on Laura Ann's white gown, an elegant but simple throwback to the grace of a bygone era, a return to simpler times. "You're beautiful," she said, brushing back one of Laura Ann's bangs. "Just so you know, I envy you. Ian. The farm. Something stable."

"Envy *me*?" Laura Ann exclaimed.

"Uh-huh," she said with a little laugh. "I know I bounce around a bunch, full of energy and all. But a lot of it's just a show, cousin. There's a part of me, a part that grows bigger every day, that just wants to settle down. Wants to find someone," she said, her voice drifting off, a hand adjusting Laura Ann's tiny veil.

"And you will, Stef." Laura Ann leaned forward and gave her a hug. "But don't envy me too much. Next week I'm back in a courtroom, fighting for James." A shadow passed over her face. "Maybe more."

Stefany nudged her. "That's in the future. But you're here now, girlfriend, and it's your wedding day. Mr. Wonderful is waiting for you at the end of that aisle!"

Laura Ann took a peek through the windows again, the piano accompaniment by Pamela her cue to start walking. But something remained unsaid. She wiped at her eyes, determined that this be her happy day.

"God put you here for me. You know that, right?"

Stefany shrugged. "We've had that conversation," she said, her smile fading. "You know how I feel about all that stuff. Let's don't go back there."

"I know. But with the music playing, and Ian waiting, I still need you to know something."

Stefany shrugged and Laura Ann took her hands in her own.

"You see things that most people don't, Stefany. In people. In situations. You might not realize it, but you're like a key — you unlock secrets. You help people." She pulled their clasped hands up, drawing her cousin close. "You helped me."

Stefany's smile returned with a silent nod that said "thanks."

Laura Ann released her embrace. She took a deep breath, adjusting her veil, then pushed on the door. "You ready?" she asked.

"Got your back, cousin. Lead on."

SEPTEMBER 23

Laura Ann pressed Ian's hand. From honeymoon to courtroom. The wonder of their two days away in Parkersburg seemed so very distant. Like ripping off a scab, every moment of this trial drew pain.

"How did you learn of Ms. McQuistion's death?" Mr. Brewer asked, leaning into a walnut rail that stretched around the witness box in Judge O'Dell's courtroom. Felix Mendoza squirmed on the stand, half an hour into the questioning by Laura Ann's attorney.

"Relevance?" Mr. Whitt blurted out, his hands raised.

"Relationship to the deceased, Judge," Mr. Brewer answered without looking up.

"Proceed." Judge O'Dell waved him on as Mr. Whitt lowered his head.

"She came to thank me for knocking her up." Mendoza's eyes darted about the room, avoiding Laura Ann's glare. "Me and her, we were tight."

"You got her pregnant?"

"That's what I just said."

"And you say you were close? In a relationship kind of way?" Mr. Brewer asked.

Mendoza shrugged.

"I'll rephrase. How did you learn of Ms. McQuistion's death? You were 'tight' as you say, yet you never visited her in the hospital, she made no calls to Cincinnati during her stay in Wheeling, and you never called her." He lifted some of his own papers, pointing to the judge's desk. "Exhibit seven, judge. Ms. McQuistion's cellular and hospital phone records."

Judge O'Dell nodded and waved him on.

"So, I repeat. How exactly did you learn of her death?"

Mendoza shrugged again. "Through a friend." His eyes searched the courtroom gallery, then went back to Brewer.

"Did you visit her, or provide any manner of support during the hospitalization for her heart problem?"

"Heart problem?"

"You weren't aware of her rheumatic fever?"

"No."

"But we heard from Ms. McGehee—I mean, Mrs. Stewart—that she cared for Ms. McQuistion for the better part of a month, at home and in the hospital, through her last month of pregnancy, a month complicated by heart disease."

"Again, Judge, what's the relevance?" Mr. Whitt protested, standing at his desk.

"Relationship with the deceased, Your Honor, and justification for the decision about who would care for her child." Mr. Brewer faced the judge. "Ms. McQuistion chose Mrs. Stewart as a guardian for her son, a woman who demonstrated extraordinary sacrifice to support the deceased during her last days. From Mr. Mendoza's own testimony, he had no idea Ms. McQuistion ever experienced any heart problems, nor did he ever take the initiative to contact her, or provide material support."

"What difference does it make?" Mendoza asked, turning toward the judge and raising his hands in exasperation. "I fathered that kid."

"Please, just answer the questions, Mr. Mendoza. Anything else, Mr. Brewer?"

"One more line of questioning, Your Honor. Mr. Mendoza, do you live in Cincinnati?"

"Of course I do."

"State, for the record, your height, weight, and educational background, please."

"Judge!" Mr. Whitt exclaimed.

"Mr. Brewer?"

"In the absence of a sperm donor contract, Your Honor, I can establish, without question, that Mr. Mendoza had no interest in legal guardianship of this child, or for any other children he might have fathered as a donor."

"Proceed."

"Okay. I'm five foot nine, one hundred sixty-five pounds. I attended the US Air Force Academy."

"Did you graduate?"

Mendoza delayed, looking down at his feet, and then answered, "No."

"State your email address and phone number."

Mendoza replied with clipped words, his eyes darting from Mr. Brewer to Mr. Whitt and back.

"Thank you. I'd like to submit an additional exhibit, Your Honor. A copy of a posting on the Internet by a party whose data matches the testimony of Mr. Mendoza—exactly." He lifted a sheet of paper up to the judge who reviewed it, his eyebrows raised, then handed it back.

"Mr. Mendoza," Brewer asked, "did you compose this posting on the Internet? It lists your email and phone number, just as you've testified."

Mendoza took the paper, glancing at it for a moment, then gulped.

"Mr. Mendoza?"

He nodded, silent.

"Mr. Mendoza motions assent that this is his posting, an Internet advertisement in which he promotes his role as a qualified sperm donor. That document states, in part," Mr. Brewer said, turning to face the gallery, "that he seeks mutually fulfilling passionate experiences with women who seek to be inseminated, absent any emotional or legal baggage." He turned back to face the judge. "I question, why is it, Mr. Mendoza, that you have no interest, as a sperm donor, in what you term 'legal baggage,' yet today you're here in Tyler County petitioning for custody of a child you purported to father?"

Mendoza shrugged with a loud exhale, shaking his head. His frown deepened by the minute.

"No more questions, Your Honor." Mr. Brewer moved back

to his desk. He whispered to Laura Ann as he settled into the old oak chair. "We haven't won this yet."

Judge O'Dell dismissed the witness, paged through his materials, and then addressed Mr. Whitt. "We've heard some interesting circumstantial evidence from your team today, Counselor. But we have yet to review the results of your client's paternity test."

Whitt turned to Mendoza and conferred, whispering behind hands that shielded their mouths. Behind them, a door clicked.

Laura Ann looked back, feeling a rush of air into the room. In the open door stood Uncle Jack, slipping into a seat on the back row. She tapped Ian's shoulder, and he spun around. All eyes turned to follow his, Uncle Jack wilting under the glare of court observers.

She turned back to face the judge, breathing deep and gripping her hands while she willed her heart to slow. Her face felt hot, the sounds about her fading into a memory.

In her mind's eye, Daddy sat on the porch steps, his arms resting on his knees. "Don't ever fear the truth, Peppermint," he said that day. She couldn't remember how old she was, or what season he'd said it. Just Daddy in his overalls, speaking his mind. "Stand up for truth, no matter what the cost."

Laura Ann looked up, the judge tapping his pen on his desk while the two men to her right conferred. When he spoke, he growled.

"I'll ask again, and only once more, Counselor Whitt. Do you intend to submit the state DNA test as evidence of paternity? Yes or no?"

Mr. Whitt turned to face Judge O'Dell, standing as he prepared to speak. He gulped, looked down at Mr. Mendoza, then back up at the judge. "Yes, Your Honor. We do."

"Then may I see it?"

Mr. Whitt stood and carried a package to the front. "In

support of my client's case, Your Honor, certified results for DNA analysis of Mr. Felix Mendoza, conducted by the State of West Virginia. Probability of paternity, 99.98 percent." He faced Laura Ann. "My client is the biological father of the child James McQuistion."

He turned, seeking out a face in the back of the room, and smiled. He looked back at Laura Ann and her team, raising an eyebrow, then returned to his seat.

Judge O'Dell reviewed the case file, nodded, and handed the materials to his clerk. "It's about time."

"Your Honor?" another voice asked.

Judge O'Dell looked up to face Mr. Brewer. The attorney stood at Laura Ann's side, a manila folder in his had. She glanced at Ian, who nodded, a small smile on his face. Behind him, Stefany punched the air with her fist.

"The defense wishes to recall a witness, Mrs. Laura Ann Stewart. To allow evidence in rebuttal."

Mr. Whitt sat up in his chair, shaking his head. He looked to the back again, a clear connection with Uncle Jack.

Judge O'Dell sat back and took off his glasses, then answered. "Proceed." A head nod between the two of them communicated some unspoken message, and the judge waved her in his direction. "Mrs. Stewart?"

Laura Ann stood up, a lingering grip on Ian's hand before she walked to the front and mounted the witness stand. Seated above the rest of the court, but slightly below the judge, she saw the room from a completely different perspective. When she testified the first time, two hours ago, her heart slammed in her chest. This time, even with Uncle Jack glaring at her from the back of the room, a gentle calm overwhelmed her.

*Secrets don't become you, child.* Granny Apple's wisdom floated back, like a thought tossed across the room from her elderly friend sitting in the gallery. *You can do it.*

Mr. Brewer approached the bench. "There's one more item of evidence I wish to submit for review, Your Honor. And after this witness, an additional witness I wish to call." He handed a file folder to the judge. After a brief glance, the judge sat up a little straighter, turning to face her on the stand.

"You don't have to do this, Laura Ann," Judge O'Dell said.

"I want to, sir," she said. "I need to."

"As you wish." Judge O'Dell held the file out, motioning toward Mr. Whitt. When he shared the papers with Mendoza's attorney, the lawyer dropped the papers on his oak desk, dumbfounded. She watched the reaction as Mendoza picked up the file, wagging his head in disbelief.

The bailiff swore her in, and Mr. Brewer approached the stand, smiling. "Laura Ann Stewart, who is the biological mother of the child, James McGehee McQuistion?"

Judge O'Dell furrowed his brow, lowering his head to look over his glasses. Laura Ann faced Ian for a brief moment, his smile of affirmation spurring her on.

"I am the biological mother."

Laura Ann heard Uncle Jack's trademark *harrumph* in the back of the room. He launched up from his seat, a fist raised. "No!"

Judge O'Dell pointed a bony finger toward her uncle. "Order in my court, Jack Harris. Or I'll lock you up for contempt — in your own brother's jail." The judge let his command settle the room, then he leaned forward, both hands on the bench. He nodded to Mr. Brewer.

"Your Honor, I submit as evidence of maternity a state-certified DNA test, based on a blood sample drawn last Thursday."

He handed the paper to the clerk, who read aloud. "Combined parentage index 153.435. Probability of maternity 99.954 percent. Laura Ann McGehee, probable mother. James M. McQuistion, child."

Judge O'Dell shook his head, his mouth agape.

Mr. Brewer continued. "Laura Ann, state for the court how you came to be the biological mother of this child."

She took a deep breath, keeping her eyes locked on Ian. "Daddy and I needed money. He didn't know it, but I volunteered to be an egg donor at the Morgantown Fertility Clinic." She shivered, then continued. "I donated sixty-eight eggs over the course of four visits. What they call 'harvests.' Ms. McQuistion became pregnant using some of the eggs donated on my first trip." She bit her lip, closing her eyes a moment to recapture her calm, then continued. "She chose me using an Internet profile that was posted on the clinic website, and later came to Middlebourne to thank me for my role in her pregnancy." She pointed toward Mendoza. "Like she did with the other donor. I'd never met her until that day, nor did I know she had chosen me. But ..."

Mr. Brewer waited for her to finish the sentence, moving to the rail to encourage her.

"But it rained. On June twenty-fourth. Because of the flood, she couldn't leave, and stayed with me for a few days. We became friends, and when she got sick, Ian — my husband, but we were courting at the time — helped me take her to the hospital. After she'd been there a while, she asked me if I would consent to be the guardian for her son."

Judge O'Dell lowered his glasses from his nose and let out a low chuckle. He lifted up the stack of papers on his desk and slid them into a brown leather pouch.

Laura Ann looked at the judge, then continued. "Ms. McQuistion passed away due to heart complications," she said, biting her lip as she struggled with the words. "And her baby — James — was born premature about an hour before she died. I waited for him to be released, and met with a lactation consultant to help me nurse the child. That about summarizes it."

"One more question, Laura Ann," Mr. Brewer said, his hand

resting on the rail of the witness stand. "Was anyone else, other someone at the fertility clinic, aware of your egg donation at the time Ms. McQuistion would have become pregnant?"

Laura Ann shook her head. "No. I told no one."

"Thank you." He turned to the judge. "No more questions, Your Honor."

The judge faced Mr. Whitt, sweat beading on the attorney's brow. "Cross examine?"

Whitt shook his head, fumbling with some papers. Mr. Mendoza uttered an expletive, pushing back from the table, and some more words Laura Ann could not hear when he moved closer to his attorney.

"You may step down, Mrs. Stewart. Mr. Mendoza, another outburst like that and I'll hold you in contempt as well."

As Laura Ann made her way to the table aside Ian, Mr. Brewer approached the bench. "Your Honor, the defense wishes to call our last witness." He handed a package and briefing sheet to the judge, who shared a copy with the clerk. He handed a separate copy to Mr. Whitt. "Ms. Maggie Clark, erstwhile of the Morgantown Fertility Clinic."

Mendoza's attorney threw his hands up, blurting out his question again. "Relevance?"

Judge O'Dell looked back at Mr. Brewer for an answer.

"Your Honor, we will establish the extraordinary personal sacrifice of my client in her role as donor and biological mother for the child."

"Proceed."

A few gasps arose about the courtroom when a woman stood in the audience and walked out of the gallery toward the witness stand. Laura Ann lowered her head a bit, then raised her chin, determined to endure this. For James. And for Sophia.

"Please state your name and city of residence," Mr. Brewer said, once she'd been sworn in.

"Maggie Clark, of Morgantown, West Virginia."

"Ms. Clark, are you married?"

"I am not."

"And your employer in November of last year?"

"I was a nurse serving as a reproductive specialist and nurse anesthetist at the Morgantown Fertility Clinic, on the staff of Dr. Alexandros Katinakis."

"Thank you. Have you met Mrs. Stewart before?" he asked, motioning to Laura Ann.

"I have. She was single then. I served as the attending nurse at three of her harvesting sessions."

Laura Ann winced at the term, but kept her back straight. Ian put his hand on her forearm, a squeeze of affirmation. They would endure this together.

"Is Mrs. Stewart the mother of James McGehee McQuistion, based on the records as you knew them at the time?"

"She is. The clinic has been closed, however. I do not have the donor records in my possession."

"Objection!" Mr. Whitt exclaimed, standing up.

"Sustained."

"Alright. Let's explore another line of questioning, Ms. Clark. Do you have any children?"

"I do. I was infertile for many years before my divorce, but successfully carried a daughter to term as a result of in vitro fertilization. Dr. Katinakis was my physician."

"Relevance?" Mr. Whitt said, bounding up.

"Continue," the judge said, waving him on.

"And did you select the biological mother for your pregnancy?"

"I did." She looked in Laura Ann's direction. "I chose Mrs. Stewart. Her name then was McGehee."

Gasps arose around the court gallery, another two or three people peeking into the court, then taking a seat near the back.

Laura Ann's shivers ran from her spine to the tips of her

fingers, a shaking she could barely quell. She'd heard this pronouncement before. But Maggie's words cut just as deep now as they did last night when Mr. Brewer introduced her over dinner.

*I have a daughter.*

Ian's hand gripped her tight, his assurance so steady, so firm. She clung to her husband, her rock. Surely this revelation pierced him to the core ... yet he never flinched. More people slipped into the courtroom amid loud murmurs.

"Order," Judge O'Dell said.

"Why did you choose Mrs. Stewart? I mean, Miss McGehee?"

"She was attractive, relatively tall, and physically fit. Her IQ test scores were high, and she seemed so stable and strong. She told us her story, about how she was donating her eggs to raise money to help her father. It made me cry."

"And Ms. Clark, can you tell us why you left the employment of the Morgantown Fertility Clinic, prior to their losing their license?"

"I can." She straightened up, taking a deep breath. "I learned that two of our donors died — our patients. For various reasons, but neither of them during the performance of our care."

Laura Ann looked down in her lap, shaking her head. Ian put his arm around her. Mr. Brewer let the courtroom quiet a bit, then continued.

"Some of your donors died?"

"Yes. One girl suffered seizures as a result of the surgery soon after her third harvest. She moved away after the second trip to our clinic, and we asked her to fly back to Morgantown for a third donation. She came. But I learned later," Maggie said, her chin quivering, "that she passed away soon after. We heard it was natural causes. But I discovered, through her family, that she'd suffered a stroke." She coughed, and continued. "There was strong evidence that her drug regimen, to induce the hyperstimulation of her ovaries, may have been responsible when acting in combination with a tumor she had, but did not know about. A second client passed away from internal complications after commencing a Pergonal drug regimen, also to stimulate her ovaries."

"Objection," Mr. Whitt said. "Circumstantial evidence. We're not trying Dr. Katinakis here, or fertility treatments."

"Agreed," the judge said. "Mr. Brewer?"

"Ms. Clark, as a reproductive specialist and attending nurse, please summarize for the court the procedure and the medical complications that you presented to each egg donor before her, as you say, ovary harvesting event."

"The egg harvest is accomplished using one of two methods. An ultrasound-guided aspiration is a minor surgical procedure done under intravenous analgesia — sedation for pain control. An ultrasound probe is inserted through the vagina to image the swollen follicles of the patient's ovaries. A needle is guided through the walls of the vagina into the follicle and the ripened egg is suctioned out. In some rare cases — and this happened for Mrs. Stewart's first harvest — we have to guide the needle though the patient's abdominal wall, or through her bladder. In more severe cases, we use general anesthesia and laparoscopic surgery through an incision below the patient's navel."

"And Mrs. Stewart's harvests?"

"All of them were of the first type, sir. Intravaginal ultrasound, in two of my three sessions with her, with no penetration of the abdomen except the first time."

"What kind of impact does that procedure have on the woman?" Mr. Brewer asked.

"Nausea, bleeding, cramping, mild weight gain, and diarrhea are not unusual," she said, looking back at Laura Ann. "I know that Mrs. Stewart experienced some of these symptoms because we spoke about it. Those were the usual complications that we mentioned in the safety briefing."

"Is that all?"

"No. Bloating, swelling, and distended abdomens are common for some women. More serious complications include Ovarian Hyperstimulation Syndrome, or OHSS, as an aftermath of the drug regimen used to stimulate egg release. The ovaries become dangerously enlarged with fluid and can leak into the abdomen, with serious complications."

"Have you witnessed this in your patients?"

"Yes, sir. In some."

"Other problems?"

"Some women — we think it's a small percentage — have experienced significant scarring of the ovaries as a result of the harvesting events, particularly if they have provided more than one donation. In extreme cases, infertility can result due to damage to the ovary. Some medical studies report an increased probability of ovarian cancer, as well as suspected ties to breast and uterine cancers. These effects are still under evaluation, of course. Unfortunately, there's a tendency in this industry to publish only positive findings, and — "

"And?"

"Well, it's new and fast-moving technology, and there's not a very good way yet to follow up on the long-term health impacts of the drug regimens or harvesting events. A girl might donate today, but a year from now, or five years from now, she moves on to a new town, and finds she's infertile, or has cancer. We don't always make the connection."

"I'd like you to examine this issue from another angle, Ms. Clark. Can you share with us, from a clinical perspective, what are the impacts of egg or sperm donation on the person who is formed as a result of these donated gametes?"

Maggie took a deep breath, wiping her hand in a quick pass across a glistening cheek. She sat bolt upright, stronger than Laura Ann thought possible were she in her shoes. "The studies are still formative. Nevertheless, clinical evidence shows that donor off-spring are twice as likely to be in trouble with the law before age twenty-five, and one and a half times more likely to develop identity crises, depression, even mental illness. Why? Perhaps it's a result of their concerns about their—how do I say this?—complicated origins. What some mistakenly call a 'freak of nature' or 'a lab experiment.' Then again, perhaps it's a lack of grounding in family roots, or some angst about why the parent *paid* to buy the sperm or eggs to create them. I've heard the story, from more than one client, of donor offspring who asked their surrogate mother, 'Did you buy me?' "

"Why then, in your opinion, would Ms. McQuistion seek out Mr. Mendoza and Mrs. Stewart?"

"Objection! Conjecture, Your Honor."

"I'll allow it. Go ahead, Ms. Clark."

She nodded at the judge, took another deep breath, and continued. "For the same reason I sought her out when I learned about this lawsuit from some coworkers I knew at the clinic. To tell my daughter more about the wonderful woman who sacrificed so much to make her life possible. To give my baby girl those roots. That's why I chose her eggs in the first place, and it's why I agreed to come here today—and that's not conjecture. It's my story." She stared long at Mr. Whitt, then turned her attention back to Mr. Brewer.

"Do you continue to work as a reproductive specialist, Ms. Clark?"

"I do not." She pursed her lips, then continued. "The more I learned, the less I liked it."

"And Ms. Clark, based on your prior experience as a nurse in this industry, if your daughter were of age to make an egg donation for altruistic purposes—or for money—would you recommend it?"

Maggie wagged her head, a deep frown gathering as she expelled two words with force. "Absolutely not."

"Thank you. One more question. For the sperm donor, what are the medical side effects of a man donating a sample?"

She chuckled, looking around the room, then to the judge, a bit red-faced. "Side effects? I mean, none that I know of. The donors are provided a room with some — some pornographic movies and magazines, you know? And a sample cup. But side effects?" She shrugged.

"Did Mr. Mendoza provide samples at your clinic?" he asked, pointing toward the desk with Mr. Whitt.

Maggie nodded. "Yes. He was a frequent client." She smiled, then added, "He never complained."

"Objection!"

"Mr. Brewer?" Judge O'Dell asked.

"No further questions, Your Honor. The defense rests."

Mr. Brewer returned to the oak table where Laura Ann and Ian waited. She bent at the waist, her hands clasped together, a mental agony pummeling her insides. The sordid testimony about James's father, the explicit sexual references, and the thought of her genes joined in some way with Felix Mendoza all turned her stomach. Mr. Brewer put a gentle hand on her shoulder as he sat down, then withdrew it. Ian's arm threaded around her, pulling her close.

Laura Ann looked up as Mendoza and Whitt conferred with whispers to her right. For a long time, an uncomfortable silence hung over the court. She heard the rustle of a robe and looked up. The judge shifted about, moving some papers into his satchel.

"Well, I think we're about done here," Judge O'Dell said.

"Your Honor?" Mr. Whitt exclaimed, turning away from Mr. Mendoza, his hands raised in the air. "What is this?"

"I said, we're done, Mr. Whitt. Based on the evidence submitted by your client, and by Mrs. Stewart, in consideration of the legally binding and probated will of the deceased Ms. Sophia McQuistion, and after that enlightening evaluation of the medical risks of Mrs. Stewart's egg donation, the court finds in favor of the defendant, Laura Ann McGehee Stewart, legal guardian—and certified biological mother—of the child James McGehee McQuistion."

"What?" Mr. Mendoza exclaimed, jumping up from his chair.

"Sit down, Counselor," Judge O'Dell ordered. "Yes, the plaintiff did establish paternity. The defendant, however, has proven that she is not only the legal guardian, but is also the biological mother of this child. In addition, she may have experienced a significant risk to her health in order to donate genetic material to the deceased. The defendant has established a clear and compelling case for parental rights, in accordance with the laws of the State of West Virginia."

Judge O'Dell shook his head. "This beats anything I've ever seen. It's time to go home, folks. The court rules for the defendant. Clerk of the court, please inform Child Protective Services I'll be giving them a call. It's time to get that baby back in his mother's arms."

Judge O'Dell slammed his gavel into the desk. "Court is adjourned."

Eagles took wing, gliding on high currents of cool air above a cliff of books and along sheer walls of pictures. An aviary came to life in her imagination, seated in Judge O'Dell's eagle-strewn chambers an hour after the trial.

"Angus would be so proud of you," Judge O'Dell said, leaning forward on his elbows, his hands clasped where they supported his chin in thought. "You didn't have to do that. You might have won it based on your care for Sophia, and the probated will."

"Maybe," she said, her smile so wide it gave her cramps in her temples. "But I'm tired of carrying that secret."

"Why? I mean, why'd you do it?" Judge O'Dell asked.

"Submit for the maternity test?"

"Gracious, no. Maybe it's a little personal, but humor me. I heard what you said in there, but why donate your eggs? With all those risks?" He tilted his head in the cradle of his hands, waiting.

"Other than the bloating and pain, they didn't tell me about the rest of the physical complications. They advertised a big payment. But it wasn't what I was paid. I needed the money for medical and bank bills. And it kept us going—for a while." Her voice drifted off, and she looked down. "Four thousand dollars on my first visit. A few hundred dollars on my last visit when they couldn't harvest enough eggs. Then I stopped going."

The judge listened, all ears, not pushing her.

"I wanted to get this story out in the open, to be free of all the secrets." She shrugged. "I don't care what people think. I'd rather they knew I took a stand."

He nodded, a patient listening ear. Laura Ann could hear the screech of eagles, winging their way across the void of his office, free at last.

"I learned something very important in all of this," she said, taking Ian's hand where it dangled by her shoulder. Judge O'Dell raised an eyebrow, waiting.

"Actions have consequences. I sold part of myself to save Daddy and the farm. But that little decision affected many lives, and not all of them for the good."

Judge O'Dell wiped at his eyes, then continued. "I'm glad

for Ms. McQuistion—and for you—that she had you in her life, Laura Ann. The way I see it, these challenges you've overcome in the past months represent a sort of extended detour, a byway on a long road that leads from grace to strength." He cocked his head to the side. "But somehow, I suspect that detour is not yet finished. There are other Sophia McQuistions and Maggie Clarks out there—and surely another James."

The judge took a long breath, his bushy eyebrows furrowed in thought. "This is all very new to me. You know, I read about these issues, but they've never hit this close to home." He leaned back in the chair, hands laced behind his head.

"Your actions and this case raise some tough questions. Is a child a gift from God?" he wondered aloud. "Or have babies simply become some kind of commodity?"

Staring upward in thought, his eyes focused on the eagles that circled above, winging on the winds of change.

# CHAPTER 29

OCTOBER 1

The lobby of Tyler County Bank reminded Laura Ann of a bee-
hive. Or an anthill. A steady stream of people filed in and out
of the bank, most of them here because of the confluence of
lunchtime, a payday Friday, and the first of the month. Payments
came due, checks waited to be cashed, certificates of deposit
rolled over. Clerks moved from desk to desk, the bank's three
officers negotiating, approving, and cajoling. Laura Ann stood
on the edge of the fray, her son in her arms, and a wad of cash in
her pocket. The time had come.

Her last trip. Except for the miraculous support of Sophia,
Ian, and Granny Apple, the farm would have gone to the bank a
long time ago. The McGehee account would be emptied today.
She was a Stewart now, part of a proud clan.

Baby James stirred, bundled in his cotton blanket, fast
asleep. She needed to move quickly in the bank, get the loan
paid, and get home. She couldn't nurse him here.

Finally her turn came at the teller. Laura Ann approached
the woman, someone she'd never met. "I came to pay on my
mortgage." Laura Ann fished a wad of more than a hundred
twenty-dollar bills from her front pocket, one hand securing

321

James, the other clutching the cash surrounded by a rubber band and note with her loan number. "For this account," she said, pointing to some writing on the wrapper.

The teller nodded, took the cash, and whipped through it in rapid fashion, her rubber-coated thumb expert with the bills. She typed a number in the computer at her station and waited, then typed again.

"Are you sure this is the correct loan number?" she asked, sliding the money back in Laura Ann's direction.

"Yes. Why?"

The teller shrugged, typed the number in again, and replied, "I'm sorry, but could you wait for a moment over there, ma'am"—she glanced at the screen—"Ms. McGehee."

"It's Stewart. McGehee was my maiden name." Laura Ann's heart skipped again, like it had last Thursday when Uncle Jack stepped into the courtroom. Even though he sat in jail now, under arrest for fraud, his connivings still spooked her. "I don't understand. What's the problem?" Laura Ann asked, shaking off the memory of her uncle and his sticky threads that ran through the mountain hamlet of Middlebourne.

"My system says that there's been a change to your account, not related to the name change. You'll need to talk to a loan officer. It will be just a minute." She directed Laura Ann to a chair.

James whimpered, his stomach growing empty after a lunch two hours ago. Laura Ann kissed his forehead, her heart pounding, and prayed for some path to resolution, whatever this latest financial concern.

"Miss McGehee?"

She looked up to see an older gentleman she had met when Daddy first set up the loan.

"I'm Joe Emerson, Laura Ann. Your father and I went to school together."

Frustrated with the delays, and James's stirrings, she cut her words short. "Hello, Mr. Emerson. I tried to make a payment on my loan," she said, handing him the stack of bills, "but the teller won't take it. Is there a problem? I've changed my name—I got married," she said, holding up her ring finger. "But that doesn't seem to be the problem."

Mr. Emerson shook his head. "No. But there is something you need to know. About your account."

Mr. Emerson ushered her into his office. After rummaging through a file cabinet, he retrieved a large envelope, then slipped some papers out and handed them to her. "I'll need your signature," he said with a widening smile.

"What?" she asked, scanning the papers. More legalese.

"You may keep your money," Mr. Emerson said, sliding her cash into a sleeve and sealing it. He set the money near her on the edge of the desk, and then placed a pen in front of her. "But we'll need your signature."

"For what?"

His smile disarmed her. Laura Ann flushed, then riffled through the paperwork. On the second page, a large red label ran at an angle across the document, marked "PAID."

Mr. Emerson handed her a small envelope. "A benefactor paid your loan off last month. Her attorney asked that we give this to you the next time you came to the bank." The note read "Laura Ann."

Tears swelled in her eyes as she held the envelope in shaking hands. "Thank you," she stammered. "I don't know what else to say."

Mr. Emerson met her gaze. "We all know what you did, to save the farm and your baby. And," he said, "to uncover the fraud. You made us proud." He folded the loan paperwork and handed it to her.

"Your debt is paid in full."

———————

Back on the farm, with the baby fed and laid down for a nap, Laura Ann settled into a rocker on the porch. Tears gathering in her eyes, she carefully opened the envelope and slid out the note. As she read, a tear fell, swirling with wisps of purple, dissolving the ink of a gentle cursive. Laura Ann's hands trembled as she held the dainty card, forcing her tear to run across lines, a snail trail of wet pain running down the length of the message. A message that stole her heart.

> *Dear Laura Ann,*
>
> *You sold the gift of life to heal your father. You gave me new life and brought us both a son. You took me in as a friend, even though I was a stranger invading your special private world. I am praying for you and for our child. Your road will not be easy; I know that mine was not.*
>
> *Perhaps with this gift, you will never again need to forfeit part of your body to save someone else. I have found my dream through you—through the sacrifices you made for your father and for me, through your loving care, and through your indomitable spirit.*
>
> *As I write this my own heart is failing, Laura Ann. But you have enough heart for both of us. For the three of us.*
>
> *Hug our baby for me. I love you.*
>
> *Sophia*

# EPILOGUE

### DECEMBER 25

Up before sunrise on Christmas Day, Laura Ann laid her pen down on the kitchen table and read her own words, a new page in the leather-bound journal she'd first opened a year ago today. Ian and James slept, a few minutes remaining before her husband's usual five-thirty feeding in the barn.

> *Dear Daddy,*
>
> *It's Christmas Day, a year since my last letter. So much has happened. Where do I start?*
>
> *You remember Ian, his Saturday visits every week, helping out around the farm when he wasn't at school or at work. Ian's here every day now. I'm his bride. You were right. He'd been courting me for years and I was too blind to see it. We were married in September, at the Baptist church in Pursley. You'd have loved it. He took me to the Blennerhassett for our wedding night. It was beautiful.*
>
> *Granny Apple is still going strong. She opened up a red one-room schoolhouse, like the one you attended. She takes in homeschoolers whose parents want a return to what she calls the "old ways." And guess what? Auntie Rose is in there*

*with her, teaching and cleaning. They live together now. Granny Apple needs a little help, Auntie Rose needs a little company, and Uncle Jack is no more. He and Phyllis McIntosh wrote fraudulent crop policies for farmers who'd passed away. But you beat him at his game. He paid someone to burn our tobacco barn, and the claim he filed against it brought him down. He found a lonely one-room concrete apartment with some guards and an iron door. He'll probably be there for a long time. Phyllis too.*

*Remember Stefany? She's famous. She busted Uncle Jack's insurance fraud cases and many more related to a big flood that we had in June. You'd have hated it. The flood, I mean. It devastated West Union and Middlebourne. The water went up thirty feet at The Jug crossing and washed it out. That took months to repair, and they opened the new causeway after our wedding (and just in time for hunting season). It's nice being married to a game warden. No one comes out here to drink and shoot at night anymore.*

*I have a son, Daddy. We named him for you and I carved a new chain this year. His full name is James McGehee McQuistion Stewart. It's very Scottish. You'd love it. He has Momma's eyes. McQuistion is for his birth mom. That's where the story, and the chain, gets complex. I've never carved a chain like this, with two links hooked into one. Sophia was his birth mom, but he carries your blood, through me. It took two of us to carry a baby named James to term, I guess. That makes him twice as special.*

*We are praying to adopt a daughter in January through a birth mother Granny Apple connected us with. It's a way for Ian and me to give something back to the community, and to build a family in return. We're going to name her Hope, for Momma. She should be born any day. My doctor tells me that I have some female problems that will make it hard—maybe impossible—to have children, so we're thrilled to be able to give this little girl a home.*

*I miss you so much, Daddy. I needed you every day this past year. I lost a very good friend, Sophia. Then I lost my son to the state for a while. We almost lost the farm, but an angel saved us. I wish you could have known her. I tried to follow your advice every step of the way, listening to the Spirit—my little voice. With Ian's help, we did what you asked us. The farm is back in family hands for good.*

*This little spot on the page is a tear for you. I tried to wipe it away, but it smudged. Maybe that's a good thing, because now you know what I've spilled for you nearly every day since you left. I miss you. I always will.*

*I learned a tough lesson this year—many lessons. You were so wise in all the things you taught me, but I had to learn one special lesson all on my own. Sometimes I do the wrong thing for the right reason. You knew that. But I learned something else. Actions have consequences. It took me a while to figure that out. The good news is that God redeems our actions—if we'll trust Him and give Him a chance. There's still heartache, but He can heal that hurt, in time.*

*Be at peace, Daddy. I am married now. We have the farm. We have a son. I've added two more links to the family chain, and a third is on the way.*

*I love you.*

*Peppermint*

---

Beside her, James suckled, wrapped in a thick knit blanket, Granny Apple's newest wool creation. Blue, green, and black, the tartan of Clan Mackay, surrounded her son from shoulder

to toe while they rocked on the porch after Christmas dinner.
James squeezed her finger, his customary grip while he nursed,
one blue eye and one green focused intently on his mother.

Laura Ann laughed at the hold on her index finger, tugging
at him playfully. *"Manu forti,"* she said. "'With a strong hand.'
The motto of Clan Mackay." James never let go, his smile growing as she tugged, until he lost his latch on her, then let go of her
finger and went back to dinner. His hand lay open, waiting like
a flytrap to catch his momma.

"Your granddaddy would be tossing you in the air right
now," she said. "James Angus McGehee. That's where you get
your first name. And from James McQuistion, your honorary
father." She paused for a long time, no desire to verbalize the
next words. "Your birth father's name was Felix Mendoza." That
name still hurt, a stab of pain.

Laura Ann rocked, cuddling James against a cold afternoon
breeze. Christmas came warm this year, but too cold to spend
long on the porch feeding an infant.

"The daddy who loves you and gave you your last name is
out in the barn tuning up the tractor. He'll teach you to drive
it one day. He's a game warden. Ian Arthur Stewart. And your
birth mom, where you get your middle name? She was Sophia
McQuistion. I've got so much to tell you about her. She gave her
life for you."

"This is your home," she said, waving a hand toward the
horizon as she rocked on buckled grey boards. She cooed when
his eyes started to shut, then added, "One day The Jug will be
home to your children too." She breathed deep of the farm air,
smells from the barn of fresh hay and wintering cows, mixing
with the fertile scent of bottomland, and the waters of the Middle Island Creek.

"It will be home to you and your children. A home for generations to come."

# RECOMMENDED RESOURCES

- Scott Rae and Dr. Joy Riley, *Outside the Womb: Moral Guidance for Assisted Reproduction* (Chicago: Moody, 2011). The leading resource of its kind on the ethics of assisted reproduction technologies (ART). As one endorser states, "*Outside the Womb* is a rare blend of scientific information, biblical guidance, and empathy for those struggling with infertility."
- John Kilner, C. Christopher Hook, and Diann B. Uustal, *Cutting-Edge Bioethics: A Christian Exploration of Technologies and Trends* (Grand Rapids: Eerdmans, 2002). This excellent reference text covers a broad array of bioethical dilemmas, medical technologies, and cultural issues.
- The Center for Bioethics and Human Dignity (CBHD), Deerfield, Illinois. Located on the campus of Trinity University near Chicago, this organization is the leader for the debate and communication of bioethics issues. Their web-based newsletter provides weekly insights into news and cultural trends, and their website is populated with dozens of valuable resources. The CBHD annual conference in mid-July provides a remarkable insight into bioethics from a Christian worldview. Visit www.cbhd.org.
- The Center for Bioethics and Culture (CBC) Network of San Ramon, California, has taken a strong stand on the international exploitation of women through egg donations. Learn more about what the fertility industry is *not* telling young women about the long-term health impact of egg harvests,

practices that CBC President Jennifer Lahl refers to as "the industry's dirty little secret." Also, learn about the exploitation of at-risk women who are desperate for easy cash. The CBC video *Eggsploitation* can be obtained through their web link at www.eggsploitation.com and on their organizational web site at www.cbc-network.org.

- The Tennessee Center for Bioethics and Culture, based in Brentwood, Tennessee, provides a monthly newsletter that showcases many bioethical issues in easy-to-understand format. Dr. Joy Riley provides insightful resources and a monthly column. Visit www.tennesseecbc.org.

- The Christian Medical and Dental Association (CMDA) serves as the national voice for Christian doctors. Consult their website at www.cmda.org to learn more about resources and policy statements on issues of bioethics, and their extensive outreach through ministry and missions.

- The Nurses Christian Fellowship provides an international nexus for nurses to engage students, nurses, and patients with the good news of the gospel, and to bring God's love and healing to nurses and healthcare. Learn more about their ministry at www.ncf-jcn.org.

A detailed Reader's Guide, with discussion questions, biblical references, and additional research recommendations, is available on the author's website at www.austinboyd.com.

Follow regular postings about bioethics issues through the author's blog, hosted at www.austinboyd.com /category/blog/.

Email comments and questions to the author through his contact form at www.austinboyd.com/contact-me/.

# ACKNOWLEDGMENTS

I enjoy reading the acknowledgment page for any book, imagining all of the people who had a critical hand in bringing a manuscript to print. It's a labor of love, and a team effort ... whatever the book happens to be.

For *Nobody's Child*, I owe a special debt of thanks to Zondervan and my senior editor, Ms. Sue Brower, a woman with the vision to communicate complex bioethics issues through the power of fiction. She grasped my "bioethics suspense" concept the first time we met, and she's been a joy to collaborate with for the past two years.

My agent is friend and mentor rolled into one; I am blessed by the wise counsel of Les Stobbe. Many authors owe their entry into the world of publishing to Les, and I am one. He's an amazing man, an active participant in the Christian publishing community.

Every ship has a rudder. Since the first concept for this novel was put to paper, the Center for Bioethics and Human Dignity (CBHD) has helped direct my course for this venture. In the early days of our first concept exploration, Mr. Matthew Eppinette was a dependable advisor at CBHD. When Matthew moved on to a new bioethics assignment, Dr. Michael Sleasman emerged as a key resource, supporting many calls and meetings where we discussed the leading reproductive issues of the day. CBHD Executive Director Ms. Paige Cunningham and her staff have supported my research, conducted early critiques of the manuscript, and contributed immeasurably to the novel through their focus on the medical and emotional impact that egg donation has on women.

Other bioethicists have also played a major role in the formation of this novel. Ms. Jennifer Lahl, President of the Center for Bioethics and Culture Network in San Ramon, California, and Dr. Joy Riley, Director of the Tennessee Center for Bioethics and Culture, were essential reviewers and contributors to the novel's direction. Dr. Peter Lawler of Berry College, Dr. M. Kelly Lynn of Huntsville, Alabama, and a dozen physicians unnamed here were all part of the research for this book.

A novel is a story, and if it's not told well, it's just boring prose. I am blessed with a wonderful editorial team of friends who help me improve my writing. Sue Brower, Lori Vanden Bosch, Bob Hudson, Steve "The Novel Doctor" Parolini, and Mary DeMuth each found things in my work that needed to be changed and helped me improve this manuscript for publication. These wonderful people are trusted mentors, and through their feedback I have become a better writer.

Alicia Mey, the Zondervan lead for marketing, Jennifer Baar, Zondervan's publicist, and Katie Broadus also deserve a special mention. Once a book is in print, they help you learn about it, and help me to get it into your hands. Thank you!

To my advance reader team, I sincerely appreciate your wise comments and keen insights: Karen Lynn, Dr. M. Kelly Lynn, Jennifer Frith, Roger Spencer, Pam Cassady, Riley Wallace, my sister Carolyn Boyd, my father Walker Boyd, my son Andrew, and my intuitive wife Cindy. Your support blessed me in many ways.

I write through the inspiration of the Holy Spirit. If there's a bottom line in any acknowledgment for my books, it always goes to God. Thank you for placing me here, for a time such as this.

## Share Your Thoughts

**With the Author:** Your comments will be forwarded to the author when you send them to *zauthor@zondervan.com*.

**With Zondervan:** Submit your review of this book by writing to *zreview@zondervan.com*.

## Free Online Resources at
## www.zondervan.com

**Zondervan AuthorTracker:** Be notified whenever your favorite authors publish new books, go on tour, or post an update about what's happening in their lives at www.zondervan.com/authortracker.

**Daily Bible Verses and Devotions:** Enrich your life with daily Bible verses or devotions that help you start every morning focused on God. Visit www.zondervan.com/newsletters.

**Free Email Publications:** Sign up for newsletters on Christian living, academic resources, church ministry, fiction, children's resources, and more. Visit www.zondervan.com/newsletters.

**Zondervan Bible Search:** Find and compare Bible passages in a variety of translations at www.zondervanbiblesearch.com.

**Other Benefits:** Register to receive online benefits like coupons and special offers, or to participate in research.